Women of Verdun

Book Three

Nicolette

By

Pearl A. Gardner

Women of Verdun, Book Three, Nicolette

eBook edition
ASIN:

Also available in print version

ISBN-13: 978-1518676277
ISBN-10: 1518676278

Printed by CreateSpace, an Amazon.com Company
Available from Amazon.com and other online stores.

Pearl A. Gardner

Acknowledgements

I could not have written this story without extensive research into the lives of ordinary men and women who lived in France and Britain in the years around the time of the Second World War.

My quest for discovery took me to library archives, both in the real world and in cyberspace. I would like to thank the many thousands of people responsible for keeping records, collating and publishing files from large, newsworthy world events to small, handwritten personal accounts. Your efforts in making all this information available have been invaluable to my work.

For those readers with a more intimate knowledge of the period, locations and events portrayed in this story, I apologise if my account is not exactly historically or geographically correct. The events that happen to these characters are fictitious, and although I have endeavoured to keep the general historical details authentic, some degree of artistic license has been used to aid the flow of the story.

Contents

Chapter 1: Saying Goodbye

Nicolette gently held the frail hand in hers as tears slowly slipped down her cheeks. Her fragile grandmother was slipping further away with each shaking, shallow breath the old woman took.

'She can't hold on much longer, Mum, can she?' Nicolette asked Collette, her mother, sitting opposite her on the other side of the bed.

'At least she's not in pain now.' Her mother was holding the other hand of the desperately ill woman in the bed. 'The doctor gave her a sleeping draught. She won't wake again, Nicolette. You know that, don't you?'

'Yes, I do, Mum. I said all I had to say to Mémé yesterday while she was still conscious enough to understand me.'

'She may still be able to hear us, Nicolette. The doctor said that hearing is usually the last of the senses to go. We can still talk to her, though she won't be able to answer us.'

'I would only tell her again, how much she will be missed, and how much I love her. How I have always loved her.'

'As we all do, my child.' Collette turned to her dying mother. 'You are unique, my darling Mama. How will we live without your love and your support?' Her faintly accented voice was shaking with emotion.

Nicolette reached for her mother across the bed, and the three generations of women formed a circle of love with their joined hands. The woman on the bed took another shallow breath, the pink, satin counterpane barely rising.

'She would hate us to be sad, Mum. She'd call us maudlin, or she'd use the French word for being too sentimental. Larmoyant! She'd say we were larmoyant bébés.'

'Whichever language she chose she'd be cross with us.' Collette smiled briefly and lightly squeezed the fragile hand of her mother. 'I'm sorry, Mama, but you mustn't be angered by our sadness. You have been the backbone of this family for many years, and we will all find it hard to continue without you.'

'We will follow your example, Mémé.' Nicolette glanced across at her mother and took a deep, settling breath before speaking to her grandmother again. 'Your courage and your heart will live on with us. We will grow strong again after you have gone, and we will survive whatever is to come in this world. You can leave us now, my darling grandma. Go in peace ma chérie.'

6

'Oh, Nicolette. Mother is really going to leave us, isn't she?'

'I think she has taken her last breath, Mum.'

Both women watched the counterpane for signs of movement, but it remained quite still.

Collette clasped her hands to her mouth to stifle her sobs and Nicolette quickly skirted the bed to gather her mother into her arms. 'Courage, Mum. Be brave for her sake. She was ready to leave us.'

'I know, Nicolette. My tears are for us, not for her. She's gone to a better place while we have to find a way through this war without her. She lived through the last war and suffered, as we all did. She thought she'd given her family the chance of freedom by bringing us to England but now we are facing another war, and we are outsiders in this foreign land. We'd have been better off back in France, I'm sure.'

'You can't know that for sure, Mum.'

'No, I can't, but from what I hear, Elizabeth does not seem to be suffering in Verdun as much as we are here in London. It would have been so much easier if we'd stayed there.'

'I know how difficult it was for you, Mum, when you first came to England. You were pregnant with me and had just lost my father, but Grandma Belle was convinced it was the right thing to do, and we've forged a good life here, haven't we?'

'It was right for Belle and right for you too, Nicolette, but I'm still not sure it was the right move for me. I left so much behind when I came here, and nothing could ever replace what I'd lost in France, Nicolette.'

'I know, Mum, but I thought you were happy here.' Nicolette was shocked by the revelation that her mother wasn't as happy as she had always appeared to be. 'I thought you loved living in England. What about Dad? You wouldn't have met him if you hadn't moved to England. He was the love of your life, or so you kept telling me.'

'Maurice was a lovely man. I knew none better here in this country. He was a loving and devoted husband. He became a father to you and, with Maurice, I was happier than I'd been since leaving France.'

'It saddens me that I have no memory of him, Mum.'

'He died when you were very small. We only had a few years together. His love saved me from the torment of grieving for your real father, and when we had Joseph, I felt our lives were complete. He lived his life around you children. You meant the world to him, even though you weren't of his blood. I wish you could have known him longer. You were seven when he died, so I would have expected you to remember something about him. Joseph was only three and, of course, remembers nothing of his father. Are you sure you have no memory of your stepfather?'

Nicolette had hazy recollections of a laughing man, but couldn't flesh the memories with details. 'Sorry, Mum. I can see a smiling face, but that's about all.'

'That is a shame. I wish! I wish! Oh, it's no good wishing for something that can never be.' Collette sighed. 'Life was cruel to me. I lost two good men who both loved me very much, and you lost two fathers before you got a chance to know them.'

'I feel I know them both, Mum. You and Aunt Flissy talk about Antoine and Maurice often. I love to hear your stories about how things were for you in France, and when Joseph and I were small.'

'Stories! That's all my past is reduced to. Will my mother only be remembered through stories? It seems so much less than she deserves. We endured so much pain, Nicolette. There is no justice in a world where such a brave woman has her life end like this.' Collette stroked her mother's still face.

Nicolette's tears slipped down her cheek. 'We'll never forget Belle, Mum. Her memory will live on in us long after today has passed into history. You still remember your first love, don't you? My father has been dead for years, but Antoine's memory lives on in your heart. He lives in me, too.'

Collette gazed at Nicolette. 'I wish you looked more like him. Your hair is the same as your Grandmother Elizabeth's blonde curls, but everything else about you is from my side of the family.'

'I'm a mixture, Mum. I have Belle's blood running through me, too. Her memory will never die while I live.'

'So many good people die before their time in a war. It is expected, and we accept it, but to lose Belle this way seems wrong, somehow.'

'Don't dwell on her pain, or the way she died, Mum. She's at peace. Come, now. We have to let the others know she's gone.' Nicolette gently lifted her mother from the chair and steered her to the door. As they descended the staircase, Nicolette kept her arm around her mother's waist, guiding her steps.

Nicolette opened the door to the living room where her fiancé and brother were waiting, together with her Aunt Felicity and Uncle Edwin.

'Has she gone?' Felicity was the first to speak. 'I'm sorry I couldn't be there. I couldn't bear to see her like that. I've seen my share of suffering on the wards and in theatre, but it is very different when the one who has pain is someone you love so much.'

'She didn't suffer, Aunt Felicity. She drifted away while she slept. It was very peaceful, wasn't it, Mum?'

'Are you all right, Nicky?' Robert asked.

Nicolette turned to her fiancé. 'Yes, darling, I'm glad I was able to be there for Mémé. I'm sad, and I'll miss her. She won't see us get married or know our children, and that makes me even sadder. I can't imagine a future without her there. She had a peaceful end, though.'

'No person can live forever, Nicolette, though seventy years doesn't seem long enough for a spirited woman like Belle.' Her Uncle Edwin came to hug her. 'I'm sure her spirit will be hanging around for as long as it can. She won't want to miss being involved in your life, and I know she'll be watching you from heaven.'

'What a nice romantic notion, Edwin.' Collette smiled through her tears at her brother-in-law. She turned to her son. 'How are you, Joseph? You're very quiet,' she asked him.

'I can't believe she'll never play chess with me again, or come to support the cricket team. She's really gone, hasn't she?' The eighteen-year-old glanced from his mother to his sister, and then back to his mother. 'How are you, Mum?'

'Sad, you know. But we have to organise a funeral now and tell the doctor. There is so much to do, where do we start?'

'I'll let the doctor know, Mum.' Nicolette went to get her coat from the hallway. 'Will you come with me, Robert?'

'We can call at Brooke's on the way back.' Robert suggested. 'You did say you wanted them to do the arrangements, didn't you, Collette?' he asked.

'That would be a big help, Robert, thank you.' Collette smiled at her future son-in-law.

'What about the venue for the wake?' Edwin asked. 'She always liked the Royal Oak, and they do a good spread there.'

'We can ask them this evening when they open, Edwin.' Felicity suggested. 'If you're sure that's what you want, Collette.'

'My word, it seems I will have nothing to do if you all continue to take over.'

'I'm sure they don't mean anything wrong, Mum.' Joseph looked nervously at his Aunt.

'Of course, we only want to help, Collette.' Felicity looked edgy. 'If you think we should step back, we will.'

'She was your mother too, Flissy.' Edwin pointed out, defensively. 'Your sister wants to be included, Collette. It's a small thing to ask. We can organise the wake, and it would be our contribution to the expense of everything.'

'That's very kind of you Edwin, but mother left us well provided for, as well you know.'

'Time enough to talk about finances after the funeral, Mum,' Nicolette said, shrugging into her coat. 'We won't be too long. Is anyone hungry? We could call for some fish and chips on the way back.'

'It seems wrong to think about food when Grandma is lying dead upstairs.' Joseph looked at the ceiling.

'Life goes on, son.' Collette smiled wryly. 'Fish and chips would be good, Nicolette, thank you. Will you stay to lunch, Flissy? You could help me plan the funeral service.'

Nicolette left with Robert, and they hurried down the leafy avenue of Thames Ditton. The wind blew clouds of leaves from the branches and spots of cold, November rain began to fall.

'I never could understand your family, Nicky. What is it between your mum and Felicity? There always seems to be tension in the air between them.'

'Sibling rivalry, I think. They are close in age, only fourteen months between them. There was always competition between them for Belle's attention when they were children, I think. Not so much when they became adults and moved over here, though.'

'I think there's more to it than that.'

'Like what?'

'Oh, I can't put my finger on it, exactly. There's some resentment between them; I can feel it when they are together. I hear it in their voices.'

'You've always struck me as being far too sensitive for a man, Robert. But I think you're wrong on this one.'

'Too sensitive, am I?'

'Don't worry! It's not a bad thing to be, Robert. I love you for being caring and sensitive. Most men I know would be more afraid of showing emotion than of having a bare-knuckle brawl in the street.'

'How many men do you know, Nicky?' Robert chuckled and nudged her side as they hurried along, hunched together against the wind. 'I thought I was your one and only true love.'

'You are! Silly moo.' Nicolette nudged him back. 'But I know a lot of men from work, and there's Uncle Edwin and Joseph.'

'You can't compare me with your brother or your uncle. Joseph is a boy, and Edwin is an old-school gentleman, though, he has a rough edge to his dialect.'

'That's because he comes from Yorkshire. I think Aunt Felicity must be a very strong woman to put up with his archaic views.'

'What do you mean?'

'She has her career, which is surprising considering how Uncle Edwin sees the world. In his opinion, men should go out to earn the money and women should stay home to do the housework and look after the family.'

'Perhaps his views had to change because they never had children?'

'Maybe, but I have a feeling that Aunt Flissy would have followed her dream even if she'd given birth to a brood of youngsters.'

'Do you think she is sad because she couldn't have a child?'

'She has Joseph and me. Aunt Flissy has been like a second mum to me. Uncle Edwin has always tried to play the father figure to us, but he has no idea about children, really. His ideas are so old fashioned. He's a big believer in a woman knowing her place and, according to Uncle Edwin, that place is very firmly in front of the kitchen sink.' Nicolette giggled.

'Just the place for you, my darling.' Robert ducked away from her playful slap. 'Only joking!'

'You'd better be, Robert Wainwright. I'll have you know that I have no intention of becoming a slave to the kitchen. I've applied to join the Women's Auxiliary Air Force, to help the war effort.'

Robert stopped abruptly. 'What!' He took hold of her shoulders and spun her to face him. 'You can't!' he protested, looking shocked.

'Why not?'

'We're getting married next year!'

'Well that won't change things much, will it?'

'You'll have to move away! We won't be together, and, and, oh, Nicky! Please tell me you haven't done anything about joining up yet, have you?'

'Robert! What's wrong with you?' She pulled him into a shop doorway to shelter from the rain and turned to face him. She took his hand in hers. 'Listen to me, will you? Some said this war would be over before that first Christmas and they were wrong, weren't they?

Others have warned that it might last longer than the last one. Mum is worried that our family will be victimised because she's foreign. You know how some people can't tell one foreign accent from another? French, German, Italian, it's all the same to them, which is why they are suspicious of Mum and Aunt Flissy. If I enlist, that will show our neighbours that we're British now, and willing to fight for this country that we now call home.'

'My, you've got it all worked out, haven't you?'

'You'll be joining up too, Robert, won't you? It's the only topic of conversation for the young men on the factory floor at work. Some of them have already left Mason's to fight in the war. I thought you would want to enlist too and, if you do, I don't want to sit at home and twiddle my thumbs waiting for you to come home to me. I want to do something too.'

'You're worrying for no good reason, Nicky.' Robert looked a little sheepish. 'I haven't given much thought to enlisting. I'm above the age limit for compulsory registration by two years. I don't have to go, Nicky. You don't have to worry.'

'I know you don't *have* to, Robert.' She couldn't believe what she was hearing. 'I thought you would *want* to!'

'Why would I? I'm happy at Jackson and Tweed, and in a couple of years I'll be finished with my training and they promised they'd consider me for a partnership after I gain some experience. In ten years or so, we'll be set for life, my darling. You can't want me to give it up now and go and fight in this awful war.'

Nicolette felt confused. She had thought that her fiancé would feel as she did about defending Britain and was disturbed to hear that they were poles apart on the issue of patriotism. She looked into his eyes and, for the first time, felt uncertainty. Her heart did a somersault. His words had sown the first seeds of doubt about her view of him. How could she love a man who did not share her passion for this country? A myriad of thoughts flashed through her mind in a second, and she quickly turned away, to hide her disillusionment from him.

'You do understand, don't you, Nicky?' Robert gently pulled her around to look into her eyes. 'I'm thinking of us, my darling. Our future won't be worth much if I don't get my papers. It's all I've ever wanted to do. Being a solicitor, and perhaps progressing to be a barrister eventually. Becoming a partner in the firm is all I've dreamed of since I was in school. My uncle pulled strings to get me into the firm. Positions like this don't come along every day. You know how much this career means to me. It's our future, Nicky!'

'Our future won't be worth anything if the Germans overrun us. Your precious papers won't amount to more than fish and chip wrappings if we lose this war.' She could hear her voice rising and bit her lip to stop more hurtful words tumbling from her mouth.

'I think we should focus on the here and now, Nicolette. Your grandmother has just passed away, so I can see how that would affect your thinking. Let's just deal with our errand and talk about the future later when we're a little calmer. What do you think?'

Nicolette nodded because she didn't trust herself to speak, and they began to walk again, their steps leading them to the doctor's surgery. She knew that her grandmother's death had nothing to do with the conflicting emotions rolling around inside her. She thought she loved Robert. They'd been together since she was eighteen. She'd celebrated her twenty-first birthday in April. She had spent the last three years getting to know this man, but now she was beginning to understand that she didn't know him very well at all.

'Here we are, let's get this over with, Nicky.' Robert guided her through to the small reception and took charge of informing the receptionist why they were there.

When the doctor came out from his consulting room, he smiled sadly and shook their hands, offering condolences as he shrugged his coat on. 'I'll make my way to your house now and write out the certificate. Mr Brookes will take care of the rest of the arrangements. You will be instructing Brookes, won't you? I'm sure Belle told me that was who she wanted.'

'Yes, doctor. We're going to call there next.' Nicolette told the older man.

'Good. Good. Tell him he can collect her in about half an hour.'

'Collect her?' Nicolette didn't understand at first and then realised that the funeral director would need to take her grandmother's body to the funeral home for preparation. 'Oh, yes. Of course.'

'Was she peaceful at the end, Nicolette?' the doctor asked.

'Yes, thank you. Your sleeping draft made all the difference to her. She didn't seem to have any pain, and simply slipped away about an hour ago.'

'Good. Cancer is a terrible curse, and we doctors don't have much in our medical bags to combat the monstrous symptoms, but we do what we can to ease the suffering. It's not always enough, though. I'm glad I was able to help Belle. She was a feisty lady and didn't deserve to die at such a young age.'

'She was just over seventy, doctor.' Robert pointed out.

'That's not so old from my perspective, young man.' The doctor smiled and wiggled his eyebrows. 'Though, I suppose you'll think it's a good old age to achieve. Your thoughts on life expectancy might change when you get to my age.' The doctor hesitated and aimed a sympathetic smile at the young couple. 'Although with this war, I'm guessing not many young men will be so fortunate as to live out their natural life-spans.'

Robert's face blanched, and Nicolette watched his Adam's apple bob as he gulped for air. She clutched his arm to offer some support and felt him shaking. 'We have to get on, Doctor Martin. Mum is expecting you.'

'I'll see you out.' The doctor walked them to the door and said his goodbyes.

'Are you all right, Robert?' Nicolette asked, still clutching his arm as they walked away from the surgery.

'I'm perfectly fine.' Robert's voice was shaky. 'I just didn't like to hear that my days might be numbered because of this damned war. I don't want anything to do with it. I'm not a fighter. I'm a pacifist. Why can't politicians sit down together and have an amicable discussion to settle their differences?'

'I think they've already tried that a few times, Robert, but you can't reason with men like Hitler.'

'Then our politicians didn't try hard enough, and now we're going to have a repeat of the war that was meant to end all wars. Will they never learn?'

'Going to war wasn't a choice that was easy to make, Robert. Surely you can see that. Chamberlain didn't make ultimatums to Hitler without a great deal of thought to the consequences.'

'And still he made them, so he can't have thought it through enough. A whole generation of men died in the last war, and it's going to happen again, Nicolette. Do you want me to die?'

'Of course, I don't!' She was beginning to feel anger building inside her. 'But I don't want men like Hitler to rule over us and impose their insane doctrines on our way of life. Do you?'

'So you think I should follow in the footsteps of all those noble souls who gave their lives for our freedom? You want me to throw myself into the bosom of whichever armed service will have me so I can do my duty for King and country?' Robert sounded tense and resentful, and his footsteps quickened.

'I want you to do what you feel you should, Robert. If staying in the background and finishing your solicitor training makes you happier, then that's what you should do, but I will be enlisting as soon as they'll have me.' She wanted him to understand the depth of her feeling but didn't want to pressurise him into doing something he obviously was not happy to do. She didn't want him to die, of course, she didn't, but to think he might be a coward at heart made her feel very uncomfortable.

'You're impossibly stubborn sometimes, Nicky. If it makes you happy, I'll look into what I can do to help in this war. Maybe they'll need part-timers at home who can man the fort and defend the homeland while the war is fought on foreign soil. Would that be enough for you?'

'Would that be enough for *you*, Robert?' She couldn't help turning the question back at him. 'After all, it's your conscience you must consider, not mine.'

'Why do you have to be so mulish, Nicolette?'

'I'm merely stating the obvious, Robert. This war is taking over our whole lives, for goodness knows how long, and we have to make up our minds how we are going to live through it. I'm going to help, in any way I can, to make sure Britain emerges triumphant, and Hitler and his gang are firmly put in their place. You will do whatever you think you ought to, and your decision should have no bearing on what I do, what I believe, or what you feel I might think of you.'

'Are we falling out over this, Nicky?'

'I hope not, Robert, but if I can be honest with you, I do think this war might change us as people. Bearing that in mind, maybe we should wait a little longer before we get married.'

'Wait! No! We have the arrangements agreed, and some of those are partly paid for. We're to marry on your twenty-second birthday! We can't postpone.'

'The wedding is still six months away, of course, we can postpone. It's not as if we're walking down the aisle next week!' Nicolette felt her anger building again but didn't want to argue about this in the street, especially as they were almost at the funeral director's premises. 'Can we talk about this later, please? I don't think I can deal with this now, on top of everything else I have been through today.'

'We'll postpone this conversation, Nicolette, but I'll not

postpone the wedding until we have discussed this further.'
'Very well.' Nicolette unhooked her arm from his and led the way through the door to speak to the funeral director.

Chapter 2: Funerals and families

Nicolette couldn't sleep. She'd spent half the night in the cellar with the rest of her family listening to the heavy drone of aircraft and the distant booming of dropping bombs. From the direction of the thundering racket, she had a good idea that the East of London and the dockyards would have taken a pounding in the raid. The all-clear sounded around three in the morning, and they had all trudged, wearily, back to bed.

Her Grandmother Elizabeth had arrived from France the previous day, and her frightening introduction to life in London under threat of being hit by Hitler's bombs was evident to see. The elderly woman sat upright between Felicity and Collette in the gloomy cellar, gripping their hands tightly. Elizabeth had bravely endured a perilous journey through occupied France before embarking on a clandestine sea crossing on rough waters to make it to her friend's funeral. Nicolette was in awe of her paternal grandmother's courage. She barely flinched at the repeated bangs, rumbles and shakes, as the bombers did their worst. Only when the all-clear sounded, did she admit being afraid.

'I've already lived through a terrible war, but I never experienced anything so frightening in my life,' she had said as they helped her back to bed. 'How do you cope with this horror every night?'

Nicolette remembered her mother soothing the old woman with words of encouragement. 'They don't aim their bombs at Thames Ditton, Belle-Mére. They are determined to flatten the centre of London and our industrial areas.'

Her grandmother had replied in a firm, strong, American accent, 'Then I hope their aim has improved since the last war.'

Nicolette didn't offer to inform her grandmother that many thousands of homes had been destroyed already. Londoners were suffering greatly. Those who hadn't died in the bombings of their houses were now homeless and lived in shelters or overcrowded conditions with relatives. She couldn't understand how Robert could turn a blind eye to the evidence of Hitler's cruelty. How could he stay focused on his personal future when the whole of Britain was being intimidated by such a despot?

The rain was beating against the blacked-out window, echoing the tears that trickled down Nicolette's cheeks. The confusion in her heart was unbearable. She had been so sure of her future with the man she thought she loved with all her heart, but now that love had suffered a serious knock. She was no longer convinced that she wanted to marry him because she was no longer sure what she felt about her fiancé. Her faith in their love was diminished by Robert's attitude to the threat she saw from the enemy. She could not understand why he didn't feel the same way about defending their freedom, but that bewilderment was overshadowed by the devastation of losing her beloved Mémé. Her grandmother was to be buried later that day, and Nicolette could not believe she would never see or talk with the old lady again.

Belle had always been a huge part of her life. Nicolette's earliest memories involved baking and making exquisite dishes with her grandmother. As they worked in the kitchen, Belle would describe her life in a French chateau and her stories helped to colour Nicolette's view of that country. It was obvious to Nicolette that Belle loved France. She often spoke of her home near Verdun and her flamboyant American friend, Elizabeth Armaud, or Elizabeth Duval, or Elizabeth Dubois, depending on which husband's name she favoured at the time. Elizabeth was Nicolette's paternal grandmother, and she had met her often.

Nicolette had travelled, with her mother and Aunt, almost every year to visit the chateau in France. Elizabeth came to England every spring to shop in the fashion houses of London and stayed with them in the house in Thames Ditton that Belle had inherited from Henry Whitmoor.

The two elderly women would talk in English and switch to French mid-sentence. They seamlessly conversed in their unique language, and only someone with a depth of knowledge in both, could understand them. Nicolette had been speaking French and English since she learned how to talk and could easily follow the conversation of the older women. They laughed and reminisced but didn't talk much of the hardships they endured during the last war. She often overheard her mother and Aunt Felicity talking about those awful times and learned enough to know it hadn't been easy for any of them.

During the war years, the chateau grounds became home to a hospital that was inundated with wounded soldiers. Australian nurses and various high-ranking officials were stationed there. Belle volunteered her skills to the kitchens to help the army cooks, but her fine cuisine was reduced to mass catering for the hungry soldiers and hospital staff.

Shortly after news came that Belle's estranged first husband had been killed in action, the flour mill she part owned, was bombed. Many lost their lives, but Belle and her two girls were lucky. They survived the war. Nicolette's grandmother had been a brave and spirited woman and earned the admiration of many, including an English Major, who had acquired a taste for her French cuisine while staying at the chateau. Major Whitmoor took it upon himself to take Belle and her family under his wing, offering her work at his home in London after the war.

She persuaded her recently widowed and pregnant daughter, Collette, to leave her home country of France, believing that Britain could offer them a better future. Felicity was eager to live in England, to train to be a theatre nurse. She needed no persuasion to join them in their plans to leave France.

Belle spoke fluent English and loved her work for the Major who often entertained, giving her the opportunity to show off her skills in the kitchen.

Nicolette often wondered whether there had ever been anything more to the relationship between her grandmother and the Major, but no amount of probing would get her beloved Mémé to admit anything more than friendship.

If only she had asked more questions, while Belle was alive. Nicolette resolved to ask her mother and aunt to tell her as much as they knew. There were so many blanks in her grandmother's history, and Nicolette wanted to know more about the woman who had such a big influence on her. From her earliest recollections, she remembered that Belle instilled a strict sense of right and wrong and emphasised the importance of good manners, cleanliness and respect for elders.

Belle spoke in English but lapsed into French when she was excited, which was a joy to witness, or when she was angry, which wasn't often. Nicolette loved to speak French with her grandmother. As a child, she felt as if she were speaking a secret language that only her family knew. As she grew older, she came to know the truth about her background, and her French roots. She excelled in languages at school, though her French accent was different to the classic French of her teacher. She spoke with the regional dialect of Lorraine, which gave her spoken French a more natural lilt. Belle helped her when she studied the German language, explaining how to perfect the guttural pronunciation of some words. Her grandmother was fluent in all three languages and had been an excellent tutor.

The rain ceased, and Nicolette's mind was enticed back to reality by the sound of birds waking. She knew the sun was rising, though she couldn't see the lightening skies because of the blackout curtains. She'd barely slept at all, and had no desire to leave her bed. Today was going to be horrendous, and she was in no great hurry to start it.

Robert was coming at ten; before everyone else was due to arrive at eleven. He told her he wanted to support her through this sad day, but she would much rather he didn't. She was unhappy with his decision not to enlist, and she was perplexed by how his choice of passive action changed the way she felt about him. He argued that he was not required to register because he was older than the age limit the government had set. It didn't seem to upset him that most men his age were ignoring the compulsory limits and enlisting anyway. Robert seemed prepared to sit it out and hoped it would all be over before he was required, by law, to do anything.

She was ashamed to discuss his position with her colleagues at work, fearing they would condemn him publicly as much as she did in her heart. She hadn't told her family either, for the same reason. She would have to face the truth of her feelings and tell Robert soon. She couldn't tie herself to a man who didn't share the same values that she had, and he deserved to know that his future was not going to turn out as he planned.

Fresh tears escaped her eyes as she realised that her future would be changed too. All she'd imagined for the last couple of years was spending her life with him. Now it seemed that life, with a coward, was the last thing she wanted.

Was he a coward or was he standing on his principals because he truly believed he was right? Was his reasoning sound? Nicolette tried to give him the benefit of the doubt, but each time, she remembered the tremor in his voice. She recalled the shaking of his arm after the doctor had pointed out the possibility of an early death for him due to the war. His fear was obvious. He was afraid of fighting and afraid of dying.

Death is such a simple word. Am I afraid of death, she asked herself? Was Belle afraid of dying? Her grandmother faced death stoically, only whimpering when the pain was at its worst. She'd been brave throughout her life, and all through her illness. Death did not seem to scare Belle, and Nicolette knew she had faced it more than once. She remembered her grandmother telling her that death is merely a transition from one state to another. She explained that life was short and said that when it is over there is more beyond the veil of death. Belle believed there were great new experiences waiting in the afterlife.

'Death is the greatest adventure of all, Nicolette,' she had said. 'Make the most of every minute of life you live here. It is your duty to live your life as if death is just around the corner.'

When Nicolette had asked why, Belle explained, 'That way you live life to the full and won't let an opportunity slip by unnoticed. The more experience you gain in this life, the better prepared you will be for the next one.'

Nicolette had been young and naïve at the time and had questioned her grandmother's words further. 'What kind of opportunities will I have to look for?' she had asked.

'If I knew that, I would be Queen of the world, child. Look for opportunity everywhere. You'll have many chances of happiness, excitement, and adventure. You may get the opportunity to do good works, to be fulfilled, to live your dream. When you arrive at a crossroad in life, always take the one that moves your heart most, and you won't go wrong.'

Nicolette could hear her grandmother's words in her mind. She never forgot the conversation they had that day. Belle had gone on to explain that her simple philosophy had steered her through many decisions she had to make, not least the one she made in coming to England.

Nicolette knew she was at a crossroad now. One road led her to marriage and a settled and predictable life with Robert, another was pointing to an unknown future without him because of his attitude to the war. Would she still want to go down the path to marriage if Robert had unhesitatingly rushed to enlist? She couldn't answer the question she posed to herself. She had thought she loved Robert. She had felt she belonged to him and they were meant to be together, but a few words had changed everything, and now she felt she'd been set adrift on a stormy sea.

'How are you bearing up, Nicky?' Robert asked as he wrapped his arms around her.

'I'm keeping it together.' She disentangled herself from his embrace. 'Come and see Grandma Elizabeth. She has arrived from France. Can you imagine how she managed to do that? I still can't believe she organised her crossing on a fishing boat. If the Germans had caught her, she'd have had a lot of explaining to do.'

Her American grandmother still lived near Verdun in France. Nicolette's mother had sent a telegram with the news of Belle's death and was surprised by her mother-in-law's response. Elizabeth replied and had insisted Belle's funeral should be delayed until she managed to arrange passage to England. Fortunately, the old woman's money helped to speed her departure from France and pay the huge fee needed to secure her a safe crossing on a small fishing boat out of a quiet beach north of Dunkirk.

The rest of the family considered the old woman was foolish to attempt the journey, but Nicolette thought she was brave. Her paternal grandmother had endured a long train journey to the French coast and then boarded a small boat in the dead of night to cross the choppy, wintry sea. Uncle Edwin had collected her from Hastings. He'd stayed in a boarding house and visited the docks every day, hanging around for hours to wait for her unscheduled arrival. Eventually, he'd found her arguing with the local officials who had never seen an American passport. His Northern good humour had smoothed the way for her to enter the country, and he had driven the last leg of her journey to Thames Ditton.

Nicolette took Robert's hand and steered him to an elderly woman seated beside Belle's coffin in the parlour. Elizabeth had her age marked hand on the glossy wood, and she was staring out of the window at the cloudless blue sky.

'Mémé Elizabeth?' Nicolette spoke softly to get the old woman's attention. 'You remember my fiancé, Robert, don't you?' She felt odd to be speaking of Robert as her betrothed when her heart was set on ending the relationship but felt today would not be an appropriate time to rock the family with more bad news. Belle's funeral was going to be difficult enough to cope with, without the added stress of a broken engagement.

Elizabeth turned unfocused eyes to Nicolette. She seemed to come to her senses and glanced at Robert.

'It is nice to see you again, Madam. I'm sorry it is under these sad circumstances.' Robert put out his hand formally.

Elizabeth took his hand and gave a small smile. 'Ah, yes. Belle told me you planned to marry our young Nicolette next year.' The old woman's voice was strangely accented by American and French influences.

'Yes, we have everything arranged for her birthday. I hope this war won't prevent you from coming to our wedding.'

'It didn't keep me from Belle's funeral.' She reached to touch the coffin again. 'We fought them before, didn't we, old girl? We won't let them rule our lives. We can't!'

'Grand-Mère Elizabeth and Belle helped the French army in the last war.' Nicolette explained to Robert, who was looking a little uncomfortable. 'Belle was not afraid to die, even back in those days. She took food convoys to the front line.'

'Your mother helped her, you know.' Elizabeth looked at the two sisters consoling each other on the sofa. 'Collette took a bullet in her shoulder on her first trip, but that didn't stop her from going again.'

'M, my g, goodness!' Robert stammered. 'I didn't realise your family were so involved in the last war.'

'There is a lot you don't know about my family, Robert.' Nicolette didn't like to see him squirm, but pointing out the bravery of her family members seemed to make him more of a coward in her eyes.

'Felicity began her nursing career at the casualty station in the grounds of my home, you know.' The old woman said proudly. 'The sights that poor girl witnessed!'

'Aunt Flissy wants to volunteer to go back to ~~France~~ the front, Mémé. She thinks her skills as a theatre nurse will be needed at ~~the front,~~ there but Uncle Edwin doesn't want her to go. He says she's too old.'

'Too old! Pah! Belle and I were of a similar age in the last war, but that did not prevent us from doing what we could to help.' Elizabeth shook her head. 'Age is merely a number. You are as young as you feel inside. Age should not be a definition of ability. Look at me, my birth certificate proclaims me to be seventy-five but did that stop me from coming to pay my respects to my friend?' Elizabeth reached her hand to Nicolette. 'Help me up, my dear, will you?'

Nicolette helped her grandmother get out of the chair. The old lady used a walking stick as she made her way to the grieving sisters, but her agile movements proved she did not need it. 'Don't cry for Belle, girls. She was ready to go, you know. We exchanged letters in the last few months, and she told me that her work here was done.'

'What work, Tante Elizabeth?' Felicity asked. 'She hasn't worked since Major Whitmoor died and left her this house. She hasn't needed to.'

Elizabeth chuckled as she looked at the two women. 'Always

the practical one, weren't you, Flissy? Work doesn't always mean the paid kind, you know. She worked tirelessly to keep her family safe. She stayed in England for your sakes; you know that.'

'What do you mean, Mémé Elizabeth?' Nicolette asked.

'Belle's heart was in France, yet she put her needs aside to help you girls out of a particularly complicated situation after the last war, did she not? That takes a special kind of work, you know. She worked at keeping your secret, but it was at the great sacrifice of her needs.'

Nicolette watched her Aunt Felicity blush.

'Belle-Mère, please!' Nicolette's mother took hold of the older woman's hand. 'This is not the place to launder our dirty linen.' Collette's eyes flickered around the room full of mourners and came to rest on Nicolette. 'Belle would not like to hear you discussing the past in this way.'

'Don't worry, Belle-Fille, I have no intention of rocking your boat. Your secret is safe.' Elizabeth looked directly at Nicolette, but her brief smile was fleeting and did not reach her eyes, which seemed unusually cold and hard.

Nicolette did not have long to wonder what the short conversation had been about. The clop of horse's hooves sounded from outside, announcing the arrival of the hearse. The funeral director's men ushered the mourners outside, and then loaded the coffin into the carriage for Belle's final journey to the church at the end of the road.

Elizabeth walked between Collette and Felicity at the head of the column of people dressed in black. The three women held their heads high. Nicolette followed with Robert and her Uncle Edwin, wondering how she would manage to stay brave and keep her tears at bay. She watched the horse-drawn hearse, carrying her beloved Mémé Belle, with an incredible heaviness in her heart. If Belle's best friend and two daughters could hold it together, then she could do no less. She lifted her chin and set her shoulders back as she walked slowly behind them.

The service seemed to go on forever, with hymns, eulogies, and prayers. Nicolette switched off to most of it. Religion had never been important to her. Belle had taken some comfort in her Sunday outings to the church, but she had never insisted that anyone accompany her. Apart from the early years of attending Sunday school, Nicolette had not enjoyed the rigid structure of worship. She believed in a simpler God who did not need the constant display of devotion and fear of damnation from his followers.

When Elizabeth was helped to the lectern, Nicolette lifted her head. She was interested to hear what her paternal grandmother would have to say about her maternal grandmother. The two women had been friends for many years. Her American grandmother knew things about her family. She'd already alluded to knowing some secret, and Nicolette determined to question the old lady before she returned to her home in France.

'Belle. My Belle!' Elizabeth began in a trembling voice. 'Where do I start?' She read from a shaking sheaf of papers in her hand. 'You were my best friend from the moment we met. We helped each other through life, through love, through war, and peace. I supported you when you lost your babies in the first years of our friendship. You supported me when I lost my sons in the dark days of the First War. Through the years we cried together, laughed together, plotted and planned our schemes together. What will I do without you?'

She paused to wipe a tear and gazed at the congregation. When she began to speak again, her voice was firmer and strong.

'Belle meant so much to all of us gathered here today. She touched us all in various ways. She touched many lives. Belle's heart was so large.' Elizabeth smiled and looked at Collette and Felicity sitting on the front pew. 'The spirit that made "The Little Cabbage of France" will live on. Your mother was one of the bravest people I ever knew. She was given that name by the French soldiers she helped to feed. Others called her, "The Woman of Verdun" but she never believed she deserved the acclaim. She did what she thought would help her country. She helped to raise moral. She put her life in danger to bring comfort to the boys in the trenches around our hometown. She earned respect, love and admiration from the youngest boys still wet behind the ear, to the Army Generals who recognised her great contribution to the well-being of the troops.'

Elizabeth paused again and shuffled her papers. 'Belle would not have been happy to know that we are again at war. If she'd been healthy and strong, she would be making her way back to France to do it again, I'm sure of it.'

A ripple of subdued laughter echoed through the congregation. Nicolette glanced sideways at Robert. His face was pale and his jaw tightened as he stared, unblinking, straight ahead. She turned her attention back to Elizabeth.

'She leaves behind two daughters who I know she was proud of. Collette helped, in her mother's quest to comfort the soldiers in the last war, and Felicity nursed the sick and injured men as they streamed into the casualty station from the front line. Since that war left a great mark on all our lives, I hope you will forgive me for dwelling on that awful time.'

Again, she paused to wipe away a tear and turned a page.

'When Belle moved to England, we thought we would only be separated for a short time. She intended to return after Nicolette was born, but Collette met Maurice and wouldn't be persuaded to leave the second love of her life. Felicity met Edwin and she began her training in London. Belle was caught up in their lives, and couldn't live her own as she wanted to.' She went on quickly, 'Please don't think she was a martyr, girls.' She aimed her comments to the front pew. 'You were her life. She was always the best mother you could have had. Not like me.' She huffed a laugh. 'We often discussed how different we were. We both loved our children, but Belle seemed to love everything about them while I found the caring and nurturing part of motherhood a boring chore.' She shrugged. 'It didn't mean I loved them less or that Belle loved them more. Our children knew two mothers and had the best parts of us both.'

Nicolette had already heard snippets of the family history from her mother and aunt, but Elizabeth was throwing new light onto the shadowed past. She listened with increasing interest.

Nicolette was disappointed that Elizabeth didn't speak much more of the past, and she finished her eulogy with a few words. 'And so I bid farewell, to my beloved Belle. Rest in peace my dear. Give my love to Patrice and Norman. I'll see you all again soon.'

Chapter 3: Calling it off

Nicolette was dreading her meeting with Robert. She was going to break off their engagement during the planned walk through the park. Robert had suggested they spend the evening with her family as Elizabeth would be leaving in a few days, but she didn't want an audience for what she was about to do. She knew she was doing the right thing. She couldn't tie herself to a man who didn't share her values. Part of her still loved him. Part of her was beginning to think he was not a coward. Perhaps he was braver than most because he was standing his ground against strong opposition. Most young men poured scorn on conscientious objectors, no matter what their true reasons were for not joining the fight.

Robert would not be swayed. He firmly believed the war would be over in a matter of months, and thought he would be wasting his time even considering leaving his position and his training. It didn't matter that one of his superiors had already left to join the Royal Air Force. It didn't count that Nicolette was waiting to join the Women's Auxiliary Air Force. Nothing was more important to him than finishing his training and securing his future in a firm of solicitors. Nicolette now realised that she did not want the same future. She would have been happy to go along with Robert's dream, but the war was changing everything. She couldn't understand why he didn't share her appreciation of the situation. They were worlds apart, and she could no longer see a future for them.

Spending time with her paternal grandmother had strengthened her resolve to end her engagement. Belle had always followed her heart and encouraged Nicolette to do the same. Until the last few days, Nicolette had not realised just how strong willed her Grandmother Belle had been. Listening to Elizabeth had brought Nicolette closer to understanding Belle, and she felt she knew her better now than when she'd been alive.

Her grandmother Elizabeth had reinforced Belle's philosophy by telling stories of the old times. She already knew that Belle had left her first husband when Collette and Felicity were infants. She was astounded to hear the circumstances of abuse that the family had endured because of Belle's first husband's brain injury. She was aware her grandmother had conducted an affair for years with Patrice before she married him in Verdun after her husband's death in the trenches. She thought the affair had started before her mother was born. She had always presumed Patrice was her grandfather from the way Belle spoke of him. She was shocked to learn the truth. Why had no one told her? Why did no one explain?

She heard more about her family in the last few days than she had learned in all the years she had spent growing up with the three women she thought she was closest to. She heard about her great-grandfather Joseph, who fought in the French Eighteen-Seventies War. She discovered more about Julien, her true grandfather who had drive and ambition until he was injured in an accident. Her father, Antoine, and her Uncle Pascal died in the last war, and Elizabeth had been inconsolable at the loss of two of her sons. She admitted being cheered to learn that Polly, her daughter, was expecting a child, even though that first grandchild would be born in America. Charles was born a few months before Nicolette.

'So there is only a month between our ages, Grand-Mére?' Nicolette asked.

'Yes, that's true.'

'Were you happy to hear that Collette was pregnant? After all, I would be Antoine's child. It must have been a consolation for you to learn that I was on the way, after losing my father.'

'Yes, dear. Of course, it was.' Elizabeth patted her hand but didn't make eye contact.

'You must have been upset when Belle brought them all to England.'

'Yes, I suppose I was.'

'Why did they leave Verdun, Grand-Mére?' Nicolette thought there must be more to the story than her grandmother was telling her. Why would a pregnant woman make a rough sea crossing to give birth in a strange country when her husband's family were settled in France? The war was over. Why take unnecessary risks? She had asked Belle the same question many times but had never been given a straight answer.

'You must have been told about the major, Nicolette. He offered you all a home and a secure future. Belle thought it was for the best.'

'I've never understood her reasoning. How could it be better for my mother to leave you? I can understand Aunt Felicity wanting to come here to study nursing, but what did my mother have to gain?'

'It's all in the past, Nicolette. Your mother would never have met Maurice if she hadn't come here. There was nothing for her in France after Antoine was killed.'

'What about you? I can't understand why she would leave her mother-in-law. You were both grieving for my father. Surely, you would have needed her to stay and comfort you. How could she consider taking your unborn grandchild away from you?'

'I had Norman and Francoise to keep me company. Francoise married Sabine, and they gave me three more grandsons before my Norman died. You know all this. You played with your cousins on visits. I don't blame your mother for taking you away from France. Even though you lived here in England, I don't feel I missed your childhood, Nicolette.'

'I feel I missed getting to know you, Grand-Mére.'

'You had Belle. I'm sure she made up for both of us.'

'I'll miss her.'

'Me too. I will miss her chatty letters.'

'What about the rest of your family in America? Do you hear from them?'

'Yes, I write to Polly often. Frederick can't send letters now. He has dementia, you know.'

'I'm sorry to hear that. He's your cousin, isn't he?'

'Yes, that's right.'

'Did he ever marry? Do I have more relatives out there?'

'No, my dear. Frederick never married.'

'What about Polly's children? What are they doing now?'

'Well, Charles,' Elizabeth became animated while discussing her other grandchildren. 'He's the one born just before you. He recently joined the American Air Force. I think he has ambitions to come over here and help fight the Huns.'

'Do you think America will join the fight?'

'It can't be avoided, Nicolette. They helped in the last war, they'll want to do the same thing again; I'm sure. No matter what Roosevelt said in his election campaign.'

'What about the other three cousins? They are all younger than me, aren't they?'

Nicolette listened patiently while her grandmother told her about her American cousins. Polly had four children, and Elizabeth was proud of them all. She took the time to describe each of them, but Nicolette had already stopped listening.

She had a whole family out in America that she had never met, and there were dark secrets hidden in the family closer to home that Elizabeth would not be drawn to talk about. Like Belle, she had avoided explaining the reasons for Belle's escape to England with her daughters. Nicolette had always thought it strange that a pregnant woman would leave her home and the place her husband had been killed. Collette left her mother-in-law and everything familiar, to settle in a foreign land to have her baby.

Something didn't add up, but she couldn't find out what it was if no one was prepared to talk about it. She had asked her mother, but Collette had always shrugged and blamed Belle for whisking her away to live with the major. Felicity and Collette seemed to think there was something going on between Major Whitmoor and Belle, but Belle had always denied it. Nicolette could find no evidence to suggest anything more than friendship between the older couple, so what was the real reason they came to England?

Elizabeth squeezed Nicolette's hand, bringing her back from her thoughts to focus on her grandmother. 'So there you are, Nicolette. Now you know all about your American family.'

'I should like to meet them one day. Do you think it may be possible?'

'Perhaps, after this war has been won and the world can get back to normal again. Travelling to England used to be easy, but now, there are Germans everywhere in Europe. I hope my return to France will be trouble free.'

'I wish you'd change your mind and stay with us, Mémé. We'll keep you safe here in England. Uncle Francoise will understand if you decide to stay.'

'Safe! Oh, Nicolette, you are funny.' Elizabeth chuckled. 'I've only been here a week, and there have been six air raids in that time. I've slept in the cellar with the rest of you more times than I've slept in my bed. Didn't the Germans just miss the school down the road with the bombs they dropped two days ago?'

'But we're safe in the cellar!' Nicolette pointed out. 'And we always get warnings in time to get down there.'

'I'll be much safer in my chateau, dear girl. The Germans don't bomb what they already think they own.'

'Perhaps you're right, but I can't help worrying about your journey home. Are you sure the fishermen can be trusted?'

'I pay them well enough. Francoise has already travelled to the coast on business. We planned for him to stay at a hotel, so my escorts will take me there after we land at the small beach near Dunkirk. The Germans think they know everything, but the French locals love to get the best of them, you know? They are very helpful, especially when I make it worth their while in French francs.'

'You're enjoying this adventure, Mémé, aren't you?'

'If the reason for my journey were pleasant, I would have enjoyed it better, I think.' She looked thoughtful for a few moments. 'Belle would have enjoyed hearing about my trip.'

'You two were so brave in the last war.'

'We did what we had to do to survive, my child, No more.'

'That reminds me; I have to go out, Grand-Mère.' She remembered the reason she had arranged to meet Robert. 'I'm sure Mum will look after you.'

'Are you meeting your fiancé?'

'Yes, I'm meeting Robert, and, well, you should know that I'm going to break it off with him.'

Elizabeth gasped. 'But why?'

'He's not who I thought he was.'

'You are so like your mother!' Elizabeth's eyes turned cold for an instant, and then she smiled a little too quickly. 'Collette was always impulsive.'

'Was she?' Nicolette thought that her mother was the prim and proper one. Felicity was the impulsive sister. 'Anyway, this is not an impulsive move. I've been giving it a lot of thought. I haven't come to this decision lightly, you know.'

'I'm sure you know what is best for you, Nicolette. Does your mother know what you intend to do?'

'Not yet, but I will tell her as soon as I've done the dead.'

'I'll keep your secret, then.'

'This family are good at keeping secrets, aren't they, Mémé Elizabeth?'

'I have no idea what you mean, girl.' Elizabeth looked uncomfortable and avoided Nicolette's eyes.

'I wish I had time to ask you more about the past, but I have to go.' Nicolette bent to kiss her grandmother's cheek. 'There is still so much I don't know.'

'Knowing everything is sometimes more a curse than a blessing, Nicolette. Don't get too nosey. You might not like what you uncover.'

'Belle always said that one whole truth is better than a dozen half lies.'

'She would! She was the best liar of them all, you know.' Elizabeth grinned mischievously and raised her eyebrows.

Nicolette was astounded. 'What do you mean?'

'Don't be late, Nicolette. Poor Robert should be put out of his misery before it gets much later.'

'I haven't finished with you yet, Grand-Mère.' She smiled and kissed the old woman again. 'You are full of mysteries and secrets, but I'll have to postpone my questions for now. I can't wait to hear more.'

'You may have a very long wait, child.'

'I'll see you later.'

Robert was waiting by the bandstand. He was smoking a cigarette and pacing the path. She watched him from the cover of the trees and felt the familiar pull of attraction. He was a handsome young man. His taller than average height, coupled with his waving light-blond hair, set him apart from other men. His athletic build added to his allure.

She'd been in love with him for so long; she found it difficult to deny the memory of those feelings for him. She realised that she had been seeing him through eyes blurred with emotion, but now her vision was clear. He had revealed his true colours, and she found she didn't like what she saw. She sighed deeply and began to walk towards him.

Robert's face brightened when he saw her, but his smile was soon replaced by an anxious frown when she didn't return his good-humoured welcome.

'What's wrong, Nicky? Has something happened? Is your Grandma Elizabeth all right?'

'Everyone is fine, Robert.' Everyone except me, she thought. 'I have to talk to you. Let's sit in the park shelter.'

'It's freezing, Nicky. Wouldn't you rather we went to the pub?'

'This won't take long, Robert. Come on.' She didn't take his hand, but he fell into step beside her.

'You're scaring me, Nicky. What's going on? Have you heard from the WAAFs? Are you leaving?'

'Yes I have, but that isn't what I want to talk to you about.' She took a seat on the wooden bench in the shadows of a three-sided shelter by the bowling green. She patted the hard, wooden slats. 'You might want to sit down, Robert. You won't like what I have to say.'

He perched on the edge of the bench and turned to face her. 'I'm listening.'

Now she was here, and he was waiting for her to speak, she felt guilty and uncertain how to start. She'd rehearsed her speech so many times in her head, but now the words wouldn't come. She was sure that what she was about to do, was the right thing. She intended to end their relationship. There would be no going back. She'd arrived at the crossroad, and she knew she would be following a one-way street from here. She swallowed nervously but lifted her gaze to look him in the face. 'I'm ending it, Robert. I don't want to marry you.'

'What? You can't mean it. Why?'

'There are lots of reasons, Robert.'

His face took on a sympathetic expression. 'You're not in your right mind, Nicky. You're depressed about the death of your grandma. Belle's passing has unsettled you. It's understandable. You just need some time, my love, to get over this. Perhaps—.'

'Robert! Stop!' She interrupted his litany of excuses. 'I've never been more certain of anything. I'm breaking off our engagement because I don't love you any longer. I thought I loved you very much, but I was wrong. I don't love you enough to marry you.'

'What changed? Is it the war? Is it because I won't enlist?'

She couldn't answer him. She didn't want to use his cowardice as the reason for her decision, but she couldn't deny what he said was true. She gazed at the damp leaves skittering around her shoes.

'I'll join the army! I will!' He reached for her hand. 'Look at me, Nicky!'

She lifted her face.

'I'll join the army or the navy or the air force if it will make you happy. I'll train for war, and I'll fight and risk my neck if that's what it takes to keep you. I want to marry you, Nicky. I want you to be my wife. I love you!'

'I don't want you to join the bloody army, Robert!' She could barely get the words through her tightly clenched teeth. She pulled her hand from his grasp and jumped from the bench, to create some distance between them. 'The thing is; we want different things from life. I thought we were well matched. I believed you wanted the same things I did, but you don't.'

'What things, Nicky?'

'I can't explain it, Robert. I just know you are not the man for me.'

'That's not fair, Nicky. You can't tell me you don't love me without telling me what's changed. You loved me last week! At least you said you did when we were snuggling on your sofa.'

He came to take her hand again, but she wrenched it away and turned her back to him.

'What do you want, Nicky? Do you even know?'

'I know what I don't want, Robert.'

'Well, that's a place to start. What don't you want?'

'I don't want you! I don't want to be stuck in Thames Ditton, married to a dull solicitor, with no life of my own other than what you can give me! I don't want to be a suburban wife bringing up a brood of children in a comfortable house. I don't want to be responsible for having your dinner on the table at six every evening and your slippers warming by the fire. I want a life, Robert. I want. I want…. I want more,' she finished, lamely.

'Well, that sounds pretty comprehensive.' He went to lean against the damp wall of the shelter and crossed one leg over the other. He reached into his jacket pocket for another cigarette and offered her one. She shook her head. 'How long have you been feeling like this?'

'Since Grandma Belle died.'

'I knew it!' He blew the smoke from his mouth in an exasperated sigh. 'You'll change your mind when the grief passes, Nicky. All this talk of her bravery and the exciting life they profess to have lived during the last war has unsettled you, just as I thought it might.'

She shook her head in denial of his words. 'You're wrong.'

'You don't understand how terrible it was for them, do you? You hear the thrilling stories, but you don't hear about the fear and the danger they lived through. War is not glamorous, Nicky, no matter what your aunt and mother say. They see their history through rose tinted spectacles. Time has skewed their memories, and they convince you they had a fabulous time of things and it was all a great adventure. Life is not like that. War is not like that. Can't you see? The evidence is all around us. Look what is happening to London. War is brutal, Nicky.'

Nicolette sighed and absently kicked a pile of wet leaves. 'You don't understand.'

'I think I do, Nicky.' He tossed his cigarette into a puddle and came to take her by the shoulders. He shook her gently and made her look into his eyes. 'You see the future with me as boring and uninspiring because your Grandma Elizabeth has stirred up a desire for adventure. The truth is; you'll join the WAAFs and spend the war in some dusty office counting paper clips. When it ends, you'll be out of a job, and you'll be alone. At least with me, you have a secure future. I can look after you.'

'I don't *want* you to look after me, Robert.'

'I can even give you an adventure if you like. I'll take you travelling. We'll go to Paris and Rome after the war. I can make you happy, Nicky. I know I can.'

'And I know you can't, Robert.' She shrugged his hands off her shoulders. 'I won't change my mind, so don't expect me to. I didn't want to be blunt because I didn't want to hurt your feelings more than I had to, but you have to know that I don't love you any longer.'

'How can you be so sure of that?' His eyes were dark with emotion as they looked into hers.

'Because I can't love a coward!' There, she'd said it and the words hung between them like a bloodied knife blade.

Robert stepped back as if she'd slapped him. 'You think I'm a coward because I won't fight in this bloody war?'

'No, Robert. I think you're a coward because you don't *want* to fight for what is good and right. You aren't prepared to give anything of yourself to fight the evil in this world or to try to make this country a better place for the next generation. If I were a man, I'd be over there right now. I wouldn't waste a minute on qualifications when I know there's a monster out there determined to ruin any other kind of future I might have planned.'

'So I'm a coward because I don't think the same way you do?'

'No, that's not it!' She closed her eyes and sighed. 'Well, yes. Perhaps that's one reason. Not that I think you're a coward, Robert. Not really.'

'That's big of you.'

'You're entitled to your opinion, but most people with your attitude to the war are called cowards by everyone else.'

'So you listen to the crowd instead of making up your own mind about me? You know my reasons for not wanting to fight. It's pointless. Fighting never solves anything. This war will be another disgustingly atrocious waste of life.'

'I don't share your opinion, Robert. I think the sacrifice is worth it to stop men like Hitler.'

'What if he can't be stopped? What if we throw this generation of young men to the battlefields, and he still gets here to take over? We'll have gained nothing for the sacrifice.'

'We have to try, though, Can't you see that?'

'No, I don't share your opinion on this.'

'Oh, Robert! That's the whole point. We don't think the same way. We don't want the same things. We're done. It's over.'

'Is that what you truly feel?'

It was happening. She was splitting up with Robert. She was surprised to feel emotional about leaving him. The lump in her throat threatened to choke her, but she couldn't let him see that she was upset. She didn't want him to think she was having second thoughts. She had to be strong. She couldn't trust herself to speak and simply nodded.

'Look at me, Nicky. I want to see your face.'

She blinked her tears away and lifted her head to stare into his eyes. She pushed her emotions deep inside. She didn't want him and she had to make sure he understood that this was the end. If she gave him any hint that she might change her mind, he would grasp at the chance and the breakup could become protracted and messy. She wanted a clean break.

'You are sure about this?'

She nodded.

'Is there nothing I can say to change your mind?'

She shook her head.

'Don't you have anything else to say to me? Is that it? After three years of loving each other and planning a future together, all you can give me is a head shake!'

'I'm sorry, Robert. I've told you my reasons. There's nothing more to say.'

'I hope you find what you're looking for, Nicky, but I don't think you will.'

'Perhaps I won't, Robert, but I won't give up hope.'

He sighed and turned from her. His shoulders drooped, and his steps were slow as he walked away from her. He didn't turn around. She waited until he was at the park gates before she let her tears flow. He was far enough away and wouldn't see them, even if he did turn to wave a final farewell. She might never see him again, but although he would leave a large hole in her life, she knew she would be stronger without him. She would have to be. Her papers had arrived from the WAAFs. She had an appointment in a few days with the recruitment office at the Air Ministry in Kingsway.

Chapter 4: Enlistment

Nicolette was helping her grandmother prepare for the trip back to France. She was checking the older woman's room to make sure nothing had been left unpacked. The family had tried to persuade Elizabeth to stay in England for her safety, but she wouldn't hear of it. Nicolette tried again before she carried the suitcase to the door.

'Are you sure you won't stay with us, Grand-Mère? You know Uncle Francoise will understand.'

'I have already told your mother I'll be quite safe, Nicolette. The Germans are not interested in an old woman travelling alone. If they question me, I am simply returning home from a visit to the French coast. I also carry a good deal of cash to placate the most inquisitive officers. Just in case, you know?' She tapped the side of her nose and winked.

'Oh, Mémé! You are enjoying this, aren't you?' Nicolette couldn't help smiling, despite her worries about her grandmother's safety.

'I must confess I haven't enjoyed as much excitement since the last war.' Elizabeth chuckled. 'But it should be easier on the return journey. Francoise plans to meet me at a little hotel we know on the outskirts of Dunkirk.'

'Come on, let's get you downstairs.' Nicolette carried her grandmother's case as she followed the old woman down the stairs.

'How safe is it to travel in France? Don't you get stopped and questioned in every town?' Collette asked as Elizabeth entered the living room. 'I worry about you, Belle-Mère.'

'You are in more danger here than I will be. When will you all see sense and move to the countryside? The Germans won't stop this infernal bombing until London is flattened. How can you bear to be cooped up together in that cellar night after night?'

'They won't drive us from our homes, Tante Elizabeth.' Felicity called as she helped her husband into his coat. 'They can bomb the whole of England, but they won't break us.'

'Brave words, Flissy, but where will Collette and her family live if they bomb this house?' Elizabeth asked. 'Where will you live if they bomb your home?'

'We try not to think about it, Mémé.' Nicolette held the old woman's coat out and gestured for her to put it on. 'Come, Uncle Edwin is eager to set out. He'll want to get back before the blackout. It's no fun, driving in the dark without headlamps.'

Elizabeth shrugged. 'If that is all he has to worry about, he's a lucky man. I have a rough sea crossing ahead of me with all the thrill of possible capture by submarine or German patrols.'

'Now, Belle-Mère, that is enough!' Collette admonished her mother-in-law. 'Edwin knows your risks are greater than his. None of us will rest until we hear you are safe at home. You will send a telegram as soon as you can, won't you?'

'I will if the lines work. You know how unreliable they are these days. Saboteurs are everywhere.'

Nicolette hugged her grandmother. 'Take care, Mémé.'

Joseph waited in line, to hug the old woman. 'I know I'm not your blood, but you're the only grandmother I have now. Take care, Elizabeth.'

'I will, Joseph.' She patted his back gently and turned to Felicity. 'If you do get to the front lines, to nurse the soldiers, promise me you'll take care.'

'I will.' Felicity kissed the old woman on both cheeks.

'We should go.' Edwin opened the door and the family filed out to the street.

They waved as they watched the car pull away.

'I hope she'll be all right.' Nicolette sighed wistfully.

'Don't waste your energy worrying about Elizabeth, Nicky. She's a tough old bird.' Joseph put his arm around his sister. 'I pity the German that tries to get in her way, don't you?'

Nicolette smiled. 'Trust you to see the funny side.'

'There is no funny side to any of this!' Their mother snapped. 'I hate this damned war!' Collette hurried inside with her hand over her face.

'I'll go to her.' Felicity offered.

'Phew, what did I say?' Joseph asked his sister.

'Don't worry, Joe. Mum is bound to be a bit emotional.'

'She's going to be worse when she knows what I've done.'

'What have you done?' Nicolette could guess, but waited for him to tell her.

'I've enlisted. I leave on Friday.'

'So soon!' Nicolette was shocked. 'Army? Navy? Air Force?' She blurted. She felt excited for her brother, but apprehensive at the same time. He'd be in danger, no matter which service he'd applied to.

'The RAF. I went for my medical and initial tests a month ago and I have to report to Uxbridge on Friday.'

'Why didn't you say anything before now?'

'I couldn't, could I? What with Belle's funeral, Elizabeth staying longer than expected and you breaking things off with Robert, it's been pretty hectic around here, hasn't it?'

'Mum's going to be livid that you kept it from her until the last minute. You're a dark horse, Joe.'

'She won't be too upset. You'll still be around to keep her on her toes.'

'No, I won't, Joe. I have an interview at the Air Ministry on Thursday.'

'And you call me a dark horse! What are you hoping to get into?'

'Oh, I haven't given it much thought. I'll do anything, really. I'll probably be counting paperclips for the duration. That's what Robert told me.'

'Someone has to do it, I suppose.' Joseph reached to ruffle her hair but she ducked. 'Nice reflexes, Sis. Those paperclips had better watch out! You'll have them counted and filed away in no time at all.'

'Oh, you!' She pushed him and they tussled together as they made their way into the house.

'Children! Do stop this foolish behaviour. You're both adults but you wouldn't think so, they way you two carry on.'

'Don't be stuffy, Mum. We're only letting off steam.' Joseph released his loose stranglehold on his sister. 'Nicky has something to tell you.'

Nicolette pulled a face at her brother and stuck out her tongue for good measure. 'You go first, Air-Ace.'

Collette frowned. 'What's going on? What does she mean, Joseph?'

'I'm going to train as a pilot. I'm going to Uxbridge on Friday.'

'What!' Collette and Felicity said together and turned worried faces to him.

'You can't!' Collette said.

'Why didn't you tell us?' asked Felicity.

'I'm eighteen, Mum. I can.'

'But you're too young.' Collette dropped on the sofa as if her legs would no longer support her. 'You can't leave me.'

'You'll have Nicolette, Collette. You won't be alone.' Felicity glanced at her niece's awkward expression. 'Or is there something we should know about you, too?'

39

Nicolette took a deep breath. 'I have an interview to join the WAAF on Thursday.'

'No! I won't allow it. You can't both go to war.' Collette's face was pale. 'I can't lose you.'

Nicolette went to sit beside her mother. 'You're not losing us, Mum. We're doing what you would have done if you were our age. We want to help the war effort just as you did. Just as Aunt Flissy did, and Belle and Elizabeth. You can't stop us. I'm sorry if you're upset about it, but you have to see we are only doing what we feel is right.'

'You didn't bring us up to be cowards, Mum. We have your example to follow, don't we?' Joseph added.

'You can't argue with that, Collette.' Felicity pointed out. 'I should have said something before, but I also have an interview next week. I've applied for a position with the Queen Alexandra's Nurses. I'd like to work in the casualty clearance stations again. I'm hoping my experience will count toward them accepting me despite my age.'

'What does Edwin think to that?' Collette asked.

'He doesn't know, yet.'

'He won't let you go.' Nicolette said.

'He won't have a choice.' Felicity lifted her chin. 'I'm at the sharp end already at work. We get the casualties from the bombing raids and it's heartbreaking to see the young children and women with horrific injuries.'

'So why do you want to put yourself in more danger when you're already helping victims of war here?' Collette asked.

'Because I want to help our soldiers. '

'What will Edwin do when you're gone?' Collette raised the question that Nicolette had wondered about.

'He's already joined the Local Defence Volunteers. He goes to drill in the church hall every evening. If he were younger, he'd be in the army, by now. He wants to help too, but he's too old for the regulars.'

'I'll be all alone in this big house. I'll be a sitting duck for the German bombers. What will I do without you all?'

'Oh, Mum.' Nicolette took her mother into her arms. 'Why don't you do voluntary work? I'm sure the soup kitchens would welcome your skills. Didn't you help to feed the army in the last war?'

'You'd have me serving soup to the homeless?'

'Why not, Collette?' Felicity asked. 'It would be the perfect job for you.'

'And you'd be helping all those poor, bombed-out people, Mum.' Joseph encouraged his mother. 'Think what a difference you could make. I'm sure the slop they serve now could be improved by your expertise in the kitchen.'

'I wouldn't know where to start. Who would I have to see?'

'Why don't you come into town with me on Thursday, Mum? Perhaps we could ask around to see what is already being organised.'

Collette sighed. 'Looks like you already organised me.'

'So here we go again, Sister. You'll be feeding the masses, and I'll be repairing them.' Felicity chuckled. 'Just like old times, eh?'

'Except, we will be worrying about the children this time instead of our mother.'

Chapter 5: Interview

Nicolette waited impatiently in the long corridor. She'd counted the windows, the squares on the linoleum floor and the number of doors that punctuated the walls. She resisted chewing her nails. She didn't want to appear nervous. About half an hour had passed, and there was still no sign of the young woman who had taken her papers and disappeared through a wooden door.

She'd been given sheets of forms to fill in and was then shown into a room with about twenty other young women. They were all given a pencil and told to sit at a desk, to fill out the paperwork. They now sat in a line in the corridor, waiting to hear whether their form-filling had been successful.

Nicolette had left her mother near Covent Garden, a few streets away. Collette intended to call at the churches and ask where she might be able to volunteer her services. They had arranged to meet for lunch at a café they liked near the Theatre Royal on Drury Lane. Nicolette glanced at her watch. If the Air Ministry didn't hurry up, her mother would have to eat alone.

'Are we keeping you, Miss Armaud?' The young woman appeared at her side as if from nowhere.

'No, err, of course, not.' Nicolette stammered.

'Please follow me.' The young woman turned quickly and marched along the corridor.

Nicolette gathered her gloves and bag and hurried after her, feeling the curious eyes of all the other seated young women watching her. She was shown into a small office with one desk and two chairs. The room had no ~~and no~~ other furniture. It looked dismal and felt cold. She shivered.

'Please take a seat.' The young woman indicated which chair she should sit on. 'Someone will be with you shortly.' She left and closed the door behind her.

Nicolette sighed. More waiting around! How much longer would they keep her? She lifted her hand to her mouth, hesitated, and then clenched her fist. She would not bite her nails. She lowered her hand and clutched the handle of her handbag tightly. Stay calm, she told herself. They called you first so it can be either good or bad news. They will tell you they don't want you, and then you can go. Perhaps they do want you, and then you'll find out where you are to be stationed to count their paperclips. Hold tight. They won't keep you waiting much longer.

Pearl A. Gardner

She turned when she heard the door open. A very good-looking man walked into the room and smiled at her. His dark eyes danced over her, from her head to her toes and she felt self-conscious under his scrutiny. She felt herself blushing and noticed he held her forms in his hand.

'Your answers to some of our questions have intrigued us, Miss Armaud.' He switched to French and asked her what she thought she was doing here.

'I beg your pardon?' She answered in English.

He asked again, in French, and added, 'You have us all in a spin if what you wrote on here is true.' He shook her forms.

She answered in French. 'I would like to join the WAAF to help win the war. I'll do all I can to help defend Great Britain. If that means counting paperclips, then so be it. I'm your girl.'

He switched to German. 'What do paperclips have to do with fighting Germany?'

She answered in German. 'You tell me! It seems you have them in abundance according to my ex-fiancé. He thinks all I will be good for is counting them for you.'

'Bravo, Miss Armaud.' The man put her forms on the desk and applauded quietly. He spoke in English, 'What part of France are you from?'

'I've lived in Thames Ditton all my life, but my family lived near Verdun before I was born. My grandmother still lives there and I have visited often.'

'Verdun, eh?' He scratched his chin. 'How familiar are you with the area?'

'I know the town of Verdun quite well and I am very familiar with the small village where my grandmother's chateau is situated. I visited Reims and Nancy once or twice and I've been to Paris once.'

'Good. Nice and concise. That's what we like. No rambling with unnecessary details.'

Nicolette lifted her chin. She watched him as he read more from her form. His hair flopped over his forehead in a wave of golden brown. He needed a haircut. He had a lighter coloured moustache, badly in need of a trim, sitting on his upper lip. His skin was clear, with a hint of a tan. His fingers were long and slim. The hands of an artist or a piano player, perhaps, she thought.

'Are you scrutinising me, Miss Armaud?' His eyes lifted from the papers and he grinned at her.

43

'Sorry, I didn't mean to stare.' She quickly looked at a dark stain on the opposite wall.

'No, I'm interested in your assumptions. Please tell me your opinion of me.'

'I have none.' She was beginning to feel embarrassed. 'I've only just met you.'

'Still, you will have already started to make some assessments. Tell me what they are. Don't hold back and don't try to be polite.'

'Is this part of the test?' she asked.

'If you like.'

She sat back in the hard, wooden chair and tried to look relaxed even though her heart was beating wildly. Something about the man was unnerving her. He was creating waves of unease in her insides. 'I thought you had the hands of an artist or a piano player,' she began. 'But then I realised that you've probably recently seen action in a warm climate, so your skills might be more suited to warfare these days. Maybe you're a sniper or a pilot who was shot down over enemy territory.'

'What makes you think I've been in a hot climate recently?'

'You have a slight tan and your hair has hints of gold as if bleached by the sun.'

'Very observant, Miss Armaud. Go to the top of the class!'

She hesitated but decided to be bold. 'You were probably away from civilisation for about six weeks.'

'Now you have me intrigued.' He leant back in his chair and looked at her quizzically. 'How could you possibly know that detail?'

'You need a haircut.' She suppressed a smile by biting her lips together.

'Well, I'll be blowed!'

'Am I right?' She was desperate to know whether her powers of observation were as good as she wanted them to be. She knew she had it in her to do more than count paperclips.

'Yes you are, but I can't tell you where I was, why I was there, or what I was doing.'

'Of course, sir. I wouldn't expect you to.'

'Deferential to superiors too, you just get better and better, Miss Armaud.'

She felt her insides contracting with pleasure from his praise. She knew she was blushing and lowered her eyes.

'You'll do, Miss Armaud. How do you think you'll cope with sharing a bunkhouse in basic training?'

'I'm sure I'll manage as well as the other girls.'

'Make sure you do. I'll see you when you get through the first stages. If you survive the basic training, you'll be sent to a remote training camp in Scotland. When you get there, make yourself known to me.'

'Won't you remember me, sir?'

'Don't flatter yourself, Miss Armaud. I see hundreds of hopefuls such as you.'

'Who should I ask for, sir? I don't know your name.'

'Mr Brown.'

She sucked in her cheeks, to suppress the laugh that bubbled from her chest. 'Is that your real name, sir?'

'What do you think, Armaud?'

'I don't think anything, sir.'

'Good! Keep it that way.'

'Yes, sir.'

'You can go now.'

'Where should I go, sir?' She felt a little confused. Had she been accepted? Would she have to go to a training camp now? Right now?

'Go home, Armaud. We'll write to you with details of what will happen next.'

'Oh, yes, of course.' She stood and moved to the door.

'One thing before you go.'

She spun to face him. 'Yes?'

'Don't say a word about this interview. The other girls will have a very different screening to the one you just had. They are the ones who will count our paperclips.'

'Of course, sir.'

'And another thing.'

She paused with her hand on the door. 'Yes, sir?'

'Work on suppressing that blush. It could get you into all kinds of trouble.'

She looked puzzled. Why was blushing wrong? How could she stop her face from colouring when she was embarrassed? Why should she even try?

'That will be all.'

She pulled the door open and stepped into the corridor. The number of girls still waiting to be seen had halved. She walked down the row of chairs with shaking legs. One girl put out a hand to stop her.

'How did it go, pet?'

'Not bad. I think I passed the test.'

'Hope to see you at Bridgnorth, then. That's where they'll send us for basic training, you know. I'm Peggy Stanley.' She stuck out her hand for a handshake.

'Nicky Armaud.' She said as she took the girl's hand.

'Are you a Londoner? You don't half sound funny to my northern ears.'

'Yes.' Nicolette didn't want to jeopardise her future by admitting her French roots to this girl. 'Where are you from?'

'Newcastle. I came down on the train last night and slept at the tube station. Well, when I say slept, I don't know how any of you Londoners can sleep with that racket going on all night. Bloody Germans!'

'Will you go back today?'

'Yes. I'll get home past midnight, but it will all be worth it if I get in. It's exciting isn't it, being able to help our boys fight this war?'

'Yes, it is.' Nicolette was beginning to feel the first thrill of adrenaline running through her veins. She was excited. She couldn't wait to start her training, and she was determined to get through it, whatever she had to do. She couldn't wait to go north and meet Mr Brown again. 'Hope to see you at Bridgnorth then.'

Chapter 6: Basic training

Nicolette stared at the letter addressed to her. She knew it would contain her instructions and travel arrangements. Joseph had already left to begin his training to become an aircraft pilot. He wanted to fly fighters but knew that only the best would be chosen for that specialised form of combat. He'd confided that he would be just as fulfilled flying bombers or even cargo aircraft, so long as he was doing something worthwhile to shorten the war. She knew that whatever her brother did, she would worry about him, and their mother would worry about both her children.

'Aren't you going to open it?' her mother asked. 'Put me out of my misery and tell me when you are leaving, won't you?'

Nicolette tore the envelope open and pulled out the letter. She scanned the instructions quickly until she saw the date. The sixteenth of December jumped out from the page. A fortnight from now which meant she wouldn't be at home over the Christmas period.

'Oh, Mum. I didn't think it would happen so quickly. I thought they'd let me have Christmas at home first.'

'Let me see.' Collette took the letter and sat on the couch, to read the details. 'Well, that will give us two weeks to ensure you have everything you need before you leave.'

'I won't need much by the sound of things.' She leant over her mother's shoulder and pointed to the list of essentials she would be allowed to take with her. She read, 'No civilian clothing, other than the clothes I will be wearing.' She glanced at her mother. 'What's that supposed to mean, Mum? What about a change of underwear? They can't expect a girl to make do with one pair of knickers for goodness' sake! I'll need more than one pair of shoes too, won't I?'

'Perhaps they will provide those things for you.' Collette suggested. 'After all, you'll be expected to wear a uniform, won't you?'

'At least I can take my own toiletries, so it won't be all that bad.'

'Joseph didn't take much with him when he left. He said the Air Force would kit him out, and I'm sure they'll do the same for you.'

'We'll all be in uniform, Mum. You have your WVS overall, and Aunt Flissy will soon be kitted out in the Queen Alexandra's uniform. Has she heard when she might be shipped out?'

'She couldn't tell us, even if she knew, Nicolette. I don't think it will be too long. Edwin is furious with her, but his anger and sulks will not dissuade her from going. She's determined, you know.'

'What will he do without her, Mum? How will he manage? He can't boil an egg.'

'I told him he can come to me for his evening meal. We'll both be alone when you've all gone, so it makes sense to pool our rations.'

'How does Aunt Flissy feel about that?' Nicolette knew that there had always been friction between her mother and aunt where Edwin was concerned, though had never really understood why.

'It doesn't matter what she feels. She won't be here!'

Nicolette decided not to pursue the matter. It appeared her mother had everything worked out and now seemed less concerned that her family were leaving her. She took the letter from her mother's hands. 'What else does it say?'

On a cold December morning, Nicolette boarded the train for Bridgnorth. She wore her best wool coat over her tweed suit and cotton blouse and had her brown leather ankle boots on her feet. She carried an overnight bag with a few toiletries, half a dozen pairs of knickers, and a spare brassier, an extra pair of stockings, two nightdresses, a knitted twinset of top and cardigan and some stout shoes. She also carried her gas mask and a small handbag that held some money, sandwiches, a flask of water, lipstick and a comb. Her mother had thought of everything when she helped her pack the previous day.

The train was crowded with no spare seats, so she stood in the corridor and stared at the passing scenery as the train sped along. Other passengers hurried by trying to find seats, calling to friends and bumping against Nicolette as they pushed through the narrow corridor. Families, men in uniform, and a few old people shuffled along the moving carriage trying to find some place to settle down for the journey.

'Going far?' A young man in a grey greatcoat asked her.

'Bridgnorth.'

'You might get lucky then. You'll be changing at High Wycombe, and the next train should be quieter. You might get a seat the rest of the way.'

'I hope so.'

'What's in Bridgnorth, a boyfriend, is it?' The young man asked.

'Erm,' She lowered her eyes bashfully and cursed her

unaccustomed shyness. She felt strangely tongue-tied. He was very attractive, but she didn't know what to say to the inquisitive airman.

'It's all right if you don't want to tell me. My pals are always saying I'm too nosey for my own good.'

She smiled but kept quiet.

'Not the talkative type, are you?'

She flicked her eyes up to look into his face. His eyes were full of warmth as he looked at her, and she smiled. He was just being friendly.

'You didn't say where you were going.' She decided to be polite to the young man. He seemed nice, and she didn't want to appear rude. Conversation with an interesting stranger might help to pass the time on the journey.

'Same as you. Bridgnorth. I caught a bullet and some shrapnel a few months ago that stopped the war for me. I can't fight anymore, so I'm only good enough to train others to do the job. I'm to be in charge of the next intake of WAAFs at the training camp. I ask you! What am I going to do with a bunch of girls?'

Nicolette started giggling and put her hand over her mouth. She turned to the window, to hide her blushes.

'What did I say?'

She could see his confused expression reflected in the train window. She giggled again but was unsure how to proceed.

'Oh, no!' The young man slapped the side of his head with the flat of his hand. 'You're one of them, aren't you?'

She nodded and tried to suppress her laughter.

'Look, miss. I shouldn't be talking to you. Under the circumstances, I'd better leave you to it.'

'Please don't go,' she blurted. She didn't want him to leave. 'I won't tell a soul we already met, I promise.'

'But I'll be...'

'What can anyone do? Who would know that we spoke on the train? What difference will it make?' She was warming to the young man and wanted to spend more time with him.

'You'll find out when I start giving you orders. I'm a devil on the parade ground.'

'You'll be teaching me to march, I expect.'

'Among other things.'

'Have you trained women before?'

'You'll be my first bunch, and I'm nervous if I'm honest, but please don't tell the others that. I have to look as if I'm in control and full of confidence in front of raw recruits.'

'My lips are sealed.' She smiled. 'I don't know your name. Should we introduce ourselves, do you think?'

'Sergeant Bradley.' He stood to attention and saluted. 'At your service, miss. At least until we get to camp, and then you'll have to call me sir and do everything I ask of you or you'll be in big trouble.'

'I'm very pleased to meet you, Sergeant. I'm Nicolette Armaud.' She held out her hand expectantly.

He hesitated before taking it, but his handshake was firm and warm. 'What a pretty name. Shame I'll have to call you Private Armaud.'

'I won't mind, sir.' She held his hand a little longer than she should have. It felt good and solid in hers.

He grinned and gently took his hand from hers. 'What are your plans for after training? Wireless operator? Clerk?'

'Well, I thought I'd be counting paperclips, but I've already been told I'll be sent to a remote place in Scotland after training.'

'Don't tell me any more, miss.' The sergeant put up his hand and touched his fingers lightly and briefly to her lips. 'Careless talk costs lives and all that.'

'What did I say?'

'Have you been told why or where you'll be sent after training?'

'No.' She shook her head and wondered what he might know that she didn't.

'Look, miss, it's not my place to speak out of turn, but I'm guessing you've got some special talent that attracted the big boys' interest when you first applied.' He put his hand up again. 'No, don't tell me. I don't need to know. It will only complicate things for me.'

'But I'm not special at all. At least, I don't think I am.'

'Listen! Most girls have some idea of what they want to do in the services. They see the young women in newsreels at the cinema and take it into their heads that they can do the same thing. I bet that's what made you decide to enlist, wasn't it? The glamour of it all! The important-sounding titles! Radio operator, radar plotter, barrage balloon operator and the like.'

'Not at all!' she protested. 'I want to help win this bloody war.' She didn't like to be spoken to in such a patronising tone. 'People are dying, not just the young men on the battlefields, but women and children are getting hurt in our towns and cities!' She wanted the young man to understand how passionate she felt about what she was about to do. 'I want to help stop Hitler and his mob. If counting paperclips for some important high-ranking officials will help in that cause, then that's what I will do.'

'You don't have a clue, do you?'

'About what?'

He took a deep breath and let it out slowly. 'It's best you don't know, for now.'

'You're scaring me.' She began to feel nervous. 'What do you know?'

'I know that I will do my very best to make sure you get through the training. I'll be hard on you, Miss Armaud. Probably more than I would have been if I hadn't known what you just told me but remember it will be for your own good.'

'Now you're really scaring me. What's in store for me at Bridgnorth?'

'Bridgnorth is where you'll get a proper grounding in discipline, attention to detail, and physical endurance. We'll make something of you, I'm sure.'

'All that, just to count paperclips!'

'Oh, I think you'll be doing far more than that, Miss Armaud.'

'There you go again, being all elusive and mysterious. Can't you tell me anything?' She couldn't help flirting with him, but he didn't seem to mind.

'A word or two of advice, miss. Keep a low profile in training. Don't tell anyone else what you know about where you'll be sent. Do everything asked of you without question and do whatever it takes to get through it.'

'Yes, sir.' She saluted him. 'Anything else, sir?'

His face was deadly serious. 'Keep to your cover story of counting paperclips. Being a clerk is the safe option, if anyone asks what you enlisted for, that's what you tell them.'

The train hissed and began to slow.

'We're coming into High Wycombe,' he told her. 'We change trains here. I think it might be best if we separate now. I can't get involved with you. Much as I'd like to get to know you better, Miss Armaud—.'

'You would?' Nicolette interrupted him and felt her heart miss a beat. He liked her.

He continued as if she hadn't spoken. 'It's impossible for me to be friends with a recruit.'

'Would you prefer that we hadn't met?'

He smiled softly, and she noticed the small scar on his temple. She instinctively reached to touch it, but he moved his head away from her hand. 'Is that where you took the bullet?'

'I'm going to leave you now, miss. Try to sit near the front of the next train and I'll sit at the back.'

'If you say so.' She sighed.

'Believe me. It will be better in the long run if we don't speak again in public.'

'How can we avoid talking when you're going to be training me?'

'I don't talk when I train. I shout.' He grinned. 'And I don't care for back-chat.'

'I'll remember that.' She smiled at him and felt saddened that she couldn't enjoy his company for the next stage of their journey. 'I can pretend I never met you if you like.' She said impulsively. 'If it will make it easier for you when you're training me, I swear I won't say a word.'

'Who did you say you were?' His severe expression didn't falter, but his lips twitched as if he were containing a smile. 'No don't tell me. We never met, did we?'

'No, sir.' She watched him turn to leave the train. 'We never did.'

As he walked away, she noticed he had a pronounced limp. Perhaps that's where he was injured, she thought. Poor man. He must have been in the first battles of the war. She shook herself and lifted her overnight bag from the floor.

When she finally alighted from the train in Bridgnorth, she found herself surrounded by young women who were gazing in bewilderment around the station platform, looking as lost and confused as she was. Nicolette saw a familiar face and called, 'Peggy!' She hurried to join the girl she'd met at the Air Ministry.

'Nicolette! Am I glad to see someone I know! It's bloody bedlam here, isn't it?'

'I don't think any of us know what to do. The letter gave us instructions to get to Bridgnorth, and here we all are, but what now?'

'LADIES!' a voice yelled from the crowd. 'QUIET, PLEASE!'

Nicolette saw her sergeant friend step out from the crowd and stand before the milling women. She wanted to catch his eye but remembered her promise. Nevertheless, she couldn't help feeling a little disappointed when he ignored her completely.

He stood to attention and barked at the assembled young women. 'Those of you with papers for entry to the WAAFs at RAF Bridgnorth, please form an orderly line and follow me.' He turned on his heel and limped to the station exit.

A voice called out from the crowd, 'You heard the man. Come on, girls.'

Nicolette grabbed Peggy's hand and joined the line of women. They gave their names when asked by a young woman in uniform and were told to climb aboard a large lorry. When they were seated on the wooden benches, Nicolette finally had a chance to take stock of her companions. The women were from all kinds of backgrounds, judging from their state of dress. Some wore threadbare coats and down at heel shoes, others wore silk stockings and had feathers in their hats.

'We're a proper mixed lot, aren't we, Nicky?' Peggy whispered as she elbowed Nicolette in the side. 'See that one over there? I bet you a bob she doesn't last a week.'

Nicolette smiled as she looked at the thin girl dressed in a satin frock and matching jacket. 'She looks frozen stiff, poor thing. Let's make room for her between us.' She gestured to the girl, to join them. 'Move over, Peggy.'

'Thanks, I was feeling a bit lonely. I don't know a soul here. Did you two join up together?' The slightly built girl squeezed between them.

'Not exactly.' Nicolette explained. 'We met at the recruiting office in London. This is Peggy, and I'm Nicky.'

'My name's Ethel, but most folks call me Kit because I like cats.'

'Pleased to meet you, Kit.'

Nicolette held out her hand the girl shook it quickly and turned to Peggy.

'Nice to meet you, Peggy.' She shivered. 'Wish my Mam hadn't made me wear my best outfit. I told her it wasn't warm enough for this weather, but she wouldn't have me going off to war in anything but my Sunday best.'

'Snuggle up, lass.' Peggy put her arm around the slim shoulders. 'We'll soon have you toasty and warm.' She grinned over the girl's head at Nicolette.

When the lorry was packed with young women, they were transported to the base where they disembarked on a large square of concrete at the end of the road. The square was surrounded by low wooden buildings. The girls were divided into two groups by the female who'd taken their names earlier. Nicolette's group were shown into a hut, lined with beds. She realised that this hut would be her home for the next few weeks.

'Stand by your beds!' Sergeant Bradley called from the doorway. 'Shut your mouths and open your ears!'

All the girls found a bed and stood very still as the sergeant limped slowly down the centre of the room.

'Now these are the rules. Break them and you'll be on toilet cleaning duty for a week. Understand?'

They all nodded.

'The response is, yes, sir! Nice and loud, please, so I know you all heard me.'

'Yes, sir.' They chorused, noisily.

'Rule number one, lights out at ten, no talking after lights out. Number two, you will all have completed your ablutions and be dressed and ready to march to the mess hall by eight in the morning. Lateness will not be tolerated. Understand?'

'Yes, sir.' The girls called together.

'You can all see your beds have three, large, square cushions. These are called biscuits. You also have a straw-stuffed pillow, two sheets and three blankets. You'll be shown how to make your bed for sleep and how to stack it in the morning. Take care to listen to Corporal Mendip when she instructs you how to do this. I'll be inspecting your efforts first thing.'

As he spoke loudly, he limped down the line of women with his hands behind his back. 'Any deviation from the standard stack will be punished. Understand?'

'Yes, sir.' Nicolette straightened her back and held her head high as he passed her. She noticed his eyes flickered in her direction briefly, and she smiled to herself.

He spun to face her, his face stern and disapproving. 'Got a problem with that, Private?'

'Err, no, sir,' she stammered.

His eyes stared into hers, but she didn't see any warmth in them this time. He spun away from her and shouted, 'Drop your bags by your beds and follow Corporal Mendip's instructions. Before supper, you'll be shown where to put your belongings and how to make and stack your bed. I'll see you all in the morning.'

'Goodnight, sir.' Nicolette whispered. She knew he'd heard her when she saw the back of his neck flush red, but he didn't acknowledge her words and simply limped briskly out of the long hut.

'Right, girls. Unpack your bags and put your things into the boxes at the end of your beds.' The female corporal instructed. She went to the nearest bed to the door and unfolded the bedding stack while the girls quickly unpacked.

'All done?' the corporal asked. 'Gather round, then. Don't waste time. The sooner we get this done right, the sooner we can all go to supper.'

The young women hurried to form a circle around the first bed in the long room.

'Watch carefully, now. I'm going to show you how to make your beds. You should follow my example exactly. Understand!'

A few girls chorused, 'Yes, sir,' uncertainly. Some substituted, miss for sir. Others stayed silent, unsure what to respond to the corporal.

'Yes, Corporal, will do, ladies.'

They called the correct reply.

'Right! First you'll need to unwrap your bedding and place the biscuits on the pallet, like so. Then place one sheet on top, fold it like so.' She demonstrated the correct way to make up the bed and followed the demonstration by folding it again into a neat pile. 'Now you lot do the same thing. Remember, I want to see nice neat creases at the corners and no wrinkles!'

'Yes, Corporal,' Nicolette called with the others as they returned to their beds.

All the girls followed her example and soon the beds were all made up and looked ready to sleep in.

The corporal walked down the line of beds, pointing out sloppy creases and wrinkles. 'This won't do, ladies. Let's try again, shall we?' Her voice was syrupy smooth, and Nicolette flinched when she shouted, 'Now stack your bedding! Woe betides any of you if I see any wrinkled blankets!'

'What?' Peggy looked at the corporal.

'Are you questioning my orders, Private?'

'No, sir, I mean, miss.' Peggy began to roll up her blankets.

'No, Corporal will do, Private.'

'Yes, Corporal.'

Nicolette followed Peggy's lead and all the girls soon had their bedding stacked neatly, as it had been, or so they thought.

'Not one of you took any notice, did you?' The Corporal marched down the line of beds sneering at their handiwork. 'Let me show you one more time and this time you had better listen and learn. I'm hungry, and I don't want to be eating cold rations tonight!'

She shook out the nearest girl's bedding and showed them the correct way to stack the biscuits, fold the sheets, roll the blankets and wrap it together with the folds showing to the front.

'Now, ladies, let's see you do it again.'

It took three more attempts before the corporal was happy with their efforts. 'At last! Now you can make the beds ready for sleeping in them, and then we can go for supper.'

Nicolette suppressed a groan and glanced at Peggy, who was exchanging silent eye rolls with Kit. 'Don't let the corporal catch you doing that,' she whispered. 'She'll have your guts for garters!'

'She can have 'em. My guts aren't worth anything at the moment. I'm so hungry.' Kit said as she smoothed a wrinkle from her top blanket.

'All right, ladies, let's get a move on. Supper won't wait much longer, you know! This way.' The Corporal marched from the hut, and the girls fell into line behind her.

'I hope we don't have to sleep to attention in those beds!' Kit said as they hurried along, and the nearest girls laughed nervously. 'I'll be afraid to move all night in case I cause a dratted wrinkle!'

The smell from the mess hall was not particularly appetising. The aroma of boiled cabbage added nothing to their anticipation of a good, hot meal.

'Liver and bacon with mash and cabbage!' Peggy grinned as she took the plate from a woman in a green overall. 'What a treat.'

'Are you sure?' Kit asked uncertainly, as she took her plate.

'Well, I'm hungry enough to eat a horse, but this will have to do.' Nicolette carried her plate to one of the long trestle tables in the dining hut. She looked at the watery gravy soaking into the lumpy mash and sighed. 'My mum would have a fit if she saw what we had to eat.'

'My mum would be jealous.' Peggy sat down quickly and forked a pile of soggy mash into her mouth and swallowed. 'She can't cook to save her life. This is proper nosh.'

'Are you sure?' asked Kit.

'Try it, you'll like it.' Peggy encouraged.

'If you say so.' Kit lifted a fork to her lips and took a nibble of cabbage. 'Ugh, it's cold. I can't eat this.'

Nicolette glanced around the room full of girls pulling faces at the cold and unappetising food. 'Well it looks like this is all there is, and I suspect we won't get anything else until breakfast, so we'd better eat it all up.'

'Wise words, Private.'

Nicolette swivelled her head. She hadn't seen the sergeant come in. She watched him move down the line of seated, eating, young women. 'Eat up, girls,' he shouted. 'You'll need to keep your strength up for drill tomorrow. I'll see you all on the parade ground at one sharp.'

The following day they were woken at six, shown where to complete their ablutions and marched to breakfast. Each girl was served a rubbery fried egg and a slice of fatty bacon in a thick slice of bread. They all wolfed it down without complaint. Tea was served in buckets, and they each had to dip their tin mugs into the lukewarm brew.

After breakfast, they were given a huge bag of bits and bobs of uniform and told to share them out. Black silky knickers in all sizes were soon snapped up, but the thicker, grey woollen bloomers were left in a heap on the floor. Some girls were fortunate to get a full uniform of a skirt, blouse and jacket that fitted, but others couldn't find anything to fit and had to wear their own clothes. They were all given a pair of stout black shoes and told to polish them until they shone like glass.

The day continued with a drill in the afternoon where they learned how to march in step. They were taken to the medical block where they stood, in line, to receive injections. After the inoculations, they were taken to a schoolroom where they were shown the different shapes of aircraft and had to repeat the names of each until they could name them all correctly.

One day rolled into another, each following a similar routine of cleaning their hut, shining shoes, and washing and pressing what uniform they had managed to scrounge. Each day they marched, exercised and attended the schoolroom for lessons. They learned how to recognise an aircraft by its silhouette. They memorised the emblems of ranks until they could tell the difference between a corporal and a warrant officer at a glance.

Two weeks had passed in a blur of activity and Christmas was only one sleep away. They were informed there would be no leave granted for the Christmas holidays. On hearing this, some girls were so homesick they dropped out and went home for good. Consequently, Christmas Eve was a miserable evening.

The girls had arrived back at their hut after two hours of marching up and down the parade ground while being buffeted by a freezing, gale-force wind. Sergeant Bradley had seemed to enjoy making them repeat the formation-marching endlessly. He'd picked on some girls for not keeping in step on the turns, and Nicolette had come in for a particularly stern admonishment for tripping over a loose shoelace.

Bradley had yelled above the howling gale. 'There is no excuse for undone shoelaces, Armaud! Lack of attention to detail like that could cost you your life! Don't let me see you with loose laces again or you'll be cleaning the latrines for the rest of your time here in Bridgnorth.' He raised his voice even louder to shout in her face, 'DO YOU UNDERSTAND!'

'YES, SIR!' she had yelled back, defiantly.

She had felt more miserable than ever, but had squared her shoulders and followed the marching commands quickly and precisely after that. She was determined to show the sergeant that his pitiless treatment would only make her stronger.

His cruel and relentless orders continued for hours. She thought his voice must surely give out before their stamina, but he shouted louder, demanded more and only stopped the drill and dismissed them when the wind brought a deluge of freezing rain.

'Anyone got a plaster?' Peggy called to the room of morose girls. 'This blister is giving me hell!' She rubbed her heel, gently.

'I think the NAAFI ran out of plasters, Peggy.' Kit sat beside her friend on the bed. 'I've got some Vaseline. That might help.'

'Thanks, pet.'

Corporal Mendip came into the hut carrying a box of letters and parcels. 'Santa came early, girls. Stand by your beds!'

The young women stood at attention by the end of their beds. Nicolette hadn't heard from her family since she left home. She'd sent letters to her brother and mother to let them know how she was and hoped there were some replies in the box the corporal carried. She could feel the excitement in the room as Corporal Mendip called out names and handed small parcels and envelopes to the waiting girls who tore them open eagerly.

'Private Armaud!'

'Yes, Corporal!' Nicolette stood taller and wondered what the box might hold for her.

'Here you are.' The corporal handed her a small packet and two envelopes.

'Thank you, Corporal.' She sat on her bed and began to rip open the parcel.

'What you got, Nicky?' Peggy asked.

Nicolette glanced up to see that her friend had nothing to open. Peggy hadn't received anything. She turned to see Kit watching her expectantly.

'Here.' Nicolette handed the torn parcel to her two friends. 'Open this for me, will you. I want to see who has written to me.'

They didn't need any more encouragement to rip the parcel open. Both girls eagerly tore the paper to expose a tin box.

'Shall we see what's inside, Nicky?' Kit asked. 'It has a note that says, "Happy Christmas, with love from Mum".'

'Yes, open it.' Nicolette had seen that her first letter was from her mother, and she started to open the second letter.

'It's biscuits!' Peggy grinned. 'They smell delicious.'

'I told you my mum was good in the kitchen, didn't I? We'll save them for after our dinner tomorrow, shall we?'

'You'll share them with us?' Kit asked, sounding surprised.

'Of course, I will, silly moo.'

'Who wrote to you?' Peggy asked.

'Mum and my brother.' She quickly scanned the letter from Joseph. 'Joseph will be posted to RAF Binbrook in January to continue his training. He's got leave for Christmas, lucky thing. He'll be with my mum and Uncle Edwin now.' She sighed and smoothed the wrinkled paper. 'I wish I could see them all.'

'Hey, let's have none of that homesickness, Nicky. It's Christmas, let's not be sad. We have each other, don't we?' Kit sat beside her and put a comforting arm around her shoulders.

Peggy came to sit at her other side and hugged her. 'And I'm hoping the mess will be serving something good for supper this evening.'

Nicolette smiled. 'Trust you to think of your stomach!'

'We'll wait until you've read your letters, Nicky.' Peggy shrugged. 'It'll probably be bully beef slop as usual.'

Nicolette put her letters aside. 'No, my letters will keep. Let's see what they cooked for us.'

The mess hall was noisier than usual when the three girls walked in. The aroma of roast pork greeted them and made their mouths water.

'Is that proper meat on the menu?' Peggy pointed to the metal serving trays filled with thick slices of roast pork.

'Make the most of it, ladies.' Sergeant Bradley called from a nearby table. 'It's not often we eat this well.' He pointed to the end of the serving benches. 'Grab yourselves a bottle of beer too. The alcohol is courtesy of the top brass to raise moral.'

'Don't mind if we do, Sergeant!' Peggy grabbed a plate from the serving woman. 'Ta, pet.'

Nicolette shook her head in amazement as she took a seat with her friends. She couldn't believe the change in the sergeant in such a short time. Less than an hour previously he'd been treating them all to his most foul temper and issuing punishing commands in atrocious conditions. Now he was chatty and polite as if the whole terrible afternoon had not happened.

She stared at her plate with no appetite. What was she doing here, anyway? What did she hope to achieve? How could she think she could really make a difference in this war?

'Not to your liking, Private Armaud?' The sergeant called. 'The cooks went to a lot of trouble to get that pig. Don't waste it.'

She put her head down to whisper, 'I wouldn't dare! You pompous idiot!'

'I think he likes you, Nicky!' Kit grinned.

'You're insane. He hates me!' she said before stuffing a forkful of meat in her mouth.

She had an hour before lights out to read her letters, and the other girls were already re-reading theirs quietly. The ones who hadn't received anything were gathered at the end of the room around the wood burner, chattering quietly. One girl began to sing a Christmas Carol and the others joined in. '… Holy Night. All is calm…'

Nicolette concentrated on her mother's words.

My dearest Nicolette,
I hope this finds you well, and I hope you are making friends and fitting in. It must feel strange to you, to be housed with so many young women after having your own room at home. The training sounds frightful. Why would you have to learn to march? You won't be sent to war, and so marching would not be a skill you would need to have. I don't understand how young ladies should be made to do such unladylike occupations, but I suppose the authorities think such things have a purpose.

Pearl A. Gardner

I heard from Joseph. He is enjoying his training and making friends, just as you must be. He hasn't been near an aircraft yet and sounds disappointed. He'll be home for Christmas, and although I will be very happy to see him, I will still be sad that you can't join us. What a shame it is that you must stay in Bridgnorth.

I'm settling in quite well to the Women's Voluntary Service. They have me cooking soups and stews during the day for the homeless. Sometimes I help to serve them from the back of a large truck they let us park in Leicester Square in the evenings.

We have to abandon everything when the siren goes off, and we all run for the underground with everyone else. We sit and wait on the platforms and wonder what we'll emerge to find.

One night, we came out after the all-clear to find someone had stolen the whole lot! We couldn't find the truck. There hadn't been a bomb in the area. There was no rubble and no damage to the surroundings. It had just vanished. The warden said it had probably been stolen, soup and all! We reported it to the police but don't expect to get it back. Black-market racketeers are everywhere. The truck is probably broken up for spare parts by now, and the soup will be filling the bellies of criminals.

Uncle Edwin is like a lost sheep. I do what I can for him. He keeps himself busy with the Home Guard. They play at being soldiers and help to clear up after the raids. It keeps him occupied, though I know he misses your aunt terribly. Felicity went off to war last week. We thought she'd get Christmas at home, but, like you, the authorities in charge of organising this war had other ideas and sent her off to a casualty station abroad. We have no idea where she is. I expect we'll hear from her when she is settled. I'll let you know.

We still have had no word from your Grandmother Elizabeth. I worry that she didn't make it back, but Edwin says that no news is good news, and we shouldn't worry. Elizabeth is a resourceful woman, so I'll try not to worry about her. My mother-in-law could always take care of herself. Again, I'll let you know if we hear anything.

Robert called around in the hopes that you might be home for Christmas. He wanted to arrange to see you, but I told him you won't be here. He asked me to let you know that he has joined the Navy and will be leaving in January. I suppose it was only a matter of time before he would be called up anyway. I'm still sad that it didn't work out for you two. I think Robert hoped he could change your mind. I told him that war changes people. It makes us assess ourselves and

61

forces us to think differently about what we want from life. I hope you can find happiness when all this is over, my dear.

I wish you a happy Christmas, Nicolette. I sent you a taste of home and hope my parcel reaches you in time.

All my love, Mum.

Nicolette folded the letter and tucked it back inside the envelope. The letter from Joseph was full of his news, and he wrote of his excitement about his imminent posting to Binbrook. She knew the station flew Wellington Bombers. He would, at last, be seeing his beloved aircraft, though it would be quite a time until he was allowed to actually fly one. He ended his note with an affectionate three crosses in a row and the words, *"Take care big sister, TTFN, Joe."*

She sighed and felt a moment of self-pity. She wished she could be with her family, but everything had changed now. She was becoming a serving member of the British forces and would soon be given duties to help in the fight against Hitler. She could sacrifice family time for the cause. Thousands of men were already doing much more than that. She remembered her mother's words about Robert. He had joined the Navy. After all his protestations, about not wanting to be involved, he had finally chosen to ignore his noble principles. She hoped he hadn't done so for her sake. She knew she didn't want him back. She couldn't share her life with Robert. She wanted more than he could give her. She didn't know what that would be, but she had a feeling that she would soon find out.

Chapter 7: Moving on

By the end of January, some girls had already been selected for their trades and now spent time each day in the various technical training huts, acquiring the basic skills they would need. Peggy was learning Morse code. Kit, surprisingly, had always been interested in mechanics and was learning how to service and repair engines. Nicolette stuck to her cover of wanting to be a clerk and attended lessons in shorthand. They were still drilled to within an inch of their endurance, were summoned, daily, to Physical Exercise class, and had to keep their hut and uniform spotless at all times. By nightfall, the rule of no talking after lights out was easy to follow. They were too tired to do anything but climb into their beds and sleep.

Nicolette had done her best to keep her word to Sergeant Bradley. She didn't want to get him into trouble, but she was finding it difficult to avoid being affected by him. He was everywhere. He inspected their bed stacks daily. He supervised their drill, barking orders at every turn. When they stood to attention, he inspected the ranks, criticising them. He ridiculed their sloppy stance, their wrinkled blouses or the length of their hair, which had to be worn above the collar. He always found something on which to pass judgment. She tried to stare straight ahead when he came near, but when he looked directly into her eyes, her heart always beat a little faster.

'What happened to your hair, Private Armaud?' His fingers flicked the stray strands that had escaped her attempts to pin them into a roll.

'I washed it last night, Sergeant, and it just won't behave this morning.'

The other girls close by, began to giggle but the sergeant gave them all a stern, warning look, and the giggles soon faded to silence.

'Perhaps you should try using Brylcream to keep those curls under control. It works for me.' He flashed a brief smile and continued along the line.

Nicolette's eyes flew wide. She couldn't believe he had said something nice instead of giving her an extra duty to perform. She glanced at Peggy, who was standing beside her, grinning mischievously.

'Now I *know* he likes you,' she whispered.

'Don't be daft,' she hissed back.

'Shush, he's coming back up the line,' Kit said from behind them.

All three stood very still as he marched, awkwardly past them with a limp. Nicolette watched him take a sheaf of papers from the corporal and wondered what they would be asked to do next.

'Ladies!' he began. 'I have the list of your postings. I'm sure you'll be sorry to hear that you'll be leaving us in a few days to continue more specialised training in your chosen fields.'

A murmuring began in the ranks, and he waited for them to stop whispering.

'We've been tough on you here, but I hope we have instilled in you all, a sense of pride in yourselves that will stand you in good stead in the months and years to come. It has been a pleasure, ladies. We wish you well in your future roles.' He turned to the female corporal. 'Would you like to read out their fate, Corporal?'

'Yes, Sergeant.' The corporal took the papers from him, and he left the parade ground. The corporal appeared to read the first few papers, and then called to the assembled young women, 'When I call your name, march smartly from the ranks and approach me. First up, Private Anderson.'

A well-rounded young woman stepped two paces from the front rank, turned on her heel and marched to the corporal.

'You'll go to Leighton Buzzard to plotter's school. Collect your travel warrant tomorrow from the office.'

'Yes, Corporal. Thank you.'

'Private Armaud!'

Nicolette stepped from the ranks and marched to the corporal.

'You'll be sent to Scotland.'

'What will I be doing there, Corporal?' Nicolette asked.

'I suppose you'll find out when you get there, Private! Collect your travel warrant tomorrow.'

'Yes, Corporal.'

She marched back to her place and waited until all the girls had been given their orders. It seemed to take hours and all the while she wondered what was in store for her. All the other girls were assigned further training and told exactly where they would be going and what they would be doing. Peggy got her wish to train as a wireless operator and was to travel to London, to attend the radio school. Kit got RAF Binbrook, where she would continue her training in the motor transport section there. Nicolette briefly wondered whether Kit might bump into her brother there.

She listened with mounting unease to the other girls' postings. No one else had been given such unclear instructions. All Nicolette had been told was that she was to go to Scotland. She had no idea where, in Scotland, or what she would do when she got there. She began to worry what the other girls would think of her obscure and unexplained posting, but she needn't have been concerned. They each seemed too excited about their own news to have remembered the vague orders she'd been given.

'Where are you going, Nicky?' Peggy asked quietly. 'I forgot what she said to you.'

'I'm to go to Scotland, to work as a clerk.' She whispered the first thing that came to her mind and hoped it would be enough to satisfy her friend's curiosity.

'Now for some good news, ladies.' The corporal clapped her hands to get their attention as the murmurings had grown louder since the last girl had been given her orders. As the women quietened, the corporal grinned. 'You've all got a four-hour pass from seven tonight. You can go into town and let off steam.'

The ranks broke as cheers erupted, and berets and caps flew in the air.

'We can go to the pub! At last! I thought I'd have to spend the rest of the bloody war without a glass of stout.' Peggy hugged Nicolette. 'Come on, girls. It's almost half past six. We have to get ready for a night on the town!'

Nicolette watched her friends laughing and flirting with some young men in RAF uniform at the bar. She had tried to join in the fun, but her heart wasn't in it. She didn't feel the excitement as the other girls did. They were all certain of their future, but hers was hazy and unclear. She still didn't know what to think. The noise of the bar was beginning to give her a headache, and she was considering sneaking away from the din.

'Penny for them!' A familiar voice broke her reverie, and she glanced up into Sergeant Bradley's face. 'Can I buy you a drink?' he asked.

'I thought you weren't supposed to fraternise with the likes of me, Sergeant.'

'Well, that was before you got posted. You'll be officially released from under my care shortly, so we can be friends until you go.'

'What?' She didn't understand.

'How about that drink?'

She smiled and tried to relax. 'Thanks, I'll have a glass of stout.'

'Coming right up.'

She saw Peggy winking at her. 'I told you he liked you, didn't I?' she shouted from the bar.

Nicolette grinned at her friend. The evening had suddenly become more interesting. She watched the sergeant as he took the two glasses from the landlady and turned to bring them back to the table. He smiled, and her heart did a flip. It seemed months, not weeks, since she'd broken up with Robert, and she knew it was too soon for her to become involved with anyone else. She wasn't looking for love and romance, but she couldn't deny the affect her sergeant was having on her.

'Thank you.' She took the glass of dark ale from his hand.

'I thought you'd be a gin and tonic kind of girl.'

'Can't stand the stuff.' She laughed. 'I prefer wine, but pubs in England don't serve much of my favourite tipple. The ones that do seem to think any old wine will do and don't seem to appreciate the various qualities...' She didn't finish her explanation because she realised she was rambling and possibly giving away too much information about her background.

'Wine, eh? Never tried it.' He took a long drink from his glass of beer. 'Now, that's better.'

She took a sip of her stout and grimaced. She didn't like the taste of the bitter brew but had said the first thing that came to mind when he asked her. She'd been drinking lemonade before his offer.

'Not to your liking?' He pointed at her glass. 'I can get you something else.'

'No. Really. You don't have to,' she assured him. 'I think it's an acquired taste, but I'm sure I'll get used to it.'

'Rather like wine, I'm told.' He winked and grinned at her. 'Where did you learn to appreciate fine wines?'

'In France, where else?' She laughed.

He leant close to whisper, 'Ah! So that's why the Baker Street Irregulars are so interested in you.'

'The Baker Street who?'

'Not here, Nicolette. Keep your voice down.'

She huffed an impatient sigh. 'Look! If you know anything about what they want me to do next, tell me,' she hissed. 'I'm totally in the dark about my future with the WAAFs, and I can tell you that I'm not happy about it.'

'All right. You win.' He put his head close to hers. 'I did some digging and found out that your mother is French. You speak French and German like a local, I believe.'

She nodded and waited.

'You can't tell me that you haven't worked it out.'

'Worked what out?'

'What they want to train you for.'

'Well, I know it's not counting paperclips.'

'You'll be working as an interpreter. For the top brass, possibly. It could be very exciting. You'll get to meet some high ranking officials, maybe even the prime minister himself.'

'Oh, my goodness!' She gasped. 'I had no idea that speaking French could be so important. I always took it for granted.'

'I think your skills with the German language will be more important, don't you?'

'Possibly.' She nodded. 'But I'm a bit rusty. I haven't spoken German for months. Not since my grandmother became ill and we couldn't continue our lessons.'

'Your grandmother taught you!' He looked alarmed. 'Was she German?'

'No, she was French but did business with Germany before the last war. She spoke the language fluently. Much better than I can.'

'You said 'spoke', not 'speak'. Does that mean she's no longer with us?'

Nicolette stared into her glass as tears suddenly filled her eyes. She nodded.

'Was this recently?'

She nodded again.

'I'm sorry. You must miss her.'

Nicolette nodded and stared at her hands. 'Every day,' she admitted.

'Tell me about her.'

She looked into his face and saw genuine interest in his eyes. Her heart filled with something indescribable, and she realised that it would be too easy to fall in love with him. She couldn't let it happen, though. She'd be leaving in a few days. She might never see him again. What good would come of getting too close to him now? She shrugged. 'You know too much about me already. Tell me something about you. I don't even know your first name!'

He smiled. 'That's easy. It's David.'

'That's a good, solid, English name. It suits you.'

'I'm glad you approve.'

She steered the conversation to safer, more general topics, and they chatted for the rest of the evening about inconsequential trivia. When the landlady rang the bell for last orders, Nicolette couldn't believe how fast the evening had flown by.

'Oh, goodness, I'd better get a move on. My pass runs out in half-an-hour.'

'I think you'll find the camp has put on some transport for you and your friends.' He stood to help her on with her coat. 'There's a truck waiting outside.'

'How thoughtful.' She glanced at the other girls who were saying goodbye to groups of young men. She looked up into David's face and smiled. 'Did you have anything to do with arranging our safe return to camp?'

'Maybe I did.'

'Thank you. I'm sure they'll all appreciate how thoughtful our sergeant can be after all the pain and suffering you caused us in the last few weeks. I've still got the scars of blisters on my feet from all that marching.'

'Sorry about that, but I had my orders.'

'I'm not complaining. I've enjoyed my time here at Bridgnorth.'

'I've enjoyed it too.'

Nicolette saw his eyes darken. She would only have to lean towards him and his lips would be on hers. She pulled away abruptly and began to fasten the buttons on her coat. 'I expect there'll be another batch of raw recruits coming in next week to keep you on your toes.'

He looked disappointed. 'They arrive on Monday.'

She held out her hand. 'Well, it has been nice knowing you, Sergeant.'

He took her hand but didn't shake it. Instead, he lifted it to his lips and kissed her palm. 'I hope our paths cross again, Private.'

Peggy's raucous voice interrupted the moment as she pushed her way between them. 'Come on, Nicky. We don't want to get into trouble in our last few days here, do we?'

'I'd better go, Sergeant.' Nicolette said.

'Goodbye, Private.'

Chapter 8: Scotland

Nicolette was the only one to leave the train at Arisaig. Her long journey terminated at the small platform in the early morning and she was still rubbing the sleep from her eyes as she disembarked the cold carriage onto the frosty platform. She had no idea what to expect, but the cold silence filled her with a sense of foreboding. She watched the sparsely populated train puff steam as it moved from the station, leaving her alone.

She turned in a circle, to view her surroundings and was amazed at the beauty of the landscape beyond the wooden station building. Snow-capped mountains rose behind the building, and frosted pine trees huddled close to the rails on either side of the single track. The heady scent of pine filled the misty, morning air. She took a deep breath and closed her eyes to savour the aroma and wondered how long she might have to wait, for someone to come to collect her. She'd been told she would be met at the station, but didn't know the time of the meeting. She'd presumed the person collecting her would know what time the train would be arriving. She walked to the station building to see whether anyone was around. She looked through the window and tapped on the door, but it was clear the building was unoccupied. The sound of her knock had an empty, hollow feel to it.

She looked for somewhere to sit and wait, but there were no seats on the platform. She put her bags down and lowered herself to sit on the edge of the cold concrete, dangling her legs over the track. She thought about smoking a cigarette, but she only had two left and was in two minds about giving up the habit. She was hungry, though, and had nothing to eat, so a cigarette might help to keep the hunger pangs at bay.

She struck a match and lit the cigarette. She was about to throw the lighted match down on the rails when a voice called out in a Scots lilt, from behind her. 'I wouldn't do that, miss, if I were you.'

She swivelled her head to see who had spoken.

A man with grey at his temples, wearing a dark suit and a tartan beret was walking towards her. 'There's usually a good amount of oil on those tracks. You could end up blowing your legs off if you threw a lighted match down there.'

'Oh!' She looked at the flame working its way to her fingers, down the shaft of the match and quickly blew it out. 'Thank you.'

'No problem, miss. Glad to help.'

She scrambled to her feet. 'Are you here to collect me?'

'Well, I'd like nothing better, miss, but I have to pick up a young gentleman.'

'I'm afraid I'm the only one who got off the train. Perhaps he'll be arriving later?'

'Typical! Bloody Englishmen can't be trusted to catch a train on time.'

'Well, I caught it with no trouble and I'm English.' She couldn't help smiling at the older man's disappointment in her countryman. 'But then, I am a girl, so I'm probably more trustworthy in your opinion.'

'And you say you're the only one to get off here?'

'I am.'

He looked thoughtful for a moment and stroked his chin. 'What's your name, miss?'

'Private Armaud, at your service, sir.'

'Armaud?' He took out a card from his pocket and examined it closely.

'Yes.'

'Is your first name Nick, by any chance?'

'Close. It's Nicolette.'

'Well, you can see why we thought we were expecting a man. Sorry for the mix-up.'

'So you *are* here to collect me?'

'If you're Nick Armaud, you're the one we're expecting at the big house.'

'The big house?'

'You'll see. Come along, miss. Or perhaps I should call you, Private?' He reached to pick up her bag and she had no choice but to follow him.

'Yes, I'm Private Armaud, but I was told not to wear my uniform to travel here.'

'Quite right.' He took her to a smart, black car and held the door open for her. 'We don't get many women up here, Private. You'll have to take us as you find us.'

'What, err...?' She didn't know quite how to ask her question, so she just came out with what was on her mind. 'What exactly do you do here?'

He looked at her quizzically. 'Don't you know?'

'I haven't got a clue.'

He sighed heavily. 'What is the ministry thinking of? To send us a woman with the name of a man is bad enough, but to send us someone who doesn't know the first thing about the SOE is plain stupid if you ask me. If I were a betting man, I'd wager they made a mistake and you'll be on the next train out of here.'

'What's the SOE?'

'Well, I suppose I'd better tell you. Can't do any harm. It stands for Special Operations Executive.'

'Special Operations?' She repeated the words to see whether they held any significance for her. 'Does that have anything to do with being an interpreter?'

'Well, I suppose it might. Aye, Private. We do a bit of interpretation.' He smirked and added, 'Among other things.'

His enigmatic reply did nothing to assuage her curiosity, but his evasiveness warned her to keep her inquisitiveness under control. She'd find out soon enough what she would be expected to do.

The car journey only took a few minutes but she was able to appreciate the remoteness of the place. Rolling hills of heather stretched for miles in all directions. She saw a glimpse of what looked like the sea on one side and the snow-capped peaks towered into the distance. The scenery was beautiful but bleak. They didn't pass any other dwellings, shops, pubs or buildings of any description. Not even an animal shelter. When the car rounded a bend in the road, she was surprised to see a large grey building sitting at the end of a long grassy meadow, surrounded by thick, pine forest. It looked like a castle or manor house. It had a turret and lots of gables and appeared to rise from the misty meadow like a fairy-tale castle from a cloud. It wasn't what she had been expecting at all.

When he pulled the car to a halt, by the large, imposing entrance, her companion turned to her. 'Welcome to Arisaig House, Private Armaud. If you're hungry, they'll still be serving breakfast in the mess hall.'

'You have a mess hall in this fine old place?' She had images of the long wooden hut at Bridgnorth in her head and couldn't imagine a place as grand as this large house having anything so basic.

'Come with me, Private. We'll get our scran, and then I'll show you around.'

'Scran?' She followed him through a wide, arched entrance.

'Scran means food. I was referring to breakfast, lassie. De ye not ken you're in Scotland now?' He emphasised his dialect and winked at her.

'Oh, I see.' She giggled. 'It's a good job I'm good with languages. Seems I have to learn Scottish, now.'

'Scots!' He corrected her. 'We locals don't like to be called Scottish. We're Scots and our language is Scots too.'

'I'll try to remember that.' She could hear the low mumbling of men's voices and she could smell bacon and toast. Her stomach rumbled. 'Will we have breakfast before my language lessons begin?' She quipped.

'I'll drop your bags here for now.' He put her bag by a large oak dresser and went through some double doors, beckoning her to follow him.

He showed her into a large dining-room set with four, long, wooden tables. The room seemed crowded with men eating breakfast but they all lifted their heads when she entered. All discussion ceased as twenty or so men in casual dress turned to stare at her. She lifted her chin and tried to look confident and sure of herself, though her insides were quivering with nerves.

Her eyes flicked around the room, taking in the dresser, laden with piles of toast, a platter of crisp bacon, and a dish of eggs in shells. There was also a covered tureen and various pots of relishes, chutneys and preserves. A roaring log fire burned in a large inglenook fireplace, making the room warm and inviting. In the seconds it took her to scan the room, her companion had introduced her as Private Nick Armaud to the rest of the men seated at the tables.

They all called out a nondescript greeting and she nodded and answered a quiet, 'hello.'

'Better get something down you, Private.' One of the young men shouted. 'You'll be needing your strength for the long journey home.'

The others sniggered and Nicolette lifted her head defiantly. She didn't know why they were making fun of her but she didn't like it.

'Take no notice, Private. Come and get some scran.' He handed her a tray and began to pile a plate with bacon, two eggs in shells and some slices of toast.

She hesitated.

'There's porridge in the bowl if you'd rather have that.' He pointed to the lidded tureen. 'But we put salt in our porridge up here. You might not like it.'

'Bacon will be fine, thanks.' She heaped a few more rashers on her plate.

'The eggs are boiled but it's pot luck if they're hard or soft.' He whispered. 'Toast is good, they bake the bread here, and there's some butter at the end, over there.' He pointed, with a knife he'd just taken from a heap of cutlery in a box. 'Coffee and tea are in those urns on the windowsill.'

'Thanks.' She followed his example and soon had a breakfast fit for a king on her tray. She followed him to a table and sat beside him.

'Hope you don't mind me sitting with you,' she whispered.

'Why would I mind?'

She glanced at the other men flicking suspicious glances at her while they ate. 'The others don't seem too friendly.'

'They don't bite. They'll be fine once they get to know you.' He pointed his knife at her plate. 'Eat up. The boss will want to see you before we put you through your paces.'

Her hunger overcame her nerves and she attacked her breakfast hungrily, ignoring the rudeness of the other men who were now talking quietly and making comments about her.

'How long will she last, do you think?' one said.

'She'll be on the train home by tonight, I'll bet.' Another sniggered.

'What are they thinking of? Sending us a woman, for God's sake?'

'Is she going to train alongside us?'

'She'll hold us back. We'll be playing nursemaid—.'

'Give her a chance, why don't you?' Her companion interrupted the flow of derogatory comments. He spoke quietly, but the others fell silent to listen to him. 'She's here for a reason, same as the rest of you. She's been picked out because someone, somewhere, thinks she can help us win this war. We're in it together and we work as a team. You know this! Just because our team now has a new member, and she happens to be a woman, it doesn't make us any less of a team. Understand?'

'Yes, sir!' The men jumped to attention and saluted her companion.

Nicolette almost dropped her fork. 'Are you an officer, sir?' she asked.

'Major MacDonald, but you can call me sir.' His stern words were softened by his friendly grin.

Her recent training had instilled an automatic response in the presence of officers and she immediately jumped to her feet and saluted him.

'Admirable, Private, but you're not obliged to salute when out of uniform.'

'Sorry, sir.' She glanced at the other men who were all smirking at her slyly and resuming their seats. 'But they saluted you, and they're not in uniform.'

'I'm not in uniform, either, Private. Just in case you hadn't noticed.'

She sighed and pursed her lips with frustration. 'Is this a different kind of service up here? You don't seem to have the same rules of rank and responses that I just spent the last six weeks learning.'

'Sit down and finish your breakfast, Private.' The Major indicated her almost empty plate. 'All will become clear after you've met the boss.'

'Who is the boss, sir?' she asked before putting the last pieces of bacon in her mouth.

'Wing Commander Brendon has overall control of what we aim to achieve here, Private Armaud. I'll take you to meet him when we've done here.'

She put her knife and fork down. She was impatient to know what she would be doing while she was in Scotland and so far no one had given her the slightest idea of what that might be. The sooner she met the person responsible for her duties, the better. 'I'm done, sir,' she announced and got to her feet.

Chapter 9: Fish out of water

She waited in the comfortably furnished office on the upper floor of the grand house, pacing the carpet and glancing out of the window at the extensive view to the sea. When the door opened, she turned to face the Wing Commander and snapped to attention.

'At ease, Private. Take a seat.' He indicated the seat at one side of the large desk and went to sit at the other side, facing her. 'We've heard good reports about you. You appear to have, exactly what we need, and you seem capable of following orders and keeping your nose clean. How fit are you?'

She was surprised by the question and shrugged before answering, 'As fit as anyone else who just completed basic training, sir.'

'Well, we have a few weeks to improve on that. You'll be spending time with a team of Royal Air Force Commandos out in the field. We expect you to keep up with them, and the training will be tough. Do you think you'll cope?'

She remembered the unfriendly men she'd met at breakfast and felt a determination to prove them wrong. 'I'll give it my best shot, sir.'

'That's the spirit. Pilot Officer Brown will meet you in the cellar storeroom, he'll kit you out for this afternoon's jaunt.'

'Can I ask where I'll be going, sir?'

'Best not to ask too many questions at this stage, Private. Loose lips sink ships and all that.'

'Yes, sir!'

The Wing Commander got to his feet, and Nicolette sprang to attention from her chair.

'I know you feel like a fish out of water, Armaud, but you'll soon get the hang of how we do things. We have a lot riding on you, Private. I hope you can do what we expect of you. Dismissed.'

She hesitated before quickly marching from the room and closing the door behind her. What did he mean? What was he expecting of her? Whatever it was, it sounded important. She had so many questions running through her mind, but it seemed no one was prepared to tell her anything. What had she got herself into?

She eventually found the cellar storeroom and was surprised to find a familiar face there. She'd wondered when she might see him again.

'Mr Brown! You've had a haircut, sir.' She commented when she saw the man who had interviewed her in London.

'Very observant of you, Private.' His tone held a hint of mockery.

'I was told someone would help kit me out. Are you Pilot Officer Brown?'

'That's me.' His eyes travelled the length of her body from the top of her head to her toes, and she felt a little embarrassed by his close attention. 'What size shoe do you take?'

She suddenly realised why he'd been looking at her with such intensity. He was merely interested in her size. She felt disappointed. 'Five, sir.'

'I hope we have some boots in your size. Take a look in that box over there, will you?' He pointed to a large wooden crate. 'Rain and sleet are forecast for tonight, so we'd better get you a waterproof. Did you bring woollen sweaters with you?'

'I have a cashmere twin set, sir.' She paused in her search of the crate.

'I hope you didn't bring your pearls to match!' He quipped. 'Totally unsuitable!' He grinned and his eyes twinkled at her. 'I expect you weren't told what to bring with you.'

'No, sir, I wasn't told anything.' She desperately wanted to make a good impression on the pilot officer, but each time she opened her mouth it seemed he found something to make fun of or criticise.

'Try that on.' He tossed a thick, green, woollen sweater at her. 'And those.' A pair of heavy woollen trousers landed on the stone floor at her feet. 'These should fit you.' A rolled pair of thick socks landed close to the trousers. 'Had any luck with the boots, yet?'

'Still looking, sir.' She turned her attention back to the crate of boots and pulled one out that looked about the right size.

'Good! If you can find the matching one, we might be in business.' He smiled at her.

'Are you a pilot, sir?' She knew that the rank of a pilot officer was not just given to pilots, but suspected that this pilot officer might actually be a pilot, and she wondered why he wasn't flying.

'No, Armaud. I'm not a pilot. Why do you ask?'

'I just think it's strange that the RAF have the rank of pilot officer, flying officer, flight lieutenant and squadron leader for men who will never go anywhere near an aircraft.'

'We have to differentiate ourselves from the army somehow,

Armaud.' He stood taller and lifted his chin. He sniffed and used a pompous tone. 'We can't be like the soldiers in the army. It just wouldn't do, now, would it?'

She giggled and pointed to the army green of the clothes he'd thrown her. 'What about this uniform, sir? This is army green, isn't it?'

'Our men on the ground around here wear green for camouflage, Armaud.' He smiled and winked at her. 'Where you're going, you'll need it.'

'Where will I be going, sir?' she dared to ask, hoping the pilot officer would be able to tell her something.

'I can't tell you, but I will say that the next two days will be the most difficult ones you have ever lived through. Try those on, will you.' He pointed to the pile of clothing.

She dropped the boot and pulled the sweater over her head. The hem came down to her knees.

'Very fetching.' He smirked. 'Now try the trousers.'

She blushed, but picked them up. 'Could you turn your back, sir?'

'Of course. Sorry. I'm used to dealing with men.' He quickly turned away from her, and she was thrilled to note that his neck was flushed pink.

She pulled the trousers on under her skirt, and then pulled the sweater down over the waist. 'Ready, sir. You can look now.'

'Not exactly Parisian fashion, but at least you'll be warm.'

She tugged the waist of the trousers to keep them in place.

'You'll need a belt to help keep those up.' He went to a chest of drawers and took out some leather belts. He selected a shorter one and handed it to her. His fingers grazed hers, and she felt a tingling sensation run up her arm. She sucked in her breath. She couldn't lift her eyes to meet his. Something had just passed between them, and she wondered whether he'd felt it too.

To her disappointment, he continued speaking as if nothing had happened. 'You're to do some field manoeuvres and work as part of a team. You'll be pushed to your limit, and then some.'

'I've never done anything like that before, sir.' She tried to keep her voice even. 'What will I have to do?'

'It's a kind of endurance test. That's all I can say.'

She gulped and reached into the crate for the matching boot to the one she had just found. 'That's not very helpful, sir.'

'Sorry, I can't elaborate, Private Armaud.'

'I understand, sir.' She sat on the cold stone floor to try on the boots.

'Do they fit?'

'They're a bit on the large side.'

'Try them with the socks.'

She did as he suggested and stood to get a feel of them. She walked a few paces and rocked on the balls of her feet.

'Listen, Armaud.'

She stopped pacing and looked into his face. He had kind eyes, and she noticed a few lines around them. She realised that he was probably older than her first estimation of him, but his eyes held hers magnetically.

'If you do everything you are told to do, without question, and do it to the best of your ability, even when you have reached the end of your endurance, you'll pass through the initial assessments. Then you'll go on to the next phase of your training, and that will be a piece of cake, I promise you.' His smile broke the spell.

'You know how to give a girl some confidence, sir,' she said, wryly. 'Now, what am I supposed to think?'

'You're not meant to think at this stage, Armaud. That will come later. For now, follow orders and do your best.'

She sighed heavily and picked up the rest of her kit.

'Meet with the rest of the team on the lawn out front after lunch. Make sure you eat well.'

Lunch had been a sombre affair. Some of the other men were there, watching her with suspicion, but they didn't make any derogatory comments about her, as they had at breakfast. She ate her meat pie and mash silently and tried to ignore them. Now the men were standing around outside, and they turned unfriendly faces to her as she walked out to join them. They were all dressed in the same dark-green trousers and sweater that she wore. She saw a pile of bulky backpacks on the ground to one side, and a large truck was standing on the drive.

Nicolette's heart was beating rapidly. She had no idea what the next few hours would bring, but she was determined that she would pass this test of endurance no matter what she had to do. The Wing Commander had hinted that she could have an important role to play if she could prove herself and she wanted the chance to do something worthwhile for the war effort.

Pilot Officer Brown appeared from around the side of the

building. 'Grab a bag, men. Check the contents as I call out. Anything missing let me know.'

'Sir!' the men choroused.

Nicolette watched them each take a bag from the pile and she went to take the last one. Each man emptied the bag on the ground, and she did the same.

The officer gave her an almost imperceptible nod and called, 'Blanket.'

'Sir!' The men choroused, and this time, Nicolette joined them, noting she had a large grey blanket, rolled and fastened, with straps and buckles, to the top of the bag.

'Waterproof sheet.'

'Sir!' This time, Nicolette watched as the others picked up what looked like a large piece of folded tarpaulin and packed it away. She found hers in the pile and put it in the bottom of her bag.

By the time the bags were re-packed, it seemed everyone had what they should have, including some hard biscuits and a large flask of water. She watched the other men helping each other to load the large bags on their backs. She lifted hers and attempted to shrug the heavy load into place. The pilot officer came to help her and showed her how to fasten the straps across her chest to hold it in place. She was trembling inside, but couldn't decide whether the sensation was caused by her impending ordeal or the closeness of the officer.

She looked up into his eyes and tried to appear confident, though her insides were quaking.

'That's the spirit, Armaud,' he whispered, and then quickly stepped away.

The others were watching her again, so she stood taller and lifted her chin. The bag was heavy, but she wasn't going to show them any sign of weakness if she could help it.

'Orders are as follows.'

The men turned their attention to the pilot officer.

'You'll be dropped off twenty miles from here. Not far, I grant you, but the first group have already been dropped off five miles north of your drop off area, and they'll be looking for you. Don't let them catch you. If they take one of you, you will all have failed. Understand!'

'Yes, sir!' The others all gave Nicolette a sullen glare.

'Teamwork is the order for this exercise. I'll see you all in time for supper, I hope.' He turned to walk away but called over his shoulder, 'Though I suspect you won't make it back before lunch tomorrow.'

One of the older men started walking to the truck, and he called, 'Let's load up.'

'After you, Sergeant.' One of the men fell into step behind the older one, so Nicolette followed him and climbed aboard the back of the truck. She went to sit beside the older man on a long wooden bench down one side. The others soon joined them and sat on either side of the truck on the rickety wooden benches. When the last man was seated, the truck's engines started.

'I didn't enlist to be a babysitter.' The voice came from the end of the opposite row of seated men.

The comment was followed by a low grumbling of agreement from some of the others. Nicolette felt out of her depth but was starting to get angry with their rudeness. She couldn't think what to say to defend herself, so she said nothing. She could feel her face burning, and she pressed her lips into a tight line. She was following orders, just as they were, but unlike them, she'd never done anything like this before. It was clear that these men had experience of field manoeuvres and equally apparent that they knew she had none.

The journey was bumpy, and the ensuing silence was oppressive. She was being jostled by the men on either side of her, and she could feel the animosity oozing from them in waves.

Eventually, the man beside her began to hum a tuneless drone. The sound grew louder, but the tone didn't improve with the increased volume.

'Pack it in, Bing.' The sergeant nudged Nicolette in the side with his elbow. 'Pass it on, will you?'

She was shocked, at first, to be spoken to directly, but she did as she was asked, and elbowed the humming airman. 'Sergeant said to pack it in.'

'Trouble with you lot is,' Bing yelled above the thunder of the engine, 'You don't appreciate talent when you hear it.'

'I'd rather listen to my mother's cat screeching,' one of the other men called from the other side of the truck.

'Or fingernails down a blackboard,' another shouted.

'I'll have you know I was a choirboy, Taff, before I joined this mob.' Bing sounded indignant.

'Pity your church congregation, Bing.'

'Yeah, they must have been stone deaf.' Someone else quipped.

Nicolette grinned. This was more like it. She was used to teasing and exchanging silly banter with her brother, Joseph. She didn't quite feel up to joining the repartee, but hearing it helped to calm her nerves. The men were showing a different side to their surly natures, and it helped her feel more at ease with them.

The airmen continued to joke with each other and parried amiable insults for the rest of the journey, but they didn't include Nicolette. She didn't mind. She was happy to listen and learn more about her team members. She heard names and tried to fix the names in her mind. During some ribald crossfire of words that made no concession to the fact that she was among them, she discovered the sergeant was married and missed his marital rights. Two of the other men also had wives and came in for some teasing about the lack of sex in their lives while they were living apart from their loved ones.

When the conversation became a little more bawdy, she coughed politely to remind them they had a lady in their midst.

'Oh dear.' One of the men opposite her cocked his head to one side in a patronising manner. 'Are we offending our newest member?'

'Not in the least, Taff.' She remembered his name from the earlier conversation. 'I'm enjoying the education.'

'She has a voice!' another nameless man spoke out. 'What shall we call our new pet?'

'Her real name is Nick so how about Knickers?' one suggested.

Bing turned to stare at her and seemed to be waiting for a response. She shrugged. Nicolette was unsure what to say. She didn't want to be referred to as their pet, but if that's what it would take for them to accept her, then she decided it wouldn't hurt to go along with it.

Taff sneered at her. 'Knickers it is, then.'

'Well, you all know my name,' Nicolette grinned to prove she didn't mind their choice of nickname. 'Will you tell me what I should call you lot?' She pointed to Taff. 'I know you're Taff, and your accent tells me you're Welsh so I can see where that nickname came from.' She turned to Bing at her side. 'And you're Bing after Bing Crosby, obviously.' She pointed at the first man on the opposite row. 'What about you?'

'Baldy.' He took off his cap to show a shiny bald pate.

Nicolette smiled. 'Not very original at choosing names are you?' She quickly glanced at the rest of them, and then pointed to the next man on the bench.

'Beaky.' He touched his large, pointed nose.

Nicolette let out a gust of laughter and pointed to a tall young man with exceptionally long legs. 'No, let me guess,' she was still laughing. 'Lanky!'

'She soon got the measure of us, lads, didn't she?' The sergeant laughed. He pointed the rest of the men out to her while giving her their names. 'Bones, Ginger, Deadly and Mac.'

Nicolette smiled and nodded to each of them. 'Bones. Is that because you're chubby?' She watched him nod and smirk. 'Ginger is a redhead; I can see. I'm thinking Mac might be a Scot, but I've no idea why they'd call you, Deadly.' She looked at the one she couldn't work out.

'He's our sharpshooter.' Beaky told her.

'Never missed a shot, ever!' Baldy boasted on behalf of his fellow commando.

'Glad you're on my side, airman.' Nicolette was beginning to feel much more comfortable with her companions but was brought back to the reality of her situation when the truck stopped, and the engines were switched off.

Chapter 10: Fitting in

'Everyone out,' the sergeant whispered in the quietness. 'Heads down, fan out and take cover. Mac and Deadly are our scouts.' He grabbed Nicolette by her bag straps. 'You're with me. Stay close.'

The sergeant jumped to the ground and pulled her down beside him. 'This way,' he called.

She crouched low and hurried after him, heading for a nearby line of low bushes. She sank to the ground next to the sergeant and immediately turned to try to see where the others had gone. She felt his hand push her head to the ground. 'Head down, Knickers,' he hissed. 'We stay low until Deadly and Mac have searched the area.'

'Yes, sir!' she whispered.

'You're as green as the beret you're wearing, aren't you?' he whispered.

'Just out of basic training, sir.'

'You can call me Sarge.'

'Yes, Sarge.'

'Look, Knickers. I have no idea why they want us to show you the ropes out here, but whatever it is that you can do must be important.'

'I speak French and German. It's nothing special.'

'There must be more to it than that,' he quickly added, 'But don't tell me. I don't need to know.'

'How long do we stay here, Sarge?' She was beginning to feel the urge to relieve herself and cursed the two mugs of tea she'd had after lunch.

'Until Mac and Deadly have checked the area. The noise of the truck will have attracted the enemy if they were in earshot but if we get lucky, they'll still be miles away, and we'll be safe, for now.'

'What will happen if they find us?'

'You don't want to know, Knickers. It'll be the end of the game for you, and we'll all be sent to the front. Not a bad thing for most of the lads. They're itching to get some real action.'

'I get the feeling you'd rather stay safe, Sarge.'

'Not exactly, Knickers. I want to fight as much as the next man.'

'But you have a wife and children.'

'Lots of fighting men do. It doesn't change anything.'

'It must make you less willing to die for your country, though.'

'No one wants to die, Knickers, but if that's what it will take to keep my youngsters safe, that's what I'll do.'

'Do you miss them?'

'What do you think?'

'Sorry.' She wriggled and tried to cross her legs. 'That was a stupid question.'

'Keep still! What's wrong with you?'

'I need to pee, Sarge.'

'Oh,' he sighed. 'Crawl behind that bush and do it quietly.'

She slithered along the rough ground to the thicker undergrowth and managed to do what she needed as quietly as possible. When she emerged, the rest of the men were gathered around the sergeant, smirking as she joined them. She blushed but grinned. 'What's wrong, Bing? You never been caught short?'

'Let's get on with it.' The sergeant was spreading a map on the ground. 'This is where we are.' He pointed to a red spot on the crumpled paper. 'The enemy could be anywhere in this area.' His hand grazed the map in an arc above the spot. 'And we need to get back here.' He touched the place marked with a cross some twelve inches from the red spot.

'They'll expect us to head for the mountain, Sarge, won't they?' Beaky touched some triangular markings a few inches from the top of the paper. 'That would be the long way home, but we'd have the best chance to avoid bumping into them.'

'Maybe.' The sergeant scratched his chin. 'Is that where you'd set up an ambush to wait for us if you were in their place?'

'Perhaps.' Beaky nodded. 'But they'd have to get lucky. Those mountains have hundreds of square miles of ravines, caves, screed slopes and trails. We could take any one of those trails and still miss the enemy by miles.'

'But, on the other hand, we could be sitting ducks if they've set up camp on the very trail we choose to take.' Baldy shook his head.

Nicolette could see that the fastest route back to the house would be by road but already understood that they would be vulnerable out in the open. She couldn't see any forests or wooded areas marked on the map. She could see just a few scrubby islands of rough brush nearby. She lifted her head to look at the terrain but all she could see was an endless horizon of rolling heather, and bracken-clad countryside. She turned back to the map and saw a blue wiggly line to the bottom of the paper.

'Is that a river, Sarge?'

'More of a stream, Knickers.'

'Possibly made deeper by your recent deposit.' Bing chuckled.

The others sniggered, and Nicolette felt her neck growing hotter.

'What were you thinking, Knickers?' The sergeant asked her.

'I thought that sometimes rivers or streams lie lower than the surrounding countryside because they cut shallow valleys into the land. We might get cover by following the route of the water.'

'Give the girl a medal.' Taff laughed disparagingly. 'Do you think the enemy won't have thought of that one?'

'Sorry, I was just saying...'

'If we waited until dark, that could be a plan, Knickers.' The sergeant nodded and looked thoughtful.

'If we wait around here, we'll lose the advantage of a head start on them.' Lanky was already using his binoculars and searching the far horizon for signs of movement.

'Or we could take cover and see which way they decide to go in search of us, and then take the opposite route.' The sergeant folded the map and put it back in his bag.

'So where do we hide?' Beaky asked.

'The last place they'll think of looking. Right here at the drop-off point.' The sergeant pointed down the road to a rising hill covered in deep bracken. 'Let's go get ourselves some camouflage.' He turned to two of the men. 'Ginger and Bones! You set a false trail to the mountains. Don't make it too obvious. The rest of you, retrace the trail you already made from the truck and get back on the road.'

'It's going to be another long night in the cold!' Bing grumbled.

'You'll just have to cuddle up close for warmth, Bing.' Taff gave Bing a hefty shove in the back.

Bing recovered his footing and shot Taff a mischievous grin. 'I'll keep a lookout for a sheep for you, boyo. I'm told you Welsh boys are partial to a cuddly ewe or two on a cold night.'

'Quiet, now.' The sergeant stepped into the deep bracken. 'Spread out and tread carefully. Don't leave a trail. Fold the stalks back into place behind you as you go. We'll meet by that small overhang of rock.' He pointed higher up the hill. 'You walk ahead of me, Knickers. I'll cover your tracks. Don't walk in a straight line, do a zigzag.'

'Yes, Sarge.' She stepped from the road into the waist-high ferns and tried to put her large boots down carefully, avoiding the longer stalks. She noticed that the other men were walking slowly backward through the vegetation and tugging the bracken back into place to cover the trail they were making. It seemed to take forever, but eventually the whole group was gathered by the small overhang, sitting a few feet apart, completely engulfed by the ferns.

'What now?' she asked the nearest airman.

'We wait, we listen, and we watch.' Bing told her.

'And we keep our mouths closed!' Taff added.

She nodded and eased her bag to the ground to take the weight off her shoulders. It might be a long night, and she wanted to be ready when she got the order to move again.

'Get comfortable.' The sergeant pulled his blanket from the top of his bag. 'Get your waterproof out too. It'll rain soon, or snow. It feels cold enough!'

Nicolette unfastened her blanket and dug deep into her bag for the tarpaulin. She watched the others fold their blankets around them and cover everything with the waterproof sheeting. She did the same and was soon feeling warmer, wrapped like a caterpillar in a cocoon, under the shallow canopy of ferny leaves.

Darkness fell early in the northern late winter and Nicolette was soon shivering with cold again. A full moon appeared from time to time from behind scudding dark clouds but when it disappeared again, the world became black as pitch.

Soon after Nicolette had lost all feeling in her feet, she began to hear sounds of movement from the other side of the road. She was immediately alert but didn't need to be told to keep quiet. The moon briefly illuminated the hiding place, and she glanced through the gloom, to see that her companions were all frozen in place with eyes wide, and they appeared to be listening, just as she was.

'The truck stopped here.' A voice called softly, the noise carrying on the cold wind to them. 'See the dust has been disturbed at the side of the road?'

'Tracks lead this way, Sarge.'

They listened to the sound of boots on the hard surface, and then the softer, muffled noise of boots on grassy hillocks, moving away from them.

'It's too dark to make anything out, Sarge, but I'm betting there are about a dozen of them.' A voice echoed softly from over the road.

'Which way did they go?' another voice called.

'They gathered in those bushes. Someone took a leak. Amateurs!'

Bing giggled softly beside Nicolette but smothered his mirth with his hand.

'Looks as if you were right, Sarge. They headed for the mountains. 'B' group will pick them up in no time.'

'We'll be home in time for supper, after all.'

'Let's go. Move out, men.'

The hidden group waited, holding their breath until the last of the sounds of crunching boots had disappeared. Nicolette continued to wait and keep as still as a statue. She didn't want to be the one to break the silence and risk blowing their cover.

Eventually, the sergeant called softly. 'Time to move out. Slowly and quietly. Up and over the top of the hill to the stream in the next valley. If we get separated, follow the water downstream to the first cover of low brush. We'll regroup there.'

'How will we find the stream in the dark?' Nicolette asked the sergeant.

'We'll hear it, Knickers. Do you need to pee before we go?'

'No, Sarge.' She giggled nervously. She'd been amazed to hear that the other group of airmen had found evidence of her deposit in the bushes.

The men moved stealthily, wrapped in their blankets and waterproof sheets to keep the sleet from penetrating their clothing. Crouching low, they moved up the hill and only stood to their full height when they were safely down the other side. Nicolette followed the line of men, bending as low as she could while crossing the summit of the low hill, and the sergeant brought up the rear.

The ground on the far side of the hill was rough and stony with sparse vegetation. The gradient was steep, and the going became difficult. Nicolette staggered along, trying to keep up with the men in front. After a couple of hours of negotiating rocky ground or trudging through knee-high vegetation, the terrain became easier with low growing grasses, but the weight of her bag was dragging her shoulders down, and she stumbled. She regained her footing and halted to take a breath and get her bearings.

'Are you all right, Knickers?' the sergeant called softly.

'Yes, Sarge.' She stepped out again, following the line of moving men. She saw one of them disappear and heard a soft yell of alarm. 'What was that?' she whispered.

'Don't know, come on, Armaud. Don't dawdle.' The sergeant overtook her in his haste to get to the downed man. 'Take cover,' he called back to her. 'It might be an ambush.'

She dropped to the ground and looked around for somewhere to conceal herself, but there was no cover and nowhere to hide. She could see a small commotion ahead of her and crawled to where the man had dropped from sight. The others were gathered there, staring into a hole in the ground.

'What happened?' she asked.

'Bones fell down this pothole.' Lanky told her.

'Is he all right?' she asked.

'Don't know, he hasn't said anything yet.' Beaky looked worried.

'He's probably winded himself, or he might have banged his head on the way down.' Bing shook his head. 'Can anyone see how deep the hole is?'

'No way to tell, but it's narrow. I don't know how he got his fat backside down there.' Taff peered into the small, black hole. 'It's impossible.'

Nicolette threw off her waterproof and blanket and began to undo her backpack.

'What are you doing?' the sergeant asked her.

'Permission to check on Bones, Sarge? I'm the smallest, my aunt is a nurse, and she was always showing me first-aid techniques. I could help if you let me.'

'Who has the rope?' the sergeant asked.

Nicolette soon had a rope fastened around her chest, and two of the men were lowering her into the narrow, dark pothole. She had to feel her way down the slippery, muddy sides in the blackness. The hole widened until she couldn't feel the other side with her outstretched hand.

'Stop!' she called to the men on the rope. She listened and thought she could hear breathing. 'Bones! Can you hear me?'

She heard a groan. 'Lower away, slowly. I'm close to him.'

Her boots crunched on a slippery, gravel surface, and she crouched to feel around the place where she'd landed. To her right, the ground dropped away steeply, and she felt an updraft of air that told her the hole went deeper. She felt to the left, and her hand met rough, woollen trousers. 'Bones. Are you hurt? Where's your head?' Her hands felt his dangling boots and travelled up his legs, trying to get a feel of what was holding him suspended in the hole. 'Talk to me!' Her feet slipped on the narrow, wet ledge, and she made a grab for his legs to steady herself.

He screamed, and she swiftly let go her hold but threw herself against the wall beside his dangling legs.

'Knickers? Is that you?' His panting voice came from above her. 'My leg is smashed, and my bag seems to be caught on something.'

'Good job your bag saved you, Bones, or you'd be in a much worse state, for sure. This pothole might go down for miles.' She stood, on tiptoe to feel his neck, shoulders and back for abnormal bumps or depressions, just as her aunt had taught her in the games of nursing she had played as a youngster. 'I can't reach your head. Did you hurt anything up there on the way down?'

'Not that I can feel. My knee is throbbing a bit, though.'

She was relieved to discover there was no other serious damage that she could find above his waist. She could feel a sharp rocky outcrop above his shoulder where the strap of his bag had caught and halted his descent. 'Where did you say your pain was?'

'My knee took the worst bashing and my ankle. I couldn't breathe for a while, my chest was tight, but it seems fine now. I think I was just winded.'

She gently felt down the length of his legs and heard him breathe in sharply when her hand slipped on a patch of slick, wet fabric. She could feel a hard, pointed, stick-like protuberance from just above his knee and her heart sank. 'You have a compound fracture, Bones. Do you know what that means?'

'It means my army days are over for a good while.'

'I can't do anything about your injury down here, so you'll have a great deal of pain when they lift you out. Do you think you'll be able to stand it?'

'I don't have much choice, do I?'

'Listen. I'm going to tie this rope around you, and then I'm going to unfasten your bag.' She began to untie the rope from her chest.

'No, it's not safe, Knickers. You could fall down there.' Bones protested, pointing to the bottomless void to the right of them.

It was too dark to see very much, but they knew the danger was there. They could feel the updraft of dank air, and their voices had an eerie echo coming from below them.

'We only have one rope, Bones. We'll take it in turns to get out of here. You first. No argument.'

She quickly secured the rope around Bones' chest and called to her companions. 'Take the strain!' When the rope went taught, she unfastened the young man's backpack and let it drop into the darkness. They heard the bag crashing and bouncing for many feet before it came to a stop.

'Haul him out.' Nicolette called. 'Go carefully! He has a smashed knee and ankle.'

Nicolette clung to the muddy wall of the hole, her hand hanging to the sharp rocky outcrop that had saved the young man. Showers of dirt and gravel rained on her as Bones was hoisted from the hole. She heard the brave man trying to suppress his moans as each heave on the rope brought him more pain.

Eventually, the moaning stopped and after a few seconds the sergeant called, 'Rope coming down, Knickers!'

She lifted her face to another rain of wet grit and reached a hand to feel for the rope. She soon had it secured around her and called for them to lift her out. As she was lifted clear of the pothole, she'd never been happier to smell fresh, clean air, even though the sleet was coming at her face like freezing needles.

The whole operation had taken minutes but had felt like hours to her. She lay panting for breath beside the top of the hole, watching her companions checking Bones for any other injuries. Someone covered her with a tarpaulin.

'You daft bugger!' Ginger was prodding Bones along his spine. 'Should have looked where you were going. That hole is not even a foot wide! How could such a lard arse as you, fall into something so small? Can you feel this?' He continued his prodding.

'Ouch!' Bones hissed. 'There's nothing wrong with my back. She already checked me over down there. I told you! It's my leg!'

'We might need to make him a stretcher,' Nicolette suggested. 'And we'll have to splint his knee and thigh to stabilise the damage.'

'There's not much around to make a splint with.' Ginger called softly.

Nicolette shuffled to where she'd dropped her bag. She took her waterproof sheet and folded it to make a thick, solid square. 'What happened to the rope?'

She hurried to crouched beside the injured man. 'I'll try not to hurt you, Bones, but we have to make sure we don't damage your leg any more when we move you.'

'Do what you have to do, Knickers, I'll be a brave boy.'

'Does she know what she's doing, Sarge?' Mac asked, giving her a suspicious glare.

'Good question.' The sergeant looked at her. 'Do you?'

'Are any of you qualified as medics?' she asked.

The silence told her she was the only one with a smattering of medical knowledge. 'Listen, his leg is broken. We can all see that. I don't know how to fix a compound fracture.'

'What's a compound fracture?' Deadly asked.

'When the bone is sticking out of the skin!'

'Ouch!' Lanky cringed and turned away.

'We need to make sure it can't move around and cause more damage when we carry him.'

'What do you have in mind, Knickers?' the sergeant asked her.

'This tarpaulin is stiff and strong. I think it will do the trick.' She wrapped the folded tarpaulin around the leg with the protruding bone

Bones whimpered but didn't complain.

'Hand me the rope, Lanky.' She wound the rope around the waterproof fabric and tied a few knots to secure it.

'Well, it's obvious our Bones won't be walking anywhere. How do we get him back?' Baldy asked.

'We can make a hammock from blankets, and we'll carry him,' the sergeant suggested.

'Trust you, Bones!' Lanky shook his head. 'You're the heaviest man around, and you still want us to carry you so you can dodge the trek home.'

Chapter 11: Digging deep

The going was difficult. Darkness hampered them as much as the uneven ground they traversed, but they continued to follow the stream, carrying the injured man in turns. Bones occasionally whimpered when a man stumbled, or his hammock jolted, but otherwise stayed silent. Nicolette knew he would be in agony, and didn't know whether she could keep as quiet if she'd been so badly injured. As it was, she was weary beyond measure. Her shoulders ached, her thighs and calves throbbed, and she couldn't feel her feet. She had thought she was reasonably fit, but her lungs felt as if they were about to burst, and her heart was hammering against her rib cage like a frightened, caged bird. She felt dreadful, weak and close to tears, but she continued walking. She didn't want to let the team down.

'Shush!' the sergeant whispered urgently. 'Everyone down!'

The four men carrying the hammock lowered it to the ground and crouched beside Bones. The others immediately flattened themselves against the muddy banks of the stream. Nicolette threw herself against the wet mud, glad of the rest.

The sound came from far away, but they could all hear it intermittently as the freezing wind brought fragments of the noise to their ears. The clatter of scrambling boots on screed slopes was unmistakable.

'They must have worked out that we didn't head for the mountains.' Baldy whispered.

'What next, boss?' Bing asked.

'We have the advantage for now. The wind is blowing towards us. They can't hear us, and I'm hoping they are too far away to see us. Let's move on and hope we can outrun them.'

'We can't run with Bones.' Nicolette hissed her protest. 'We're all tired. What if you drop him?'

'We have to risk it!' The sergeant hissed back. 'It's our only chance.'

'I don't know whether I can keep up with you much longer, Sarge,' Nicolette admitted, reluctantly. 'Why don't you leave Bones with me? You can hurry ahead and send someone back for us.'

'Out of the question, Knickers!' The sergeant sighed impatiently.

'But you don't understand, sir!' She insisted, knowing she was out of order back-chatting her sergeant and questioning his orders. 'We could cause him more damage. He could lose his leg!'

'And we could lose this war!'

'It's only an exercise, for goodness' sake.' Nicolette huffed with frustration. She needed to make the sergeant understand the seriousness of the situation, no matter how much trouble she would be in for insubordination. She just couldn't see the sense in taking such a risk with Bones. 'Those men behind us are the same ones you had breakfast with this morning. They are not the enemy. Not really.'

'Oh for heaven's sake!' Bones called from his hammock cocoon. 'Will someone shut her up and get me out of here?'

Nicolette turned to the sergeant. She had reached the end of her endurance. The mere thought of taking another step, let alone running, seemed impossible to her. 'I'm sorry, Sarge, but I can't run. I don't have the strength left. You'll have to go on without me.'

'We can't leave you, Knickers!' A few voices muttered similar words in the darkness.

'You'll have to. Bones needs medical help, and I'll hold you back.' She struggled to keep the tears inside. She didn't want them to see her cry. 'I can't walk another step. I'm sorry.'

The sergeant squelched his way to her along the muddy bank and crouched by her side. 'Listen, Knickers, you have to dig deep. You have to come with us, and you have to keep up. No arguments. You *can,* and you *will* do this. Understand?'

Nicolette felt a tear escape and run down her face. She quickly wiped it away with her wet sleeve. She didn't know whether she could do what he asked, but she knew she would have to try. She nodded.

'Anyone got a plan?' the sergeant asked his men.

'I'll take the lead, Sarge,' Mac offered. 'I've been carrying him for the last few miles. I deserve a break.'

'All right, Mac.' The sergeant grabbed one side of the hammock. 'Bing, you take the rear guard. The rest of you grab a hand on this.'

'You heard the man.' Taff took hold of the hammock. 'If we all take hold, we'll make more progress.'

Nicolette took hold of the blanket near Bones' head. 'You let me know if the pain becomes unbearable.'

'It won't, Knickers,' Bones said through gritted teeth.

They set out at a jogging pace, stumbling and lurching over the rocky streambed in the dark. Nicolette kept glancing at Bones' face, but couldn't see him clearly. She knew he would be suffering, but he didn't make a whimper. Her shoulders were aching from the weight of her bag. Her legs throbbed, and her feet were stinging in a hundred small places. She was wet and cold but was warming up a little with the increased pace.

After an hour of jogging in shallow, freezing water, over stones and pebbles that threatened to turn her ankle at every step, she was ready to give up and drop to her knees. Her breath was coming in rasping gasps and her throat burned. She felt she couldn't take another step, but she did. The thought of getting Bones back to base kept her going. He needed urgent medical help.

The sergeant called out, 'Stop!'

They halted, and Nicolette realised she was not the only one who felt dreadful. All the men were panting heavily, and their heads hung wearily from drooping shoulders.

'I think we lost them for now. Listen!'

Acting as one, the men held their breaths, cocked their ears and listened to the wind. It carried no sound of their pursuers.

'How much further, Mac?' One of the airmen asked the front man.

'I think I see the ocean ahead, so we need to leave the stream and cut across the moor in a mile or so.' Mac answered.

'The sun will be up soon. We'll lose the cover of darkness,' Deadly pointed out.

'We'll cut from the stream after that rise.' The sergeant pointed to a low hillock in the near distance, silhouetted against the slightly lighter sky beyond. 'That should give us some cover for a while.'

They began to move again, but Nicolette detected a slower pace. They were all close to the end of their endurance.

'How are you doing, Knickers?' Beaky's voice whispered over her shoulder.

'No worse than you, Beaky,' she answered.

She felt a reassuring pat on her shoulder. 'That's a girl,' the man called softly.

They managed to avoid their pursuers and made it back to base an hour after sunrise. At this northern latitude in late March, the sun didn't show above the horizon until well into the morning. Pilot

Officer Brown had not been too far out in his estimation of them making it back in time for lunch.

Bones was taken to what passed as a medical room where he was assessed by the house nurse. Shortly after, he was on his way by car to the nearest hospital at Fort William. Nicolette knew it wouldn't be an easy journey, but couldn't be any worse for the injured man than being carried in the makeshift hammock for miles.

They had all waited for news of Bones and watched for the enemy group appearing on the meadow. She sat on the low wall with the rest of the team, watching the car drive away. The sergeant had suggested they should all get cleaned up before lunch, but none of them made a move to go inside.

'Well, we can't do anything more for him.' Ginger got to his feet. 'And I'm starving.'

'Come on, Knickers,' Mac took Nicolette's arm and dragged her to her feet. 'You'll feel much better after some scran.'

'I'll need to have a bath first. I'm covered in…' She glanced down at her filthy state and rolled her eyes. 'Goodness knows what I'm covered in, but I smell like a blocked drain.'

'You're no dirtier or smellier than the rest of us, lassie.' Mac grinned. 'The mess room has seen worse, believe me.'

The Scots commando put his arm around her shoulders and guided her inside. The rest followed, and they were soon seated together at one of the large tables, eating stew with steaming dumplings. Nicolette was gratefully spooning the delicious gravy into her mouth when the door opened and the enemy troops filed in, looking peeved.

'You led us a merry chase, Sergeant.' One of the men came to slap the sergeant on his back. 'That false trail almost worked, you know.'

'What made you realise it was false?' the sergeant asked.

'The fact that it petered out after a few miles gave us a clue.' The enemy airman reached to snatch a carrot from the sergeant's plate. 'It seems your men didn't try hard enough to fool us.'

'Fooled you for as long as we needed to, Sergeant Major.' Deadly boasted.

'How did the hindrance work out for you?' The sergeant major looked at Nicolette.

She lifted her face and straightened her shoulders, waiting for some disapproving comments from her team members.

'Knickers did all right.' Mac said, patting her shoulder. 'Bones was the hindrance. He's on his way to hospital now with a busted leg.'

'What happened?' One of the other men from the enemy group asked as he helped himself from the tureens of food on the long dresser.

As the enemy group took seats at the neighbouring table, the discussion continued with good-natured bantering as they told the story of the preceding night. Nicolette was gratified to learn that her suggestions and comments about taking the streambed had been taken seriously and were now being praised by her teammates.

'She rescued Bones too, don't forget.' Lanky lifted his fork in a mock salute to Nicolette. 'And she didn't complain too much when we ran for our lives after we heard you lot closing in.'

'She sounds like quite a girl!' A voice from the door made all the men turn their heads. Pilot Officer Brown stood there, smiling at Nicolette.

She felt her heart do a somersault but tried her best to keep her breathing steady to prevent the blush creeping up her face. She didn't want him to know how much he affected her.

'Don't judge a book by the cover, sir!' Bing grinned at Nicolette over his raised spoon. 'She might look a bit prim but she's got as much stamina as I have, I'll give her that.'

'She's not looking too prim and proper just at this minute, Bing.' The pilot officer smirked and put his hand to his nose as he came closer. 'Whatever did you lot use for camouflage? Sheep dung?'

The sergeant grinned at Nicolette. 'It's a long story, sir.'

'Well, the wing commander will need a full debrief, and he'll want to have a word with you too, Armaud.'

'Yes, sir. Should I go now?' She hoped the wing commander would wait until she'd finished her lunch.

The officer smirked 'I think he might appreciate it if you took your time in this instance, Armaud.' Pilot Officer Brown was grinning widely, and she got the impression he was highly amused by what he was seeing. 'Finish your lunch. It sounds as if you've earned it.'

'Thank you, sir.' She turned from him to concentrate on her plate of food. She felt a little put out. She didn't like to be made fun of, and she had the distinct impression that he was laughing at her.

'Armaud.'

She glanced up at him.

The pilot officer's mouth was twitching. 'Perhaps a bath after lunch would help to make you more presentable?'

He hunkered down beside her and reached his hand to her face. She couldn't believe he was acting so intimately in front of all the men. She could almost imagine him leaning to kiss her. He was so close.

'Excuse me,' he said. 'You have a smudge of something despicable on your nose.' His thumb wiped the end of her nose, and the dining room exploded in laughter.

She whirled to her team, intending to admonish them for not telling her, but she realised that their faces were also covered in unspeakable grime and muck. She began to giggle, and then laughed loudly, banging the table as her teammates were doing.

'You'll do, Armaud,' Pilot Officer Brown got to his feet and touched her shoulder briefly.

His gentle touch sent a bolt of energy through her. She felt she'd been struck by lightning. She froze for an instant, but then covered her reaction by continuing to bang the table, although her laughter now had a hollow ring to it. What was it about this man? Why did he have such a profound affect on her? Did he know? Did he feel it too? She hadn't felt like this with Robert. She was certainly attracted to the pilot officer, and she didn't think she was imagining it but she knew it couldn't lead anywhere.

She couldn't fall in love again. She wouldn't. Not with him. He was way out of her reach anyway. He wasn't interested in her, either. Not in a romantic way. He found her amusing. He certainly hadn't given her any encouragement to think of him in any other way but as her superior. She should forget him, just as easily as she had forgotten the sergeant at basic training. David Bradley might have stirred her heart, and had things been different, he might have been her next romance, but he was quickly fading from her memory. Pilot Officer Brown would fade too. She had no room in her life for romance. The WAAF was her life for now. Living with these men. Laughing with them, training with them and learning how to... what? She still had no idea where all this training would lead her.

Chapter 12: Combat training

Her eyes were closing, and she jerked her head to stay awake. The hot bath had eased her aching body and cleaned the grime of the moors from her skin, but now all she wanted to do was fall into bed. She hadn't slept since dozing fitfully on the night train. How long ago was that? More than thirty hours ago. No wonder she was so tired.

The door to the room opened, and she reacted automatically, jumping to her feet and snapping to attention.

'At ease, Armaud,' the wing commander said. 'Take a seat before you fall over, girl.'

'Thank you, sir.'

'I hear you did well. Though, I also hear you were argumentative and lacked confidence in yourself.' He sat in the large leather chair opposite her, framed by the window and the view of the ocean beyond. He rested his elbows on the desk and made a steeple of his fingers under his chin. 'However, we can work on your shortcomings. Congratulations are in order, quite the heroine, aren't you? I'm very pleased.' His smile was wide and genuine.

She felt a fraud to receive so much praise. 'Did they tell you I almost gave up out there?' She decided to be honest with the officer. She didn't want him thinking she was some kind of heroine with endless stamina.

'I was informed that you went beyond the call of duty in rescuing a fellow airman and that you were persuaded to continue the exercise even when you thought you couldn't make it.'

Nicolette sighed. Her teammates had painted a glowing picture of her, but the truth was not so glorious. She needed the officer to know her limitations. She didn't want to be put through anything like that again. 'Sir, I did what I had to do. No one else could have gone down that tiny hole to get Bones out. There was no room for a larger person in that small space.'

'You didn't even wait to be asked to volunteer, I hear.'

'Well, it was obvious I was the only person there that could have done what needed to be done, sir.'

'Nevertheless. You showed initiative and guts. Just what we were hoping from you.'

'I argued with the sergeant, sir.' She wanted to make sure the wing commander knew all of her failings. 'I shouldn't have. I'm sorry.' She knew she had been wrong to voice her opinions so freely in front of the others. She should have taken her sergeant's orders without question, no matter what the circumstances.

'You questioned authority for the good of your fellow airman. That showed initiative and also proved you have leadership qualities. We are not disappointed in you, Armaud.'

'You're not, sir?' She felt a little confused.

'And you found reserves of strength when required to do so. Exemplary conduct, Armaud.' He was beaming with pride at her accomplishment.

'May I ask what happens next, sir?'

'You'll receive more training here, and then you'll be sent south for more specialised instruction.'

She still had no idea of what she was being trained to do and thought that now might be a good time to ask the big question. The wing commander seemed to be in such a good mood and pleased with her. 'What exactly is it that you want me to do, sir?'

His face changed immediately. He looked sterner and his mouth set in a line. He shook his head and gave her a smile that was little more than a brief lift of his lips. 'Listen very carefully, Armaud. We are going to train you to perform in the field. We will give you the skills you'll need to survive, in the environment we'll be putting you into. You don't need to know any more than that. Each step of your training will make it clearer to you, but remember that we can fail you and send you back to civilian life at any stage. If that happens, then the less you know about our ultimate goal for you, the better. Understand?'

'Yes, sir!' She called the automated response to the 'understand' question, even though she didn't understand a word of what he'd said.

'Get some sleep, Armaud. You'll begin combat training in the morning.'

'Combat training, sir? I thought women were not allowed to fight.'

'They're not in normal circumstances, but this training will be for your safety. You'll be taught self-defence techniques among other strategies that you'll need.'

'Oh.' She couldn't think of anything sensible to say.

'Off you go, then.' He flicked his hand to the door.

She stood to attention and marched from the room.

The following weeks were filled with lessons. She ran every morning to keep fit. Her teammates ran with her and then trained alongside her. They showed her how to wrestle a man to the ground, using the opponent's weight as leverage. They shared their knowledge of close quarters, hand to hand fighting, pointing out how valuable her elbows and knees could be, to damage her opponent. She enjoyed learning her new skills and was delighted when she managed to put Lanky on the floor after only a few seconds of him feigning an attack on her.

'Great work, Armaud.' Pilot Officer Brown applauded her on his way through the large hall. 'Keep it up!'

She pushed a stray strand of hair behind her ear and watched the officer disappear through the far door. 'What does he do around here? Apart from keeping a close watch on me, that is,' she asked Lanky, reaching to give him a hand up from the floor.

'Don't worry yourself about him, Knickers. It's me you have to keep at arm's length.' He lunged for her again, and she blocked him with her elbow, ducked low to avoid his left hook and punched her right hand into his groin. Lanky doubled over and rolled away from her. 'Mercy!' he cried. 'Can someone else have a go with her? She's fighting dirty!'

'I'm doing what you told me to do, Lanky.' She went to crouch beside him. 'Are you all right?'

He grabbed her by the waist and threw her on her back, quickly sitting astride her chest and pinning her arms to her side with his legs. 'Never show mercy, Knickers. It could be the death of you.' He laughed down at her. 'I win this one, I think.'

She heaved an exasperated sigh and wriggled ineffectually to try to get away.

'No, you are trapped. No way out. I can kill you at my leisure.' He aimed two fingers at her head.

She took a deep breath and heaved her legs into the air, wrapped her ankles around Lanky's neck and dragged him over to the side until she was sitting on his chest. She quickly drew her finger across his neck, right over his jugular vein. 'My kill, I think.'

'Who taught you that move?' Deadly asked from the sidelines where the rest of the team were watching.

'My brother, Joseph.' She giggled and helped Lanky to his feet again. 'We were always wrestling when we were kids.'

'Where is he now?' Lanky asked.

'Aberystwyth, I think. He's training to be a pilot.'

'Any other brothers or sisters?' Deadly asked.

'No, just the two of us.'

'Did he teach you any other tricks we should know about?' Lanky asked.

'You'll have to find out, won't you?' She teased.

The sergeant major from the enemy team came over, clapping his hands. 'Good work, Knickers. I think we've done here for today. They want you at the firing range.'

'Yes, Sergeant Major.' She picked up her sweater and put her beret on as she made her way to the door. 'Just me?'

'Yes,' the sergeant major said. 'This lesson is just for you.'

She raised her eyebrows but didn't question further. She'd learned that some of the things she was asked to do were beyond her comprehension anyway. 'See you later, team.' She wiggled her fingers at the men she now knew as friends and made her way outside and across the meadow to a stand of pine trees.

The weather had improved in the last few weeks, and the spring sun shone warmly on her head. She'd learned a lot since she jumped down from the train on that cold and frosty platform. She knew how to kill a man, with no noise if she had to, though she couldn't imagine ever having to do so. She could handle a knife safely and knew the technique to disarm someone who intended to stab her with one. She could defend herself, if she had to, even if her opponent was twice her size.

She'd learned how to read a map; use a compass; a radio; a pistol and a rifle. She had also learned elementary Morse. She could recognise some edible plants, knew how to set a trap to catch a rabbit or a rat, and had been shown that either could be eaten. She knew how to light a fire with dry tinder and a few bits of wood. She could also set traps for larger targets, such as men, cars or tanks. She knew about explosives, detonators, and raid tactics. She knew almost everything she would need to know to be a spy in France or Germany or anywhere they wanted to send her. She had worked out what she would be doing before anyone had told her. She still had much more training to go through, but she couldn't wait to get started on the real job whatever it was they wanted her to do.

She rounded the stand of pines to see Pilot Officer Brown waiting for her. He was alone, and she was surprised. There were usually a few trainees and airmen around the firing range.

'You sent for me, sir?' she asked and gave him a salute.

He nodded and threw a very small pistol at her.

She caught it and said, 'I hope this isn't loaded, sir.'

He gave her a mocking glance and shook his head. 'The bullets are over there. Load all six and show me what you can do.' He pointed to a tarpaulin spread with boxes of ammunition. 'Before today is over, I want you to be accurate with that gun.'

This is going to be easy, she thought. She'd already done pistol training and was almost as good as Deadly with the smaller weapon. This one was just a little smaller than she was used to, but she was sure she'd get the feel of it quickly. She loaded it and pointed it at the bull's-eye target a few yards away. She held her arm out at shoulder height, took aim and fired. The hole appeared close to the edge of the target. She aimed lower and shot again, hitting the target near the centre. The next four bullets hit the target dead centre, and she turned to the officer. 'Will that be all, sir?'

He smiled at her. 'Well done, Armaud. But that was too easy.' He came to take the gun from her, and she handed it over and stepped back. She didn't want to be too close to him. He unnerved her. He was too attractive, and she could feel a connection of some kind happening between them. She fought it. She didn't want to be attracted to him. She didn't need any complications in her life.

She watched him load the tiny gun and walk to ~~the~~ face the target. He held the gun by his side and fired two shots at a time, from his hip. All six bullets hit the centre ring.

'That's some good fancy shooting, sir.' She acknowledged his skill with the weapon.

'Now you try shooting it that way.'

She could see the advantage of being able to shoot without showing the weapon, especially as she had worked out what her future role might be. She loaded six bullets and faced the target. She held her hand steady by her hip and fired the first one. It didn't even touch the target, and they heard a thud as it slammed into a tree.

'Try again.'

She took a breath and aimed lower, trying to get a feel of the angle she needed. This time, the bullet clipped the metal ring at the top of the target, ricocheted up and took some thin branches from the top of a pine tree.

'That's better, but next time try shooting one after the other. It's what we call the double tap. If the first bullet fails to kill, the second one might finish the job.'

'Like an insurance policy, sir?'

'That's the idea, Armaud.'

She took aim and fired two bullets in succession. The first hit the edge of the target, and the second slid in below it.

'Now fire the last two.'

She did as he asked and got closer to the centre.

'Reload,' he instructed.

'Yes, sir.' She stooped to pick up more bullets.

'I need you to be fast and accurate, Armaud. You might not get a second chance in the field. If you find you have to use this weapon, you must make sure there is a safe exit from the kill zone and a good chance of getting away. You do understand, don't you?'

'Yes, sir. I do.' She nodded emphatically. 'It might have taken a while for the penny to drop, but I know what is expected of me now.' She looked into his eyes and saw compassion there. 'I will probably be put in a situation where I can do some damage to the enemy or gather some information that could be useful. I might find myself in tricky circumstances and will have to defend myself or kill someone.'

'That's what we agents do, Armaud. I'm glad you finally understand what all this is about. You still have a long way to go, so let's get this part right, shall we?'

She thought she might have misheard him and asked, 'Are you an agent, sir?'

'Who told you that, Armaud?' He grinned at her. 'Loose lips and sinking ships will get us both into trouble; though I rather think you'd be worth getting into trouble over.' His eyes glinted in the sunlight. 'You're a dangerous and exciting woman, do you know that?'

She couldn't believe he was flirting with her. She turned her attention to the task at hand. She concentrated on loading the tiny gun. Her fingers trembled, and she dropped a bullet. She was now feeling uncomfortable in his company and desperately wanted to deflect his provocative intentions. She quickly picked up the fallen bullet and asked, 'Will this really be strong enough to kill someone? The bullets seem too small to do much damage.'

'Take a look at the target if you need proof of the effectiveness of that little killing machine.'

He put a hand on her waist to guide her to the wooden circle. She felt the heat of his fingers spread over her lower back and quickly moved away from his touch.

She put a hand to the deep holes in the target. She could see the bullets embedded in the splintered grain.

'Human flesh is softer than that wooden circle.' He reached to gently squeeze her upper arm. 'What damage do you think you could cause to a German officer who was intent on capturing you?'

'I see what you mean, sir.' She turned to him and took a shaking breath. 'Even if the bullet didn't hit a vital organ, it would still cause a lot of damage.' She glanced down at his hand on her arm, and then looked into his eyes. She thought she saw a glimmer of something. She swayed closer to him, expecting something more from him. She could almost believe he was about to kiss her, and she felt frozen in time, staring into his eyes, but he blinked and moved away.

'You could always aim for the knee if you had a good, clear shot.' His voice sounded hoarse.

'Why would I do that, sir?'

'If you didn't want to kill the person, but you didn't want him to run after you and catch you, that would save his life and yours.' His gaze was focused on the trees, and he avoided looking at her.

'I see.'

'Killing isn't easy, Armaud. You have to live with your conscience when you take a life.'

'Have you killed many, sir?' She was beginning to feel sorry for him. He seemed too gentle a man to be a killer.

'Too many, Armaud. But I don't lose sleep over any of them. They would have killed me if I didn't get them first.'

'I can't imagine killing anyone, sir,' she admitted.

'Let's hope you don't have to, Armaud.'

His eyes were focusing on her again, and she felt the magnetic pull of him. She almost stepped closer to him but stopped herself. Instead, she turned to the target and shot two bullets from the hip, then another two, and then the final two. Tap-tap, tap-tap, tap-tap.

The pilot officer walked to examine the target. 'I think you've got the feel for that pistol, Armaud. Reload and see if you can do it again.'

She sighed and picked up another set of bullets. The brief spark of attraction was gone. She didn't know how she felt about the pilot officer. He seemed confused too. One minute he was telling her she was exciting and seemed to want to kiss her, and the next he was giving her the cold shoulder. She shook her head to clear the thoughts. She couldn't fall for the officer. It was against regulations and would complicate everything.

She loaded the pistol and waited, for the officer to move away from the target.

'Wait, Armaud.' He jogged to the side of the target area and pulled out a cloth dummy of a man on a tripod frame. 'I'm going to set him in motion. See how you do with a moving target.'

She watched him place the dummy about ten yards away and set it swinging on the tripod. When he was clear, she fired from her hip. Tap-tap, tap-tap, tap-tap.

After inspecting the holes, she was asked to try again from a crouching position, then with her back to the target, turning to shoot as if she were running away from it. She shot the target from every angle, covering many scenarios. She didn't always hit where she aimed, but she always hit it. She was determined to prove herself. She focused on her aim, to block her growing attraction to the officer. He was obviously doing the same. His initial flirtatious manner had been replaced by cold indifference. He was instructing her, nothing more.

When the lesson was over, she helped him pack the gear away and handed back the pistol.

'Keep it, Armaud.' He placed the tiny gun back in her hand. 'This is yours now.' He handed her a box of bullets. 'Don't load it but keep it safe.'

'Where should I keep it, sir?' She didn't like being in possession of the firearm.

'Wherever you think it will be safe, Armaud. You won't need it until you get your assignment, and that won't be for a few more weeks.'

'Weeks?' She was surprised. 'I thought I would have months of training. I won't be ready!' She began to feel a trace of panic in her stomach.

'Come on, we'll go for dinner.' He put his hand behind her waist to guide her from the target field, but he didn't touch her. 'You're ready now, but the bigwigs want to fine-tune you.'

'What does that mean?' She began to walk with him, back to the house.

'You'll leave in the next few days to go to Manchester for parachute training.'

'Parachute training!' She was shocked. 'You expect me to jump out of an aircraft?'

'How else do you suppose we'd get you into enemy territory?'

She shrugged. 'The same way my American Grandmother got in

and out of France last year to attend my French Grandmother's funeral.'

'Your grandmother did what?' He spun to face her. 'How did she do that?'

'She's very rich and knew some people who smuggled her out on a fishing boat.'

'Now I know where you get your guts from. Did your grandmother realise how much danger she was in? If the Germans had discovered her destination..! Well!' He shook his head. 'I don't know what they would have done.'

'You don't know my Grandmother Elizabeth. She could talk her way out of most situations. Or bribe her way through.'

'Does she still live near Verdun?'

'Yes, why do you ask?'

'She could be a very useful contact for our operatives in the field.'

'Am I going to Verdun?'

'Not my place to say, Armaud. You could be sent anywhere.'

She felt a pang of unease at what might lie ahead for her, and she didn't want to leave the comforting surroundings of Arisaig. Jumping out of planes sounded very scary, and she didn't know whether she would be brave enough to manage such a feat. She'd coped well with the training so far. She'd made friends here, she felt she'd settled into the team, and now she would have to start again with another group of strangers.

'Listen, Armaud.' He turned to look down into her eyes. 'An agent's life is a lonely one. We don't have many friends, and we can tell nobody about what we do or where we go. Nobody! Understand?'

'Yes, sir,' she whispered the automatic response in a shaking voice.

'You're afraid, but that's natural.' His smile was soft and warm, and his lips looked very inviting. 'Once you are given your first assignment, the fear will be replaced by excitement. Harness your fear. Make it your friend. You'll be eager to get to work, I can tell.'

She swallowed audibly.

'For now, your teammates have a little something lined up for you.' He grinned and winked then steered her towards the house again. 'Word got out that today is your birthday.'

'Is it?' She'd lost track of the days in the time she'd been at Arisaig. If today were her birthday, she'd be twenty-two now, and this would have been her wedding day if she'd stayed with Robert. She walked along with the officer, crossing the meadow and realised she hadn't thought of Robert in weeks. She wondered what he was doing. Had he enlisted as he threatened he would? Her life was changed so much in the few months since her grandmother died. Would she ever feel normal again? Would life ever resume the natural course for her? Marriage and a family were all she'd ever wanted until war broke out. Now those things seemed unimportant.

They arrived at the house, and the officer opened the door. 'Hide that toy, and then join your friends in the mess. They're waiting for you.'

'What about you, sir? Will you be there?'

'Not this time, Armaud. I'm leaving tonight.'

She was about to ask him where he was going but thought better of it. Instead, she simply nodded.

'See you around,' he said.

'Yes, sir.'

She watched him walk down the long hall before running upstairs to hide her weapon among her underwear. She may never see him again, and she felt she'd lost something precious. She sighed and hung her head for a few seconds. It could never have worked, she told herself. Not in a million years.

She hurried downstairs to the dining-room. When she entered, the place erupted in a loud cheer, and her friends surrounded her, slapping her back, congratulating her, and reaching to shake her hand or kiss her cheek.

'Happy birthday, Knickers.' The sergeant handed her a glass of beer.

'Thanks.' She took the glass and took a long swallow. She was going to miss these men.

Chapter 13: Home

She'd arrived at Ringway, Manchester, a few weeks ago and to her utter amazement, had enjoyed every minute of her training there. Jumping from a static balloon had been her first taste of leaping into the air after days of jumping, attached to wires, from a high platform. Learning how to fall, land safely, and quickly cover her tracks had been an exhilarating experience.

She was now equipped to embark on her first mission. She knew how to check her deployed parachute immediately on exiting the aircraft. She knew how to tuck her knees and roll when she touched the ground. She had practised burying her chute and suit within minutes of landing, using the small spade attached to her leg. The previous day had been her first and only jump from a moving plane, and she had felt such a surge of pure elation, it lasted all the fifteen seconds it took to reach the ground. She couldn't wait to do it again but was disappointed to be told she would have to wait. The next time she jumped would be for real when she would be dropped clandestinely behind enemy lines.

Now she was on her way home. She was dressed in her WAAF uniform, freshly pressed after sitting wrinkled in her bag for the last few months. She'd been given a three-day pass to visit her mother before continuing her training in the New Forest.

She got off the train at King's Cross, and it suddenly hit her that she had been shielded from the war during her training. Arisaig had seemed an oasis of peace. There'd been a few alerts at Manchester, but no bombs had dropped while she was there. Now she walked on bomb-blasted streets with piles of rubble and smoking remnants of houses. She passed a group of gossiping women.

'Did you hear old Mrs Coldwell copped it last night?' She overheard one of them saying.

'Hey, look there's a girl who can do something about this. Hey, darlin'! You're in the Royal Air Force aren't you?' one of the gossips shouted to her. 'Tell them pilot pals of yours to give old Hitler a thump from us, will ya?'

Nicolette turned to smile at them. She gave them a wave and called, 'I'll give him one myself if I see him.'

She went to the bus stop, intending to take a bus to Thames Ditton, but she could see the road was impassable. A bus wouldn't get through until the wardens had cleared the road. She began to walk and then realised her mother might be on duty near Covent

Garden and changed direction to see whether she could find the soup kitchen Collette had told her of.

It didn't take long to find the long line of people waiting to be served at the small church hall. She walked to the front of the queue and listened to some disgruntled mumbles from the hungry, desperate, victims of war. 'Get back in line!' 'Who do you think you are, miss?' and 'We've been waiting hours!'

'Sorry, I'm not here to eat,' she tried to reassure them.

She ducked through a side door in the building and immediately saw her mother stirring a large pot on a stove. 'Mum!' she called.

Collette dropped her spoon into the broth and whirled around. 'Nicolette! Where did you spring from? Why didn't you tell me you were coming home?' She reached for her and Nicolette felt the thin arms of her mother embrace her.

She held her mother at arm's length. 'You've lost weight. You're working too hard.'

'Pah! I'm needed and work stops me worrying about you and Joseph and your aunt. Have you eaten?'

'I could eat something but I wouldn't want to deprive people of their lunch. I'll get something later.'

'You'll sit over there and let me bring you some broth.' Collette pushed Nicolette to a small table in the corner of the kitchen. 'I won't take no for an answer. We have enough for half of London so they won't miss one bowl. When was the last time you ate? You don't look too bad. Are they feeding you well? What have you been doing? I write you letters but don't get replies. Where have you been?' Her mother kept up a constant stream of questions but didn't wait for answers.

'Mum, please stop!' Nicolette laughed at her mother's enthusiastic, effusive welcome. 'I'm fine but I've been moving around a lot and I don't think the postal service is quite what it was before the war. I haven't had any letters from you since I was in basic training. We can catch up now. Tell me, have you heard from Grandma Elizabeth?'

Nicolette's mother put a bowl of broth on the table with a spoon and a slice of thick, rough bread. 'I got a telegram a few weeks after Christmas. It had two words on it. "Home safe". That's all.'

'So she got back safely, that's a relief.' Nicolette was pleased her grandmother was safe and now knew for certain that Elizabeth was back in Verdun.

'What about Aunt Felicity? Where is she?'

'She's in the desert somewhere in North Africa. I had a Christmas card from her.'

'What about Joseph?'

'He's a Leading Aircraftman now. He's on his way to Canada for more training. You just missed him, Nicolette. He was home for a few days last week.'

'Bugger!'

'Pardon?' Collette looked shocked by her daughter's use of bad language.

'Sorry, Mum. I seem to have spent too much time with... err... well, sorry.' She almost let it slip that she'd been training with lots of men and had picked up their ribald language. She would have to be more careful. 'What about Uncle Edwin? How is he coping without Aunt Flissy?'

'We rub along together, you know?' Collette put her hands to her face. 'Oh, no! You won't know, will you! You didn't get my letters!'

'What happened, Mum?' Nicolette could see it was something bad from the expression on her mother's face.

'Thank goodness Edwin was on duty when that bomb dropped. Their house took a direct hit. He's living with me for the time being.'

'Oh, that's terrible. Does Aunt Flissy know?'

'We wrote to her but there's nothing to be done about it. We make the best of things and will sort everything out when the war is over, whenever that will be.'

Nicolette spooned some broth into her mouth. 'Mm, this tastes so good, Mum. You have no idea how much I missed your food.'

'Well, I will do my best to feed you well from our meagre rations.' Collette picked up the large pot and carried it through to the serving tables. She hurried back and began to chop a pile of vegetables. 'I just need to get the next pot started and I can leave them to it. I'm off duty tonight, thank goodness. How long will you be staying?'

'I have a three-day pass, but I don't want you to use your rations on me.'

'We don't starve, Nicolette. We grow vegetables and I keep a few chickens now. Edwin wants me to get a piglet to fatten for next Christmas and he knows someone who can get me one for a good price.'

'My, you are turning into an entrepreneur before my eyes, mother!'

'It is no more or less than we did in the last war. You forget I am an old hand at this, Nicolette.'

'I'm sorry that you have to go through it again, Mum. It's so unfair.'

'What choice do we have, my love? Great men throw childish tantrums and ordinary people pay the price of the quarrel. It never changes.'

Nicolette ate her broth and watched her mother working her way through the pile of vegetables. The older woman's hands were red and work-worn. Her shoulders stooped a little more than she remembered, and her hair held a few more streaks of silver. Nicolette realised that she'd only been away from home for six short months but the physical changes in her mother were unexpected and shocking. She seemed to have aged ten years.

'Where did you say you were going next?' Collette asked, wiping her hands on a cloth.

'I'm going to be a radio operator on the south coast.' She told her cover story and left the details vague to avoid complicated explanations.

'Well, I'm sure that sounds exciting and worthwhile. Are you happy?'

Nicolette smiled to herself. Her mother was always abrupt and to the point. 'As happy as I can be for now.'

'What kind of answer is that, I ask you? You could be married by now if you hadn't been so impulsive.'

'Mum! I was not impulsive! I gave it a lot of thought before I broke up with Robert.'

'Sorry, my love. I know you did but the poor man is broken-hearted.'

'I thought he'd joined the Navy.'

'He did but he came to see me before he left. He said to tell you that he'll still be here for you when the war is over in case you change your mind about marrying him.' Collette came to sit opposite Nicolette and took her hands in hers. 'He loves you, Nicolette. You two were meant to be together, can't you see that?'

'No, Mum.' She pulled her hands away. 'Robert is not the man for me.' She knew beyond doubt that she had made the right decision. She had been attracted to two men since the breakup with Robert, and could have fallen for either of them. She knew she wasn't ready for marriage when her feelings could be so easily swayed.

Her mother sighed. 'Well, I suppose what is done, is done, but it is such a shame.'

'It's not a crime to call off an engagement, Mum. Aunt Flissy did it with that Australian Doctor, didn't she?'

Collette's eyes narrowed. 'Who told you about that?'

'I've known for years. Grandma Elizabeth told me.'

'Well she had no business telling you. That is ancient history and is best forgotten.'

Nicolette watched her mother jump up and start to tidy her workspace. She scooped the chopped vegetables into a pot and wiped down the table.

'What was he like, Mum? Why did Felicity break off her engagement?'

'You'll have to ask your aunt that question. I can't answer for her.'

'Perhaps I will ask her if I ever see her again.'

Collette took the empty bowl from the table and took it to the sink. It seemed her mother was ignoring her as Collette carried on as if she hadn't spoken. Nicolette watched her mother rinse and dry the bowl, and then place it on the shelf with hundreds of others.

She got to her feet and went to hug her mother. 'Have I upset you, Mum?' she asked.

Collette shrugged her off and shook her head. 'No, my love. I often wonder whether I will ever have my family around me again, and it is the war that upsets me. The circumstances of war are making changes to my life again and it makes me angry. Felicity has put herself in danger for no good reason. She could have stayed here, and then nothing would have changed. Oh, it's such a mess.'

'What has happened, Mum? Is there more going on than you are telling me?'

'Nothing to concern yourself with, Nicolette. Come! I'm done here. Elsie will take over when she arrives in a few minutes. I'll just tell them I'm leaving and we can go home.'

Nicolette was in her own bed in her own room listening to the low voices of her mother and Uncle Edwin downstairs. She couldn't hear the discussion but the tones suggested they were sharing endearments. There were long silences interspersed with murmured conversation and a few low-pitched giggles from her mother.

Nicolette began to suspect that something was going on between them that shouldn't have been. They'd acted very strangely at supper. It was almost as if they were avoiding looking at each other. A few times, Nicolette had caught them exchanging worried glances and she felt they were keeping something from her. The couple had been thrown together in exceptional circumstances and Nicolette could only guess at the emotions that had grown between the older couple.

She knew from her grandmothers' stories that age was no barrier to love. Her Grandmother Elizabeth married her third husband when she was around Collette's age. Her Grandmother Belle had married Patrice when she was around forty-years-old.

When had the attraction between them begun? How long had they been living under the same roof? Did it happen gradually or had they always been attracted to each other? Is that what the underlying tension between the sisters had been about? If that were true, then why had Felicity left Edwin to go and do her nursing on the front line? Surely she would have known the danger of leaving her sister and husband together. Was her mother fighting the attraction just as Nicolette had done with the pilot officer? It certainly didn't sound as if she were resisting Edwin now.

She listened intently to the quiet conversation drifting up through the floor but couldn't make out any words. Eventually, the voices quieted and she fell asleep.

Birdsong woke her the next morning and she felt more refreshed than she had in weeks. She was amazed that her sleep had not been disturbed by a night raid. She had no idea what time it was but her stomach rumbled giving her a clue that it was late in the morning. She dressed quickly and went downstairs.

'Good morning, sleepyhead.' Edwin came to embrace her. 'It's so good to see you looking well. We've been thinking about you every day, and wondering where you were and what was happening to you. You and Joseph are our main topic of conversation, did you know that?'

'Are we?' She began to rummage in the kitchen cupboards.

'Collette put some porridge in the oven to keep warm for you.'

'Oh.' She smiled politely. 'How nice.' She grimaced. She hadn't had porridge for months but cheered when she remembered how good her mother's porridge tasted.

'She's popped to the shops. She won't be long.'

Edwin watched her as she took out the pot of porridge and assembled her breakfast. 'I was sorry to hear about your house, Uncle Eddy. Aunt Flissy will be livid, won't she?'

'Nothing she or anyone else can do about it.' Edwin scratched his head. 'We aren't the only ones to lose everything in this war.'

'You'll still have each other.' Nicolette said to test the waters. 'That's the most important thing, isn't it?'

Edwin looked away and nodded.

'You don't seem so sure of that, Uncle.' She decided to ask a few questions. She wanted to know whether her suspicions were right. 'Is everything all right with you and Aunt Flissy?'

'Oh, you know how it is. It was her choice to run away to war. She didn't *have* to go.' His voice shook and he clenched his fists at his sides. 'She was needed here! London needed her just as much as the soldiers at the front. Would she listen? No, she bloody wouldn't! She only has herself to blame.'

'Blame for what, Uncle Edwin?'

He stared at her for a few seconds and she noticed a nerve twitching on his cheek. Eventually, he spoke. 'Never mind. Forget I said anything.' He moved to the door. 'I have to get going.'

'Uncle Edwin!' She was determined to get to the bottom of the mystery and decided to ask him straight out. 'Are you and Mum having an affair?'

'What! How? I, I,' he blustered. 'How dare you suggest such a thing?'

'Are you?' She pushed.

'That's none of your damned business!'

'Well, that answered my question.' She shrugged. 'But you're right. It is none of my business. Though, I'm sure Aunt Felicity will have something to say about it when she comes home.'

'If she comes home!' he hissed.

'Are you wishing her dead, Uncle Edwin?' Nicolette was amazed to realise the strength of his feelings.

Edwin seemed to sag and his shoulders drooped. 'Of course, not, Nicky. How could I?' His tone changed to one of sadness and he took a seat at the table. 'I don't wish any harm to come to her. I loved her very much, you know.'

'Loved, as in past tense?' Nicolette picked him up on his use of words. 'So you don't love her any longer?'

'It's a long story, Nicky. A story that started when you were very small.'

'I have time, Uncle. Tell me. I'm a big girl now, you know.'

'Well, you'll know the truth before long, I suppose.'

'Tell me.' She encouraged.

He scratched his head again and took some time to gather his thoughts. He sighed. 'When I first got to know your mother, she was all I ever wanted. Her French accent made her seem exotic and exciting.'

'So you met my mother before you met Felicity?'

'Yes.' He nodded. 'We had a brief affair but I found out that she had you and I wasn't ready for a family. I was young and confused. Felicity was in the background and I realised that she was just as pretty, just as exotic and she made me fall in love with her.'

'She made you?' Nicolette nearly laughed but kept her smile hidden. She knew her Aunt Flissy could be a tease and a flirt. 'Was my mother upset by your change of heart?'

'She didn't seem to be too upset at the time. Maurice came on the scene and the two of them seemed to hit it off straight away. He doted on you and that seemed to endear him more to Collette. They were married after a few months of knowing each other. Then I married Felicity and you know the rest.'

'Are you telling me that my mother would have been your first choice from the beginning if she hadn't been burdened with me?' Nicolette could understand how a young man would not want to take on the responsibility of someone else's child but the rejection still hurt.

'Yes, but I was wrong. I know that now. I realised it within months of your mother marrying Maurice. I saw lots of you because Felicity was like your second mother and I grew to love you too. I hope you know how much you mean to me, Nicky.' He reached for her hand and she let him hold it.

'I know, Uncle Eddy.' She could see tears in his eyes and knew his declaration was true. 'I suppose Mum knows how you feel about her.'

'She's always known.'

'What about Aunt Flissy? Did she know?'

'Yes.' He heaved a deep sigh. 'It's a mess, Nicky. I love them both but my heart belongs to your mother.'

'Perhaps that's why Flissy went away. Perhaps she knew and couldn't stand in your way any longer.'

The kitchen door flew open and Collette rushed in. 'That's not the way it is!'

'How long have you been listening?' Edwin asked.

'Long enough. What are you thinking of? Nicolette has no business knowing about our past.'

115

'But I think I should know what's going on under my nose, Mum.'

'What gives you the right to poke your nose into my business?'

'You're my mother!' Nicolette tried to keep her voice low. She didn't want to get angry with her mother but the woman could be infuriating sometimes.

'So I am, but sometimes you wouldn't know it!'

'What's that supposed to mean?' Nicolette asked.

'You've always taken her side in things. Aunt Flissy this and Aunt Flissy that. You idolised her and she spoilt you at every opportunity. She was always trying to prove she loved you more than I did. Sometimes I wish I'd never agreed...' She put her hand to her mouth and bit her lips together.

'Never agreed to what, Mum?' Nicolette was riveted. She hadn't realised her mother felt such jealousy towards her aunt. She thought the two women loved her equally and had always felt fortunate to have two mother figures in her life.

'Oh, nothing. It doesn't matter now.'

'It matters to me, Mum. What happened back then? I know you must have been unhappy that my father died in the war and left you with a baby but I feel there is something you're not telling me.'

'Of course, I'm unhappy that your father died, Nicolette. I was a war widow and pregnant. Of course, I was unhappy. I was heartbroken. What more could there be to it? Isn't that enough?'

'I'm sorry, Mum.' Nicolette hung her head. 'It must have been a very difficult time for you.'

'It was but we got through it.' She sighed and smiled. 'And you brightened our lives when you came along.' Her mother gave Nicolette a look of love and yearning. 'Don't think for one minute that we regret having you, my love.'

'Then, what *do you* regret, Mum? Something made you unhappy and it wasn't losing my dad in the war, was it? There's more to it than that.'

'After you were born, I met Edwin.' She glanced at the man who was looking at her with adoration in his eyes. 'We fell in love. Head over heals. Weren't we?'

Edwin nodded and his eyes glowed with unshed tears.

'Then he found out you had a baby and everything changed.' Nicolette filled in a piece of the jigsaw that Edwin had told her.

'I sometimes wish I'd never agreed to marry Maurice as quickly as I did. It was a rebound affair. We weren't meant for each other in the same way as Edwin and I were.'

'But you told me he was the love of your life.' Nicolette protested.

'I couldn't tell you the truth, could I?' Collette sighed. 'He became your father and you worshipped him. I wish you could remember him, Nicolette. He was such a good man.'

'Just not quite good enough, though, Mum. Did you still love Edwin?' She glanced at her uncle.

'I never stopped loving him, but Felicity got her claws into Edwin and didn't give him a chance to change his mind. She was just the same with Antoine but he could not be tempted away from me. She would have had him too if he'd been a weaker man.'

'Are you telling me that Aunt Felicity would have had an affair with my real father?'

Collette nodded. 'Fortunately, he loved me too much. She didn't think I noticed the way she looked at him or the way she spoke to him sometimes but I saw the lust in her eyes.'

'Wasn't she engaged to the Australian?'

'The doctor was just a plaything for her. She's always had loose morals.'

'I'm amazed, Mum. I thought you two were the closest sisters ever. I thought you loved each other.'

'We do, Nicolette.' Collette laughed briefly. 'Just as you and Joseph love each other. I know he's not really your brother but... I mean, he's your half-brother but you love him, don't you?'

Nicolette nodded. 'I've never thought of Joseph as a half-brother. He's simply my brother.'

'And you fight and argue all the time, don't you?'

'Not all the time, Mum.' Nicolette chuckled. 'No matter how much we quarrel, we will always love each other.'

'And it is just the same with your aunt and me. We have our fights, our jealousies and rivalries but we are sisters. We are of the same blood.'

'What will happen when Aunt Felicity comes home?'

Her mother and Uncle looked at each other and shrugged.

'I don't know,' her mother said. 'We'll deal with that, if and when, it happens.'

'You don't have to worry about this, Nicky,' her uncle said. 'We're the grown-ups and we'll sort it out between us.'

'You have enough to think about.' Collette took off her coat and hung it behind the door. 'Did she tell you she's going to be a radio operator, Edwin?'

Chapter 14: The test

Finishing school was nothing like she'd imagined it would be. In her mind, she'd envisaged honing her new skills of close combat, and perhaps keeping up her levels of fitness with more running and physical exercise. Instead, she was inundated with new information. She learned infiltration techniques, communication in the field, personal security and how to conduct herself if she suspected she was being watched.

She learned how to break into a locked house or room. She was taught how to operate a tiny camera and practiced taking photographs of papers, people and landscapes.

One instructor explained the advantages of disguises when trying to avoid being captured. He placed some glasses on his nose and began to walk with a limp. 'You don't have to make major changes to fool the enemy. Use a different hairstyle or wear a hat. A pretty headscarf, darker face powder and brighter lipstick often work well for the ladies.'

Nicolette absorbed everything she was taught, knowing her life may depend on remembering some of the things she was being shown.

Eventually, she was told she had an assignment, and she reported to the main office with a nervous knot in her stomach to discover where she would be sent.

'Come in, Armaud,' the warrant officer called. 'Take a seat.'

She sat opposite the older man at the long table and looked at the assortment of items displayed in front of him.

'We're setting you a test. Nothing too arduous. We'd like you to blag your way into Barclays Bank, the Colonial and Overseas branch in Gracechurch Street, London.'

'What should I do when I get inside, sir? Do you want me to rob a bank?'

'Goodness no!' He chuckled. 'Even the SOE wouldn't get away with a prank like that, Armaud.' He made eye contact with her. 'There's a filing cabinet in the director's office. Your task is to photograph the file of a man called Henry Peters.'

Nicolette felt her heart skip a beat. How on earth would she accomplish that?

'To get you started, we can give you an entry alibi. The bank has some safety deposit boxes, and we have taken one in the name of Lucille Smithson. That will be your name for the next few days.'

He slid some papers towards her. 'Your identity papers and ration book.'

She glanced at the unfamiliar name. 'Lucille Smithson.'

'That's right. You're the French wife of a British diplomat. The diplomat is a real person who has a country estate in Kent, but he doesn't have a wife. The bank staff won't know that he doesn't have a wife. You'll arrive at the bank and ask to see your box. This is the number and the bank has the key.' He passed another slip of paper to her.

His eyes met hers again as he went on, 'While you are there, you'll devise a way of getting into the director's office. I'm sure you'll think of something. Here are some of his background details to get you started.' He slid a buff envelope across the table. 'As luck has it, we discovered the director is having an affair with one of his secretaries, so it should be easy to concoct a cover story to get you in. We've been watching him for months. We thought he was collaborating with the Germans. His grandparents are German. We discovered the affair by chance and thought we could use it to get information from him but it turns out he's squeaky clean.'

'Except for the affair.' She pointed out.

'Well, that's hardly a hanging offence, but it could prove useful for you. He took his secretary to the Savoy for a dirty weekend. We suspect he bought her a diamond ring, though she's passing it off as paste. She told her colleague, one of our girls working undercover there, that she found it in the street after a raid. All the details are in that file.'

'Thank you, sir.' She took the file and the identity papers.

'This is only a test, Armaud. If you find yourself in difficulties or are apprehended by the local police, you can give the authorities this number. Ask them to call us and we'll get you out of jail, as it were.' Another slip of paper was passed to her.

'Might I be arrested, sir?' She held her breath waiting for his answer.

'Only if you're caught, Armaud.'

'Anything else I should know, sir?' she asked.

'Take this camera. I hear you're quite proficient in the use of it.'

'Thank you.'

'And here is the key to a flat in Mayfair. The address is inside.' He gave her an envelope with a key inside it. 'You're to use the flat as a safe house. You'll go there this evening.'

'Yes, sir.'

'Oh, and one last thing.'

'Yes?'

'Call at the camouflage rooms and get kitted out, you'll never get anywhere near the safety deposit boxes in that getup.'

She was about to ask what was wrong with her outfit of straight skirt and twinset but thought better of it. 'Yes, sir.'

'Dismissed. I'll see you back at base when you've completed your mission.'

Her heart was pounding as she left the room. The mission might only be a test, but she knew she would have to pass this to move on to the real work. She hurried to the camouflage room and explained where she would be going.

'Harriet!' The young man shouted to a colleague in the back room. 'Do we still have that mink stole in store?'

Nicolette walked as gracefully as she could on the high-heeled, patent leather court shoes. The heavy silk skirt was very tight around her hips and thighs, and she felt hobbled and restricted by the unfamiliar couture garment. She carried a small overnight bag that would have cost a small fortune and it contained all the items she would need to complete her mission. She took a taxi from the railway station to the address in Mayfair and paid the cabbie from the expenses allowance she'd been provided with.

Once inside the flat, she could relax for a while. The bank wouldn't open until half past nine in the morning, and she had all night to plan her moves. She stripped off the expensive clothing and checked the contents of her bag. She'd need to keep the camera to hand but out of sight. Her mink stole didn't have pockets, but she thought she might be able to make a pouch in the lining if she ripped it a little. She felt guilty to spoil such a beautiful item of clothing, but she'd been given carte blanche to do anything she needed to.

She spent the night rehearsing various scenarios and conversations she might have. She'd been given a rough plan of the building and memorised it, drawing it again on the wallpaper of the flat to make sure she could remember it fully. She then ripped the wallpaper from the wall and shredded it into tiny pieces before lighting it in the empty fire-grate and watching it burn. She couldn't leave any evidence of her mission.

She heard the sirens go off in the early hours of the morning but stayed in her bed. She didn't know where the nearest shelter was, anyway. She listened to bombs dropping in the distance and wished she could be doing something more important to stop them. Sneaking around banks in England was not doing anything to help the war effort but she understood that she had to get through this test before they would allow her near the action.

The all clear went and she watched the sunrise before she began to get ready. She took extra time with her hair and makeup. She was meant to be a very wealthy French lady spending the war at her husband's country estate in Kent. She needed to look the part. Her concocted cover story was firmly in her mind and she thought it sounded plausible. Lucille Smithson was up in London for a shopping trip and to remove some jewellery from the vault at Barclays to wear for a party at the estate.

She'd read the file on the director of the bank and thought she had a good chance of pulling off her mission. All she needed was a little luck.

The door to the bank was closed when she arrived, but she'd been warned that she might have to ring the bell for access. She grabbed the bell-pull with her gloved hand and waited. When the door swung open, a young man greeted her.

'Good morning, madam. Can I help you?'

She put on a heavy French accent, 'Yes, thank you. I 'av a safety deposit 'ere, and I would like to make a withdrawal.'

'Certainly, madam, do you have some identity with you?'

'Of course.' She opened her small bag and took out her false papers.

'Madam Smithson, please come this way.' He held the door for her and showed her into the large, imposing hall with an ornate mahogany staircase leading to the next floor on one side and down to a basement on the other.

Nicolette made a mental note of the layout, checking the details of the staircase with her memory of the plans of the building.

'Please take a seat. Do you have your box number?'

She leant forwards and whispered the number. She'd committed it to memory so she wouldn't have to keep opening her bag and risk fumbling. Her hands were shaking and she clasped them together firmly in her lap.

'Just one moment, madam.'

She watched him go through a door to the right of a reception desk where two women were working and taking sly glances at her.

She lifted her chin and stared disdainfully down her nose at them, and they quickly looked away.

The young man appeared again. 'This way, madam.'

He took her down the grand staircase to the basement and unlocked a large door. She followed him down another hall where he unlocked a second door, and a third door was beyond that one. Her nerves were beginning to get the better of her, and she took a deep breath.

'Are you all right, madam?'

'I am, 'ow you say, a little claustrophobic. I do not like to be underground,' she said quickly and hoped he would accept the hasty excuse explaining her tension.

'This won't take long, madam.'

He pushed the door open and allowed her to enter the vault. She glanced around looking for the number and began to realise that she had no idea where it was. Should she know? Would the young man expect her to know? She took a chance, 'I am so sorry, but can you tell me where it is? My husband set this up for me and I have no idea where to look.' She smiled coquettishly and fluttered her eyelashes for good measure.

'Of course, Madam Smithson. It is here. He pointed to the box. 'Would you like me to open it for you?'

'No, thank you.' She blurted a little too quickly. She thought she might have sounded a little hasty so added, in a silky tone, 'I think I can manage now.'

'I'll leave you for a few moments. I'll be right outside.' He handed her the key.

She waited until he had left before opening the box. There was nothing inside. She didn't expect there would be but she pretended to open her bag and rummage around, making sounds that would convince the young man that she was taking out something and placing it in her handbag.

She put the box back into the hole in the wall and locked the small door. Straightening her shoulders, she walked from the room, dropping the key into the young man's hand as she sashayed by him. She exaggerated the sway of her hips as she climbed the stairs in front of him and abruptly turned before she got to the top step, hoping to wrong-foot him.

She struck a pose similar to the ones she'd seen models use in magazines. With one hand on her hip and with her head slightly tilted she pursed her lips and purred, 'I do not suppose Bertrand is free, is he?'

'Bertrand?' The young man seemed flustered.

'Oh, I am sorry.' She put a gloved hand to her chest and tilted her head the other way and laughed throatily. 'You will, of course, know him as Mr Granger, the director. He is a good friend of my husband. We have sent him an invitation to our party, but I would like to invite him in person if possible. It is 'ow we prefer to do things in France. Is he free?'

'Err, I'm not sure, Madam.'

'Would you be a darling and ask for me?'

The young man gestured for her to continue up the stairs. 'I'll see what I can do, Madam.'

'Oh, and will you tell him that I 'ave a message from Sylvia's 'usband. I'm sure he will be very interested to see me.'

'From Sylvia's husband, Madam?'

'That's correct.'

'Would you take a seat for a moment and I'll check if Mr Granger is available?'

'Thank you.' She sank into a leather chair and crossed her legs. She was shaking so much that the feathers in her hat were surely trembling. Taking some deep breaths, she tried to steady her nerves. She touched the hem of her mink stole to check the camera was still in place, and then held her hands together demurely in her lap.

The two receptionists were staring at her with interest, so she gave them a friendly smile. One of them returned her gesture, but the other turned briskly and shuffled some papers on her desk.

The young man came back twisting his hands together. 'Mr Granger will see you, Madam, but he said to make sure you understood that he only has a few minutes before his next meeting.'

'A few minutes will be all I will need.' She stood to follow him up the staircase to the next floor.

The young man showed her into a large office with windows on two sides. She recognised where she was from the memorised plan in her head. A very distinguished looking gentleman sat behind an imposing leather-topped desk that was almost the entire length of the room.

'Good morning, Mr Granger.' She used her most pronounced French accent and sashayed as sexily as she could, across the room, holding out her hand. She heard the door close behind her and breathed a small sigh of relief, knowing the young man had left.

The distinguished gentleman stood and took her gloved fingers in a polite shake. 'I'm sorry, but do I know you?' he asked.

'You know my friend's wife, Mr Granger. Sylvia's husband is a very good friend of mine.'

'Err... Sylvia who?' The man's neck was colouring, and he placed a finger inside his collar to loosen it.

'Mrs Sylvia Davies, of course. Your secretary, Mr Granger.' Nicolette's legs were shaking so much she thought she might fall over, so she walked slowly across the room to take a seat by the window and glanced outside. 'Surely you haven't forgotten that weekend you had with her at the Savoy last month.'

'What!' His voice came out as a squeak. 'How do you know...?'

She tilted her head and smiled. 'I am sure your wife would be very interested to hear what you bought for Sylvia. A diamond ring, I heard.'

'How do you know about this?'

'As I said, Bertrand, I know Mr Davies very well. He didn't believe her story about the ring.'

'What do you want?' His tone was lower, and he spoke through gritted teeth. 'I won't be blackmailed.'

'Such an ugly word, Bertrand. I do not want your money.'

'What then? What will it take to make you go away?'

'Sylvia told her husband she found the ring in the street.'

'Lots of things are lost in the raids. Why does he think this is not true?'

'He had it valued at the weekend.' She lifted her gloved hand and waved it languidly in front of her face, carefully inspecting her fingers. 'She is a lucky girl to deserve such a valuable trinket.'

'Get to the point, Mrs, err, what is your name?'

'You can call me Lucille, Bertrand.'

'I'll ask again for the last time. What do you want?'

'The ring, Bertrand. I want you to go and ask Sylvia to return the ring to you. I am sure she will be wearing it today. I hear she always wears it to work. Then you can give it to me, and that will be an end to it.'

'I can't do that! She won't agree to it.'

Nicolette let out a gentle, tinkling laugh. 'I am sure if you explained the seriousness of the situation, she will 'ave no 'esitation. After all, she found it on the street. She could just as easily lose it again.'

'I can't promise I'll be able to get it for you.' He was already walking to the door.

'I 'ave every faith in your powers of persuasion, Bertrand. Do not let me down.'

She watched him close the door behind him, and she sprang to her feet. The filing cabinet was in the corner, and every drawer was labelled with letters of the alphabet. She tugged on the door marked "M to P" and discovered it was locked. She quickly took a hat pin from her head and inserted it into the keyhole.

She pushed and wiggled the pin as she'd been taught, and sighed with relief when the lock opened with a satisfying click.

She searched the drawer and found the file marked, "Henry Peters". She placed it on the floor and opened it. There were three sheets of paper, and she photographed all three, both sides. Then she tucked the camera away and put the file back. She'd just resumed her seat when Mr Grainger came back into the room. She smiled sweetly at him, though her heart was hammering enough to escape her chest at any minute.

'Did you get it?' she asked.

'I did, but first I have realised that I have been very remiss with my manners, Lucille. I have sent for some coffee.'

'That is very kind of you, Bertrand, but I would like to see the ring.' She felt the needles of suspicion prickling her throat. What if he'd sent for the police?

'It is safe in my pocket.' He tapped the hip pocket of his jacket. 'Sylvia was most upset.'

'I'm sure she was, Bertrand, but I need that ring.' She got to her feet and glanced behind her. The large window overlooked a courtyard, and there was a flat roof extending from the wall about ten feet down from the window. She assessed her route of escape quickly. 'I feel a little warm, does this window open?' She pushed the sash frame upwards and felt the cooler air drift into the room. She sat on the ledge and prepared to lift her legs over the edge.

'What are you doing?' The bank director was by her side in seconds. He grabbed her shoulder.

She jerked her elbow into his ribs, and he doubled over. She dipped her hand into his jacket pocket and pulled out the ring.

He made a lunge for her hand, and she kicked him in the groin. As he bent over, she brought her knee to his nose and sent him sprawling backwards. Blood sprayed from his nose, splattering her skirt and jacket but she didn't waste time on sympathy or mercy for the gasping adulterer.

She quickly slid through the open window on her stomach and turned to grab the ledge. She lowered herself until she was hanging by her fingertips, and then let go. She dropped onto the flat roof and rolled to the edge where she repeated the process and landed in the courtyard. She saw an iron, railed gate leading into a long alleyway, just where she remembered it should be, and she ran to it. It was locked, of course, and she could have picked the lock, but didn't think she would have enough time. Instead, she hoisted her skirt to climb over and heard the expensive fabric rip.

Safely on the other side, she pulled the skirt back into place as she hurried down the dark alley. She stopped at the end, to assess her appearance. The silk suit was now covered in blood and dirt. The expensive mink stole was grubby, but she straightened it and quickly tidied her hair. She knew she would attract attention, but had no choice. She emerged into the busy shopping street and tried to merge with the crowds.

She began to walk quickly through the shoppers, heading for the Monument tube station at the far end of the road. She didn't want to run and draw even more attention to herself. She was almost there when she heard a police whistle behind her and a man's voice shouted, 'Stop! Police!' She glanced over her shoulder, to see two policemen running towards her. They were about twenty yards away and closing fast.

She rapidly scanned her surroundings and saw a café to her right. She ran into it and hurried through to the kitchen. A few curious customers lifted their heads and the woman behind the counter shouted something, but Nicolette kept going. She dragged off her hat as she ran past the chef, took the camera from the pocket in her stole and pulled the mink from her shoulders. She hurried through the back door of the café and dumped her hat and the mink into a dustbin. She pulled pins from her hair as she ran until it was swinging loose around her shoulders. Reaching the end of an alley, she racked her brain to think of where she might find another crowd of people to hide in.

She ran around the corner of the building and stepped into a quiet street. Her heart fell. The blast of a policeman's whistle sounded in the street she'd just left. Kicking off her shoes, she sprinted to the end of the short road where a bus was just leaving the stop. She jumped on board and pretended to drop something so she could crouch low until the bus had passed the confused looking policemen. When it was safe, she took a seat near the front, away from her pursuers. The conductress asked where she was going.

'Mayfair.' She opened her bag to get out some coins for her fare.

'Sorry, miss, we go to Covent Garden. You need to get the next one. Shall I ask the driver to stop?'

'No!' She glanced behind her. The policemen were still standing on the corner of the street looking around for her. 'No, I, err, Covent Garden will do fine.' She paid her fare and sank lower in her seat.

'What happened to you? Are you hurt?' the conductress asked. 'Your lovely clothes are covered in blood!'

'Oh, some young men got into a fight and I was standing too close.' Nicolette said the first thing that came to her mind and laughed.

'Lost your shoes too, me dear?' the conductress smirked, looking at Nicolette's dirty, feet.

Nicolette laughed nervously. 'You know what it's like when you've been dancing all night.' She picked up one dirty foot and began to massage it. 'Bloody shoes were killing me!'

The conductress walked to the back of the bus laughing.

Chapter 15: First mission

Nicolette hobbled to the small church hall, hoping her mother would be on duty. The queues were absent this morning, but she slipped through the side door, as she had done before. She couldn't see her mother. Two women were stirring pots and they turned to her.

One dropped her ladle and came hurrying to Nicolette. 'Whatever has happened to you, child? Have you been attacked? Should we call the police?'

'No! No! I'm fine. Really.' Nicolette tried to reassure them, though, with her bloodied and dishevelled appearance, she could understand why the women would jump to such a conclusion. She put on a broader London accent when she next spoke. 'I didn't get to the shelter in time last night. I got caught outside, and a bloody bomb dropped right across the road from me.' She quickly hatched a cover story to explain her unkempt state.

'You poor dear.' The other woman came over, wiping her hands on her apron. 'We should call an ambulance. They were bombing the other side of the river last night. You must have been wandering around for hours if you've come from over there! Were you knocked out, me dear? Do you know who you are?'

'I, err...' Nicolette tried to think fast. She'd foolishly thought her mother would help her, but Collette wasn't here. She couldn't admit that she'd come in search of her mother. She was still undercover and couldn't mention her family now that these women were involved. They must never know of her connection with Collette. She realised she'd been foolish to think of coming here.

'I told you they can lose their memories, Elsie, when they've had a knock on the head,' the second woman whispered to her colleague. 'Bet this young thing doesn't even know who she is.'

'I heard you might have some grub going, and I'm hungry.' Nicolette appealed to their caring nature. 'I'm sure I'll feel better once I've eaten.'

'Of course, me dear.' Elsie hurried to get her some food.

'Where do you live, dear? Can you remember? We could get someone to take you home.' The other woman put a comforting hand on Nicolette's shoulders.

'You're very kind, but once I've had something to eat, I'll be fine. Really. I was out dancing,' she elaborated to show that she hadn't lost her mind. 'Me friends told me to hurry, but I had some high heels on and I couldn't run.' She giggled to reassure the women that she was all right. 'I think I tripped and the next thing I remember I was blown off me feet.' She let out a gust of laughter, and the two women began to laugh with her.

'I think she'll survive, Nellie.' Elsie carried a plate of toast and a mug of tea to the table in the corner.

'Oh, thank you.' Nicolette took the tea and drank it quickly. 'I needed that.' She wiped her mouth with the back of her hand.

'You can take a look in our clothing store when you've done there, me dear. We might have a few things that will fit you. Can't send you back on the streets in that state, now can we?'

'You're very kind. Thank you.' She took a bite of toast and sighed with relief. In a new outfit, she could make her way back to headquarters without being noticed.

'Well done, Armaud.' The warrant officer stood to greet her when she entered the office. 'Exemplary performance!'

'Thank you, sir.' She couldn't help smiling. She felt proud that she had accomplished her objective. She'd arrived back at base the previous day and had already been fully debriefed. 'Were the photographs useful?'

'Photographs?' He looked puzzled for a moment and then laughed. 'Oh, we didn't need the photographs. They were just to prove you could do the job.'

'Oh yes, of course.' She swallowed back the exasperated sigh. She'd taken risks, spent hours planning and her hard work had been for nothing.

'The dressing room girls and boys are not happy with you, however. They can forgive you for losing the shoes, but to lose the whole outfit, not to mention their prized mink stole! Well, I don't have to say more, do I?'

'I might be able to help replace the value of the clothes, sir.' She took out the ring she'd kept in her possession so she could deliver it in person to the warrant officer. 'You were right about the ring.' She placed it on the desk.

'How did you get...?' He picked up the ring and turned it in his fingers.

She was about to relate the whole story, but he put his hand up to stop her. 'No, don't tell me.' He put the ring back on the desk. 'Is it real?'

'I have no idea, sir, but I suspect it might be.'

'You could be prosecuted for theft, Armaud.'

'They'd have to catch me first, sir.' She grinned and watched the officer smile in response.

'You're ready for action, aren't you, Armaud?'

'Can't wait, sir.' She casually shrugged. 'Whenever you think I'm ready, I'll go.' She was desperate to get started but didn't want to seem too eager.

'We'll brief you over the next few days. You'll be dropped into the field of operation on Monday night.'

'Where will I be going, sir?'

'Just over the French coast. We want you to take care of a couple of things over there.'

'Such as?' She asked, eagerly.

'We want you to befriend the leader of the resistance group. Marcus will be a hard nut to crack, but we need him on your side. We'd like you to try to put a stop to all the infighting in his group.'

'How will I manage that, sir?' She couldn't imagine how she could control a group of resistance fighters. 'I've not had any training in leadership, let alone diplomacy.'

'From what I hear of your time in Arisaig, you turned a rabble of hard-faced, disgruntled airmen into your personal lapdogs.' He raised his eyebrows at her.

'Hardly, sir. We were friends. I was their equal.'

'Not at first you weren't!' He wagged a finger at her. 'Your qualities were noted, Armaud. We'll give you more tactics to add to your arsenal before you go, but I have a feeling you'll be a natural.' He scratched his chin and stroked his moustache. 'You see, the communists are flooding to join the existing groups. Ever since Germany invaded the Soviet Union, the commies want some of the action and realise they should have been working with the Maquis, to fight against the enemy, from the start. Now they want a bigger piece of the action than the organised resistance are willing to give them.'

Her eyes grew wide as she realised what the officer was expecting of her. 'So you want me to be their referee?' She was astonished to be given so much responsibility.

'You can do it, Armaud, or perhaps I should call you, Lucille, as that will be your operational name.'

'Why would they listen to me, sir?'

'Well, it's obvious that you'll have to earn their trust first. That's why we'll be dropping equipment and supplies along with you to sweeten your arrival. They are expecting the supplies.'

'So are you telling me that they won't be expecting me?'

'They know an agent is arriving. They don't know that you're a young woman.'

She swallowed and remembered that first morning in Arisaig. The Royal Air Force Commandos had been tough on her. What would the French Communists be like?

'You mentioned a couple of things, sir.' She wondered what other assignment would be added to her mission. 'What else would you like me to do while I'm in France?'

'We think the resistance group has been infiltrated by a German collaborator. We'd like you to discover who it is and put a stop to the flow of information to the enemy.'

'Am I hearing you correctly, sir?' She felt her chest flood with adrenaline. 'You want me to kill someone?'

'Only if you have to, Armaud.' The officer chuckled. 'There are other ways of dealing with collaborators.'

'Take them prisoner?'

'Perhaps.' The officer stroked his moustache. 'Though, I suspect Marcus will prefer your original idea of a permanent solution.'

She left the briefing office with a heavy heart. She'd been eager to get to work, but now she knew her what her mission involved, she was a little less enthusiastic. Killing people in self-defence was a necessity in war but she had never considered she would be expected to do it cold blood. She didn't know whether she'd be capable of such an act. Perhaps she would have to be.

The aircraft sounded very loud to her ears. Surely the German soldiers below would hear her approach and be waiting for her on the ground. She shivered. The end of July was warm in England, but the black, night sky had sucked any warmth from the air. She was freezing. She checked her parachute for the tenth time, checked her bag and made sure her pistol was easy to access. Her hand went to the spade, making sure it was attached securely to her leg. She went through the landing again in her head.

Marcus, or some of his group members, would be waiting for her. They would help her to hide her parachute and suit, and then take her to the safe house. Once there, she'd have to begin her mission of befriending the leader and earning his trust. She had no idea how she would do that.

The noise of the aircraft changed, and she was instantly alert to danger. She'd been told the pilot would avoid the populated areas and fly low to avoid the German radar but she still worried the anti-aircraft batteries on the Normandy coast might spot them. Her career would be over before it had begun.

An aircraftman approached her from the front of the small plane. 'Ready, Lucille?' He shouted in her ear. 'We're almost there.'

She nodded and moved into position near the hatch. She would be dropped first, and the equipment and supplies would be thrown out after her. Horrifying thoughts filled her mind about what might be waiting for her on the ground. What if the collaborator had informed the Germans of her arrival? What if her reception would be a hail of bullets from enemy guns? She shook those thoughts from her head and tried to concentrate on the mechanics of jumping from the plane. She hoped the aircraftman would give her enough time to get free of the aircraft before he threw out the radios, boxes of rifles and ammunition.

The aircraftman yanked the end of the pull-cord of her chute that was attached to the aircraft, to check it was secure. The lights flickered in the body of the plane, the signal that she was over the drop zone. The aircraftman pulled open the small hatch. She crossed her arms over her chest and jumped from the hole into blackness.

Her heart leapt, and her throat closed for a second until she felt the satisfying jerk of her chute opening. She scanned the darkness below for signs of movement, but could see nothing. She tried to concentrate, but scary images of enemy soldiers with rifles pointing at her filled her mind. She was petrified. This terrifying experience was nothing like the first jump she had enjoyed so much.

She looked at her feet to see the ground rushing to meet her and bent her knees. She had no more time to worry about her reception; she was on the ground and gathering her chute in seconds. The faster she could get her gear hidden, the safer she would be. She could see a torch beam flickering through the trees to her right and crouched low, holding her breath. She pulled the chute under her body and lay on top, hoping her dark flying suit would camouflage her if the lights belonged to the enemy.

'Hello!' The voice was heavily accented French, but she didn't move. She couldn't take any chances. She lay still and waited for the code words.

'We 'ave no whisky today.'

She breathed a sigh of relief and got to her knees. 'I have Scotch whisky with me, but I hear you prefer French Brandy.' She repeated the phrase, in French, that she knew her reception party would be expecting.

'C'est une femme!' The Frenchman spoke over his shoulder to another person. 'She is a woman!'

They hurried to help her with the parachute. 'Don't throw it away, we can use the fabric. French girls will give anything for this.' A young voice boasted.

Another young man added, in a suggestive tone, 'And we do mean anything!' He chuckled softly, as he gathered the precious fabric.

Nicolette laughed nervously and let them roll up her chute. The two men seemed young but very sure of themselves.

'Shall I take off my suit?' She asked, using the French language as naturally as if she'd been speaking it all her life.

'Not yet, it is good camouflage. Come, quickly.' He beckoned her to the trees. 'Others are collecting the supplies from the next meadow. We have to get out of here quickly.'

She hurried after the two young men, keeping her head low. They took her to a line of three trucks of varying shapes and sizes.

'Here, let me help you up.' The first young man cupped his hands and gestured for her to step into them to climb aboard a flat-backed utility vehicle.

She didn't question him. She did as he asked and climbed aboard. Within seconds she was surrounded by a dozen or so Frenchmen, all carrying boxes trailing ropes and small parachutes. They began to load the supplies into the three trucks, and then some men jumped in beside her. They set out in convoy, but she watched the first two trucks take different directions at a crossroad. The truck she was travelling in went straight ahead.

She tried to look at the faces of her companions, but it was too dark to make anything out. She didn't know how the truck stayed on the road in such darkness. It was a moonless night and clouds covered what faint starlight there was.

'When can we have a cigarette?' One of the men asked in the darkness.

'When we get inside the barn and not a second sooner.' The man sitting next to Nicolette hissed the reply. 'No lights!'

'But that is too long, Marcus. I'm choking on all this fresh air!'

The others laughed quietly.

'Be silent!' Marcus hissed. 'Do you want the whole of Normandy to hear you?'

'What is the panic? They will hear the truck anyway!' another voice commented.

'A lone farm truck is nothing to be concerned about, Henri, but a German soldier would be delighted to hear your loud French hollering.' He leant towards the young man menacingly and added, 'Especially when you are stuck on the end of his sharp bayonet.'

After an hour or so of travelling in comparative silence, a group of dark buildings showed on the horizon, silhouetted against a lightening sky. Nicolette realised the sun would rise shortly. She hoped they'd be safely inside by then. She felt vulnerable and exposed in the open truck.

She was relieved when she realised the buildings she had seen was the destination. The truck rolled through the large barn doors and pulled up alongside the other two trucks that must have taken a shorter route and arrived earlier. She realised they had separated as a safety precaution. If one truck was stopped, the others might still make it through.

She was helped down from the truck and ignored while the others unpacked the supplies and stowed them away under straw bales, inside covered holes in the ground and in barrels lining the walls. They moved with determination and purpose. Each man seemed to know what to do. She was impressed by their efficiency. As they worked, they called softly to each other, making comments about the new arrival. She listened carefully, mentally noting when names were used and what name belonged to each man.

'She's very young, Pierre,' an older man said to the stout comrade helping him carry a large box of rifles.

Pierre laughed and called to two of the younger men who were covering a trap door with hay, 'Too old for you, though, eh, little Rene?'

Rene glanced at Nicolette and blushed. 'She could do worse,' the young man boasted.

She recognised the voice of Rene as one of the young men who took her parachute. She smiled at him, and his blush became a deeper shade of pink.

'I think he is in love!' Pierre's companion quipped.

'Shut your mouth, Fabien.' Rene hissed at the older man.

'Enough! All of you!' Nicolette recognised the voice of Marcus and knew he was the leader of this group of men.

He went on, 'This young woman does speak our language and understands your stupid and adolescent banter.' He had their attention. 'Do you mean to upset our guest?'

The younger men hung their heads, but some older ones smirked arrogantly at Nicolette. She grinned, at the man she'd learned was called Fabien. He winked at her and burst out laughing, and she joined his laughter.

'Come. Let us get some breakfast and we can get to know our newest recruit.' Marcus came to her side. 'Nicely played, mademoiselle. You'll have Fabien eating out of your hand in no time.'

'Do you know the details of my mission?' she asked him.

'I don't envy you.' He guided her through the barn doors, and they followed the line of men to what looked like a farmhouse. 'We've fought the Germans on our terms for many months, and now the communists have joined us, they think they can come in and take over. We can barely tolerate their arrogance, but we have to put up with them, or De Gaulle will withdraw his support.'

'Is that what you've been told?'

'It is the way things are.'

'Which ones are the communist members?'

'Fabien and Pierre are the troublemakers. They like to do things their way. They are impatient, and they take too many risks.'

'In what way?'

'We tried to blow up the rail line from Le Havre to Paris last week. We had everything in place, and all we had to do was wait. We knew a German troop train was due, and I wanted to demolish the train full of troops as well as the track to cause as much damage as possible to the German plans.'

'What happened?'

'Fabien couldn't wait. He said we'd be putting ourselves in more danger by blowing up the soldiers.'

'Did you consider he might have had a valid opinion?'

'Why should I? I had assessed the risk and was prepared to take it.'

'I thought you said Fabien was the one who took risks?'

'He blew the charge too early, and the German soldiers were too close. They streamed from the carriage and began to hunt us down. We lost a man that night.'

'I'm sorry to hear that.' She felt genuinely sad to hear of the death of one of his men.

Pearl A. Gardner

'We lose men all the time.' He shrugged. 'If Fabien had waited, we could have blown them all up, and we would have lost no men.'

'What do you think would have happened if you'd killed all those soldiers?'

Marcus shrugged and showed her into the kitchen of the farmhouse. She couldn't question him further in front of the others, but she began to understand what one of the problems might be. She could imagine the Germans would have been angrier to lose a battalion of men than suffer a simple disruption to their transport system. She'd heard the enemy had slaughtered men, women and children in retaliation for an attack by the Maquis on a fuel store near Paris. She wondered what Fabien's side of the story would tell her, and she determined to ask him at the first opportunity.

Chapter 16: Earning trust

Sleep did not come easily to Nicolette. The strange bed in the attic of the farmhouse was uncomfortable, and she had listened to rats scratching in the rafters all night.

She listened to the household waking and moving around but didn't want to rise just yet. Her thoughts were jumbled, and she had to clear her head. She allowed her mind to drift to the previous day. She'd said goodbye to most of the men after breakfast and watched them leave to spend their days working at normal jobs, far away from the farm. She wouldn't see most of them until a few days later at a meeting that had been organised for her to speak to the whole group. She still had no idea what would she say to them.

She had learned that Marcus worked on the farm with his wife, Lissette, and his younger brother, Henri. Lissette showed her where everything was, but hadn't seemed particularly welcoming. Nicolette was dismayed to find her washing facility was a stained bowl with a jug that could be filled from the well in the yard. Her toilet was a zinc bucket in the corner of her attic room. She tried to keep the disillusionment from her face but when Lissette showed her the bed she would sleep in, she couldn't help a small squeak of horror escaping her mouth. The lumpy straw mattress had two, thick woollen blankets thrown over it, and the pillow was a straw roll wrapped in rags.

'It is all we can manage.' The woman explained with a barely concealed sneer. 'You probably won't last long anyway.' She added ominously. 'They never do.'

Nicolette had wanted to ask Lissette what she meant but Marcus called his wife away, and she watched the thin French woman hurry down the wooden ladder to see what her husband wanted.

Eventually, Nicolette had made her way outside into the farmyard. She was weary after being awake throughout the previous night, but her mind couldn't shut down. Her body was still flushed with adrenaline. She had too much to think about and couldn't relax. She had also known she wouldn't be able to sleep in that awful bed in daylight.

She had leant against a wall and watched the chickens pecking and scratching at the ground. Noticing a gangly mare looking at her over a fence, she went to pet the skinny horse. She rubbed the mare's nose and spoke to it in English. 'You look almost as bad as I feel. You poor thing.'

'Faites attention!' Henri called into her ear. He had crept up behind her, and his presence made her jump.

She knew what he had said to her, but couldn't understand why he had told her to, "be careful".

'Do not speak in English.' He explained in a quieter voice. 'You don't know who may be listening to you.'

'Oh, of course.' She answered in French and gave the horse a final pat. She had started to walk back to the house when Henri called her back.

'Wait!'

She stopped and turned to face him.

'What are you doing here?'

'Here in France? Or here at this house?' She wanted to clarify his question.

'Both.'

'I'm in France on orders from my superiors, and I'm here in this house because that is where Marcus, my contact, has brought me.'

'What are your orders?'

'If I told you, I might have to kill you.' She said it with a dead-pan face and then began to giggle.

His expression was one of shocked surprise and he seemed lost for words.

'I'm sorry.' She apologised through her giggles. 'I've wanted to say that to someone ever since I started training for this.'

He smiled warily. 'You are not like the others.'

'You have had other agents staying here?'

'We let some of them sleep here in the daytime, but the radio is moved every night. We have had three taken away by the Germans.'

'Radios or operators?' She asked, frowning.

'Both, Lucille. Unfortunately, we have seen many pianists, as we call our radio operators. They come and go. We do what we can, but they are too vulnerable. They get caught, and they get sent away, or they get shot on the spot, depending on the mood of the German soldier that discovers them.'

'So that's what Lissette meant.'

'She told you?'

'I think she believes I am simply another pianist and not worth spending time with.'

'Are you telling me you are not a radio operator?'

'I *can* operate a radio transmitter,' she confessed. 'But that isn't my reason for being here.'

'Can you tell me the real reason?'

'I'm to improve your security and lick your argumentative resistance group into shape and make a cohesive team of you.' She watched his pupils dilate slightly, and then he blinked. 'Does that surprise you?' she asked him.

'They send a girl to do what my brother can't do?'

'Your brother is in a difficult position. He can't see the solution because he is part of the problem.'

'I would be very careful if I were you.' Henri warned her. 'You don't intend to say that to his face, do you?'

'Not in so many words and not in public, but I will point out why he should listen to me.'

'Why do you think a man like Marcus would want to hear what you have to say? How can you know enough about our operation to have any authority over us?'

'Because I have the ear and the confidence of General De Gaulle and what the General wants, the General gets.' She was bluffing but knew enough of the current state of French politics to know her bluff could work. She also knew she would be taken more seriously if the resistance thought she really was speaking for the French leader who was living in exile in London.

She heard her name being called from below and decided she could leave her thoughts there and join the family for breakfast. She hoped her conversation with Henri had circulated to the rest of the family. If Marcus believed she *did* speak for the French general, her job would be easier.

She was to be taken to the radio girl later that night to transmit her first message back to headquarters. It wouldn't take long. She only had to send three code words. "Whisky delivered safely".

She knew she would meet the other members of the group soon. She'd learned yesterday that there were around a hundred of them in the area. Their ages ranged from teenagers to ninety-year-olds. They came from all parts of the community, from schoolgirls to ancient, respected grandfathers. Marcus had boasted about some of his raids and Henri had told of some daring feats of smuggling right under the noses of the German guards.

Nicolette began to understand that the resistance seemed to

be operating to serve the ego of its leader more than actually finding the best way to sabotage the enemy. She couldn't wait to discover more from the people she would meet later that day.

'Take a seat.' Lissette gestured to the rough, wooden table in the centre of the room.

Marcus stood beside his wife at the blackened, grease-covered stove and gave her a cold stare. 'We'll take you into town after breakfast.' He set a large plate of bread and greasy eggs on the table. 'Make sure you have your papers with you.'

Henri helped himself to a hunk of bread and piled some eggs on top. He ate from his hands. Nicolette couldn't see any cutlery. She followed his example. She was ravenous, but the eggs were not appetising. She forced herself to swallow.

Lissette placed a large jug of coffee on the table and proceeded to fill mugs with the dark, aromatic liquid.

'Thanks.' Nicolette took a sip and was surprised at the rich, mellow flavour. 'This is good coffee.' She lifted her mug in praise of the woman.

Lissette shrugged, but Nicolette noticed the corners of her lips lift slightly. She seized the advantage and pressed her point. 'You will have to show me your secret. My coffee always tastes bitter.' Nicolette knew how to make great coffee. Her mother had made sure of that, but she hoped her ploy of ignorance would gain her some ground in winning over the older woman.

'Do you use boiling water?' Lissette asked.

'Yes.' She lied.

'You will burn the coffee. You should allow the water to cool before pouring it on the grounds.'

'Ah, so that is your secret.' Nicolette smiled her warmest smile at the woman. 'Thank you. I'll remember that.'

Lissette's cheeks creased as her lips stretched into a small smile, but it didn't last long. 'Any fool would know how to make coffee.' The woman added dismissively, 'It is no great thing.'

Nicolette suppressed a sigh of exasperation and tried again, 'Perhaps in France making coffee is not classed as a skill but where I come from, good coffee is hard to find. Your brew is like nectar to my tongue.' She raised her mug and took another mouthful for good measure.

'Humph.' Lissette shuffled on her wooden chair, but her face pinked with pleasure.

Nicolette felt she'd made a small step to winning the woman

over. She needed all the friends she could get, and Lissette was just the start.

'Be quick and finish your breakfast, Lucille. We have work to do.' Marcus' tone was cold and stern.

Nicolette pushed the last of the unappealing breakfast into her mouth and washed it down with the coffee. 'I'm ready when you are, boss.' She hoped her deference to him would help to lighten his mood.

He looked at her suspiciously but didn't comment. Instead, he went to take a bag from a hook behind the door and beckoned her to follow him.

'I'll see you later, Lissette.' She left the table and called back to Henri, 'Au revoir Henri.'

As soon as they were outside, Marcus grabbed her shoulder and pushed her, unceremoniously, towards the truck in the yard. 'What was all that about?' He hissed angrily at her. 'You think you can befriend my wife to ingratiate yourself with me?' He sneered. 'It might have worked if I gave a damn about her.'

'What are you talking about?' She shrugged off his hand.

'I know what you are here for, and you don't have a cat in hell's chance. Why do they think a woman can do a man's job? Your Churchill must be demented.'

'I don't answer to Churchill.' She had expected some hostility from the leader of this resistance group and was prepared for his refusal, to accept her, but the strength of his anger was alarming. She knew she'd have to prove herself to this man if she wanted to get anywhere with her plans.

'Pah!' He spat on the ground by the wheel of the truck. 'Henri told me what you said yesterday. You think we will believe your lies about answering to our beloved leader?'

'Why wouldn't you believe me? It's true.' She stuck to her story; hoping headquarters would back her up as they had promised. The communications offer had informed her of the message she should use if ever she needed support from the SEO. Just add, "Little bird waiting to sing", to the communication.' He'd told her. 'Remember that phrase, you might need it,' he'd added. She hoped she'd get the chance to use it.

'You think we don't communicate with the great man himself?' Marcus was red in the face, and she could see his shoulders were tense with anger. 'We will soon know whether your words come from him. You think we are stupid?'

'If I thought you were stupid I wouldn't be risking my life to help you in this Godforsaken place, would I?' She raised her voice and added. 'I'm here to help you, Marcus!'

'Get in.' He opened the truck's passenger door, and then went to the driver's side.

She climbed aboard and sat in silence as he started the engine and she winced when he burned some rubber as he skidded from the yard.

'Are we headed for Lisieux?'

He nodded and reached for a packet of cigarettes on the dash.

'Let me light one for you,' she offered.

He tossed the packet to her, and she reached for the matches. It was months since she'd smoked a cigarette, but she still knew how to light one. She savoured the taste of the smoke on her lips and passed the glowing stick to him.

'Take one for yourself, if you like,' he said.

'Thanks.' She took one, despite having given them up months ago. She felt the need of a smoke.

'We'll be meeting at the Café Bleu. The owner is Pierre. The commie you met yesterday. With luck, Anna will be there. She's our radio girl, for now.'

'How long has she been in France?'

'Eight weeks. She's doing well. She's quick, and her instincts are good. If Anna says it's time to stop transmitting and move, we stop and move. No arguments.'

'Is she English?'

'Polish.'

Nicolette nodded. She knew there were various nationalities involved in fighting the Germans. It didn't surprise her that the girl was from the first country the Nazis had invaded.

The cigarette seemed to calm Marcus, and they spent the rest of the journey discussing the people closest to him. Nicolette asked about his brother, his friends and how he had become the leader of their organisation.

'We never had anything like an election. They simply looked to me to make decisions for them. In the early days, we were no more than half a dozen rebels who wanted to strike back.'

'What was it like for you when the Germans invaded?'

His fingers tightened on the steering wheel, and he took a deep breath. 'I can't easily put it into words. The Germans were everywhere. Interfering in our businesses, and preventing us from moving around the town as we'd like. They even stopped us worshipping in our Basilica of St Thérése until we got the mayor to intervene.'

'The Little Flower.' Nicolette knew 🌸 the story of the nun. She'd covered it while studying the background of her destination during the last few days. 'Didn't she write, "What matters in life is not great deeds, but great love"?'

'She did. I'm impressed that you would know such a thing.' His face contorted in a wry smirk. 'You did your homework.'

'It pays to be prepared.' She returned a sardonic smile. 'Did the mayor have any luck with his intervention?'

'He's a good man. They could have shot him for his insistence, but he convinced them they would be committing a mortal sin by preventing us from worshipping at the shrine. From then on, we have been allowed to use the sacred place. I think the Germans feared to anger God.' He laughed. 'They think He is on their side! Can you believe that?'

'Many nationalities kill in the name of their God.' Nicolette said sadly. 'The Lord's name has been falsely used for centuries to further the cause of various religions.'

'Well, whatever they think, the Germans realise how important the Basilica is for our community. We can worship in peace and Sunday is a special day. The Germans let us honour our beliefs in this one respect, so we take advantage.'

'You take advantage?' She was intrigued. 'How?'

'Our choir is err, how can I put this? Very select.'

'The choir?'

'All the members of our choir were Maquis. We were mostly farmers doing what we could to disrupt the Nazis, and we met on Sunday after services for choir practice.'

'The Germans didn't suspect?'

'They still don't, but in recent weeks the choir has grown with the communists joining us, and now it has become more difficult to keep a low profile. The choir has eighty members. Sunday will have to be our last meeting at the Basilica. It is too risky to continue with so many.'

Nicolette thought for a few moments. 'Can I make a suggestion?'

'Go ahead.' He shrugged.

'Perhaps you could select team leaders from the members? They could form the core of your choir. Your meetings would be easier to arrange and hide from the enemy with smaller numbers and the leaders could report to their teams who wouldn't need to attend choir practice.'

Marcus was quiet for a while. 'That might be tricky. Who would I choose as leaders?'

'I'm sure you'll work something out.' She knew how she would organise things, but it had to be his decision. She had to let him think he still had control. She felt it would be the only way to keep his trust and earn his acceptance.

'We'll park the truck here.' He swung the large vehicle into the road that swung around the back of a row of houses and pulled on the handbrake. 'Come! Anna will be waiting.'

Nicolette followed Marcus through the streets filled with beautiful Gothic buildings. German soldiers were on every corner brandishing guns, stopping shoppers and searching bags intermittently.

'Keep your head down.' Marcus warned. 'Don't make eye contact. If they stop me, you walk on. If they stop you, I'll wait for you.'

'Why would they stop me?' She hadn't considered how she would react if she were discovered.

'Why do they stop anyone? They will ask to see your papers. If everything is in order, you will be allowed to continue.'

She hoped the Germans would ignore her. The small pistol she carried strapped to her inner thigh, suddenly felt heavy and cold to her skin.

'The Café Bleu is on the next corner.'

They reached the café without trouble and pushed through the door into the cooler interior. Marcus guided her to a table at the rear where a girl of around seventeen sat demurely drinking coffee. Her companion was Fabien and Nicolette nodded a greeting to the older man. She took a seat and allowed Marcus to make the introductions.

'Lucille?' Anna asked confirmation of her name. 'Is that your real name?'

'No more than Anna is your real name.' Nicolette answered and smiled. 'You are younger than I expected.'

'So are you.' The girl said. 'The others were expecting a man.'

'The others? Does that mean that you thought they might send a woman?'

Anna shrugged. 'We women find it easier to infiltrate and influence, don't you think?'

'What makes you say that?' Nicolette was captivated by the young girl's mature attitude.

'We make better liars.' Anna narrowed her eyes and lifted her chin.

Nicolette consciously slowed her breathing. She felt the first traces of a guilty blush creeping up to her throat and hoped her steady control would keep it at bay. She realised there was more to this girl than met the eye. Anna was very astute.

Nicolette smiled. 'I think I'm going to like you, Anna.'

'What makes you think I want you to like me?' She fired back.

Nicolette shrugged. 'Everyone wants to be liked.'

'Not me!' The girl folded her arms. 'I don't care whether you like me or you don't.'

'Now, ladies.' Fabien intervened. 'We are not here for a cat-fight.'

'What do you have to report?' Marcus asked, lighting another cigarette.

Fabien leant closer. 'Falcon was taken last night. We need to get him back.'

'Who is Falcon?' Nicolette asked.

'He's one of yours.' Marcus explained. 'He's been keeping watch at La Havre for a few weeks. The Germans are more active than usual in the port and he thought it might be the start of a build-up to an invasion of England.'

'Has he been captured?' Nicolette was concerned for her fellow countryman.

'The Nazis took him to the town hall in La Havre. Our man on the ground said he is still there.'

'Does HQ know about this?' Nicolette asked Anna, knowing the girl was responsible for radio communications in the area.

'Not yet, they only took him last night.' The girl answered. 'It was too late by the time we discovered his fate. We had already ended the transmission.'

'We can only make one short transmission each night.' Fabien explained. 'To stay on air longer is dangerous.'

'I understand.' Nicolette aimed her words at Anna and turned to Marcus. 'What are your plans?'

Marcus took a long pull on his cigarette. 'Your friends dropped explosives and weapons last night. We can use them to create a diversion.'

'And then what?' Fabien asked in a sarcastic tone. 'We magically extricate him from a locked cell in the bowels of the town hall when he is surrounded by German guards?'

'The guards will come running to help defend the building when the explosions begin.' Marcus said.

'You can't be sure of that!' Anna pointed out.

'Some may stay inside, but we can deal with them.' Marcus boasted. 'I'll take that job. Killing Nazis is like sticking pigs for the roast. Then we'll blow the cell wide open and take the Englishman.'

'We can't blow the cell door.' Fabien shook his head in disagreement. 'We can't risk killing Falcon. We need to know what he found out.'

'I could help.' Nicolette offered. 'I can pick a lock.'

Marcus turned to her with a look of shock on his face. 'You'd go on a mission with us?'

'That's what I'm here for.' She shrugged, trying to give the impression that she did this kind of thing all the time.

'You'll have to walk miles in the dark. Stay quiet and keep hidden until we tell you when and where to move.'

'I can do that.' She remembered the exercise in Arisag, and began to realise that she really could help them rescue the agent.

'La Havre is a big town.' Fabien commented. 'A large group of men with guns will soon be noticed if we walk for miles on the streets.'

'What do you suggest?' Marcus asked, squaring his shoulders as if preparing for a fight.

'Do you still have the potatoes you harvested last week?'

'Some.' Marcus nodded. 'What do you have in mind?'

'If we had papers to deliver potatoes to the docks, we could get closer to our target. We could leave the trucks at the back of the library. That building is close to the town hall and the trucks would be hidden from view.'

'Can you get the papers with short notice?'

'Leave it to me.' Fabien boasted. 'Make sure you load the trucks with sacks of potatoes.'

'What about this evening's transmission?' Anna asked. 'Should I radio London with news of Falcon's capture?'

'Why risk sending a message with bad news?' Nicolette

suggested. 'We can contact HQ when we have him safely back, can't we?'

Anna tilted her head and pursed her lips. She smiled. 'I like your style, English woman.'

'Actually, I'm a full-blooded French woman.' Nicolette grinned.

All three stared at her with open mouths.

'My parents lived in Verdun,' she added. 'My father was killed in the final days of the last war. My mother moved to England, and I was brought up there.'

'Your papers say you are from Lille!' Marcus snapped angrily. 'Don't forget that!' he warned.

'You should not have told us.' Fabien scolded her. 'We have no need to know your true identity.'

'I trust you.' Nicolette said.

'Then don't!' Fabien kept his voice low but she could hear the anger in his tone. 'Trust nobody. We might be the best friends you have in the whole world but if we are taken and the Germans torture us, who knows what we might be made to confess to them?'

'I'm sorry.' She felt she'd been thoroughly chastised. 'I won't make that mistake again.' She realised she'd acted like a silly schoolgirl. In wanting them to accept her, she had given away vital information that they didn't need to know.

'We'll meet at the crossroad after sundown.' Marcus turned to Fabien. 'Henri will come, and I can get four more men. How about you?'

'Pierre will be no good tonight. He was up all last night and he's getting too old to do without sleep.' He glanced at the portly man behind the café counter. 'But I can get six, maybe more.'

'That should be enough.' Marcus stubbed his cigarette out in the ashtray.

'Will you take me, too?' Anna asked. 'I could help.'

'Not this time, Ma Petite.' Marcus patted her hand. 'You are too important to risk losing.'

'That is unfair. I have eyes, and ears, I can be your watchperson.' She protested.

'Who will send our transmission if anything should happen to you, Anna?' Nicolette asked.

'I'm sure you can operate a radio.' Anna replied, sulkily.

'And if we are both killed or captured?' Nicolette felt her heart jump as she said the frightening words.

Anna sighed resignedly. 'Go have your fun without me, then.' She scraped back her chair and flounced from the café.

'Will she be all right?' Nicolette asked the two men.

'Anna is a little firebrand. She'll cool off.' Fabien grinned.

'Come.' Marcus got to his feet. 'We need to prepare.' He turned to Fabien. 'Your men are the distraction team. I'll give you the explosives and detonators at the crossroad along with the potatoes to camouflage them with. We'll leave the trucks behind the library.'

Fabien smiled but said nothing.

'The town hall is only a few hundred yards from there so we won't have to avoid enemy eyes for too long.' Marcus lifted his chin as if expecting a retaliatory word from the communist. 'My men will wait until your men have attracted the German's attention. Then we'll move.'

'We will keep the soldiers occupied until we see your truck leave the library.'

'With Falcon on board.' Marcus pointed out.

'If you get him.' Fabien's tone was a challenge and he huffed a short, arrogant laugh.

Marcus scraped back his chair and motioned for Nicolette to move.

'I'll see you tonight, Fabien,' she said as Marcus grabbed her arm and began to drag her away from the table.

'Au revoir.' Fabien leant back in his chair to watch them leave.

On the journey back, Marcus was quiet. Nicolette had time to think about what she'd got herself into. Tonight she would be helping to blow up part of Le Havre and she'll be tying to rescue a fellow agent from the cells of a heavily guarded building. She blew out a long breath.

'Scared?' Marcus asked.

'A little.' She admitted.

'Good.' He smiled at her. 'Fear is strength if used wisely.'

'Someone told me something very similar a few months ago.' She remembered the words of Pilot Officer Brown. She also remembered his eyes as they looked into hers. She shook her head. She had to concentrate.

'Someone special, Lucille?'

'What makes you say that?' She asked, sitting straighter in the seat.

'The look of amour on your face gave you away.' His smirk was teasing. 'Did you leave a lover back in England?'

She shook her head. 'I have no lover, Marcus. No ties.' She stared ahead and tried not to think of the pilot officer. 'In this game, I can't afford emotional attachments.'

Chapter 17: Rescue

Nicolette was concealed in the back of the first truck with Rene and the other young men from the Maquis. They hid in wooden crates under sacks of potatoes covered by tarpaulin. Fabien's truck was behind with his communist group hiding in a false compartment under the load of vegetables. They'd crossed two German checkpoints with comparative ease and were approaching a third. Fabien had miraculously procured the papers for their cargo of potatoes and so far, the papers were helping them gain access to the port town. The German Navy was to be the recipient of the vegetables, according to the false papers.

The harbour town was busy with lots of truck movements. The Germans seemed preoccupied and not overly interested in two farm trucks heading for the docks. Nicolette listened as Marcus pulled his truck to a halt for the third time and hoped they'd be as fortunate with this checkpoint.

'Papiere!' A German demanded.

'Kartoffeln!' The German voice called from the front of the truck. 'Die Marine immer besseres Essen.'

Another German voice answered from the rear of the truck.

They heard Marcus laugh and offer the soldier a sack of potatoes. 'Werden sie nicht vermissen einen sack, mein freund.'

Nicolette held her breath. She listened to more exchanges and understood that Marcus was trying to negotiate an easy passage for them through the checkpoint by offering some of his load to the soldiers.

'Untersuchen ide last!' The German voice shouted.

She held her breath. The German had instructed someone to examine the load. Her French colleagues obviously did not understand German and did not look concerned. She couldn't warn them. She stayed still and hoped there were enough sacks of potatoes to hamper the soldiers and put them off searching deeper. She needn't have worried. The soldiers were merely taking what Marcus had offered them. Fortunately, they were satisfied with two sacks. They didn't search any deeper into the load.

Marcus pulled the truck away, and Nicolette strained to hear Fabien's truck following. They had got through. She breathed a sigh of relief. The noise of more engines could be heard all around, coming and going through the streets near the docks. Nicolette wondered whether the agent was right about a build-up of German troops in the area. They needed to get the man back from the Germans so he could send his information to HQ. Nicolette realised that she could also warn her superiors, but Falcon could fill the details and give some much-needed depth to the information. If he knew troop numbers and locations, the information would be priceless.

When the trucks halted again, Nicolette heard low voices and the sounds of Fabien's men jumping down and scattering in all directions. She stayed still until Marcus opened the crate in which she was hiding.

'Out! Quickly!' He called softly.

She followed the others. They'd been given their orders, and each knew exactly, what to do. Fabien's men were already nowhere to be seen. Nicolette stayed close to Marcus and Henri. Rene and three more youths were with them, and they stayed low, moving to the edge of the building, keeping to the shadows.

Marcus signalled them to stop. He then ran across the road and motioned for her to join him. She ran, crouched as low as she could, glancing around nervously. She could see the town hall at the other end of the road.

One by one the men regrouped and hurried around the corner to the back-streets. They headed to the rear of the objective, to the south side of the building. The plan was to approach the back of the town hall and wait, in hiding, for the commotion to begin on the northern side. Fabien's men were to blow up numerous targets on the other side of the building, away from the docks.

They reached a landscaped area and the men scattered, hiding in the bushes. Each man sat in silence, waiting. Nicolette's heart was racing, but she tried to stay calm. Harness the fear, she told herself. Clear your mind. She felt for her pistol and re-checked that it was loaded. She touched the bayonet strapped to her ankle inside her boot. She was unfamiliar with the weapon but knew how sharp it was. Her thumb bore a thin red stripe where she'd foolishly tested the blade earlier.

Her lock-picking kit of pins and metal rods were tucked into her collar. She felt the weight of them and made sure she could extract them from the hidden seam quickly.

She jumped when light streamed from an opening door at the back of the town hall, but then sat as still as a statue in the shadows. She watched two German soldiers come out from the building and stand in the pool of light. One lit a cigarette, and after taking a puff, handed it to his comrade. They spoke in low tones, but she could hear them boasting about how their officers would soon have the information from the spy. The one with the cigarette laughed. 'He won't hold out much longer. No one does!'

The other reached for the cigarette. 'Fear of drowning makes them talk every time.'

Nicolette held her breath. They were talking about torture. Falcon was being tortured. Were they doing it now? What kind of state would he be in when they got to him? If they got to him!

The blast of an explosion made the German soldiers jump. They gave a quick glance to the garden area, and then ran inside the building, leaving the door open behind them. Nicolette briefly thanked the smokers. She wouldn't have to pick the lock on that door, and that would save them valuable time.

More explosions followed the first, and the sound of running boots came to Nicolette from the front of the town hall. The sky was brighter in three directions. Fabien's men had been busy. She waited for the signal from Marcus. Every atom in her body wanted to run to help the English agent, but she knew that Marcus had more experience and would know the optimum time to move. She waited impatiently, fingering the pistol that she now held in her hand.

'Now.' Marcus whispered.

The six men hurried inside the building, hugging the wall. Nicolette stayed at the rear with Henri as she'd been ordered.

'Someone kill the light!' Marcus whispered. 'We're sitting ducks here.'

Rene reached for the light switch and plunged the corridor into darkness.

Marcus hurried to a corner and waved his men onwards. He pointed to a flight of stairs down to the basement. The men began to descend the staircase but before Nicolette could put her foot on the first step, a door opened at the bottom. The light from the basement exposed them to the German officer who had opened the door.

For half a second, the officer stood frozen with shock, and then he opened his mouth. Rene jumped to crush his hand over the officer's mouth. In one rapid movement, Rene's other hand snaked across the man's throat, a blade glinting in the light from behind the open door. Rene opened the man's jugular and blood sprayed the wall. In seconds, the officer's body sagged in Rene's arms, and the young man placed the limp corpse on the ground.

She didn't have time to reflect on what had happened. She was pulled down the stairs and hurriedly manhandled through the door, over the dead officer who stared back at her with unseeing eyes.

The men were running down a bright corridor, guns pointing to the front, searching every nook and cranny. Henri stayed by the door with Nicolette and his brother, pointing his weapon at the stairs.

Rene jogged back to them. 'No one else here, Marcus. Just the target but he's in a bad way.'

'Where is he?' Nicolette asked, already moving away from the door.

Rene led her to a cage-like structure. At first she didn't see the body of the man on the ground. She thought it was a pile of wet rags until she heard the moan.

'Oh, good God in heaven.' She was horrified by the scene of torture. In less than a second, she registered the large, filled bathtub. The liquid was pink with blood. She'd heard about the barbaric method of torture. Victims would be held under water until almost drowned, and then they'd be beaten senseless and held under again.

She tried the door of the cage, hoping the German officer had left it unlocked, but it stuck fast. She quickly took out her pins and rods and knelt by the lock. Her fingers trembled, but she tried to steady them. This man's life depended on her.

'Come on! Come on!' Marcus guarded her back, and the other men lined the walls watching the door. She glanced along the line of men. They were all watching her intently. All except Henri. His weapon was pointing to the edge of the door, ready to shoot the first person to open it from the other side.

She struggled with the pin and then switched to the stronger metal rods. She pushed and twisted with all her might and eventually felt the lock break. She pulled the handle and pushed the cage door open.

'Stand back, Lucille. We'll take it from here.' Marcus shoved her out of the way, and she fell back against the wall. She watched Marcus lift the body and stepped sideways to allow him to carry the agent out. She caught a glimpse of the man's swollen face and wondered who he was. Even his own mother would not have recognised him. He had been beaten to a pulp. His eyes were swollen and closed. One side of his face was discoloured by a large purple and red swelling. His lip was split in two places, and she could see his jaw was dislocated, giving his face a lopsided appearance.

'Be careful with him,' she pleaded.

'Move, Lucille.' Marcus growled at her. 'We have a long way to go before this mission is done.' He pushed along the corridor with his burden. 'Keep your weapons ready. Henri, open the door and lead the way.'

They retraced their steps to the back door but didn't encounter any more German soldiers. They could hear bursts of gunfire and men shouting from the front of the building. Nicolette hoped Fabien's men were giving the German's hell.

Henri held his hand up when he opened the back door. They stopped until he had looked into the darkness of the landscaped area, checking their exit was clear. All seemed quiet, and he motioned them on. They were crossing the lawn between the bushes where they had previously hidden when the lawn flooded with light, and a voice called, 'Halt!' from behind them.

Nicolette whirled around and saw two German soldiers pointing bren-guns at them. 'Nicht Bewegen!' Nicolette recognised the warning. 'Do not move.'

The group was illuminated like a line of ducks on a fairground shooting range. The French men didn't need to understand the German words; they knew they had no chance to escape. The machine guns could kill them all in seconds. They began to lower their weapons, but Nicolette had her pistol ready at her hip and she was closest to the soldiers. She knew they couldn't see her weapon. She fired two shots in quick succession. Tap-tap. Both soldiers clutched their stomachs, but she fired another two shots as insurance. Tap-tap.

She whirled again to face her comrades. 'Don't stand there gawping, let's go!' She yelled and began to run back the way they had come.

Chapter 18: Important information

Nicolette paced the farmyard in the darkness. Anna should have arrived an hour ago. The sun would be rising soon, making it too difficult to leave town without the risk of being stopped by German patrols. She worried what could have happened to the young girl. If the Germans had discovered her secret, Anna could be tortured just like the young man they'd just rescued. She shivered. The pre-dawn air was chilly but she felt cold to her core. An icy knot of guilt filled her stomach, and although she tried to reassure herself she had acted in self-defence, her first kills were weighing heavily on her conscience.

She'd killed two men and others had lost their lives in the rescue mission. She'd witnessed many German bodies on the ground when she'd hurried back to the trucks with her group. Fabien's men had waved them on through the shadows and helped load the injured man aboard.

While the casualty was hidden, Nicolette learned that two of Fabien's men had been shot and killed. They hadn't been able to retrieve the bodies. Another man was wounded and was already concealed in the truck behind the injured agent.

Within minutes, she was speeding south from the scene, leaving blazing buildings and carnage behind her. The Germans were too busy concentrating on the commotion at the north side of the town hall. The roar and clamour from German vehicles rushing to the scene blanketed the sound of their own engines and the trucks managed to slip away unnoticed.

Fortunately, most of the closest checkpoints were abandoned. Nicolette supposed the guards must have been called to help fight the many fires caused by Fabien's men. Marcus did not stop at the final checkpoint at the edge of town. The two trucks crashed through the barriers, sending soldiers scattering to either side. A few random bullets came from the German guards, but they missed their targets. Two of the guards jumped on motorbikes, to give chase, but after a few hundred yards, Henri and another man shot them, sending them toppling from their seats while the motorbikes lurched off the road. They breathed a collective sigh of relief when the trucks left the town and headed for open countryside.

Nicolette now waited outside the barn. Fabien's injured man was now being attended to by a doctor. Falcon had also received treatment from the friendly, resistance sympathiser. The doctor had informed Nicolette that Falcon should recover from his injuries in a few weeks. The British agent hadn't said anything, as yet. The broken jaw prevented him from speaking. He was barely conscious during the truck journey back to the farm but every bump and shake of the vehicle had made him moan and whimper in pain.

'You're safe now.' Nicolette had whispered, in English, close to the injured man's ear. 'We have you and we are clear of the Germans.' She searched for his hand in the darkness and held his fingers gently. 'Do you hear me?' she asked him. 'You are safe.'

He'd squeezed her hand with trembling fingers before he lost consciousness again.

She hoped he would be able to tell them something soon. Whatever he knew must be important and she couldn't wait to pass the information on to her superiors.

She heard a door squeak and looked to the farmhouse. Lissette beckoned to her from the open door. Nicolette glanced to the barn where the injured men were being cared for behind a wall of bales of hay. There was nothing more she could do for now and she decided to go the house.

'Marcus said I should feed you.' Lissette guided her to sit at the table. 'It isn't much, but barley ragout is all that we have. It will warm you.'

'I doubt I'll ever feel warm again.' Nicolette confessed.

'You've had a busy night. You are in shock. This is expected.' Lissette hesitated and added, 'Marcus told me what you did.'

Nicolette rested her elbows on the rough, wooden table and put her head in her hands. 'So many died tonight, and for what? Was one man worth so many other lives?'

'Don't waste your sympathy. We are at war. Men die all the time. Women too.' Lissette's tone was harsh. 'Killing is now like slaughtering our chickens or our pigs.'

Nicolette lifted her head and looked at the older woman with barely concealed disgust. 'How can you be so callous?' she asked her. 'They are all human beings.'

'It's clear you have a lot to learn so I'll let that go for now.' Lissette placed a bowl of something on the table. 'Eat that.'

Nicolette stared at the bowl of broth swimming in grease and began to spoon it into her mouth. Between mouthfuls, she asked about Anna. 'Have you heard from her?'

'No, but that is not unusual. If there has been too much activity around Lisieux, she will not take the transmitter from hiding.'

'HQ will be worried if they don't hear from me soon.'

'It is better to wait. I'm sure our General De Gaulle will not be too concerned if you are silent for a while.' Lissette smirked and leant against the dirty stove. 'Others will be filling his ears with news of France. Your voice is only one of many. You are not as important as you think you are.'

Nicolette sighed. Would she ever win the confidence of these people? Marcus' wife still did not trust her. She hoped Marcus might have reappraised her after she killed the German soldiers. Had her actions managed to convince him that she could be entrusted to help him organise his band of rebels? She continued to eat her broth and began to feel weary. Sleep was the last thing on her mind, but her eyelids were beginning to feel heavy.

'Come.' Lissette took her arm. 'You are exhausted. For two nights, you have been awake. You should sleep.'

Nicolette briefly wondered why the woman was thinking of her welfare but allowed Lissette to guide her to the foot of the wooden ladder. 'Will you wake me if Anna arrives?'

'We won't see her until tomorrow night. Dawn is here now and she won't leave town with her radio in daylight.'

Nicolette wanted to say more but Lissette put a grubby finger to her lips.

'Shush. Get some sleep.' The older woman urged her to climb the ladder.

Nicolette gave up and went up to the scruffy bed in the attic. She didn't undress. She lay down, dragged the blankets over her and closed her eyes. The last sounds she heard were the rats scratching above her head but she no longer cared about sharing her room with vermin. Sleep claimed her exhausted body in seconds.

She felt a rough hand shaking her shoulder and opened her eyes. The sun blinded her through several small holes in the wall and she closed them again.

Henri shook her again. 'Lucille, wake up! He's asking for you.'

'Who is?'

'Falcon.'

'Is he talking?' She sat up and rubbed her eyes.

'No, he can write, though he writes in English and we can only understand your name.' He pushed a scrap of paper into her hands. 'Read this.'

She tried to focus on the crumpled paper covered in scribble. "Get Lucille, I need to see her".

'You see!' Henri pulled the thick blanket from the bed. 'Hurry, it may be important.'

She allowed Henri to go down the ladder first and hurried after him. The sun was high in the sky and she guessed it was mid-afternoon. She'd been asleep for hours and still felt a groggy. She shook her head to clear it.

Two of the bales of hay had been removed from the improvised wall to allow Henri and Nicolette to enter the makeshift hospital ward. Marcus waited for them inside the small space. He was sitting on a bale of hay next to the agent's pallet bed. She was cheered to see the British agent sitting up but her heart went out to him. His face was a mess. The doctor had bandaged his jaw back in place but obviously hadn't been able to do anything about the swellings on the man's eyes and cheek. His head looked too large for his shoulders.

She glanced to the other pallet where Fabien's man lay sleeping. 'Will he pull through?'

'Karl is tough. He'll make it.' Henri nodded.

Marcus leant forwards. 'Ask Falcon what he can tell us. We have no time to waste.'

Nicolette crouched by the agent's bed. 'How are you feeling?' she asked.

The agent shook his head gingerly. He scribbled a few words on a notepad and handed it to her.

She read the words and gasped. 'Is it you?' She whispered in English. 'Is it really you?' He'd written, "Scotland was nice in springtime. I hear you listened well to my tap-tap lessons".

The agent wrote again and she took the pad.

"Do I look as bad as that, Lucille?" He wrote. "So bad you can't recognise me?"

She glanced at his face. 'Worse, I'm afraid,' she whispered, feelIng her heart doing somersaults in her chest. 'I hear you'll mend, but you might lose your handsome good looks.'

'Lucille!' Marcus interrupted her. 'Ask him what he knows about Le Havre. Anna will come to the rendezvous tonight and we have to prepare our transmission in as few words as possible. It will take some organising. We need the information.'

'Of course.' She turned to Pilot Officer Brown. 'You heard the man. I know you speak French but I'm guessing you can't write in that language.'

The patient scribbled and handed the pad to her. She read, "Not well enough to get my point over".

'Go ahead and write in English. We'll burn the paper.' She handed the pad back to him and watched him begin to write. She lowered herself to the ground by his side. Her legs were trembling and her heart was thumping. This man still had the power to affect her emotions, even when he was badly disfigured. She would feel sorry for any injured person but this was different. She felt an overwhelming attraction to him. She wanted to reach out and touch him. She wanted to take his pain away. She wanted to look after him, take care of his injuries and help to make him better. She didn't feel the same way about Fabien's man. What *was* it about the officer? Why did he have such a profound affect on her?

The officer ripped a page from the pad and handed it to her. He continued scribbling and she read what he'd written, translating it to French so the men of the resistance would understand. 'He says the Germans are running submarines from Le Havre. German troops are arriving daily by rail and road and being sent to billets around the area. They are being housed in barns, factories and warehouses at the docks. He's written some of the locations, here.' She passed the paper to Marcus and pointed out the names of streets, town districts, farms and other locations.

Falcon ripped another sheet from the pad and she took it from the officer's hand.

'He says Le Havre is not the only place where troops are building up. He's also seen tanks and big guns being loaded into transporter trains heading for Dieppe and Calais. He thinks they may be planning a coast-wide invasion of Britain from many points across Normandy.'

She looked into the officer's mangled face. 'How long do we have, do you think?' she asked him.

The agent shrugged and held up three fingers.

'Three months?' she asked.

He shook his head slowly.

'Three weeks?' She couldn't believe what he was telling her.

He nodded and wrote on the pad.

She read his words as he wrote them. "I heard German orders from Hitler. I listened at the door of the communication room before they got me. Hitler's war on Soviets is meant to throw us off the scent. His primary aim is Britain. Troops are to move over the channel on August twentieth. Will have support from air and sea". When she finished reading, she asked him, 'Are you sure?'

The pilot officer gave a small nod.

They all turned when Lissette entered the makeshift room carrying a tray set with bowls of steaming liquid.

'I have brought broth for our guests.' Lissette explained. She handed a bowl and spoon to the pilot officer and turned to the man on the other bed platform. 'Karl, can you wake up for me?' she urged the sleeping man. 'You need to eat.'

Nicolette ignored the woman and turned to Marcus. 'Where is Anna? We need to send this information immediately.'

'Impossible.' Marcus shook his head.

'Why?' Nicolette asked. 'The Germans won't be expecting us to transmit in daylight. We could take advantage of their ignorance. They won't be prepared and won't be searching for a radio signal.'

The officer put down the bowl and scribbled again. He handed the pad to Henri, who was closest. Henri glanced at the paper and passed it to Nicolette. 'He can write in French, see.'

She showed the paper to Marcus. 'He says we should do as I suggest.'

'Then what are we waiting for?' Henri jumped to his feet.

Nicolette turned to the man on the bed. 'Thank you, Falcon. We'll take it from here.' She felt an overwhelming urge to bend down and kiss him but she resisted. Instead, she hurried from the small space and began to pace nervously down the outer wall of the barn.

Marcus joined her and placed a hand on her arm. 'Do you know what you are asking?'

'Do you realise what's at stake?' she asked.

'He has it wrong.' Marcus insisted. 'The Germans don't have enough men to fight on all these fronts. Do you know how many have been sent to Russia?'

'I know how many could be ready to cross the channel in three weeks' time if we don't do something to stop them. Those are the only figures that concern me right now.' She rounded on the French man. 'HQ needs to know where they are! We have to risk a transmission in daylight. Time is of the essence!'

'What if Falcon is wrong? How can Germany spare that many troops?'

'What if he is right? Can we risk it?'

Marcus lit a cigarette and took a long pull from it.

Nicolette grew impatient. 'We have the locations of thousands of troops, thanks to that man in there! Will you allow his efforts to go in vain? We have to transmit as soon as possible.'

Marcus threw his cigarette to the ground and heaved an exasperated sigh. 'I'll get Anna. Do you have your codes to transmit?'

She nodded. She would use the poem she had memorised to code her message. Her poem had a number and she would transmit that first so the receivers would know the key to her message. Even her new friends would not know what the message contained.

'Work on the message as you go. Keep it brief. Keep it safe. Tell Henri to take you to the rendezvous.'

'Now?' she said, hopefully.

'Yes!' he hissed. 'We'll meet you there in one hour.'

'Thank you, Marcus.'

The Frenchman shrugged. 'If you are stopped, you must destroy the messages. Eat them if you have to but don't let the Nazis see them. They'll kill you.'

Nicolette swallowed and nodded. She understood how dangerous this mission was but the safety of her country now depended on her sending the message. She hoped she would get the chance to warn her superiors.

Chapter 19: Messages and missions

The sun was still high in the sky when Marcus arrived at an animal shelter, in the middle of nowhere, with Anna. Nicolette suspected that he had abandoned his truck just as Henri had, under a canopy of trees a few miles away. They had walked through fields of chest-high crops to get to the green pasture dotted with sheep and knew that the new arrivals would have done the same. *she*

Anna carried a large canvas bag on her shoulder, and her face was pale as she ducked under the beam above the wide entrance to the low, stone building.

'Did you have any trouble leaving Lisieux?' Nicolette asked.

'Not today.' Marcus answered. 'I noticed fewer soldiers on the streets. Something is brewing. Falcon could be right.'

'Did you notice any troop movement overnight, Anna?' Nicolette asked the girl.

'I heard nothing and saw nothing.' Anna busied herself setting up the radio and hanging the wires over a beam. 'Did you condense the information as Marcus instructed?'

'Yes.' She handed a sheet of paper to the girl.

'This message is too long.' Anna frowned. 'Can you make it shorter?'

'I don't see how.' Nicolette had reduced the message to the bare minimum.

'Tell me what it says and I'll know where you can cut it.'

Nicolette hesitated.

'Lucille, you can tell Anna, we trust her with our lives.' Marcus reassured.

'The numbers at the top set the key to the code.' Nicolette pointed to the first words written in code. 'The second gives news of Falcon's rescue and information about the build-up of troops.'

'We can cut the part about the rescue. They don't need to know his fate.' Anna handed a pencil to Nicolette and indicated for her to draw a line through the appropriate part of the message.

Nicolette took the pencil and drew the line through the coded words that explained Falcon was safe.

'What next?' Anna looked at her expectantly.

'The next part gives the locations of the troops with information that heavy equipment has been sent to Dieppe and Calais as Falcon said.'

'We need to keep that in.' Marcus nodded and turned to Nicolette. 'What comes next, Lucille?'

'I let them know about submarines operating from La Havre.'

'They will probably know about that already.' Anna suggested. 'In any case, La Havre is a port and would be a target whatever we tell them. Scrub it out.'

'But...' Nicolette didn't want to leave any vital information out of the message, but Marcus and Anna were glaring at her menacingly. She drew a line through the words.

'What is this last bit about?' Anna asked.

'I ask them to confirm to Marcus that I am working under orders of General De Gaulle.'

'We don't need that either.' Anna took the pencil and scratched out the last sentence.

'But—.'

'It is not important, Lucille! You are here, and you are doing the job.' Marcus interrupted her protest. 'We are all taking a massive risk in sending this message. The less time we spend on air, the better!' Do you understand?'

'Yes, sir,' she answered automatically and gave the paper to Anna.

'Do you want to check it before I send it?' Anna asked, handing back the coded message with lines drawn through the text.

Nicolette scanned the coded words, taking her time to make sure the message said as much as she needed it to. How could she convey the importance of her message in so few words? Would HQ realise what she was telling them? Would they trust her judgement? She held her hand out for the pencil and after a second's hesitation, Anna gave it to her.

'What are you adding?' The Polish girl asked.

'One word. That is all right, isn't it?'

'What word is that?' the girl asked.

'You don't need to know.' Nicolette had merely added Falcon, written in code, to give the message gravitas. She hoped HQ would presume Pilot Officer Brown had sent the message.

'Get on with it, Anna.' Marcus glanced through the opening to the pasture beyond. 'Be quick.'

Nicolette watched the girl turn on the radio and flick some dials and switches while she waited for it to warm up. Nicolette recognised the procedure. She knew how to operate a radio and could have done the transmission herself, but the resistance members had their own way of doing things, and she had to follow their rules, for now.

Anna established the connection and began to tap her finger on the contact to start the transmission. She sent a series of coded dots and dashes over the airwaves. If any German mobile detectors were in the area, they would be able to track the radio signal down in minutes.

Marcus began to fidget as Anna continued to send the Morse Code. 'Hurry, Anna!' he hissed.

She glanced up to give him an exasperated sigh but continued her work without interruption.

'Calm down, Marcus.' Henri looked at Nicolette and shrugged. 'He always gets nervous during a transmission.'

'Don't we all?' Nicolette tried a small smile, but her lips trembled.

'I'm done.' Anna quickly dismantled her equipment and packed it into the canvas bag.

'Don't you wait for a reply?' Nicolette asked.

'Are you serious?' Anna gave her a look of disgust. 'We need to move!'

'Come, Lucille.' Henri took Nicolette's arm and guided her out into the sunshine. 'Keep low but hurry.'

Nicolette followed Henri as he ran, at a crouch, around the edge of the pasture, keeping to the hedgerow. She glanced behind to see Marcus and Anna heading in the opposite direction. The message had gone, and there was nothing more she could do.

They heard the truck before they saw it and had time to take cover behind the hedgerow.

'Keep down!' Henri hissed. 'How did they know we would be transmitting at this time of day?'

Nicolette peered through the thicket of brambles to see four German soldiers leaving the truck and start heading for the animal shelter. They had rifles at the ready and were scanning the ground for signs of disturbance.

She felt her heart thudding heavily and sweat began to trickle down her back. She swallowed and watched them hurry from the shelter and run down the path that Marcus and Anna had taken. Then she realised that Anna still had the paper copy of the message. Nicolette knew she should have taken it back to destroy it but now had to rely on the girl, to take care of the evidence. She hoped Marcus could evade the German soldiers. If they caught the radio operator, everything would change. Would Anna destroy the message? Would she talk under torture? Marcus trusted Anna, so Nicolette decided to trust her too, for now. She was obviously an experienced pianist and would know what to do with the paper evidence. Marcus would do his best to make sure the Germans didn't catch them.

'Come.' Henri grabbed her arm. 'Hurry.'

She ran for her life, crouching low and keeping close to the bramble hedge until they were sure the Germans were far behind them.

The Sunday morning sky was dark with stormy clouds. Nicolette ate her breakfast of rough bread and cheese while she stared at the threatening clouds through the dirty window. The weather had been hot and sultry for the last couple of days, and now thunderstorms were brewing. She'd spent the last two days helping to take care of the pilot officer and Karl.

Marcus had managed to keep Anna safe after the daylight transmission, and he'd boasted about leading the Germans all over the French countryside before losing them. Lissette had not been happy to hear that her husband had almost been caught. 'There will come a day when you won't be so lucky, and then what will I do?' Her voice had been full of venom. 'You are always selfish! You think only of the glory. What good are brave deeds when you are dead? You know I can't run this place alone!'

'You wouldn't be alone!' Marcus raised his voice. 'Henri will be here.'

'And if they torture you, and you tell them about this place?' Lissette had shouted. 'None of us will be safe!'

'What would you have me do?' Marcus yelled. 'I can't sit back and do nothing while France is controlled by Nazis.'

Lissette rounded on her husband. 'Sometimes I think you have more love for France than you have for me!'

'Then you would be right!' Marcus cursed. 'Merde, woman! Your mean spirit and petty, unfounded jealousies will be the death of me!'

'Jealousies!' Lissette's face was red with anger. 'You tell me there is nothing going on between you and that Polish girl! You think I was born yesterday?'

'I keep telling you; there is nothing between us.' Marcus shouted. 'Why don't you understand that Anna is like a daughter to me?'

'Oh, that's right! Rub it in, why don't you?' Lissette's face contorted with pain. 'You think it is my fault we didn't have children! Now you taunt me with your fatherly affection for a stranger. How does that make me feel?' She threw a ladle at her husband. 'Do you ever stop to think how I feel?'

'Why should I?' Marcus glanced fleetingly at Nicolette and gave her an imperceptible shrug of apology. 'You make it difficult for me to feel anything for you, Lissette. Your bitterness has poisoned you.'

'Is that so surprising?' She yelled. 'Anyone would be bitter, living with your coldness!'

Nicolette had excused herself and ducked out of the kitchen to get away from the row at that point. From then, she avoided spending too much time with the bad-tempered woman and helped more in the makeshift ward with the injured men. The French communist resistance member was eating and drinking and growing stronger. His bullet wounds were healing. Pilot Officer Brown's face was turning yellow and purple, and the swellings were going down a little. He still couldn't talk and communicated with paper and pencil, destroying each sheet in a candle flame in a metal bucket beside his bed when Nicolette had read it.

She learned of his daring mission along the Normandy coast. He'd been working alone, gathering evidence of Hitler's plan and sending snippets of code back to HQ as and when he could. The Germans had discovered his transmitter hidden in a railway siding and that had been the end of his communications. He'd continued to gather information, keeping watch and getting closer to the German officers when they gathered for meetings and discussions. He told Nicolette how he would listen to conversations by hiding under the floors of wooden huts or simply eavesdropping at windows. He'd planned to contact Nicolette's team when he was certain his information gathering was sufficient, but then he'd been captured.

"I was foolish and took one risk too many", he wrote.

'You're safe now.' Nicolette had smiled at his discoloured face, seeing the handsome features she remembered. 'You'll soon be on your way home.'

She had already hatched a plan to get him back to England. He would soon be fit enough to travel, and she hoped to have everything in place by then.

To attempt to cross the English Channel from the Normandy coast would be out of the question now that HQ knew what was going on there. The British would be putting plans into operation to disrupt the flow of troops to the area and destroy the locations she had sent them. She knew she couldn't send the pilot officer home by the shortest route because, for the next few months, it would also be the most dangerous one.

Fabien wanted to send the officer back with his people via Brest, and then by boat across the Channel. Nicolette had pointed out the danger of sailing too close to the Channel Islands and told Fabien it was too risky. 'The Germans hold the islands and any boat sailing from Brest in the direction of the English coast will come under scrutiny by their patrols,' she had insisted.

She then told Marcus she had an idea how she could get Falcon home, and the Frenchman had shrugged. 'Do it your way if you must.' He'd not offered any help, but she hadn't expected him to.

Nicolette could not trust the resistance with organising Falcon's travel plans. Until she knew who the informer was, she couldn't trust anyone. She knew she would have to organise transport and papers through the contacts of Marcus and Fabien, but she hoped to keep the pilot officer safe from falling into a trap.

She intended to speak to Fabien when she met him at the Basilica later that morning. Today would be the day she addressed the 'choir'. She had rehearsed what she would say to them, going over the speech in her head, but was not sure any of them would take notice of what she had to say. Pilot Officer Brown had encouraged her to use her charm. "You'll have those French men rolling over so you can tickle their tummies in no time", he'd written.

'I wish I had your confidence,' she'd said.

He'd made a coughing, choking sound that she interpreted as a guttural laugh, and he wrote, "Remember to smile. Your smile will charm them".

If only it were that easy, she thought.

'Are you ready?' Lissette asked Nicolette when she came into the kitchen wearing a dark-green dress that was slightly cleaner than her everyday one. She wore a dark, wide-brimmed hat and carried a large black handbag.

'Yes.' Nicolette rose from the table. 'Though, I feel a little underdressed.' She glanced at Lissette, and then at her own dusty trousers and striped, man's shirt.

'You are supposed to be a farmhand, so you should look like

one.' Lissette peered down her nose at Nicolette. 'Going to worship is not a fashion show. We are going to pray to our Little Flower, Saint Thérèse. She would not care what you wear.'

'Yes, of course. You are right.' Nicolette smiled cheerfully at her hostess, though she found the woman infuriating. 'Shall we go?'

Marcus and Henri were waiting outside with the flat-backed truck.

'I'll jump on the back, Lucille,' Henri suggested. 'You can ride in the cab with Marcus and Lissette.'

'I'm happy to ride with you, Henri.' Nicolette hoisted herself onto the familiar wooden boards at the back of the truck. 'I hope the rain will hold off until we get to town.'

'We have the tarpaulin.' Henri pointed to the waterproof canvas that had concealed them on the trip to Le Havre.

'If you're sure?' Marcus asked, opening the door to the cab.

She nodded. She couldn't bear to listen to the couple bickering as they always seemed to do.

The drive to town was uneventful. She shared a cigarette with Henri, and they kept glancing at the dark clouds above them.

'The storm will be a good one.' Henri stared at the ominous sky. 'With luck, the thunder will help to disguise our meeting.'

'Do the Germans keep a close watch on the services?' She began to worry that her speech might be overheard and realised that she was taking another huge risk to help these people.

'They leave us alone, mostly, but occasionally they will send a party of soldiers to sit at the back of the congregation.'

'What do you do when that happens?'

'We sing, of course.' Henri laughed.

'I wonder why the Germans haven't worked out that the choir is bogus.'

'Because we allow the ones with good voices to sing, and the stone deaf members mime the words. We're not stupid, Lucille.'

'I never said you were, Henri.'

'Yet, by being here, your presence infers that we can't run our operation without interference from London.'

'Why would you say that?' she asked.

'Marcus said you are here to take over from him. You intend to charm Fabien and his men to fall under your leadership, and we will have no choice but to follow.'

Nicolette shook her head. 'Is that how Marcus sees things?'

'Are you telling me he's wrong?' Henri raised his eyebrows.

'Yes. Marcus is wrong.' She wanted to elaborate, but the truck had just entered the town. She became interested in the German soldiers who were stopping and searching people as they entered the town. The truck was waved over, and Henri reached into his pocket.

'What are you doing?' Nicolette asked.

'They will want to see your papers.'

'Oh, of course.' She felt foolish as she pulled out her documents. She'd half expected Henri to pull out a weapon.

The German soldier stood by the truck and examined the papers that Marcus handed him. He then moved to take the papers from Henri and Nicolette.

'Quelle est votre destination?' he demanded.

Nicolette knew he'd asked where they were going.

Henri answered. 'We are going to the Basilica.'

'Ah!' the German waved them on with his rifle.

'Phew, that was easy.' Nicolette breathed a sigh of relief.

'Don't look so nervous, Lucille. If you act confident, they will not suspect you. If you appear like a frightened schoolgirl, you will give them reasons to investigate you further.'

'That's what they told me in training, Henri, but it is so much harder to seem cool when a German soldier has you at gunpoint.'

She sat on the hard pew between Lissette and Henri, kneeling to pray and standing to sing, following the rest of the congregation as the priest took them through the service. The hymns and sermons washed over her. Her mind was concentrating on the mission. She had to try to win these people over, and she still had no idea whether her words would be enough.

After the priest had given them his blessing at the end, she watched most of the people leave. The ones that stayed moved to the front and Nicolette had a chance to appraise her audience. She was surprised to see some women and young girls among the men. She saw Anna and smiled at her, but the young Polish girl lifted her chin and looked away without returning the gesture. Nicolette's heart sank for a second. If she couldn't even get the people who knew her to respond, how was she going to get through to the rest of them?

Fabien came to her side. 'Don't look so terrified, Lucille.' He placed a friendly arm around her shoulder. 'These people are curious to hear what you have to say.'

'They might be curious, Fabien but they look like a pack of hungry dogs to me, and they are eyeing me up for their dinner.'

'Can I give you some advice?'

'Please do.' She was ready to accept any help she could get.

'Don't speak for too long. These meetings only last a few minutes. We have to pay lip service to hymn singing for the benefit of the Germans, and most of the French women have dinners spoiling in ovens all over town.' He leant close to whisper, 'I don't know which is worst; the suspicion of the German guards or the anger of a French woman when your sermon means her ragout gets ruined.'

Nicolette laughed. 'I'll heed your warning, friend. Thank you.'

A man she did not know walked to the altar and beckoned another man to sit at the organ. 'We will begin with hymn seventeen in the book.'

The organ music began, and the choir sang the first lines of the hymn. Nicolette joined the singing but was beckoned to the front before the first verse had finished.

'The voices will stop, but the music will continue.' The choir master explained. 'We have a boy outside at the front and another on the side door over there. They will warn us if we need to start singing again.'

Nicolette nodded to show she understood, and then turned to face her audience. She heard the first rumble of thunder and hoped the storm would help to disguise the sound of her voice from prying ears outside.

'I won't keep you, my friends,' she began. 'I'm told your numbers have grown, and that is a great thing. You don't know how happy it made me, to hear how many more of my fellow French patriots have joined the fight. We might be living under the rule of the Jackboot for now, but we will never capitulate.'

She spoke as a French woman in the French accent she had grown up hearing and speaking all her life. She didn't want these people to think of her as an English usurper.

'However, much as it pleases us to have so many members to do the work, the increase in numbers has brought problems.'

She saw faces exchanging glances and went on. 'I do not refer to your differences. It doesn't matter to me whether you began your resistance career in the Maquis or whether you have communism in your heart. We are all French under the skin.'

She let her statement sink in for a few seconds. 'The problem we face is one of logistics. There are too many of us. Security has become a prime concern. Too many people know too much about the organisation. If any one of you is caught and questioned, well, my friends, you know what that could mean.'

She watched the audience glance around with frightened expressions.

'My aim is to keep you safe. I discussed this with Marcus, and he agrees that to continue meeting here and operating with so many members would be foolish. We are practically inviting the Germans to arrest us. I understand they have been lenient to the choir so far but we can't rely on their goodwill for much longer.'

'If at all!' A voice called softly.

She searched the crowd for Marcus and spoke directly to him. 'It was Marcus' idea to choose team leaders who can meet here and pretend to be members of the choir. They will be your eyes and ears, and they will report back to their teams.'

'Who will be the leaders?' a voice from the crowd asked her.

'Marcus and Fabien will choose them.'

A murmur rumbled around the large group.

Fabien came to stand at her side. 'I will agree to this proposal by Marcus.' He beckoned Marcus. 'Come, my friend. Let us discuss the details while Gustav takes the choir practice.'

'Well that was easier than I had anticipated,' she confided to Marcus when they were in the vestry.

'Using my name was a clever move, Lucille, but I'm not sure I like your tactics.' Marcus narrowed his eyes at her. 'Who will make the final decision on our plans? Am I to be the leader, still?'

'There will be many missions for you to take on, and no one person will be responsible for all of them.' Nicolette explained. 'Fabien, you have shown great leadership qualities and your men respect you—.'

'My men respect me too!' Marcus snarled. 'What are you suggesting, Englishwoman?'

Nicolette took a quiet breath. 'Marcus, you are also a good leader, but your skills are more suited to hit-and-run missions where Fabien is more of a diplomat. There is room for both of you to be leaders. You could also promote more of your group to help you. We need to create smaller operational cells to minimise security risks. One cell will not know anything about another cell's members or operations. If any unit becomes infiltrated by German agents, they will not be able to compromise the rest of you.'

'She's right, Marcus. You can't dispute it.'

'We need your expertise, Marcus, but we also need Fabien's talents with planning and strategic attacks. Together you would make a formidable team.'

'I won't take orders from a communist!' Marcus curled his lip as he looked at the older man.

'I'm not asking you to.' Nicolette knew she would have to placate Marcus. She couldn't let things get out of control. 'Orders will now come from London, directly through Anna's radio. She will report to both of you, and you will then pass the information to your team leaders who will help to organise the raids and missions.'

'From London, eh?'

'From the great general himself,' she boasted.

'General De Gaulle?' Fabien looked astounded.

'Who else?' Nicolette asked. 'He has heard of your heroic efforts and has great pride in your movement. He has asked people like me to help make you even more effective in your fight against the enemy.'

'Pah, we still only have your word for this.' Marcus stared at her with hostile eyes.

'If you'd let me communicate with HQ, I could prove my position in an instant, but we all know how difficult that would be. For now, I ask you to trust me. Am I asking anything of you that you would not want to do?'

'I'm not happy taking orders from London.' Marcus insisted.

'Then let me prove I have the authority of your general. You can't refuse General De Gaulle himself, can you?' Nicolette knew it was a dangerous claim on her part, but if it were the only way that Marcus would accept her, she would have to take the risk.

Fabien shrugged. 'She has a point, Marcus.'

Marcus heaved a frustrated sigh. 'We meet tonight at the school near Glos. I know the caretaker, and he'll keep watch.'

'I'll bring Anna,' Fabien offered.

'Perhaps we don't need her.' Nicolette suggested. 'I can operate the radio.'

'Anna will be there.' Marcus said, firmly. 'I can trust her to pass the messages correctly.'

'Are you suggesting that Lucille would lie to us?' Fabien asked.

'Can't you understand Morse?' Nicolette asked, beginning to understand why Anna was so important to them.

'We'll meet tonight.' Marcus repeated and walked from the vestry.

Nicolette sighed as she watched him go. She could appreciate his reluctance to accept her, but she didn't understand why he was so angry. 'What is wrong with him, Fabien? Why can't he take me at my word? What more do I have to do? I jumped out of a plane to be here, and that is no easy thing to do in the dark. I kill two Germans in cold blood to save our necks and still he doesn't trust me.'

'He is afraid of you, Lucille.'

'What?' She was astonished.

'He is a simple farmer who can't read or write but has men who look up to him and follow his orders. You threaten his way of life, Lucille. You are educated and refined and could easily take his little empire away from him.'

'That's not what I'm here to do,' she explained. 'I've tried to tell him that we need him. Why won't he listen?'

'He will. Give him time.' Fabien draped an arm around her shoulders. 'Come, Lucille. Join our singing and forget your troubles for an hour.'

'He can't read or write?' she whispered to the older man. 'How does he manage?'

'With great difficulty, I suspect. That's why he appears angry. He is frustrated by his limitations.'

'How long have you known?'

'Long enough to understand the man.'

Marcus drove them to the schoolhouse close to midnight. Anna and Fabien were waiting in the basement of the building, and the caretaker was keeping watch outside.

'We can't send a long message tonight,' Anna warned. 'Keep it simple.'

'Can we accept a reply if we keep it brief?' Nicolette asked.

'That's what we are here for,' Marcus pointed out.

'Then send this. No need to code the message.' Nicolette composed her thoughts for a few moments. 'Lucille being doubted. Confirm she is acting on French General's orders. Little bird waiting to sing.'

'There is no need to send the last bit. What does it mean?' Anna stopped her fingers tapping.

'That is my call sign.' Nicolette insisted. 'If you fail to add, "Little bird waiting to sing", they will not believe the sender of the message is genuine and will not send an answer.'

'Very well.' Anna hit the Morse key and tapped out the last sentence.

Within a few minutes, the reply was heard. Nicolette could decipher the dots and dashes but left Anna to translate to Marcus and Fabien.

'She's the real thing. Lucille speaks for General De Gaulle. Work with her.'

'Send this, Anna,' Nicolette asked. 'Waiting for your orders will check-in each night.'

The Polish girl tapped out the message.

'Now we go before we are discovered.' Fabien helped Anna pack the transmitter into the canvas bag, and they all hurried outside to the waiting trucks.

'Anna will receive orders from London now.' Nicolette explained. 'HQ will tell you what they want you to do.'

'What about you? Will you leave?' Fabien asked.

'I need your help.' Nicolette whispered to the older man. 'I need documents for Falcon. I want to take him home.' She didn't want to say too much about her plans in front of Anna. She didn't completely trust her and felt the feeling was mutual.

'I'll see what I can do. I'll come to the farm in a day or two.'

'Thank you.'

Nicolette jumped into the truck and waited, for Marcus to get in and start the engine. He spent a few minutes thanking the caretaker and saying goodbye to Anna before he opened the cab door.

'I thought you were in a hurry to get away from here?' she asked.

'I see no Germans, we're safe.'

'What if they are hiding in the bushes over there?'

'They would not be hiding. They would have captured or shot us by now.'

'How reassuring.' She couldn't keep the sarcasm from her voice. 'Tell, me. How long has Anna been operating as your pianist?'

'A couple of months or so.' Marcus started the engine and pulled away from the school. 'Why do you ask?'

'You don't think it is odd that she hasn't been discovered yet?'

'Why would I think that? She is good at covering her tracks and doesn't take risks. She's the best we've had so far.'

'How many radio operators have you worked with?'

'I don't know. I lost count after the first four or five.'

'How long did they last, in general?'

'It varied.' He turned to her. 'What's your point?'

'I'm not sure I trust her, Marcus. She's either very lucky, or she has friends in high places.'

'German friends?' His mouth dropped open. 'No! You are wrong!'

'I hope I am because if I am right, the Germans will know everything we know.'

'Anna is not a double agent! She is like a daughter to me.'

'Perhaps I'm wrong, Marcus. I hope I am.'

'I *know* you are wrong.' He stared ahead at the dark road.

'Then who is the traitor? We know there is a leak. The Germans know some of your movements and are waiting for you. How many men have you lost in the last month?'

'Too many.' His shoulders drooped.

'You must suspect someone, Marcus. Think!' She implored him. 'Do you have any idea who might be letting the enemy know what your plans are?'

'If I knew,' He thumped the steering wheel. 'I would kill them with my bare hands.'

'Keep your eyes and ears open, Marcus. We can't afford any more leaks.'

'Is your mission here finished?' He changed the subject. 'What does your HQ want us to do for them?'

She sighed with frustration. She didn't know what else she could say. Whoever was sending information to the Germans had to be stopped, but how could she find out who it was? She'd have to rely on Marcus. She couldn't do anymore. She had to get the pilot officer back to London, and she couldn't trust Marcus' group to help. The informer would probably lead him straight into a trap. She would have to think of a solution to that problem. For now, she needed to keep Marcus happy. 'London will expect you to act on their advice. They'll set you up with targets and objectives. It's up to you how you deal with each mission.'

'They'll supply us with weapons?'

'Everything you need.'

He lit a cigarette and inhaled deeply. 'So have you now fulfilled your purpose in coming here?' He handed the cigarette to her.

'Mostly.' She took a pull and inhaled. She grinned as she blew the smoke from her mouth. 'My primary mission was to get you and Fabien talking instead of fighting each other.'

Marcus flashed a smile at her. 'Well, we have always talked.'

'You've not been very good at listening, though, have you?'

'Perhaps not.'

She handed the cigarette back to him. 'Now that you know how important it is to work together, I'm sure you will achieve great things together.'

'You think so?'

'Listen, Marcus. My aim was to get the Maquis to work with the communists. We need you to operate a cohesive underground offensive, hitting the enemy in specifically targeted areas for maximum effect. You can only do that if you communicate effectively.'

'I understand, Lucille. I'll try to be a good dog from now on.'

Nicolette laughed. He wasn't exactly rolling over to let her tickle his tummy, but she felt she had turned a corner with the resistance leader.

Chapter 20: Back to Verdun

Fabien had been true to his word and supplied Nicolette with papers for her and Falcon. He'd told her of a system of safe houses that a young Belgian girl had organised, throughout France, to help British airmen get home after being shot down over enemy territory. She was given one address on the outskirts of Paris but wasn't given more in order to protect the rest of the line. If she only knew one address, she could not betray the whole operation, even under torture. The thought sent shivers through her body. She had witnessed the kind of torture the Germans were capable of.

She checked her railway tickets. The train would leave Lisieux at ten and would arrive in Paris a few hours later. Fabien and Marcus believed she would contact the safe house later that day but, in fact, she planned to travel much farther. She had enough French currency to purchase more tickets in Paris. By early evening, with luck, she and Falcon would be arriving at the destination Nicolette had planned.

She preferred to keep the details of her journey secret from the group. She had been tasked to look for an informer in their midst but so far hadn't worked out who it was. Anna was her prime suspect but Marcus had vouched for the Polish girl. Nicolette couldn't take any chances. Any member of the group could be responsible for passing information to the Germans. The less anyone knew about her real plans, the better.

Marcus and Fabien had been warned to look out for the informer. She felt she had done as much as she could do, for now. Getting Pilot Officer Brown home was her priority. His knowledge of the situation developing in Normandy would be essential to the SEO. They would already be in possession of the facts but the officer's skill and experience in obtaining that information would be required again. The faster they could get back, the better-equipped Britain would be.

She knew her grandmother had contacts with the French underground and Nicolette was planning to take Pilot Officer Brown to Verdun to ask for her help. She hoped her Grandmother Elizabeth would help organise safe passage for them, through neutral Spain, to London.

The rail journey had been fraught with danger. German soldiers boarded the train at every stop, checking papers and asking questions. Their cover story had worked, so far. They were travelling as husband and wife. The newlyweds were eager to visit family in Metz. Their home was in Paris. Nicolette was a seamstress and the officer was a travelling salesman, selling office supplies. They were taking time from their work to enjoy a short honeymoon in the country.

Nicolette had purchased tickets to take them all the way to Metz as a cover for her intended destination. She would leave the train at Verdun, and then try to get some transport from there to her grandmother's chateau. She hoped the Germans would not question her change of travel arrangements too closely.

'Do you have an excuse ready if we are stopped?' the pilot officer whispered when the train halted in Reims.

'I will tell them I feel unwell, travel sickness.' She whispered, close to his ear. 'I will say I need some air and you will come with me because you can't bear to be without your new wife for a second.' She snuggled closer and giggled for effect before whispering, 'We will conveniently forget to board the train in time before it leaves the station and we will be stranded in Verdun.'

'That sounds too easy, Lucille.' He used her code name, the same one that was written on her false papers.

'But, Pierre!' Her lips brushed his ear as she spoke in her quietest tone, 'I was taught that the simplest solutions are always the best. No room for mistakes over small details if there are no details to trip us up.' She used the name on his papers and leant to rest her head on his shoulder. She was happy to play the part of his wife. She had the perfect excuse to be close to him, and she was finding she enjoyed the contact.

'I hope you are right, my darling.' He whispered, in perfectly accented French, and squeezed her gently. 'Our lives will depend on it.'

'I know, my love.' She sighed, and snuggled closer to the officer, keeping up the pretence of being madly in love with her new husband.

The other passengers in the carriage had witnessed the intimate display for many hours, though would not have heard their whispered conversation. Their fellow travellers were now ignoring the young couple's affectionate behaviour, averting their eyes politely.

They heard heavy boots marching on the platform outside the carriage and all eyes turned to the window.

'Have your papers ready!' a loud German voice shouted in French.

The passengers shuffled and reached for bags. Nicolette held her breath and tried to look relaxed and happy as the soldiers worked their way through the train.

'Papers!' A young soldier demanded, holding out his hand to the passengers in their carriage.

Nicolette handed three sheets to the soldier and smiled shyly. 'I recently changed my name; we just got married.' She explained the extra paper. At first she had questioned Fabien's logic in adding this small complication to their papers. When he'd explained that the Germans would be so tied up in the changed details that they would not think to check further, she had to agree that his reasoning sounded feasible.

The soldier checked the papers and handed them back with a smile. 'Congratulations.'

'Thank you.' The pilot officer gave the soldier a tight smile.

Nicolette held the sigh of relief until the soldier had left the carriage. 'How will we keep this up?' she asked in a whisper.

'You are doing fine, Lucille.' The officer put his arm around her shoulders and pulled her close.

She breathed the scent of him and felt comforted by his warmth. She knew she shouldn't get attached to this man, but was beginning to realise that all her good intentions had been in vain. It was too late. She looked up at his smooth face. The shadow of a beard was dusting his chin but all traces of bruising had disappeared. Fabien had advised them not to travel until the officer's face was completely healed. A beaten-up agent would rouse suspicion, no matter what story they could concoct to explain the bruises. His jaw still looked slightly lopsided but not so much that it would draw attention. She was tempted to stroke his face but resisted. Instead, she rested her head against his chest and closed her eyes.

'Wake up, Lucille.' Nicolette felt a hand on her shoulder and woke with a start. 'Shush, nothing to worry about,' the pilot officer quickly reassured her and whispered, 'We are entering Verdun, I thought you might like to get ready.'

'Oh, of course.' She put a hand to her mouth to stifle a yawn. 'You should not have let me sleep so long, Pierre,' she admonished him in a tone just loud enough for the other passengers to hear her. 'I feel a little out of sorts now.'

'Do you, my darling?' His face was a picture of concern. 'Perhaps your travel sickness is troubling you.'

'It always happens if I sleep while travelling. I think I need some air.'

'We'll be stopping soon; perhaps we can take a short stroll on the platform.' The officer suggested, for the benefit of the other passengers.

'I wouldn't do that if I were you, young man.' An elderly woman cautioned. 'The Germans won't like it at all!'

'Oh, Pierre, I do feel quite ill.' Nicolette put a hand theatrically to her brow. 'I don't care what the Germans think; I need some air.'

'Open the window.' A young man suggested.

'Err, thank you.' The pilot officer watched the young man struggling to open the window and breathed easier when it proved to be stuck.

The train began to slow and Nicolette jumped to her feet. 'Please, Pierre, I have to get off this train or I will be ill and embarrass myself.'

'Let me help you, my dearest.' The pilot officer grabbed their bags and guided her to the corridor. 'Keep it up, Lucille, we're almost there.'

Nicolette kept her hand over her mouth and clutched her middle dramatically.

'Please make way,' the pilot officer called. 'My wife is unwell.'

Other passengers were waiting to disembark but moved to allow Nicolette to hurry past them.

Once on the platform, they merged with the passengers moving to the exit.

She turned away, to flop on a wooden bench.

'What's wrong?' the pilot officer sat beside her.

'German soldiers are everywhere. They are checking the tickets. They will ask why we are leaving the train here instead of going to Metz.'

'Leave it to me, I will explain.' He took her elbow and guided her to the soldiers.

'Tickets!'

'Hello, sir,' the pilot officer gave the German a polite smile. 'I wonder whether you could help us. My wife has been taken ill.'

The soldier glanced at Nicolette. She pulled a sad face and sighed for good measure.

'We are meant to be meeting relatives at Metz but as you can see, my dear wife cannot travel more today. We need a hotel for the night. Could you suggest somewhere?'

The soldier was taken aback and only gave their tickets a cursory glance. 'The Imperial is not too far.' He pointed to the left of the exit. 'I hope you feel better soon, Madam.'

'Thank you. You are very kind.' Nicolette said in a small, frail sounding voice.

When they were out of sight of the station, they hurried to a café that Nicolette remembered well from her previous visits.

'Are you sure about this, Nicolette?' The pilot officer sounded tense. 'The owner might not remember you and if he does he may not be willing to take risks for you.'

'Monsieur Louis is a friend of my grandmother. He will help us. I would stake my life on it.'

'You *are* doing!' he reminded her, sternly.

'I like you much better when you are the doting husband.' Nicolette gave him a nervous smile. 'I don't care for the doubting Thomas.'

'You are too trusting, Nicolette.'

She stopped in her tracks. He'd used her real name and it sounded so good to hear it from his lips. 'Lucille, Pierre!' She reminded him. 'My name is Lucille!'

'Of course. How stupid of me.' He glanced around the empty street. 'Is that the café?' He pointed over the road.

'Yes, come.'

The café owner not only remembered her but went out of his way to help them. She didn't tell him any details, and he didn't question her. Nicolette explained that she had to see her grandmother. The man agreed to take them when he'd closed for the evening. He served the couple a meal and made small talk between attending his other customers. Two German officers arrived and ordered coffee, but they didn't seem to notice there were strangers in town.

Eventually, the café owner drove them to the chateau and refused Nicolette's invitation to come in and say hello to her grandmother. 'I'll see her at church on Sunday,' he called as he drove away.

'You didn't tell me your family owned a chateau.' The pilot officer tilted his head to stare at the grand old building. 'This is quite a place.'

'It belongs to Elizabeth's children. My father's share will pass to me on her death. I hate to think of selling this to divide the equity between us but I'm afraid we'll have no choice.'

'It would be a shame,' he agreed.

Nicolette took the officer's arm and approached the front door. It opened before they reached it and Elizabeth had gasped with surprise. 'Nicolette! What on earth are you doing here?' She spoke in English with a heavy American accent.

'Shush!' Nicolette warned, glancing around at the shadowed garden. She expected German soldiers to be everywhere. 'Grand-Mère Elizabeth, we are travelling incognito and we need your help.'

Elizabeth ushered them inside and took them into a large reception room. She listened to Nicolette's story with wide eyes. Nicolette told her grandmother the truth about her work as an agent and explained the officer's recent brush with German interrogators.

'We could have used the safe houses and relied on the resistance but I suspect we might not have got very far. They have an informer in their midst.' Nicolette explained. 'I thought we'd be safer in your hands, Grand-Mère.'

Elizabeth shook her head and pressed her lips together. 'You are just like your mother. She also took liberties with my good nature.'

Nicolette was confused. She thought her grandmother would be eager to help them. She glanced uncertainly at her companion.

Pilot Officer Brown coughed. 'We don't want to put you in danger, Madam. If you think we ask too much, we'll leave now.'

'No, Mr Brown. I'm sure my Grandmother will help us.' She turned to the older woman. 'You will, won't you?'

'Of course, I will.' Elizabeth sat straighter in the chair. 'What do you take me for?'

Nicolette smiled with relief. 'Thank you, Grand-Mère.'

'It is late, and you both look exhausted. Let me get Martha to make up a bed for you.'

'Please don't, Madam. The fewer people who know we are here, the better.'

'He's right, Grand-Mère. We can make up our beds. Which rooms would you like us to use?'

'Oh, I presumed you were a couple. Forgive me.'

'We've been play-acting the part all day so it's not surprising you jumped to that conclusion.' Pilot Officer Brown grinned at Nicolette.

'Come, I'll show you to your rooms.' Elizabeth got up and

waved at the door. 'The others are already in bed. I'll have to tell the family that you are here and the servants will soon realise we have guests. What do I tell them?'

Nicolette shrugged. She hadn't thought so far ahead.

'Could we be visiting from the South of France? Perhaps we could be relatives of your late husband,' the officer suggested.

'That might satisfy the servant's curiosity. Good thinking.' Elizabeth nodded.

'Are Uncle Francois and Aunt Sabine here?'

'Of course, they are, where else would they be? Come.' Elizabeth took them upstairs and began to walk down a long corridor. 'Shush, your aunt and uncle are sleeping in there.' She pointed to a heavy oak door. 'I'll put you two down at the end. Try not to make too much noise.'

'Where are the children, Grand-Mère?' Nicolette didn't want to disturb her cousins.

'Antoine is putting himself in danger every day. Sabine is consumed with worry. Your two older cousins are involved with the underground, and, while we don't like what they do, they are probably your best hope of getting out of France. Gaston is fourteen, and still a child, but he is eager to be involved too. Fortunately, his brothers don't allow him. He's asleep in the room next to his parents.'

'Antoine and Pascal are active in the resistance?' Nicolette was astounded. 'But they are children!'

'No, Nicolette. They are not children. Antoine is nineteen and Pascal is seventeen. If France had some backbone, they would be in the army and fighting the Nazis but as it is, they are content to run around the countryside causing mayhem.'

'Are they home now?' Pilot Officer Brown asked.

'They are out.' Elizabeth opened a door and showed them into a bedroom. 'I never ask where they are. It pays not to know.' She pulled open a drawer in a large dresser. 'The sheets are in here. That door is connected to the next room, but you'll remember that from your previous visits, Nicolette.'

'Thank you, Grand-Mère.' Nicolette said, quietly. 'We're very grateful.'

The pilot officer took a set of sheets from Elizabeth and went to the connecting door. 'Get some sleep, Nicolette. I'll see you in the morning.'

When the door closed behind him, Nicolette turned to her

grandmother. 'What did you mean earlier, when you said I was just like my mother?' Something had always niggled Nicolette about her grandmother's attitude to her. 'You've said something like that before to me, and I never understood what your problem was. I thought you loved Collette. Why would you think she'd want to take advantage of you?'

'Not tonight, Nicolette. It is late. Get some sleep. We'll talk tomorrow.'

'Please, Grand-Mère. I won't sleep now. What are you keeping from me? What is your problem with my mother?'

'Very well.' Elizabeth sighed and sat on the bed. 'You are an adult now. You should know the truth. Especially as Collette is too wrapped up in her own affairs, to think how her actions will affect anyone else. Felicity has abandoned her husband in the belief that she is doing Collette a huge favour. I will never understand those two sisters.'

'You know about my mum and Edwin?' Nicolette was surprised. 'How did you find out?'

'The world may be at war, Nicolette, but bad news still travels fast.'

'I don't see it as bad news, Grand-Mère. As far as I've been told, Aunt Felicity stole Edwin from Mum in the first place and according to Edwin, she would not be too upset by the news that they are together.'

'Well, that does not surprise me, given Felicity's history.' Elizabeth took a deep breath.

'What do you mean?'

'Felicity has always been flighty. You should prepare yourself, Nicolette. What I'm about to tell you will come as a big surprise.'

'I'm intrigued.' Nicolette couldn't wait to hear the details of the family secret concerning her aunt. She'd always suspected something but no one would tell her anything about the past.

'Very well.' Elizabeth took a deep breath. 'Felicity had an affair with an Australian Doctor. She got pregnant but didn't find out until the doctor had left. She said she didn't want to marry him anyway.'

'But Aunt Flissy can't have children.' Nicolette was confused.

'Oh yes she can, and she did. The problem with fertility must have been Edwin's. There was nothing wrong with your aunt's ability to have a child.'

'So where is the child now?'

Elizabeth looked at Nicolette and lifted her eyebrows. 'She's staring at me.'

Nicolette took a few seconds to understand what her grandmother was saying. 'No!' The word came out as a strangulated moan.

'You are not my blood, Nicolette. Your mother is Felicity. Collette is your aunt. Your father was not my beloved Antoine, but an Australian doctor called Alain Bernard.'

'Why the secrecy? Why pretend?' Nicolette's head was spinning. She was searching her memory, looking for evidence that could have shown her the truth. 'Why did my mother? I mean, Collette. Why would she take on someone else's child, even if it were her sister's baby? Why would she do that?'

'You have to understand the history of the sisters, Nicolette. Felicity had an uneasy upbringing. Your grandfather, Belle's husband, never believed Flissy was his child.' She hastened to add, 'She was, of course, but his head injury affected his thinking. He disowned her.'

'That's awful! Poor Aunt Flissy.' As she said the words, she realised that she was speaking of her mother.

'Collette took her father's side for many years and enjoyed flaunting her special relationship with him. In later years, Collette came to understand how much her sister had suffered and thought she owed a debt of honour to Felicity.' Elizabeth reached for Nicolette's hand and pulled her down to sit beside her. 'Antoine had recently been killed. Collette was a war widow. Her emotions were in turmoil. She was distraught with grief, and I don't think she was thinking clearly, but Belle saw it as the perfect solution.'

'What did Belle have to do with this?' Nicolette asked.

'She organised everything. Collette suggested that she could pass off Felicity's baby as hers. As a war widow, who had recently spent time with her husband, it would be perfectly natural. On the other hand, Felicity, as an unmarried mother would never have been accepted in French society. Her life would have been over.'

'Is that why Grand-Mère Belle took them to England?'

'It was easier to hide the truth there. Major Whitmoor helped them.'

'So Felicity is my mother?' Nicolette could see how the sisters would have found it difficult. They both loved her but she could remember the many disagreements between her aunt and mother.

They constantly argued, about the best way to bring her up. Now she knew the reason.

'So that's why you compare me to Felicity, who has always been less than perfect in your eyes. You probably resent the fact that everyone thinks I am your son's child when *you* know that I'm not.'

'Can you blame me?'

'Did you ever love me, Elizabeth?' Nicolette began to remember the small instances when she had felt her American grandmother had been harsh or cold towards her. 'I won't blame you. I can appreciate how difficult it must have been for you.'

'Nicolette, I *do* love you.' The American squeezed her hand. 'But Belle would have been the first to agree that I am not the most demonstrative person when it comes to matters of the heart. I try to treat you as I do my other grandchildren. I'm sorry if my failings upset you.'

'I can't ever remember a time when you upset me, Grand-Mère.' Nicolette realised that she had no claim to Elizabeth as her grandmother. 'Sorry, I can't think of you as anything other than my grandmother.'

'Then don't, Nicolette. What's in a name?'

'I don't have any claim to you or this lovely old house, either, do I?' Nicolette's eyes filled with tears. She had always loved the chateau.

'Not officially. No.' Elizabeth raised her eyebrows. 'But when you inherit, with your cousins, I won't be around to contest your claim. There's no reason anyone else should know the secret.'

'Who *does* know?'

'Just me, your mother and your aunt. Belle and Major Whitmoor are gone and they were the only other people who knew.'

'So my real father is Australian?'

'That's right, Nicolette.'

'I didn't think I'd sleep knowing you were hiding something from me, but now I don't think I'll sleep because I know what it was.'

'You must sleep, Nicolette. Tomorrow, I will help you and your friend. It might be a long day.'

'Thank you, Grand-Mère.' Nicolette leant to hug the older woman and was surprised at the strength in the arms of her grandmother when she returned the gesture.

'Does Collette know you are in France?'

'No, of course, she doesn't. She thinks I am a radio operator on the south coast of England.'

'Are you allowed to write to her?'

'I think HQ sends her fake messages from me from time to time to keep her happy. I'm not sure, really.' She hadn't given it much thought but now realised that her mother, or rather, her aunt, would be concerned that she hadn't heard from her.

'Perhaps I'll try to get word to her that you're safe.'

'No, Grand-Mère. Please don't. No one should know where I am.'

'Collette cares for you as her own, Nicolette. She won't be satisfied with a few lines of nonsense from a stranger pretending to be you.'

'I'll be home soon. She can wait.'

'Good night, Nicolette. Try to sleep.' Elizabeth patted her shoulder and moved to the door. 'You'll need your strength for crossing the Pyrenees. I hear it is a strenuous trek.'

'The Pyrenees?'

'The mountain passes are the only safe route into Spain. From there you'll make your way to Gibraltar, where you'll be able to fly or sail back to Britain.'

'We have a long journey ahead. How long will it take?'

'A few weeks, perhaps.' Elizabeth paused at the door.

'We have to get back as quickly as we can. Pilot Officer Brown will be needed.'

'What about you? Don't they need you too?'

'Perhaps, but he's more important than me.'

'Don't be too sure about that, Nicolette. A woman's place in war is always underestimated. Mostly by the woman herself.'

'Why do you say that?' Nicolette asked.

'How would your officer have got here, without your help?'

'He would have gone by the safe house route that the resistance offered.' Nicolette then realised that the route was not as safe as had been suggested. 'But we know there is an informer. I think he would have fallen into a trap.' The officer would probably have been picked up in Paris. The informer would certainly have alerted the Germans to their movements.

'Don't you know who this traitor is?' Elizabeth asked.

'Not yet.' Something crystallised in her mind. What was she thinking? She couldn't leave without completing her mission. 'But I intend to find out if it's the last thing I do.'

She needed to discover who the informer was. She realised that she couldn't go to Spain with the pilot officer. 'I have to get back to Lisieux.' She had a responsibility to stop the informer before he or she could do more damage.

Chapter 21: Separation

'You can't go back to Lisieux, Nicolette. It's too dangerous!' Pilot Officer Brown beseeched her 'The German soldiers may recognise you. We made ourselves quite conspicuous on that train, didn't we? What if one of them should remember you?'

'I could go in disguise. I'll cut my hair short. Or perhaps I don't have to use the train. Antoine will get new papers for me.' She turned to her cousin for confirmation.

'I'm not sure I could, Nicolette,' the young man admitted. 'It's not as if my contacts can magic them from thin air.'

'I'm sorry, Antoine.' Nicolette sighed and looked to Elizabeth. 'Can we go over it one more time? I want to be sure I'm leaving Mr Brown in safe hands.'

'We know the plan by heart, Nicolette.' Elizabeth shook her head and sighed heavily. 'We take Mr Brown to Antoine's contact in Nancy and from there he will be passed along the line to the mountains.'

'I'm not thrilled about crossing the Pyrenees; I have to admit,' the officer said.

'Conditions shouldn't be too bad at this time of year. The snow doesn't get bad until after September.' Antoine told them.

'A guide will take you over the border and hand you to our man in Spain.' Pascal added and turned to Nicolette. 'You have nothing to worry about, well, no more than expected. We can't guarantee the Germans won't interfere with our plans for your man.'

'I'll have to take my chances where the Nazis are concerned,' the officer said. 'Though I wish you'd reconsider and come with me, Nicolette.'

She looked at him with sadness in her heart. He had used her real name frequently in the few days they had spent at the chateau. She was no longer Armaud, or Lucille, or Private. She had learned that his name was James but hadn't felt brave enough to use it when speaking to him. He was her superior officer and, even though she felt closer to him than any man she'd known, she still couldn't use his first name to address him. 'You know I can't come with you,' she told him. 'I have to find out who is disclosing our secrets. We know about the damage they are causing. Antoine told us that Britain tried to attack Dieppe and the Germans were waiting for them. Someone is telling the Nazis our every move. Their actions are costing lives. I have to stop them.'

'Let me come with you,' the officer suggested. 'Two heads will be better than one.'

'We both know you are needed at HQ.' She wished she could agree with him. It would be wonderful to spend more time in his company but she knew it was impossible. 'They can't spare both of us to uncover the traitor.'

'If you hadn't got me out of La Havre we wouldn't be having this conversation, Nicolette.' His eyes held hers hypnotically. 'HQ would have had to manage without me.'

'But we *did* get you out, and you *have* to go back,' she insisted.

'We are talking in circles here.' Antoine interrupted them. 'Mr Brown leaves tonight. I will take him to Nancy by car. We shouldn't encounter any problems, but we have our cover story.'

'Yes, Antoine.' Mr Brown nodded and repeated the cover story. 'We are to attend a wedding in Nancy. Our car broke down and delayed us, and that is why we are travelling late at night. Antoine has to get to his bride in time for the ceremony.'

'The war is turning us all into accomplished liars.' Pascal commented. 'I hope the Nazis will fall for it.'

'How will you get back to Lisieux?' the officer asked Nicolette.

She shrugged. 'Perhaps the line of safe houses will work perfectly well in reverse for me?' She looked at Antoine. 'What do you think?'

'I don't see why not. Perhaps our grandmother could take you to Reims and set you on your way. It would take you longer to get back than a simple train journey, but it would be a safer route for you, Nicolette.'

'Take the safe route, Nicolette. Listen to your cousin,' the officer said.

'How soon can I leave?' she asked.

'As soon as you like.' Elizabeth answered. 'We could go tonight. I'm sure Antoine can make some arrangements.'

Nicolette nodded. It was decided. Today would be the last time she would see James Brown until who knew when. 'Until tonight, then.'

Nicolette persuaded her grandmother to cut her hair. It wouldn't harm to alter her appearance for the journey back. She was pacing the orchard, planning the strategy she would use when she arrived back in Lisieux. She had an idea and wanted to work out the details.

She was deep in thought and didn't notice the pilot officer approaching her.

'Nicolette, why are you hiding down here?'

'Oh, I, err, I was just thinking about things.' She turned to stare into his eyes. 'I was... I was working through some ideas for trapping the informer.'

'Don't tell me,' he warned. 'If I'm caught, I can't guarantee I wouldn't drop you in it.' His smile took the sting from his words. 'I like the new hairstyle.' He put a hand to her short curls.

She felt the pull of attraction and moved away from him, to give herself some space. She couldn't let him know how she felt.

'This orchard is one of my favourite places in the world.' She said the first thing that came into her head. 'My brother and I used to play here with my cousins.' She pointed to a sturdy, old apple tree. 'That tree was the best one to climb. We'd hide in the foliage when we played hide and seek.' She was rambling to cover the conflicting emotions she felt. She couldn't fall for this man, but every atom in her body was aching for his touch.

'I'm going to miss you, Private Armaud.'

She caught her breath and turned to face him. 'Don't call me that. I like it better when you use my given name.'

'You never use mine!' he accused in a teasing tone.

'It wouldn't be appropriate.'

'Why not?'

'It's obvious. You're an officer and I'm not.' She dragged her eyes away from his. 'We shouldn't get too friendly.'

'I think it's a bit late to worry about that, don't you?' He moved closer and put his hands on her shoulders.

She gazed into his face. 'Don't, James,' she pleaded. 'We can't. We shouldn't.'

'Who will know?' He leant to place his lips on hers.

Nicolette hesitated for a second but couldn't resist any longer. This man had captured her heart. His lips moved gently and her insides responded in ways that surprised her. She'd never felt as aroused so quickly by any man. The strength of her emotions overwhelmed and scared her. She pushed him away.

'This is wrong!' she said firmly. 'What are we thinking?'

'Sometimes it's better not to think at all. We can't deny what we have between us, Nicolette.'

Pearl A. Gardner

'We must deny it,' she insisted. 'Emotions will complicate everything. We have dangerous work to do and... and...' she ran out of excuses.

'As your superior officer, Armaud, I order you to stop thinking too deeply about the future.' A soft smile hovered around his lips, but then he frowned. 'Listen, Nicolette. We only have today. Hopefully, when this mess is over, we might survive to see where these feelings could take us, but for now, well...' He fell silent for a few seconds. 'You do feel something for me, don't you? Please tell me I haven't got this wrong.'

She didn't trust herself to speak and simply nodded. She couldn't deny what she felt.

He pulled her close and held her tightly. 'Keep safe, Nicolette. We'll meet again.'

She smiled and began to sing in a low whisper, into his ear, 'Don't know where, don't know when, but I know we'll meet again, some sunny day.'

His arms squeezed her more tightly. He laughed and snuggled his cheek against her throat. 'How can you be flippant when I'm baring my soul to you?'

'Don't you like Vera Lynn?' She giggled.

'You are impossible, Nicolette Armaud, but I love you.'

She was startled. 'You love me?'

'That's what I said.'

'You can't! I won't let you.'

'Why not?'

'Because, because...'

'Do you love me?' he asked.

Nicolette hadn't allowed herself to think too deeply about the emotions and feeling she had for this man. She knew that love was something that ran deep and overshadowed everything else. She thought she'd been in love with Robert but the feelings she had for her former fiancé were not half what she now felt for James.

She hadn't considered how deep her feelings were for the pilot officer. She'd had too many other issues clouding her mind, not the least of which was her priority to keep him safe. She now realised that her love for him had influenced everything she had done since he'd come back into her life.

'You're taking a long time to think about it, Nicolette.' She watched his Adam's apple bob as he swallowed nervously. 'Am I reading this wrong?'

193

'No!' she quickly reassured him. 'I just hadn't realised what you meant to me until now.'

'Really?' He grinned with relief.

'I love you, James Brown,' she declared and reached to taste his lips again.

After a while, they realised they would have to return to the house. The afternoon was growing chilly and the sun was low in the sky. In a few hours, they would begin their separate journeys and may never see each other again. Nicolette's heart was in turmoil. She was ecstatically happy to learn the pilot officer felt the same way about her as she did about him but she was distraught at their impending separation and scared for their future. The last few hours spent with him had been the happiest of her life. They'd kissed and talked and talked and kissed but neither of them felt they should take things further.

'Life is uncertain,' James had said. 'And, although making love to you is all I want to do right now, we shouldn't.'

'I know.' Nicolette felt a little disappointed but understood his reasons. She felt the same way. 'We'll have all the time in the world, one day,' she said, hoping she was right.

'I hope so, Nicolette.'

Chapter 22: Proof at last

The heat of the soil was warm against her thighs as she waited, flat on her stomach, in the wheat field. The night air felt chilly, but the ground still held the heat of the day. She'd been waiting for an hour but would wait longer to make sure she got the evidence she was looking for.

The war had escalated in the last year since she returned to Lisieux. America had joined the fight in December after the bombing of the Hawaiian harbour by Japan. The summer of nineteen-forty-two had seen terrible losses for the British forces in their attempts to invade the Normandy coast. Plans had been made, and Operation Jubilee was launched on August the nineteenth. The Germans were waiting and were ready for the attack. Someone had warned the enemy.

Nicolette was close to discovering the identity of the informer. She knew the traitor had been responsible for the deaths of thousands of Canadian and British men. She would not let it happen again. Three times in the last few months she felt she was getting close to discovering who the spy in their midst was, but last-minute doubts prevented her from taking action against the traitor. If she got it wrong, an innocent person could die while the real culprit would still be at large. She had to be sure.

Throughout the year, she'd been involved in minor skirmishes with Marcus' men. They'd destroyed enemy fuel depots, blown up German barracks full of soldiers, cut communication wires and derailed trains carrying tanks and heavy equipment but they could have done much more. Three times, she'd narrowly escaped being captured when the Germans were already on the scene of the target. The enemy troops had been waiting for the attack and were prepared.

Now, Nicolette sent scouts to the targeted areas to report back before sending in the main operational force. She organised this with no help from Marcus or Fabien. She now had her own band of loyal supporters, and they were happy to do her bidding. Young Rene was her chief scout, and she knew she could rely on him. The scout's job was to report any increased enemy activity at the objective and warn the raiding party before the mission could take place.

She was acting as the scout this evening to keep security as tight as possible. The cell planned to intercept a convoy taking supplies to the barracks in Lisieux. Men had been watching the route for months, reporting on regular truck movements and gathering information about the cargo.

Nicolette was waiting for the convoy to pass on the road beside the field. The main attack force would be in position two miles away. She was using a new piece of equipment to contact them with her report. The walkie-talkie had been dropped in with other supplies a few weeks previously and was proving a valuable piece of equipment. Short messages could be sent easily and replies received instantly. She would send a message of one word on a prearranged frequency. She would say, "Go", if her suspicions were unfounded but she would say, "Abandon", if she were proved right in her assumption that the convoy had been warned of the attack.

She checked the heavy battery was securely fastened to her chest, and then ensured that she had selected the correct frequency. Everything was ready, but she felt sure she would have to order the men to stand down. She had a sinking feeling in her gut. She had made her plans carefully and knew that if she were right, her suspicions would be proved beyond doubt tonight.

The resistance was operating as a more secure force since her arrival. Small cells functioned in isolation from the rest of the group, with small chains of command. Each cell leader was given orders directly from Marcus or Fabien, in meetings arranged at various places around the town. Occasionally, Anna would be asked to contact the leaders of cells based farther out from town by radio. She would transmit from various locations, with either Marcus or Fabien by her side.

Each unit would then carry out the instructions without involving any other cells in either the planning or the undertaking of the commands. This way, the whole organisation could not be compromised if one cell was captured. This particular operation, of intercepting the convoy, had been organised in the same way with one slight deviation.

Anna had been Nicolette's prime suspect from the beginning. The Polish girl's unfriendly attitude, coupled with her knowledge of every move the resistance planned, and every message sent or received from London, made her an obvious target of suspicion. For months, Nicolette had shadowed the girl, followed her back to her apartment in town after transmissions and watched her every movement. Anna never put a foot wrong or gave any sign of collaborating with the enemy. She now trusted the girl and had even grown fond of her. She had wasted valuable time by concentrating on the Polish girl. Nicolette then had to look elsewhere to find her informer.

As Nicolette's cell was directly involved in this particular operation, the initial plans had been discussed at the farmhouse. The informal meeting was attended by Marcus, his brother and Nicolette. No radio messages were sent regarding the mission. Orders had not come from London. The arrangement was a local operation. The only other person present at the planning stage was Lissette.

Nicolette had been reluctant to accept that Marcus' wife could be the traitor. What would the woman have to gain? She would be putting her husband and brother-in-law at risk by informing on them. Then Nicolette had begun to keep records of the times that Lissette was present at meetings or discussions she'd had with the brothers. They often talked about the contents of the transmissions from London in the kitchen of the farmhouse. They had all presumed the intimate discussions with only family present, were safe.

When Nicolette cross-referenced the resulting raids that had been compromised, with the times that Lissette would have known the plans, she had her suspicions confirmed. Lissette had been clever. She never informed on raids that her husband or his brother would be attending, or at least those missions were usually successful with little or no activity from the Germans to indicate they'd been warned.

This raid would prove or disprove Nicolette's suspicions. If Lissette was the informer, she was the only one who could have passed the information, and the Germans would be prepared. Marcus and Henri were busy with the harvest and could not be spared for this mission. Lissette had known that Nicolette's band of men would be responsible for destroying the convoy.

She felt the ground under her stomach begin to vibrate before she heard the rumble of trucks on the road. She lifted her field glasses and trained them on the road. The moon was bright, and the trucks were silhouetted against the lighter sky as they came over the small hill. She counted seven vehicles, and each appeared to have three soldiers in the cab, including the driver. She thought that looked odd. A food convoy would not usually be guarded as heavily. The first tendrils of excitement wriggled in her tummy. Could Lissette have warned them?

Nicolette rolled on her side. She couldn't see much from this angle and wanted to look into the back of the trucks. She waited for the first to rumble past the field and lifted the binoculars to her eyes. The moonlight illuminated the open-backed, canvas-covered wagon. She saw a row of soldiers, sitting side by side, along a bench inside the truck. One was smoking a cigarette; she saw the lighted end glowing in the shadows.

The next truck came into view, but the canvas was tied shut. She moved position to focus on the next one. Two soldiers were sitting at the back of the third truck, pointing their rifles to the road. She crouched lower. She was right. This convoy seemed prepared for an attack. Only three of the seven vehicles were closed. The other four were open, creating an easy and speedy exit for the cargo of German troops.

She waited until the last truck had rounded the bend in the road and lifted her walkie-talkie. She cranked the handle and spoke one word. 'Abandon.' She hesitated. Would they understand? 'I repeat. Abandon. Confirm!'

The box crackled and a disappointed voice called, 'Understood. Standing down.'

She flopped on her bottom and began to pack her equipment away. Her insides were in knots. She was happy that she knew, at last, who the informer was, but she was afraid where her discovery would lead her. She now knew, without a shadow of a doubt, that Lissette was the informer, but she didn't have the first idea how she would tell Marcus that his wife was a traitor.

Nicolette found the two men finishing for the night after a long evening in the fields. She came straight to the point. She couldn't afford to waste any more time.

'You don't expect me to believe you?' Marcus was appalled by her accusation. 'What proof do you have?'

'Who else knew of my mission?' she hissed. 'Think about it, Marcus! Did you speak to anyone else about the attack on the convoy tonight?'

Marcus shook his head and spat on the ground.

'Did you, Henri?' Nicolette asked the brother.

'Of course, not!' Henri ran a hand through his hair. 'It could have been one of your men.'

'Why would they call the enemy down on themselves? Not one man cried off tonight. They were all ready to ambush that convoy. Don't you think the informer would have made himself scarce under the circumstances if he had been one of my team?' She turned to Marcus. 'Look, I know this isn't easy for you, Marcus. I didn't say anything until I was sure. I double-checked everything. She's been telling the Germans everything she's heard for months, if not years. Think about it. Have you or Henri ever been compromised as badly as the rest of us?'

'She has a point, Marcus.' Henri scratched his chin.

'What about when we almost got shot taking out that electricity supply line?'

'Two guards were on duty that night, Marcus.' Nicolette pointed out. 'You knew they'd be there. You expected them to be there. You just got careless.'

'Are you saying I'm no good at my work, now?' Marcus was angry.

'Of course, not!' Nicolette knew she would have to calm him. 'You are one of the best operators we have. Anyone is allowed to have an off day. I almost got shot myself when those Germans discovered us making the transmission to London last month, remember?'

'Poor Anna had to run for her life.' Henri pointed out. 'They nearly had all three of us.'

'But you were waiting for them, Marcus. Your bullets stopped them following us.' Nicolette put her hand on his shoulder. 'We can't manage without you. You know this.' She flattered him, hoping to win him around.

'But Lissette! What you say? Are you sure this is true.'

'I'm sorry, Marcus, but I'm one-hundred-percent sure.'

'What will you do?' Henri asked his brother.

Marcus lifted his head and stared at the dark sky. 'I will do what has to be done. She is no wife of mine.'

'You would kill her?' Henri was obviously shocked.

'What else would you have me do?' Marcus spoke through clenched teeth. 'She is a traitor and traitors are shot.'

'Wait, Marcus. Perhaps I can give you another solution.' Nicolette had hoped Marcus would want to be lenient to his wife and was as shocked as his brother to hear what he intended to do.

'I'm listening.' Marcus stood as stiff as a board with tension.

'We can pretend we don't know of her activities. We can feed her false information, send the Nazis on wild goose chases, and play her to our advantage. What do you think?'

'Could you continue to live with her after this?' Henri asked. 'She must never suspect that you know what she's doing.'

'Think about this carefully, Marcus,' Nicolette warned. 'You would have to continue your marriage as if nothing had changed. Could you do that?'

Marcus smiled a thin, wry, lift of his lips. He nodded. 'What's that old saying? Keep your friends close but your enemies closer? I think I could do it.'

'Good man.' Nicolette clapped him on the back. 'But if you find it too difficult, if you give yourself away, you must let me or Henri know so we can help you.'

'You don't have to worry, Lucille. My wife will not suspect a thing.'

Chapter 23: Going home

Nicolette was exhausted. She'd spent the last two years in the field in Normandy, working with Marcus and Fabien to disrupt the Germans as much as possible. Now she was on her way back to England for some much-deserved leave. She was on board a tiny fishing vessel sailing from a small cove west of Brest. They were heading for neutral Ireland, where the captain had arranged for some people, to help her. Thanks to Fabien's contacts, she had been spared the long trek south through the mountainous route to Spain.

She hoped the vessel was small enough to go unnoticed by the enemy patrols. The Atlantic was a vast ocean and tonight; the swell was heavy. The captain had assured her this was the best kind of weather to avoid being picked up. It wasn't the best for her stomach, though. She heaved for hours before falling into an uneasy, fitful slumber filled with nightmares.

It was the middle of December, nineteen-forty-three. She felt she'd been running around Normandy for years, trying to keep one step ahead of the enemy. She'd seen friends shot, captured and taken away, and although she'd pleaded with Marcus and Fabien to try to get them back, it wasn't always possible. She dreamed of her friends being tortured, and then she would wake, listening for the sound of jackboots in the yard outside the farmhouse. Nicolette couldn't remember the last time she'd slept soundly throughout the night.

She'd passed hundreds of messages to HQ during her time in France, including information about troop movements, the location of radio transmitting stations, and where the enemy was positioning heavy artillery. She worked closely with Anna, who became one of her best friends in the field until she was shot just after Easter earlier that year. They'd made a transmission in the basement of a café in town. As usual, Marcus and Nicolette followed Anna, at a safe distance, to make sure she got home safely. Anna would usually hide the transmitter in one of many safe places around town before going on to her apartment. Nicolette was tired that night and had been hoping Anna wouldn't take too long about hiding the radio as she wanted to get back to her bed.

Nicolette and Marcus were fifty yards behind Anna when two Germans came out of nowhere and roughly pulled the girl to one side. Marcus dragged Nicolette into the shadows of a building and put his hand over her mouth. If he hadn't been there, she knew she would have tried to save her friend. Nicolette's hand was already on her small pistol. It would have been a foolish move. Within seconds, more soldiers poured out of an alleyway to surround the Polish girl. Poor Anna didn't stand a chance. The girl knew if she'd been taken alive they would torture her. Nicolette watched, helplessly, as Anna threw the canvas bag at one of the soldiers and made a run for it. The other soldiers shot her in the back before she got three strides away from them.

Nicolette was distressed, but Marcus was heartbroken. He blamed his wife for betraying the girl. They had no proof, though. Anna's death was a bitter blow.

Nicolette became the pianist for the group until Anna could be replaced. Every time she operated the radio, she would think of her and feel anger bubbling inside at the senseless loss of her life. She couldn't help but blame Lissette. Marcus's wife was still passing information to the Germans. Nicolette suspected the woman of betraying Anna because she was envious of her husband's affection for the Polish girl. The Germans would only need to know who Anna was, what she did and where she lived. They could then watch her movements and catch her with the evidence. Lissette would know just what to tell them.

Nicolette had always disliked the woman intensely, and since she discovered her duplicity, she hated her but after Anna was shot, she wanted to kill Lissette herself. She knew Marcus felt the same. Instead, they had to be content to continue to use her.

She and Marcus had played Lissette as if she were their puppet. They told her lies that she would then pass on, helping them make important gains against the enemy. They fed her many false pieces of information and felt satisfied when they realised their ploy was working. The first successful falsehood was when they discussed the British intention to drop supplies on a certain date in fields south of Glos. Lissette sat by the fireside, knitting, and seemed to be taking no notice of their conversation. Later that week, on the night they'd mentioned, German troops were dispatched to the scene and were distracted all night, searching the skies for incoming aircraft. During their absence, one resistance unit sabotaged their weapons store, and another cleared out the German garrison's food stores.

Nicolette was roused from her thoughts by the captain. 'We are almost at the coast, Lucille.'

She sat up and pulled her coat closed. The wind was bitter cold on the water. She could see the Irish coast in the distance. When she reached there, she would be safe. Ireland was almost home. A train ride would take her from Cork to Dublin and from there she was to fly home. Someone was coming to meet her. She hoped it might be James. She hadn't seen him in over two years. She knew he'd made it back to London but didn't know where he might be now. He'd sent her a cryptic message at the end of a transmission a few months after she'd left him in Verdun. 'Falcon home. Stay safe, my little bird.' She knew it was from him. He hadn't sent any other messages. She didn't hear from him again.

Nicolette hadn't had contact with her mother in all the time she'd been in France. She knew she would create a stir when she turned up on the doorstep, as she planned to do shortly. She'd have to be fully debriefed at HQ first, but after that, she presumed she'd be free to visit her family before being given another mission. Britain was experiencing some dark days, and the war showed no signs of ending soon. She knew she'd be sent back to France in the New Year but had no idea where she might be needed most.

The captain helped her ashore and handed her to a young woman who took her to the railway station. 'I hope you have a safe journey, miss,' her escort said as she left her boarding a train for Dublin.

Nicolette savoured the feeling of safety. No German soldiers were waiting to question her every move. She was free to speak English without fear of being overheard and arrested. She was free. She allowed herself to wallow in the unfamiliar sensation. She'd lived under a cloud of constant anxiety for such a long time that the sense of freedom was intoxicating. She smiled and couldn't stop smiling for most of the journey. She travelled through beautiful, green countryside, and she wasn't afraid that every tree or hedgerow hid German soldiers. When she caught sight of her smiling reflection in the train window, she grinned even wider. Freedom felt wonderful.

After five or six hours, the train eventually pulled into Dublin station, where she knew that HQ had arranged for someone to meet her. She'd been hoping it might be her pilot officer but realised that would be too much to expect. She gazed out at the busy platform but didn't see anyone she recognised. She saw a few men in uniform, which surprised her as she knew Ireland was a neutral country. Then she realised that a good percentage of the population had crossed the Irish Sea to Britain to enlist, despite the political position of their government.

Nicolette picked up her small bag and made her way to the door of the carriage. She was about to step down to the platform when she heard her name called. The voice was familiar but at first she couldn't place it.

'Nicky, over here!'

Then she saw him. Joseph looked taller than when she'd last seen him, but he looked years older. His eyes had dark circles, and his cheeks were leaner than she remembered. She couldn't believe he was there. He was expecting her. Why was he here? Why was Joseph meeting her? She began to worry that he was bringing bad news from home. Had something happened to her mother, to her aunt? All these thoughts flashed through her mind in an instant, and then she jumped from the train and was running along the platform. She flung herself into her brother's arms and clung to him tightly with tears rolling down her cheeks.

'What a welcome!' He hugged her, and then held her at arm's length. 'Why the tears?' He laughed. 'Aren't you happy to see me?'

'You've got no idea, Joseph.' She gazed into his mature looking face. 'But why are you here?'

'A friend of yours sent me. It seems you have friends in very high places.'

'Pilot Officer Brown?' She hoped James might have managed to pull some strings for Joseph to come to Ireland.

'Who?' Joseph had obviously not heard that name before. 'Come on, Sis. I've been given the loan of a car to take us to the airfield. We can talk on the way, where we won't be overheard.'

Joseph took her bag, and she linked her arm through his. He took her to a large, black Bentley parked by the kerb and opened the door for her.

'My goodness, we are travelling in style,' she said as she slipped into the luxurious interior.

'Courtesy of a friend of an old acquaintance of yours, I believe.' Joseph told her as he jumped in the driver's seat.

'I can't think who!' She was intrigued.

'Do you remember Group Captain Brendon?' Joseph started the engine, glanced over his shoulder and pulled away from the railway station. 'He said to remind you of your time in Scotland. That's where he first met you, apparently.'

'Wing Commander Brendon sent you?' Nicolette was surprised. 'Why?'

'Well, he's a group captain now. I guess he was promoted since you last saw him.'

'I guess?' She laughed at the Americanism. 'You spent too much time in America, little brother.

'I was there about a year before they sent me home. I then spent some time flying Wellingtons, but I'm working for your lot now, Sis.'

'You're an agent!' She couldn't believe what he was telling her. 'But you trained to be a pilot.'

'I *am* a pilot, silly.'

'Then you're *not* an agent. Thank goodness!' She breathed a sigh of relief.

'You sound glad that I'm not an agent. Was it really bad for you over there, Nicky?' He gave her a quick, concerned glance.

'Bad enough.' She didn't want to talk about the horrors she'd been through. 'What about you? What are you doing for the SOE?'

'I drop the agents and equipment to the boys on the ground.'

'How did you get into that game?' she asked.

'Same way as you, I suppose.' He shrugged. 'I was flying Wellingtons out of a base in Yorkshire. We got shot down over Belgium, but most of us managed to parachute out of the crate before it hit the ground.'

'Oh, Joseph! What happened?'

'We had help from some very brave men and women.' He glanced sideways at her. 'We spent weeks, ducking and diving from one place to the next. I think it helped that I can speak French like a native. I talked my way out of a few scrapes; I can tell you. I even chatted with the Gestapo at one point but I managed to fool them, and they let me go.'

'You make it sound like a holiday, Joseph. I know how scared you must have been.'

'I've never been so afraid in my life, Nicky.'

'Does Mum know what you went through?'

'Of course not, silly moo. Why would I go worrying the old dear with stories like that? She's been worried enough about you. Two years and nothing but a few typed messages from you. She's always complaining that WAAF's don't get leave. Anyway,' he went on, 'When I made it back to Blighty, I was called in to see your group captain friend. He'd heard what I'd done, and he offered me a job.'

'Did he tell you about me?'

'He asked whether I was any relation. Armaud isn't exactly a common name in England, is it?'

'What did he say when you told him I was your sister?'

'Not much. He didn't tell me what you were doing. I had no idea you were in France, Nicky. I didn't know until this morning. I got a message from HQ yesterday, to tell me to report to Biggin Hill for a special assignment.'

'Am I your special assignment?' She was amazed.

'By order of the group captain himself.' Joseph turned to grin at her. 'You're very highly thought of, Sister. What have you been doing to earn such first class treatment from the big boys?'

'My job.' She laughed but didn't know what to make of it. 'All this fuss! I can't believe it.'

'I hear you've been mentioned in despatches. You must have done something special, Nicky.' He smiled and raised his eyebrows. 'Though, I suspect you won't be able to talk about it.'

She thought back over the last two years to try to pick one mission where she might have earned the honour but couldn't think of one. She shrugged. 'I'm not sure why I would be singled out. I worked in a team.'

'Perhaps the group captain will tell you more when you see him this evening.'

'So soon?'

'We'll be flying back to England in an hour. I'm your pilot, so you'll be safe as houses.' He chuckled. 'Well, as safe as a house can be these days. You should see London! It's a mess, Nicky.'

'I know about Uncle Edwin getting bombed out. Is he still living at Mum's house?' She wondered whether Collette and her uncle were living as a couple by now but didn't want to ask Joseph for intimate details.

'Last time I saw them they seemed happy together. I'm sure there's something going on there, Sis. Don't know what Aunt Flissy will think when she gets back but I'm betting there'll be fireworks.'

'Is she coming home?'

'Aunt Flissy?'

'Who else, silly!'

'Isn't she somewhere in North Africa?' Joseph asked.

'That's where she was the last time I spoke with Mum, but that was two years ago.' She felt odd now, referring to Collette as her mother when she knew the truth.

'Mum is going to be so happy to see you, Nicky. I was sworn to secrecy. I couldn't tell her I was coming to get you. Had to keep it to myself and it wasn't easy, I can tell you. I was glad she was still in bed when I left this morning. The group captain would have had my guts for garters if I'd so much as mentioned your name.'

'You stayed at Mum's last night?' She thought it strange, to hear about something so natural and ordinary.

'It seemed sensible. It's only an hour's drive away from Biggin, and I have a motorbike now.'

She felt she'd fallen asleep and woken in a strange reality. Hearing Joseph speaking about home, their mother and normal, everyday things, seemed a whole universe away from the life she'd been living for the last two years.

'Why don't you close your eyes, Nicky?' Joseph suggested. 'You look exhausted and we have almost an hour before we get to the airport.'

'I still have so many questions, and it seems ages since I saw you. I don't think I could sleep; I'm too excited.'

'Questions can wait, Sis. Close your eyes.'

She did as she was told and was soon drifting away, lulled by the throb of the engine on the expensive car. She didn't think she'd been asleep for more than a few minutes before she was roused.

'We're here, Nicky.'

Nicolette jerked and opened her eyes. She was instantly awake and reaching for her pistol. It took her a few seconds to understand where she was, and then she relaxed.

'Come and see the crate they gave me to bring you home.' He guided her across the concrete pan to a grassy area where a small plane sat alone.

'I've been in one of those.' Nicolette recognised the plane she flew in when she was dropped into France.

'The Lysander is one of my favourite crates to fly.' Joseph patted the fuselage and opened the door. 'She handles like a dream. Hop in.'

'Will we be wearing parachutes?'

'I have some, but we shouldn't need them on this trip.' He laughed. 'I can land this plane, you know.'

'I hope so.' She chuckled. 'I've only taken off twice, once in training and once for real, and both times I made my own way down.'

'Well, this time, you'll have comfort all the way. Sit back and enjoy the ride, Sis. We'll be landing at Tangmere in a little over an hour.'

'That's where I flew from when they sent me to France.'

'It would be. That's my base.'

Nicolette was confused. She thought he'd flown out from Biggin Hill. 'Didn't you fly from Biggin Hill?'

'That's because I needed to collect this crate from there. The bigwigs are cooking something up, Nicky. Don't know what it is, but we're getting more planes and pilots on the base.'

'Best not to ask too many questions, Joseph. The less you know the better.'

'Do you know what's going on?' he asked.

'If I did, I couldn't tell you.' She grinned and watched him check his instruments. She had no idea what was being planned, but she hoped she'd get to see her family before they sent her back to France.

Chapter 24: Old friends

The debriefing lasted two days. She'd answered hundreds of questions, and studied dozens of maps, pointing out strategic German locations, giving additional information where she could.

She listed the operations she'd been in and the ones that she organised others to do. Nicolette was proud to report that she had discovered the informer and Group Captain Brendon was pleased that the resistance was now using Lissette against the Germans.

'We have had no significant leaks of information since you uncovered the traitor. It's a great shame you couldn't identify her sooner, Armaud. Our first concentrated attacks on the Normandy coast in forty-two were disastrous because the enemy were waiting for us. We suspect your informer was responsible for the death of thousands of men.'

'I know, sir. I wish I had discovered the evil woman earlier. It took me months to even consider her because she is the wife of one of the leaders of the underground. She was above suspicion. That's why she got away with it for so long.'

'What about her husband? Can he be trusted?'

'Marcus is a good man, sir. I'd trust him with my life.' She went on to explain, 'It's not too difficult for him to keep up the pretence of normality with his wife, sir. They don't have the best of relationships.' She remembered the rows she'd witnessed between the couple. 'I think he would have killed her himself when we found out if I hadn't suggested we could use her.'

'Mm.' The group captain stroked his moustache. 'Well, now, Armaud. I know you're eager to see your family, but we'd like you to hang around for an extra day. We're sending some men into your area, and we'd like you to talk to them before they go. Give them a heads-up on the terrain, the people, the enemy, that sort of thing.'

'I'd be happy to, sir.'

'Your brother is still in camp, I believe.'

'Yes, sir.' She'd had breakfast with Joseph earlier.

'I take it he knows nothing of your exploits, Armaud.'

'No, sir. He didn't ask, and I didn't tell him.'

'Keep it that way, Armaud.'

'Of course, sir.'

'Good. That will be all for now. Get yourself some lunch.'

'Thank you, sir.'

She left the group commander's office feeling deflated. She'd been hoping she could leave immediately after the meeting to travel home. Now she would have to stay here at Tangmere for an extra night. Christmas was almost here, and she'd hoped to be with her family for the holiday.

'Knickers!' A voice boomed from the stairwell. 'Is that you?'

She glanced over the banister. 'Lanky!' She grinned at the tall man. 'What are you doing here?'

'If I told you, I'd have to kill you!' he called, laughing.

She ran down the stairs and hugged him.

'What have I done to deserve this?' he asked, holding her at arm's length.

'I'm just happy to see a friendly face.'

'Well, I can make you even happier. Come and see the rest of the lads.'

'Are they all here?' She followed him out of the building. 'What about Bones? How is he?'

'Bones is doing fine, thanks to you, Knickers.' Lanky punched her gently in the shoulder. 'He's all fixed and training youngsters to follow in our footsteps.'

'He's not with you?' She was disappointed that she wouldn't see Bones. 'What about the others?'

'See for yourself.' Lanky took her into the mess hall and shouted, 'On your feet, lady present.'

A voice called from the back of the room, 'That's no lady! That's our Knickers!'

She was surrounded by a sea of uniform and received hugs and slaps on her back from the group of air force commandos she'd trained with. Eventually, she sat with them, gazing happily at their familiar faces. She noticed a few were missing, and asked, 'Where's the sergeant and Beaky?'

Lanky sighed and looked at his feet. 'They bought it in forty-two, Bing and Baldy were injured at the same shindig. They're doing fine, but they're both out of the mob now. Mac took a bullet to the head a few months ago in Africa.'

Nicolette allowed the news of her friends' deaths and injuries to sink in. 'I'm sorry to hear that.'

'We got replacements.' Ginger's voice was cheery. 'Come and meet Vera, Charlie and Brick.'

Nicolette forced a smile on her face to greet the newer members of the group. There was little time to mourn the loss of life in war. 'Don't tell me!' She held a hand up. 'Let me guess. Can Vera sing?'

'Like a canary.' Vera laughed.

She saw a small man with a moustache like Hitler's. 'That has to be Charlie; he looks like Charlie Chaplin.'

'Well, we couldn't call him Hitler, could we?' Deadly called out. 'I said he should shave it off, but he won't have it. Says it'll help if he ever gets caught, he can tell them he's the Fuhrer!'

Nicolette laughed with the rest of them. She scanned the other faces until she saw another unfamiliar face. The man was large, and she got the impression he would be a force to be reckoned with, in a tussle. 'You must be Brick, but why would they call you that?'

Ginger called, 'Because he's built like a brick shi—.'

Deadly interrupted him. 'Lady present, Ginger!'

'That's no lady,' Ginger grinned, and the others joined in with, 'That's our Knickers!'

'I can't believe you are all here. It's so good to see you.' She felt she'd been surrounded by family.

Someone coughed behind her, and the airmen all came to attention. She turned to see who had joined them and was about to snap to attention too, but instead, caught her breath and brought her hand to her throat. She swallowed. Her instincts were urging her to throw herself into his arms, but her training, and her sense of duty made her straighten her shoulders and salute.

'At ease men.' Pilot Officer Brown ordered. 'As you were.'

Nicolette felt his eyes boring into hers. She couldn't believe he was standing in front of her. She drank in the sight of him. He looked thinner. She saw a hint of grey at his temples. Was that a scar on his throat? Her heart raced, and she tried to calm her breathing.

'I see you still can't control that blush, Armaud.'

'Sorry, sir.' She found her voice. 'I'm still working on it.'

'Can I steal her away for a few minutes?' He addressed her friends.

'You're the boss, sir.' Lanky pointed out.

'I won't keep her long. She'll be briefing you this afternoon so you'll be seeing her again soon.'

'You're our briefing agent?' Taff asked and let his mouth fall open. 'You've been in Normandy?'

'Two years straight.' She boasted over her shoulder and followed the officer from the mess hall.

When they were outside, Nicolette shivered. The dark, December day was cold and frost sparkled on the ground.

'Let's get back inside quickly. It's freezing out here.' The officer guided her to a long, low hut at the other side of a patch of concrete. 'This is the briefing room.' He stood aside to allow her to enter first, and then stepped inside and closed the door. 'We need to go through the brief together. Those men will be dropping into Normandy, near Lisieux, in a few days. It's up to you and me to let them know what they might expect from the locals.'

She gazed around the long room. A chalkboard filled one wall at the far end, and the floor of the room held rows of chairs.

The officer turned to face her. 'I'm sure you'll have lots to tell them.'

She hesitated. Things were happening too quickly. She couldn't take it in. Was this the same man that had kissed her in the orchard in Verdun? Two years ago she'd been in the arms of this man. Two days ago she'd been in a war zone. It didn't seem real.

'Where have you been?' She reached to touch the pink line on his throat. 'I've been so worried about you.'

'Not nearly as worried as I have been about you, Nicolette.' His hand reached for hers. 'You've been in so much danger. When I heard about Anna, I thought they might have taken you too.'

'They would have if Marcus hadn't held me back.' She felt tears sting her eyes. She still couldn't think of Anna's death without feeling a knot of bitter anger inside her.

She felt his warm arms wrap around her, and his head dropped onto her shoulder. 'You're safe, now.'

'So are you.' She hugged him fiercely. 'Though, I suspect we'll be sent back soon.'

'What makes you say that?' He lifted his head to look into her eyes. 'Has someone been talking?'

She shook her head. 'I can read the signs. There's something big in the air.'

'That doesn't mean you'll be part of it.' He stroked her hair. 'I'll do everything in my power to keep you safe on British soil.'

She pulled away from him. 'And I'll fight you tooth and nail to get back to France.'

'Why?' He sounded shocked.

'I want to be there to see my job through to the end. Surely you can understand that?' She couldn't explain her reasons any simpler. 'You can't deny me the satisfaction of seeing the Germans defeated.'

'You think that will happen soon?'

'It has to.' She pulled away from his embrace to pace the floor behind the rows of seats. 'We can't let them win. If they ever bring their brand of brutality to these shores…' She let the words hang between them. 'We have to stop them, James. I have to be a part of that. You can't stop me.'

'I can see I couldn't stop you if I tried, Nicolette.' He stepped closer to her. 'Though, all I want to do is keep you safe.'

'I feel the same way about you, James but our lives are not important. Nothing else matters if we can help bring this horror to end.'

'Your time in France has changed you, Nicolette. You seem harder.'

She reached to cup his face in her hands. 'I'm not hard, James. I'm just more realistic. I know we are both lucky to have survived so far, and we'll be pushing that luck to go back, but we have to, don't we?'

He nodded. 'You're right, I know, but…'

She put a finger to his lips to stop him speaking and then touched his throat. 'What happened there?' She traced her finger along the thin pink scar.

'I almost got my throat cut, but my attacker got a blade in his stomach and decided against taking my life.'

'Oh, James.' She pulled him closer. 'I couldn't bear to lose you.'

'So you do know how I feel, then?' His tone was lighter. 'I was beginning to think I'd imagined those words we said in Verdun.'

'What words were those?' She teased. She remembered each word as if they'd spoken only yesterday.

'I believe we spoke of love.' He nuzzled her ear, and his lips moved in small kisses, over her cheek to her mouth.

She pressed herself against him, drowning in the feel of his mouth on hers. Her body responded instantly, filling her with a longing for more of him.

His hands dropped to cup her buttocks, and she pressed herself against his hardness. Her hands raked through his hair, and she threw her head back when he kissed her throat.

She wanted to give herself to him completely. She'd never made love properly with any man. She'd never felt such intensity of passion until this moment. The inexperienced fumbles with Robert had been nothing compared to this fire in her insides. James was at the centre of her being. She needed him to take things further.

213

'How long do we have?' she asked him.

He lifted his head and stared into her eyes. 'We shouldn't be disturbed for an hour or so.' He paused, sighed, and then pulled away from her. 'But we do have to prepare for the briefing session.'

'James, I, I...' She didn't know how to put her feelings into words.

'I know, my darling, I feel the same and if things were different...'

'You mean, if you weren't an officer or if we weren't at war.' She offered.

'Both of those things and much more.'

'Such as?' She wanted to understand his reluctance. She had been prepared to let him take her and couldn't quite understand why he was backing off.

'I hope one day we'll have all the time in the world to complete what we just started.'

'What if we don't?' she asked. 'What if one of us doesn't make it? Won't you regret not taking things further?'

'If I die, you will meet someone else, eventually. Won't it be better for you if you don't have the memory of a fumbled session in a wooden hut to compare him with?'

'And if I die?'

'Then I'll remember the sweetest love I ever knew.'

'But I want you so badly.' She confessed. 'Don't you want me, too?'

'More than anything but it wouldn't be fair to you.'

Nicolette began to pace again. The boiling emotions he'd created in her body were beginning to subside a little. She couldn't understand his reasons. Life was precious and all too often cut short. She wanted to take what she could from life if she were destined to die soon, but she had to respect his feelings.

Reluctantly, she pasted a smile on her face and turned to him. 'Pity, I was beginning to enjoy myself.' She grinned impishly.

'Behave yourself, Armaud. You could get me into serious trouble.'

'You told me once I'd be worth it.'

'You are. Believe me!' His smile melted her insides. 'But we have a war to win.'

Chapter 25: Home for Christmas

Nicolette and her brother were both granted leave for Christmas and travelled from Tangmere to Thames Ditton on the train together. Their mother was expecting Joseph but they'd decided to keep Nicolette's visit a surprise.

She raised her hand to knock on the door but Joseph stopped her.

'Let's sing some carols,' her brother suggested. 'Then they'll answer the door and get the surprise of their lives.'

They quickly decided on Away in a Manger and broke into song. Nicolette was nervous. She would have to pretend that she knew nothing about the secret of her birth. If she said anything, she would have to explain how she had managed to speak to her grandmother in France when she was supposed to have been on the south coast. She'd become a good liar in the last two years. She would have to rely on her experience in the field to get her through the next few days without letting anything slip.

She hid behind Joseph, as they'd planned, when the door opened. Collette sprang to embrace her son.

'Oh, it's so good to see you again so soon, Joseph. I'm glad they let you home for Christmas.' Then she noticed Nicolette and screeched. 'Oh, Mon Dieu! Edwin!' she called. 'Nicolette is home!'

Nicolette felt Collette's arms enfold her in a bear hug. 'Where have you been? Why didn't you visit? Two years with barely a word and here you are! I can't believe it. Come in! Come in!' She ushered them inside and continued berating Nicolette. 'Elsie's daughter seems to come home on leave every two minutes and you can't manage a single visit in two years! Don't you think I worry about you? Don't we deserve to know what you're doing? Where you are? Who your friends are? Two years and all we got were a few cryptic messages that could have come from anywhere and have been written by anyone. You never answer my questions—.'

'Mum!' Nicolette interrupted. 'Stop! You're like a runaway train!'

'Can you blame me?' Collette stood in the kitchen and stared at Nicolette. 'You look different. You cut your hair. You've lost weight. You—.'

Joseph intervened. 'Mum, will you at least let us take our coats off before you start lecturing us. Nicolette has travelled a long way to be here. I think a cup of tea would be nice, don't you?'

Edwin sprang to his feet and pulled Nicolette into his arms. 'I thought I was seeing things for a second. Is it really you?' He drew back to look at her face. 'You look more like your Aunt Flissy with short hair,' he commented.

Nicolette glanced at her mother, searching for a reaction, but Collette turned her back and began to fill the kettle.

'I'm sorry, Mum,' she began. 'I should have written more.'

'You can say that again!' Collette huffed and clattered some teacups. 'I wasn't sure whether you were receiving my letters. You never answered them.'

'They keep us pretty busy, Mum.' She knew it was a poor excuse, but she couldn't offer any other.

'Well, she's here now, Mum.' Joseph went to put his arm around Collette. 'Can't you just be happy that we can spend Christmas together?'

'Perhaps,' Collette said grudgingly. 'But you have some explaining to do, Nicolette. I want to know everything.'

'If she told you, she'd have to kill you.' Joseph joked and then blushed. 'Careless talk and all that,' he quipped.

'Have you been involved in something we shouldn't know about?' Edwin asked.

Nicolette stared at the floor, and then gave her brother an exasperated sigh. 'Why did you have to say anything?'

'Don't you worry, Nicky.' Edwin pulled out a kitchen chair and gestured for her to sit. 'We're not going to ask you any more questions, my love.'

'I couldn't answer if you did, Uncle Edwin.' She flopped onto the hard chair. 'You already know too much, thanks to Joseph.' She glared at her brother.

'Well, at least I got them to back off, Sis.' Joseph pulled out a chair and sat beside his sister. 'You know what Mum's like. She wouldn't have given up until you confessed all. She's like the Gestapo once she gets going.'

Nicolette smirked. 'No, Joseph, she's worse than any Gestapo I've ever met.'

Collette whirled from the stove. 'You haven't!'

'No, Mum.' Nicolette lied. 'I've never had the misfortune to meet a member of Hitler's SS. My duties are a little more mundane than that.'

'I'd love to know what you do, Nicolette.' Collette placed the teapot on the table. 'Do you receive secret messages from the front?

Are you involved in deciphering secret codes and sending important information?'

'Now, Collette.' Edwin warned. 'That's enough. The poor girl can't talk about what she does. Leave it at that.'

'She can write about the ordinary things in her life. What stopped you from telling us what you were doing outside of your duties? I presume you have a social life?'

'Not much of one, Mum.' She spooned some sugar into her tea.

'Steady with that,' Collette moved the sugar bowl away from Nicolette's spoon. 'We don't have much to spare.'

'Sorry, I didn't think.' Nicolette dropped the spoon into her saucer.

Collette snapped, 'Don't you have rationing where you've been stationed?'

'Of course.' Nicolette didn't know what else to say. 'I'm sorry.'

Collette sighed. 'I'm sorry too. It's been such a surprise to see you after all this time. I've been so worried about you. Two years with no word from you! What was I supposed to think?'

'Now, Collette. That's not exactly true.' Edwin jumped to Nicolette's defence. 'We have had some letters.'

'Two typed lines every few months with stupid messages! "Dear Mum, I'm fine. They're feeding me well and I've been to a dance". I ask you? What's a mother supposed to make of that?'

'I'm sorry, Mum.' Nicolette was running out of excuses. 'I couldn't write. I can't tell you why. You'll just have to take my word for it.'

'So I was right! Those letters didn't come from you?'

'No, Mum. They didn't come from me.'

Collette's face drained of colour. 'Then where have you been, Nicolette? Even Felicity is allowed to write home from somewhere in Italy. We got a Christmas card from her.'

'Flissy is in Italy? How is she?' Nicolette grasped the change of subject eagerly. 'I thought she was in North Africa.'

'Well, after Rommel got a beating, Monte thought he'd give the German army a run for their money in Italy.' Edwin told her. 'Don't you know about the war in Italy?' He looked puzzled. 'Where have you been? We've been following the progress of our boys on the radio for the last six months.'

'As I said!' She shook her head in frustration and stared at her tea. 'I've been busy.'

'Sorry, love.' Edwin reached to squeeze her hand. 'It's difficult not to ask questions. I'll try harder not to ask you anything else.'

'Is anyone hungry?' Joseph asked. 'I could get us some fish and chips.'

'The chippy was bombed last week, Joseph,' said Collette. 'I could do you some Spam fritters.'

'Spam fritters sounds wonderful, Mum.' Nicolette felt her mouth watering. 'We haven't eaten since breakfast.'

Collette sprang to her feet. 'Why didn't you say so?' She reached into cupboards and began to prepare a meal. 'Here we are talking in riddles about secrets we have no business in knowing and you're both starving!'

Edwin chuckled. 'That's more like it, Collette.'

After they'd eaten, Edwin suggested taking Joseph for a drink at a pub three streets away that had survived the bombing so far.

Collette looked disappointed. 'Couldn't we all go?' she asked.

'I thought you might like some time with Nicolette.' Edwin looked a little cagey. 'You might have some things to discuss without us men listening in.'

'Such as?' Nicolette looked at her mother.

'I'll tell Joseph over a pint.' Edwin hustled Joseph from the kitchen. 'We'll see you later.'

Nicolette watched them leave and turned to Collette. 'What's going on, Mum?'

Collette sighed and began to clear the table. 'You're not the only one with secrets, Nicolette.'

'If you're referring to you and Edwin getting together, you told me about that the last time I was home.'

'But you don't know that Flissy wrote to give us her blessing, do you?'

Nicolette was astonished. 'She did what?'

'She and Edwin are getting a divorce. When it's finalised, we can marry.'

'I don't believe this!' Nicolette felt the rug had been pulled from under her. 'What will people think?'

'We don't care what people think, Nicolette.' Collette began to wash the dishes. 'It is our life and we will do as we wish.'

'What about poor Aunt Felicity?'

'Oh, don't you go feeling sorry for your aunt, Nicolette.' Collette rattled the pots through the water with more vigour. 'She knows she did us both a disservice by making a play for Edwin all those years ago. She took long enough to come to her senses but now she admits that she didn't really love him, after all.'

'She said that?' Nicolette was incredulous.

'Well, not in so many words, but Edwin knows their marriage was not the happiest. I think Flissy wanted children and was always disappointed that she couldn't have them. She blamed Edwin, you see.'

'Yes, I can see why she would.' Nicolette mused aloud without thinking.

Collette paused in her enthusiastic dishwashing. 'Well, it could have been either one of them, you know.'

'But we both know that's not true, don't we?' Nicolette decided to come clean with her mother. 'Haven't there been enough secrets in this family, Mum?' She went to take Collette's wet hands and brought her to sit at the table. 'Or should I call you, Aunt Collette?'

'What are you saying?'

'I can't tell you how or why, Mum, but you'll just have to take my word for it. I know about Aunt Felicity's affair with the Australian doctor. I know that I'm her child and that you took me as yours. I know all about the secrecy and the reasons you thought you owed her.'

'Did Belle tell you?'

Nicolette shook her head. 'Elizabeth explained everything.'

'Oh, no!' Collette put her head in her hands. 'Did she disinherit you?'

Nicolette laughed. 'No, of course, she didn't, though I thought she might.'

'Did she tell you after Belle's funeral?'

Nicolette thought for a few moments and nodded.

'So you've kept this to yourself all this time?'

She shrugged. 'We had enough drama going on at the time, didn't we?'

'I suppose so.' Collette glanced up. 'What with Belle's funeral and you breaking up with Robert.' Collette gasped. 'Oh, you won't know about him, will you?'

'About Robert?' Nicolette felt her heart skip a beat. 'Is he all right?'

'Yes, he's fine. He was home on leave in the summer. He called around to let us know that he'd got married. I think his wife had a baby last month.'

219

'He didn't waste any time.' Nicolette didn't know whether to feel cross or happy for her ex-fiancé.

'Well, you made it clear that you didn't want him, Nicolette. What did you expect?'

'I'm glad he's happy, Mum.'

'Are you happy, Nicolette? Is there anyone special in your life?'

Nicolette thought about mentioning her feelings for James but didn't want to tempt fate. Any relationship they hoped to share would have to wait until after the war.

'You look so sad, my love.' Collette squeezed Nicolette's hands. 'I always loved you as my own, Nicolette. I hope you know that.'

'I do, Mum.' Nicolette hugged the woman she had always known as her mother. 'Nothing will change there. You're my mum as much as you're Joseph's mum and he's my brother and always will be.'

'Does he know?'

'No.'

'Will you tell him?' Collette looked concerned.

'Not if you don't want me to.' Nicolette realised that no good purpose would be served by telling her brother that he was not her brother but her cousin.

'Thank you.'

'So Uncle Edwin will be our stepfather?'

'He's always been like a father to you both, nothing will change there, either.' Collette smiled.

Chapter 26: Murder

Christmas passed too quickly, and Nicolette reported back to Tangmere to receive her orders. She barely had time to process the changes in her family relationships. Not only was her mother her aunt, and her aunt was her mother, but her uncle would soon be her stepfather. The confusion was too much to take in. She'd think about the future of her family dynamics when she was sure a future existed for her.

Joseph was already flying missions, dropping supplies over Normandy to her friends on the ground. Group Commander Brendon had briefed her on the basics of what was to come and, although she was nervous, she was determined to play her part.

She was sent back to the New Forest for further training in advanced combat techniques and to brush up on her knowledge of German insignias of rank.

'Do we know who my target will be?' she asked her trainer.

'He might seem inconsequential, Armaud, but we need to take him out.'

'I've never done anything like this before. I'm not sure I can carry it off,' she admitted.

'That's not what I heard, Armaud.' The officer grinned. 'I read your file. That stunt you pulled at the International branch of Barclays in London was a classy piece of work. You're a natural.' Her trainer handed her a gun disguised as a pen. 'And you're as accurate with this as you are with a rifle. You'll have no problem shooting your way out of any compromise.'

'I hope you're right.' She took the concealed weapon and put it in her handbag. 'At least I look the part, thanks to your people at Borehamwood.'

He took a long, slim blade and twisted the short, enamelled handle. The handle flared into half-a-dozen, razor-sharp spikes. He twisted again to re-align the spikes into the slim blade and inserted it into a tube of satin in the centre of a cluster of feathers adorning a small hat. The decorative handle became part of the design. 'Ingenious invention, don't you think?'

'Very clever.' She took the hat and pinned it to her hair.

'I've never seen a more stylish French Mademoiselle.'

She looked in the full-length mirror and swayed from side to side. 'I hardly recognise myself.'

'That's the general idea, Armaud. The first part of your mission is to attract attention, is it not?'

'Well, I can see I won't be a shrinking violet, that's for sure.' She felt the flutter of nerves in her tummy as she thought about what she had been tasked to do.

'Your good looks and natural charm will get you through the door, Armaud.' The officer assured her. 'If you were a plain Jane, you wouldn't stand a chance of getting close to the target. Indeed, you wouldn't have been considered for the mission.'

'Getting close won't be the problem.' She admitted. 'It's the getting away after the deed is done, that worries me.'

The officer looked at her with sympathy. 'We already discussed that this could be a one-way mission, Armaud.'

She nodded and swallowed.

'You have the cyanide pill safe?'

'Yes, sir.' She touched her jacket collar where the suicide pill was concealed in the seam.

'I hope you don't have to use it, Armaud.' The officer took a deep breath. 'You must try to organise a window of escape before you make your move. Give yourself time, Armaud. Play your man and make him trust you. This isn't a race. Take as long as you need to do the job. If you need a day or a week, it's all the same to HQ, but you must get him before he can pass on his suspicions about Rommel.'

Nicolette nodded.

'We know he has tried to blackmail Rommel. His greed has given us valuable time. Gruppenführer Cramer has given the Field Marshall a fortnight to get the money together.'

'So I have a week left, to complete the mission.'

'At the very most.'

They'd been over the plan of attack many times in the last few days. She knew the name of every officer under the target's command and could recognise each of them by their photographs. The Gruppenführer held vital information about Rommel, and it was only a matter of time before he took that information to his superiors.

It had recently been discovered that Rommel was involved in an assassination plot against Hitler. If Rommel and his group were successful, Hitler's death would bring about the end of the war much sooner than anticipated, and with the minimum amount of bloodshed. Nicolette's target had discovered Rommel's plot and was threatening to make it public knowledge unless Rommel paid him a vast amount of money.

She had to get close enough to the target to kill him. If she could do it without anyone else noticing, all the better but if not she would have to kill the man quickly and make her escape or take the suicide pill. It would be up to her, and her alone, to make the decision.

Nicolette tried to slow her breathing. She felt more uncomfortable with every passing minute. Her expensive skirt and jacket were becoming wrinkled under her flying suit. Sweat soaked the silk blouse she wore. The inside of the Lysander was freezing, but her teeth were chattering from nerves more than from the cold.

'Are you ready?' the young airman asked. 'Target in three minutes.'

She checked her canvas bag for the tenth time since take off. It contained everything she would need for the next week or so. Anything else would have to be provided by Marcus or Fabien on the ground. With no time to waste, she was to be taken straight to a café in Lisieux where she would make herself conspicuous to the German officers who frequented the place. Her friends in the resistance had sent messages to assure her that she would have the best chance of meeting her target there tonight.

They'd been watching Gruppenführer Cramer closely and recording his habits. They noticed he had an eye for the ladies, though local French girls were suspicious of encouraging his advances, fearing reprisals from their neighbours. He frequented the same café three or four nights of the week and his favourite drink was cognac.

'Time to go.' The airman tugged her ropes to make sure they were secure. 'Good luck.'

She launched herself into the black night and felt the yank of her parachute opening. She glanced up to check the canopy was fully opened, and then looked down. She bent her knees and scanned the ground rushing to meet her. Then she was rolling, gathering the ropes of her chute as fast as she could.

'Lucille!' A familiar accent called softly.

'Marcus? Is that you?' She was never happier to hear his voice.

He hurried towards her with two other men.

'Hello, Rene.' Nicolette greeted her young friend. 'I'll leave my chute in your capable hands.'

'Go, Lucille and Godspeed.' The young man relieved her of the ropes and flapping canopy.

'Hurry, we don't have long.' Marcus took her elbow, and they ran to a waiting truck. 'The café will close in one hour. We can't risk breaking the curfew.'

'Is he there? Do you know?'

'He was there earlier. He usually stays until closing time. Are you ready?'

'I will be.'

She kicked off her heavy boots and put them into the cab of the truck Then she inspected the silk stockings. Fortunately, they were unscathed. She smoothed the skirt of her suit and straightened the jacket before climbing into the truck.

'Need a cigarette?' Marcus offered her one that he'd just lit.

'Thanks, I will.' She took the glowing stick and drew some smoke deep into her chest. As she exhaled the calming vapours, she said, 'That's better.'

He started the engine and pulled onto the dirt road. 'Take the packet; I think you'll need these more than I will tonight.'

'Thanks, Marcus.' She took them and put the packet in her bag.

'Can you do something with your hair?' Marcus grinned. 'Jumping from the plane did you no favours.'

'Do I look a fright?'

'Perhaps a little dishevelled and pale. Maybe we should wait until tomorrow and give you more time to compose yourself.'

'No, we have to get things moving.' She emptied the contents of her canvas bag into her lap. She dragged a comb through her short, curly hair and reached for the small, feathered hat. She pinned the hat in place and opened a compact. 'There, that's better.' She took another pull on the cigarette and handed it back to Marcus. 'A touch of rouge and lipstick and I'll be fine.'

'What about shoes?'

'I have them here.' She pulled out a pair of high-heeled courts.

As the truck entered the outskirts of Lisieux, she lifted an arm to check her body odour. 'Wish I'd brought some perfume.'

'You smell fine, Lucille.' Marcus assured her. 'The German pigs will not notice a little perspiration.'

'I hope you're right.'

German guards stopped them at the first checkpoint. Marcus handed over his papers and joked with the guards. 'My niece thought she could avoid the curfew by spending the night at her boyfriend's house.'

The German soldier gave Nicolette the once over and smirked. She lifted her chin defiantly, acting the part of a chastised young girl.

'You'll have to watch her, old man. She'll run rings around you if you're not careful.' The German laughed and handed the papers back to Marcus.

Nicolette sighed with relief when he started the engine and moved on. 'How did you get the paperwork to make me your niece?'

'I've had these since your first visit. Always pays to have a back-up policy, Lucille.'

'How many more policies do you have?'

'I have three for you. After this mission is completed, you will be my nephew for the journey out of town.'

'I couldn't pass as a man!' she protested.

'You'll have to. The town will be crawling with Gestapo looking for an elegant French lady if you are successful.'

'You know I may have to take, you know...' she had trouble finishing her sentence, but then said, 'If, if I'm compromised.' She couldn't imagine taking the suicide pill, but she would if she thought she might be captured. She couldn't risk the Germans discovering the details of her mission. She had no idea how brave she might be under torture.

'If you are careful, you'll make it back to me, Lucille.'

'I'll do my best, Marcus.'

'I'll drop you at the end of the street. You just have to walk around the corner and down the road for about fifty yards.'

'Café Noir.'

'It will be the only café open at this time of night. It will close at ten. You don't have long. Remember, this will just be the first meeting. You only need to attract his interest tonight, and then arrange another meeting with him if you get the chance.'

'I just want to get it over with.'

'Don't rush this, Lucille.' Marcus warned. 'You should leave by a quarter to the hour. They would suspect your intentions if you stayed out after curfew.'

'Thanks, Marcus.' She knew all the details by heart but appreciated the reminder from her friend. 'Will you be waiting for me?'

'I'll be right there at the rendezvous point, Lucille. I will park the truck behind the Basilica in the usual spot.' He drew the truck to a halt at the kerb. 'I'll stay there all night if I have to, but if you make it back before ten, I'll stay with you at the apartment we rented for you. They would suspect my reasons for driving on the road after ten.'

'What about Lissette? Does she know where you are?'

Marcus sneered. 'She is too easy to fool. She thinks I am robbing bread from a food convoy. I can't wait for the time when I can expose her traitorous soul to the whole of Lisieux.'

'Well, we hope that won't be too far off.' Nicolette checked her appearance one last time and opened the door of the truck.

'Take care, Lucille.' Marcus warned.

She nodded and walked on shaking legs to the corner of the street. She lifted her chin, tucked her bag under her arm and strode out, looking confident and self-assured on the outside, while her insides were contracting painfully with fear.

She saw the lights from the café spilling onto the street before she heard the sound of music. A piano was being played inexpertly, and someone was singing in German. She took a deep breath, pasted a smile on her face and pushed the door open.

She sashayed to the counter and asked for a coffee, speaking in French.

'Of course, mademoiselle.' The man behind the counter pointed over her shoulder. 'Please take a seat and I will bring it to your table.'

'Merci.' She turned from the counter and realised that most of the customers were German officers, and they were all staring at her. She smiled at one or two of them and walked towards an empty table near the wall.

One German officer jumped to pull a chair out for her.

'Merci,' she said the "thank you" in French.

'What brings such a beautiful woman here alone and so late tonight?' the German asked in slightly accented French.

'I have had a long day on the road, and I need to relax before I go home,' she explained, remembering her cover story.

'You live alone?'

'With my mother.'

'Ah!' The German officer smiled. 'Would you mind if I took a seat?'

'I have no objection.' She smiled for good measure and gazed around the room. Her target was watching the small interchange with interest. She aimed an evocative smile at him.

The waiter brought her coffee and placed it on the table. 'May I get you something, Oberführer?' he asked.

'A whisky, merci.'

'Drinking on duty, sir?' she asked in a teasing tone. 'Would your superior condone such a thing?' She looked pointedly at her target and flashed another smile at him.

'I am not on duty, mademoiselle. Gruppenführer Cramer may have the reputation of a disciplinarian, but he does allow his staff to relax from time to time.' He took out a silver cigarette case and offered her one.

'Merci.' She concentrated to stop her fingers from trembling as she reached for a cigarette. She held it to her lips, and he flicked open a silver lighter.

She drew on the cigarette and narrowed her eyes to blow out the smoke. She caught the target watching her and tilted her head a little. She turned her attention back to the officer at her table. 'This is good tobacco.'

'A perk of my rank.' He smiled.

'And what other advantages does your rank get you?' She looked at him from beneath lowered lashes and tried a sultry smile.

'The right to entertain beautiful women.' His lips curled suggestively.

'Do the perks get better the higher you climb?' She glanced at the target and quickly returned her attention to the Oberführer.

'I have no idea.' The German laughed. 'Why do you ask?'

'Because your Gruppenführer can't seem to take his eyes off me. I'm sure he's envious of you.' She leant closer to the Oberführer to whisper conspiratorially, 'He gives me the impression he would eat me for breakfast if he could.'

'I'm sure he is simply envious of my good fortune. He won't like it that I got to you first.'

'You make me sound like a prize attraction at a carnival.' Her smile was guarded this time.

'Beautiful women don't walk into our café every day, mademoiselle.' The German man's eyes glowed with interest as he stared at her. 'Don't you realise how much curiosity you have stirred just by being here?'

'I'm flattered, Oberführer.' She dimpled coquettishly.

'Seriously, though, where have you come from? Why have I not seen you before?'

'I travel around. My work takes me all over France.'

'What work do you do that gives you such a glamorous lifestyle?'

'It's not so glamorous, sir. Staying in hotels and eating the meagre rations that restaurants charge a fortune for is not an ideal way of life but I make a living.'

The waiter brought the whisky. 'Will that be all, sir?'

'Can I get you something stronger?' the German asked.

'No, thank you.' She added, 'Not this time,' to keep him interested.

'So tell me, what do you do?'

'I am a travelling saleswoman. Cosmetics are still important to French women, despite the constraints of war.'

'Fascinating.' He toyed with his glass and stared into her eyes.

Nicolette saw the target rise from his seat. She thought she might lose the opportunity to make contact. As he neared her table she reached for her cup, knocking it over.

'Oh, goodness, how clumsy of me.' She watched the coffee run into her lap and jumped back, straight into the path of her target.

Gruppenführer Cramer coughed impatiently.

'Oh, excuse me, sir.' Nicolette began brushing her hand over the wet skirt.

The Gruppenführer handed her his handkerchief. 'Would this help, mademoiselle?'

'You are too kind, merci.' She took the proffered handkerchief and dabbed at her skirt. She lifted the stained cloth and pulled an apologetic expression. 'I'm so sorry. I'm afraid your handkerchief is ruined, Gruppenführer.' She offered it back to the officer.

'Keep it.' His smile was warm. 'It is of no consequence.'

The Oberführer looked uncomfortable. Nicolette's heart was beating rapidly. She had only a few more seconds to secure the contact. 'Oberführer? Will you please introduce me to your very kind Gruppenführer?'

'I would if I knew your name, mademoiselle.'

'Forgive me.' She held out her hand to the senior officer. 'Lucille Rivard.'

After a second's hesitation, the Gruppenführer took her hand and raised it to his lips. 'A pleasure, Mademoiselle Rivard.'

She had to act quickly; time was ticking away. 'Would you care to join us, sir?' She beckoned the waiter over. 'I feel I need to make amends for ruining your lovely handkerchief.' She moved her chair to make room for another at the table. 'Please allow me to buy you a drink as recompense.'

'No need, mademoiselle.' The Gruppenführer pulled a chair close to hers. 'Your company is recompense enough.'

'I insist.' She turned to the waiter. 'Two cognacs and a whisky, please.'

'Very well.' The Gruppenführer rested his hand close to Nicolette's hand on the table. 'One drink, and then we must leave.'

'So soon?' Nicolette tried to give her attention to both men at her table, but knew she should concentrate on her target.

'The curfew, Mademoiselle Rivard.' The Oberführer glanced at his superior nervously.

'Oh, I think we can forget a silly time constraint this once.' The Gruppenführer patted Nicolette's hand. 'This beautiful woman will not be stopped by our guards while in my company. I'll ensure your safety on the streets of Lisieux, mademoiselle.'

Nicolette flirted outrageously with both men. More drinks were ordered, and she began to hold her glass in her lap, surreptitiously pouring the cognac down her leg and into her shoes so she wouldn't get drunk. She needed a clear head for what she planned to do.

She listened to the conversation when the officers spoke in German, pretending she didn't understand a word. She pouted and protested that they were rude to leave her out by not speaking in French, while, in truth, she was learning more about their opinions of the British and the German plans for France.

Close to midnight, when the café was almost empty, the Gruppenführer turned to the Oberführer and spoke in German. 'Make yourself scarce, Herman. This is my party now.'

Nicolette breathed an inward sigh of relief. She would soon be alone with her target. Now all she had to do was arrange a convenient kill zone.

The Oberführer excused himself reluctantly. He kissed her hand and nodded, curtly, to his superior. Nicolette expected him to give the Nazi salute, but instead, he stalked out of the café looking deeply annoyed.

Nicolette began to worry about Marcus waiting in the cold for her. She knew he'd be worried and would be wondering what had happened to her. He couldn't check on her because the curfew had been in force for hours, and he would be stopped, searched and questioned if he was seen on the streets.

Shortly after the Oberführer left, Nicolette realised that she and the Gruppenführer were the last remaining customers of the café. As the waiter began cleaning the tables, her fear grew. She was hoping she'd get the opportunity to complete her mission tonight, but the thought of actually killing a man filled her with dread. Would she be capable?

She was feigning intoxication and flirting outrageously with the officer who was quite drunk. He let it slip that he lived with his housekeeper. Nicolette could not afford the risk of going back to his place. She didn't want an audience if she could avoid it. If she could get the man alone in some secluded place in town, that would be all the opportunity she would need.

'You must allow me to walk you home, Lucille.' He stood, wobbled, and took hold of her chair to pull it out. 'We can't let my ambitious soldiers put you in a cell for the night, for breaking our curfew, now, can we?'

'That's very sweet of you, Gunter.' She picked up her bag and swayed towards the German officer. She put a hand on his chest and looked up into his face. 'I'm sure I will feel very safe in your delightful company.'

'Come!' He licked his lips. 'We can continue this party somewhere much more comfortable.'

'Where do you suggest?' She slurred her words and stumbled against him as he guided her from the café. 'My mother would not like it if I came home with a man. No matter that you are such a handsome fellow.'

'Not to worry, my dear.' He placed his arm around her waist to guide her down the dark street. 'My house is not far.' He squeezed her a little too hard. 'A ten-minute walk, my dear, and we can open another bottle of some good French Cognac.'

'Oh, I don't think I can wait.' She reached to touch his face and lifted her lips to his. She felt sick to her stomach but made herself kiss him with passion.

He paused, and then pushed his tongue into her mouth and groaned. He drew away and stared at her with bleary eyes. 'You are a temptress, Lucille. I could take you right here on the street.'

'You are too handsome, sir.' She snuggled close against him. 'I can't wait for you to make love to me.'

'All right, Lucille.' His eyes flared with excitement. 'We'll play it your way.' He hurried her down the street and guided her to an alleyway. As soon as they were in the darker shadows, he pushed her against the wall. 'Is this what you had in mind?' He thrust his groin at her and began to lift her skirt.

'Oh, Gunter. Yes. Yes.' She felt his hands creeping up her thighs and fought to keep control. His touch made her shudder with revulsion. 'Please don't stop,' she pleaded.

With the officer's lips dribbling wet kisses on her throat and his hands on her stocking tops, she knew she wouldn't get a better opportunity. She reached into the decoration on her hat and pulled out the slim blade. It glinted behind Gunter's head for a second before she thrust it deep into his ear and twisted the short handle.

The officer staggered backward, his hand grasping ineffectually at his ear, an expression of confusion on his face. Within seconds, his eyes and his face went blank.

Nicolette watched the Gruppenführer's eyes glaze over before he crumpled to the ground. She waited a few more seconds before checking his pulse. When she had confirmed that he was dead, she twisted the handle and pulled her weapon from his ear, wiped it on his uniform and replaced it in the decoration of her hat. She crouched low to pull his limp body closer to the wall, then checked her surroundings and got to her feet.

She took off her brandy-soaked shoes and ran in bare feet to the entrance of the alleyway. The street was clear and she hurried back the way she had come, passing the café that was now in darkness. She arrived at the rendezvous point, behind the Basilica, to find a shivering Marcus in the foot-well of the driver's side of his truck. She opened the door and climbed in, ducking low on the passenger side.

'You have blood on your hand, Lucille.' Marcus grinned.

'It is done.' She stared at the deep-red stain on her fingers and swallowed back the bile that rose in her throat.

'Now we have a choice.' Marcus said through chattering teeth. 'Should we make our way to the apartment or spend the night in the back of this truck?'

'We can't risk being caught in the curfew. Especially now. Many soldiers saw me in the café. They won't take long to work out what happened, once they find the body.'

'Where did you leave him?'

'He's in the alley at the end of the road. I pushed him up against the east wall so his body will be in the shadows until mid-morning.'

'Then we sleep in the truck and leave early.'

231

'Let me get out of these clothes first.'

Marcus kept watch while she changed from the stylish suit into the clothes he had brought with him. He then lifted a manhole cover in the pavement and thrust the bundle of clothes she gave him deep inside the sewer. Her empty handbag and shoes were thrown in too. She now wore the trousers, shirt and rough wool jacket of a peasant boy. Her face was devoid of makeup, and her blonde hair was streaked with dirt from the road to make it appear darker. She wore the cap of a working man with the peak pulled down to her eyes. She looked like a young man on his way to work in the fields.

'Come, Lucille. Let's get comfortable. The sun will rise in a few hours, and we can soon be on our way.'

They climbed into the back of the truck, and Marcus pulled the tarpaulin over them.

'Try to get some sleep, Lucille. I'll keep watch.'

'I don't think I'll ever sleep again, Marcus.'

'Come here.' He held his arm out, and she cuddled into the older man's side. 'You did well tonight, little one.'

'I can't stop shaking.'

'Hush, I'll keep you safe. You're safe now.'

Chapter 27: Reunited

They set out from the town just after the six am curfew was lifted. They were stopped at two checkpoints, but the disinterested German soldiers only gave a cursory glance at their papers. Lucille kept her head down and pretended to be asleep. Only when the town was behind them, and the rolling countryside was ahead, did she lift her tired eyes.

'We made it.' Nicolette sighed. 'Where to now, Marcus? Your place?'

He shook his head. 'Too risky. Lissette must not know that you're here. Once word gets out about what you did, she will take great pleasure in letting the Gestapo know exactly where you are.'

'But she'd be getting you and Henri into trouble too.' Nicolette didn't think the French woman would be that stupid.

'I think she hates me enough to do that now, Lucille. We can't trust her.'

'Then where are you taking me?'

'To a rendezvous with Falcon. He has made arrangements to get you far away from here.'

'Falcon?' Her heart jumped. 'I didn't know he was here.'

'He's been working south of here with some of your commandos. He tells me the end is in sight. There's to be a big operation soon. I'm told your men are preparing the ground in readiness.'

'I heard the same thing, Marcus.' Nicolette remembered briefing her friends before Christmas. Could the boys from Scotland be here too?

After two hours of bumping along dirt roads through barren fields sparkling with frost, Marcus pulled the truck into a yard surrounded by derelict buildings. Nicolette quickly scanned the immediate area and saw the barrel of a rifle pointing at them from a broken window.

'Stay put, Marcus,' she warned in a whisper. 'This could be a trap. Keep the engine running.'

She heard the click of a safety catch being released next to her passenger side window. Her instincts, coupled with her training, made her shove the door wide, knocking a soldier to the ground. She shouted to Marcus. 'Drive!'

Someone shouted from inside the building. 'Wait!'

She turned her head in time to see Lanky waving to her.

233

'Stop! Marcus,' she shouted. 'It's all right. It's our men.'

Marcus screeched the truck to a stop, and she jumped out. Deadly was limping up to the truck rubbing his shoulder and the others were beginning to appear from hiding places around the yard.

'Nice move, Knickers.' Deadly winced as he rotated his arm. 'You almost took my arm off.'

'Sorry, Deadly. Are you all right?' She went to give him a hug and was soon surrounded by the group of commandos.

'Is it really our Knickers?' Ginger asked, flicking the peasant's cap from her head. 'Oh, yes. There she is!'

The men laughed and began exchanging silly banter.

'She's had a makeover.'

'Knickers is a boy!'

'She still packs a punch!' Deadly rubbed his shoulder again.

'Oh, I didn't hurt you that badly,' she punched him on the good shoulder.

'Did you see that?' Deadly sulked and turned to his pals. 'Now I'm completely out of action!'

'Quite the commando, aren't you, Lucille?' Falcon walked towards her smiling, and it was all she could do to stop herself from running into his arms. 'How did it go?' he asked.

'Mission accomplished, sir.'

'You took him out?' He looked surprised, worried and proud all at the same time.

She nodded and swallowed. She didn't like to think about what she'd done and how she'd done it. She felt sick to her stomach and didn't trust herself to speak of the brutal murder she'd committed.

'Lucille did well, Falcon.' Marcus came to her side and put a protective arm around her shoulders. He gazed at the airmen surrounding her with suspicion.

'It's all right, Marcus. These are my friends.' She introduced him one by one to the commandos. 'I trained with them a few years ago. They're harmless,' she assured him.

'No, we're not!' The largest commando, Brick, pouted like a sullen child. 'How can she say we're harmless?'

'Well, Deadly was a pushover, wasn't he?' Nicolette laughed.

'Now, children, play nicely.' Falcon grinned at Nicolette, and she felt her insides warming.

'Could you eat something, Knickers?' Vera asked her. 'I mean, it didn't spoil your appetite or anything, did it? Killing that Nazi?'

'I could eat a horse, Vera,' she lied to keep the pretence that everything was normal and as it should be. 'What you got?'

'Hard biscuits or bully beef?' he suggested.

'No horses?' she quipped.

'Sorry, we're all out of Gee-Gees.' His lopsided grin made her smile.

'I'll pass then.' Her gaze went back to Falcon. 'What have you got planned for me next?'

His eyes glowed, and his lips twitched before he said, 'I could think of a hundred things, but you fly back to Blighty tonight.'

'Fly?' she was astounded. 'But how?' She wondered how a plane could take off from the fields here in France. 'I mean, well, yes, I mean how?'

'We made a runway over there. These boys will light the path for the aircraft to land, and you'll be taking off again immediately. We'll deal with any enemy attracted to the landing and keep them occupied until you're safely away.'

'Is there much chance of enemy soldiers coming near?' she asked.

'There is always a chance, Lucille,' Marcus said. 'We have to be prepared for anything.'

'I won't go!' She shook her head vehemently. 'I won't put you all in danger, not to mention the pilot who would risk landing here. I can still be useful to you! You can't send me back!'

'I have my orders, Lucille.' Falcon's mouth was set firm with no hint of a smile. 'HQ ordered me to send you home when your mission has been completed.'

'They won't know. You haven't had time to transmit. I could stay longer. Nothing has been arranged yet, has it?' She was grasping at straws, but she didn't want to leave just when things were beginning to come together.

'You don't understand, Lucille.' Falcon's eyes bored into hers. 'The Gestapo will be scouring the country to find you. You murdered one of their top officers. You'll be shot on sight.'

'They will be looking for the glamorous Lucille Rivard! She doesn't exist. Look at me! Do I look like a cosmetic saleswoman?'

All eyes turned to Nicolette, and the commandos began to laugh.

Even Marcus grinned and nodded. 'You have to admit she has a point, Falcon.'

'I'll cut my hair shorter. I'll walk with a swagger. I'll be a man. They'll never suspect a thing!'

'Where will you stay?' Falcon was faltering. 'Who will take responsibility for you?'

'I will,' said Marcus at the same time as some of the commandos said, 'We will.'

Nicolette grinned at her friends. 'I won't let you down.'

'Look's like I'm outvoted.' Falcon pulled Nicolette to one side and whispered, 'Do you know what you're doing?'

'Don't send me back, James. I've been part of this for so long.' She desperately wanted to touch him, to feel his warmth, but she resisted. 'You can't deny me a ringside seat for the finale.'

'It's not my decision to make, Nicolette. I have to inform HQ of your successful mission.' He stared into space, avoiding eye contact with her. 'I'll pass on your request. That's as much as I can do.'

'Tell them I know more about troop movements at the coast. Tell them I know the Germans aren't taking the threat of invasion seriously. Tell them I heard the Gruppenführer boasting of not being deceived by Britain's double bluff.'

Falcon stared at her in amazement. 'How can you know these things?' He spluttered. 'You've been here less than twenty-four hours!'

'I have eyes and ears, and my understanding of conversational German is excellent.'

Falcon heaved a heavy sigh. 'Please don't make me regret this, Nicolette.'

She went to hug him but thought better of it. Instead, she curled her hands into fists and punched the air.

'Does that mean you're staying, Knickers?' Charlie called.

She whirled around to face the others. 'Looks like you're stuck with me.'

Nicolette asked Taff to cut her hair with his razor-sharp bayonet. He gave her a short back and sides as good as any barber could have done. She mixed a paste of soil and engine oil and smeared it into her short blonde curls. When she washed the mess out, her hair had darkened considerably. She didn't recognise herself and was confident that any German officer would not recognise her either.

Marcus gave her the papers that stated she was his nephew, and Lucille became Louis in a matter of a few hours.

Marcus returned home to organise his resistance members.

Nicolette stayed with Falcon and the commandos. For the next few months they wreaked havoc with the German communications lines, blew up electricity substations, telephone exchanges and fuel stores.

They gathered information about troop movements, artillery placements and the locations of anti-aircraft batteries. They slept in abandoned farm buildings, eating food stolen from the enemy or donated by friendly locals.

Nicolette lived rough with the unit and acted as their pianist, reporting to the SEO as often as safety would allow. Each night, the commandos tuned to the BBC broadcasts on a tiny crystal radio that Ginger carried in his backpack. They listened for the coded phrases that would tell them when to increase their activity. On the evening of the first of June, nineteen-forty-four, the message came. "The dice have been thrown".

'This is it, men.' Falcon passed a packet of cigarettes around to celebrate. 'The beginning of the end.'

Within the next week, the skies were full of British bombers. Nowhere was safe. The commandos stayed in the countryside away from major towns where the German soldiers were concentrated. Caen was almost obliterated. More than seven-hundred died in Lisieux, and Le Havre was flattened.

The commandos gathered in an abandoned railway tunnel to listen to the BBC broadcast. The newsreader read lists of gains made by the Allied soldiers in France, and then told of the destruction done to French towns and cities in the Normandy region.

'The French people will hate us for this,' Nicolette said when she heard of the massive losses caused by the Allies. 'Don't they realise who they are killing with their indiscriminate bombing?'

Falcon looked up from cleaning his rifle. 'You know there is always collateral damage in war. The bombers are acting on information that we supplied. German lines of communication; the location of the garrisons, and the local headquarters of the Gestapo. These places will all be targeted.'

'But the Gestapo HQ in Lisieux was next to a school.' Nicolette wrapped her arms around herself and rocked back and forth. 'What have we done?'

'We are bringing an end to this, Knickers.' Taff put his arm around her. 'The killing will end soon.'

She turned tear-filled eyes to her friend. 'I hope you're right, Taff. I hope all this death will be worth it.' She went outside to stand under the stars. She couldn't imagine what it must be like for the people of Lisieux. She had many friends there. Would they still be alive? Where was Marcus? What was Fabien doing? What about young Rene? She brushed a tear away and stared at the sky.

'Nicolette?' James took her elbow and guided her to the shadows near a stand of trees. 'Please don't be upset. We knew how this would end.'

'I know, but they are killing innocent women and children.' She shuddered. 'When will it stop?'

James put his arms around her, and she clung to him. They had kept their feelings for each other a secret for months. Nicolette had ached to feel the comfort of James' arms around her but had to be content with the warmth of his smile. Nicolette understood there was no room for romance in a unit of tough commandos. She lifted her face and placed her lips on his. The kiss was bittersweet and brief.

He drew back from her and glanced at the entrance to the tunnel. 'We can't Nicolette. Much as I want to, you know we can't do this. Not now. Not here.'

She nodded and stepped away from him. 'What happens now, James?' She looked up at the night sky. 'What happens when the bombs stop?'

'The Allied soldiers will be advancing on foot. We'll help clear the way for them.'

'Where do we start?'

'We head for Le Havre. You heard the transmission. Our orders are to clear the pockets of German resistance from the port.'

'When do we go?'

'At first light. We'd better get some sleep.'

Chapter 28: Justice

For the next two months, Nicolette worked with the commandos, flushing remnants of scattered German troops, tracking down snipers and living hand to mouth while making the towns and roads safer for the advancing Allied troops. She moved from Le Havre through Caen to Cherbourg, and wished she could go to Lisieux. She was so close, but Falcon's orders kept them away from the town where she would be most in danger of being recognised by the enemy.

One hot August day, they were ordered to be the advance patrol of a battalion that was marching to liberate Lisieux. Nicolette was excited to be going to the town at last but apprehensive about what she might find there. She hadn't heard from Marcus since he left her with the commandos.

Entering the ruins at the outskirts of town after dark, Nicolette was devastated to see how many buildings had been destroyed. The silhouette of the Basilica stood out against the moonlit sky, and she breathed a sigh of relief. She felt grateful that the shrine had been spared.

Over the next two days, they scouted the town, furtively investigating the German strongholds. Nicolette was happy to meet Rene on the fringes of town. The young man was laying explosives at the base of a bridge over the river.

'Hey, Rene!' she called softly. 'Blown up any Nazis lately?'

The young man flattened himself against the bridge before raising his rifle and pointing it in her direction.

'Don't shoot me, you silly peasant!' she called and laughed. 'It's me! Lucille!'

Rene tilted his head away from the sight of his rifle. 'Lucille?'

She stepped into a clearing and waved him over. 'Come meet my friends.'

With Rene's help, the commandos contacted the local resistance group. Marcus and his men arrived a few hours later and Nicolette couldn't believe how pleased she was to see the leader.

'Marcus!' She hugged him and kissed him firmly on both cheeks. 'I'm so glad to see you.'

'I'm happy to see you too, nephew.' He grinned and ruffled her short, dirty curls. 'I see you've been busy.' He nodded at the men behind her.

'You haven't exactly been idle, Marcus.' She inclined her head to the bridge. 'When did you plan to blow that?'

'Right, when the German soldiers decide to make a run for it. That's the route they'll take.'

Falcon moved forwards. 'How can you be sure of that?' he asked.

'Because the Allies are heading here from the east. The main garrison is two streets that way.' Marcus pointed. 'This will be their quickest escape route.'

'I like your thinking.' Falcon grinned and slapped Marcus on his back. 'Carry on, friend. Don't let us keep you from your work.' He went back to his men, leaving Nicolette to talk with her old friend.

Marcus waved Rene back to the bridge and pulled out his cigarettes. 'Here, Louis, or Lucille, or whatever name you are going by now. Do you want a cigarette?'

'I'd love one, Marcus.' She took one from the packet, and then leant in for him to light it for her. 'How is everybody?'

'We lost many good men and women, Lucille. I can't count how many.' He stared at the ground and inhaled deeply from his cigarette.

'Fabien?'

'No, he's still kicking around somewhere.' Marcus laughed.

'Henri?'

'No!' Marcus shook his head and spat on the ground. 'I'm sure Lissette was behind him getting captured. If I could prove she was to blame, she'd be a dead woman now.'

'He was captured?'

'He didn't talk.' Marcus was quick to reassure her.

'How do you know?'

'They shot him within hours. They don't shoot canaries.'

'Canaries?'

'The ones that sing.' Marcus explained. 'They will have done their worst and Henri would not have given them anything.'

'Poor Henri.' Nicolette's eyes filled with tears as she realised what the poor man must have been subjected to before the Germans killed him.

'It will all be over soon, Lucille. The bastards will get what they deserve.'

'What more can you tell us about them, Marcus? Where are they? We found a few pockets hiding around town, but I think we're missing something.'

Marcus guided her back to Falcon. 'I hear you might need some information about our Nazi neighbours.'

'I'm all ears, Marcus.' Falcon smiled at Nicolette.

They learned that there were still hundreds of enemy soldiers garrisoned in and around the town. Some were occupying positions on strategic crossroads. Some were hiding in the Basilica, along with hundreds of the local population who had sought refuge in the strongly built building after their homes had been destroyed.

'The cowards are using the Basilica and the people as a shield. They know we would never attack the shrine.'

'Don't be too sure, Marcus.' Falcon warned. 'We'll do whatever we must, to make them surrender.'

Marcus shook his head sadly. 'I understand. War is war.' He turned to Nicolette. 'I'll see you on the other side of hell, little one.' He began to walk away, followed by a group of his men but he turned to wave and shouted, 'Stay safe.'

'I think he has a soft spot for you, Knickers.' Brick commented.

'He's not the only one.' Deadly pointedly looked at Falcon.

'Shall we get started?' she asked, to deflect their interest in the pilot officer.

The Allied soldiers arrived on the evening of the twenty-second of August. They met stiff resistance and battles raged through the town. The Germans were not giving up easily.

A line of Allied tanks waited to advance, but couldn't get through to the centre of town. They were kept back by German machine gun posts in the square. Falcon contacted the tank commander and within minutes, Nicolette was crawling on her stomach with the rest of the commandos, making their way to the square. Knowing the area, she directed the men to various alleyways and side streets, most of which were mere piles of rubble. Using a three-pronged attack, they took out the machine gunners, leaving the way clear for the tanks to roll into town.

Heavy German artillery began to fall near the Basilica, and Nicolette heard more gunfire in the distance and knew that Marcus would be dealing with the artillery position. No more shells were fired after the gunfire stopped.

The fight was long and exhausting with small, intense battles being fought ferociously at intervals throughout the night. Sporadic gunfire and shouts could be heard from various places around the town. Nicolette hurried from one location to another, firing he r rifle at enemy positions and dodging returning fire as she helped the Allied soldiers advance.

After twenty-four hours, the British appeared at the edge of town. Falcon took his men to brief the newly arrived troops. Nicolette was alarmed to hear that the British Commander intended to destroy the Basilica.

'You can't allow him to shell the shrine, Falcon!' Nicolette implored the pilot officer. 'There are civilians in there! Hundreds of them!'

'The German officers are in there too! We have to!' He took hold of her shoulders and moved her out of his way.

'Wait!' She shrugged off her officer and ran to the British Commander.

'You can't shell the Basilica. Please!'

'Who do we have here?' The commander looked down at her and laughed. 'I know you mean well, son, but war is a business for grown-ups. I know what I'm doing.'

'But you don't!' she insisted.

'Nicolette!' Falcon called her by her given name, and she turned to him for an instant. He was shaking his head and mouthing the words, 'Don't do this.'

'Get out of my way.' The commander pushed her to one side, and she almost fell over.

The deafening sound of an explosion made Nicolette cover her ears. She looked to the west of town where a large plume of smoke was rising. 'The bridge!' she shouted. 'They've blown the bridge!'

She scrambled after the commander. 'Please. Sir!' She tugged on the commander's sleeve. 'Please give me a minute. Just one minute. I beg of you!'

'Well, you're a persistent little upstart, I'll give you that.' He peered down at her. 'What do you know about that?' He pointed to the plume of smoke.

'The resistance have blown the bridge, sir. They said they would only blow it up when it was full of retreating German soldiers. They are leaving! The Germans are leaving!'

'What do you know of the resistance?'

She stood taller to introduce herself. 'Please, sir. I am Private Armaud, 3761, I've been operating in France since forty-one. The resistance group in this town are my friends.'

'You're a British soldier?'

'I'm a WAAF, sir.' She grinned.

'You're a woman!' The commander looked stunned.

'I can vouch for her, sir.' Falcon came to her side. 'She's been in France for years, helping the underground. Now she's under my command. She can be trusted, sir. I believe the Germans are in retreat, as she says.'

'Well, I never!' The commander turned to his officers. 'Send a team to investigate that bridge.' He spun back to Nicolette. 'You stay there; I haven't finished with you yet.'

'Yes, sir.' She glanced at Falcon uncertainly. He raised his eyebrows at her but stayed by her side.

She wished she could hold his hand. She felt like a naughty schoolgirl waiting for the head teacher to dole out her punishment.

They heard gunfire in the distance, followed by more explosions.

'Marcus will be giving them hell.' Falcon whispered. 'Wish we could be there to see it.'

'I'd rather be facing the Germans, than waiting for the commander to "finish with me", as he put it.' She watched the senior officer giving orders, and then he began speaking into a field telephone.

'I think he's coming back.' Falcon whispered. 'Now you're for it.'

His grin didn't give her any confidence. She knew she'd been insubordinate to a very high-ranking officer. She would be in a lot of trouble.

'Well, it seems you were right, Private Armaud.'

'You mean you won't destroy the Basilica?' She knew she was pushing her luck to ask, but couldn't stop the words tumbling from her mouth.

'No need to. As you said, the Germans have left. Our units to the west are working with your friends, to mop up the stragglers.'

'Is it over, sir?' she dared to ask.

'It is for this town. Though, there is still work to be done in the south.'

'Has Paris been liberated yet, sir?' Falcon asked.

'Last I heard they were still fighting. It won't be long, though. Days at the most.'

Nicolette felt an upwelling of emotion. The war was coming to an end. After all these years of fighting and killing, it was almost over. A tear escaped and ran down her cheek.

'What are your plans now, Pilot Officer Brown?' The commander asked Falcon.

'Perhaps a little time off to celebrate, sir?'

'When did you last have time off, son?'

Falcon turned to Nicolette and shrugged. 'I can't remember, sir.'

'Then you'd better take your men.' He looked at Nicolette. 'And women, to some quiet spot for a few days. No doubt you'll be back in the fray before long. This war isn't won yet.'

Nicolette hesitated. 'Does that mean we can go, sir?'

The commander laughed. 'Off you trot. Well done, Armaud. Well done.'

She walked back with Falcon to the others waiting at the side of the road. She could still hear gunfire and was desperate to know whether Marcus and his men were safe. 'Could we go—?'

'Just what I was thinking.' Falcon shouldered his rifle. 'Let's see whether Marcus needs a hand, shall we?'

'But he said we could stand-down, sir!' Ginger complained.

'Do you want to miss the fun?' Deadly fell into step behind Falcon.

The group of commandos marched through the town, heading towards the bridge. As they neared the Basilica, their way was blocked by hundreds of civilians streaming from the huge building. Some had tears on their faces, others smiled. Children clung to the hands of adults; old people were being helped to walk.

Nicolette began to realise what had happened. These people had been so close to being blown to bits, but she had delayed the commander long enough to save them. They would never know what she had done, but she knew she would never forget their faces.

They heard a commotion of screaming and shouting coming from the rear of the Basilica.

Charlie pointed his rifle towards the noise. 'Something's going on over there, sir. Should we investigate? We might get ourselves a few German soldiers to play with.'

Falcon nodded and followed the commando.

A woman was screaming while two men held her down. A third was shaving her head, not too gently. She was covered in blood.

'What is going on here?' Falcon demanded.

'Marcus!' Nicolette recognised the resistance leader. 'What are you doing?' She looked at the woman with pity until she realised who it was. 'Lissette! Is that you?'

'Don't interfere, Lucille.' Rene warned. He was one of the men holding her down. 'You know she deserves this.'

'Everyone will know her as a traitor now.' Marcus threw the bloodied razor into some bushes. 'She's a collaborator and deserves to die, but I think she'll suffer more by exposing her to the wrath of people who thought of her as a friend.' He pushed his wife in the back. 'Go! Show yourself to the people of Lisieux!'

'Mercy, Marcus. I'm your wife.' The bald woman pleaded.

'You are no wife of mine!' He shoved her again, pushing her into the flow of people streaming from the shrine.

The crowds parted around her, staring at the disfigured woman with revulsion.

'I never want to see your face again, woman. Do you hear me?' Marcus yelled. 'Don't make a murderer of me. If you show yourself at my home, I'll kill you, so help me, God.'

Nicolette watched Lissette staggering through the crowd of confused people. Gradually, as word spread, they began to berate her. 'Traitor!' one shouted. 'Collaborator!' Another shoved the woman to her knees.

Nicolette began to feel sorry for the thin woman until she remembered what she had done. Lissette struggled to her feet and began to hurry away from the baying crowd.

Marcus was panting, and his face contorted with anger. Nicolette went to him and took him in her arms. 'Come, Marcus. Let me take you home.'

Chapter 29: Proposal

The war in Europe struggled on for a few more months but the Allies knew it was only a matter of time before Germany would have to capitulate.

Nicolette and her band of commandos had spent those months helping to gather German equipment and paperwork from the liberated French towns. They uncovered mountains of evidence against the perpetrators of brutal tortures. They found files of incriminating correspondence detailing the inhumane treatment of local populations. The German penchant for record keeping would lead to the downfall of many.

Nicolette was sickened to discover more torture chambers in town halls and civic buildings across the country. She worked, with Falcon, to gather photographic evidence of multiple atrocities. The evidence was being gathered to use against the officers and men who committed heinous crimes. Churchill had vowed to bring them to justice and put them on trial for the unimaginable atrocities they were responsible for.

The group of commandos was close to Reims when Falcon received orders to bring the unit back and return home with the evidence they'd gathered. He broke the news while they were relaxing in a café surrounded by happy, smiling people. The war already seemed over for the French, and the local people were celebrating.

Nicolette felt she'd never be in the mood to celebrate again after what she'd witnessed in the last few months.

'Come on, Knickers. We're going home! Smile!' Deadly encouraged her.

'Sorry. You're right.' She dragged a hand through her untidy hair and pasted a smile on her face. 'It's just that, after what we saw this afternoon, well, I don't have to explain, do I?'

'Don't dwell on it, Knickers,' Vera said. 'We got the photos and the paper trail. Those bastards will get what's coming to them.'

'I hope so, Vera.' She sighed and tried to put the horrific images of instruments of torture out of her mind.

'We're going home!' James put his arm around her and pulled her close. 'We can come clean, at last. We don't have to hide our feelings any longer. We can start to live an ordinary life.'

The other commandos grinned and began to nudge each other and chuckle.

Nicolette glanced at Deadly. 'What's so funny?'

'You two!' He smirked. 'Thought you were so clever, didn't you? Hiding your feelings! Pah! Who did you think you were fooling?'

'You knew?' James asked.

'Well, you made it too easy, boss.' Ginger grinned.

'All those meaningful looks at each other under the stars!' Taff laughed and put on a falsetto voice, 'Oh, James!'

'Oh, Nicolette!' Deadly copied the theatrical tone. He gasped and clutched his hand to his chest. 'Please! We can't! We shouldn't't!'

'Behave, Deadly!' Nicolette blushed and giggled. 'Did you spy on us?'

'Who are you accusing of being a spy?' Charlie began to laugh loudly. 'That's rich, coming from you two!'

'What shall I do with them?' James asked her.

'Shoot them at dawn, I'd say,' she quipped and leant to kiss his cheek.

'Woo-hoo!' Taff shouted, and all the heads in the café turned to them.

'We'd better get an invite to the wedding. Knickers.' Brick said.

'You can all be my maids of honour.' She laughed.

'I haven't asked you yet.' James tried to look stern, but the corners of his mouth twitched.

'Go on!' Charlie nudged the pilot officer. 'Ask her now.'

'Yes, why don't you?' Nicolette turned to James. 'You know you want to.'

'Not here!' James' face flushed pink.

'Oh, Mr Brown!' She giggled. 'You really should work on that blush. It could get you into all kinds of trouble!'

'Oh, you're impossible, Private Armaud!' James shook his head and grinned. 'I'd planned to ask you after this mess was all over. I wanted to buy you a ring and take you somewhere nice.' He took her hand. 'I pictured you at a fancy restaurant in London. You'd be wearing a blue dress and—.'

The other men roared with laughter.

'What's so funny?' Nicolette asked, and then realised what she must look like and began to laugh with them. She hadn't had a decent bath in weeks. She couldn't remember the last time she'd had enough water to wash her hair. She still wore it short. The oil stains had grown out, but her blonde curls were unruly and frizzed easily. She still wore the dirty rags that Marcus had given her, and although she'd washed them, they'd never be really clean again. She looked like a teenage ruffian, and her appearance was a million miles away from the image that James was picturing.

'Oh, dear.' She tried to stop laughing long enough to say something. 'I'm sorry, James.' She took a moment to get her breath back. 'Perhaps you should wait. I can't expect a proposal, looking like this, can I?' She felt the laughter bubbling up again.

'I don't care what you look like, Nicolette.' James told her. 'I'd marry you even if you walked down the aisle in that get-up.'

She threw her arms around him, and they kissed to the sound of applause as the whole café joined in the congratulations.

Later, they were settling into the town hall for the night. The others were setting up camp in the courts of justice rooms. She'd been allocated a small office at the rear. She spread her blanket on the tiled floor and went in search of James. She found him poring over some paperwork in a side office, and she stood outside the door, watching his profile for a few seconds before knocking and entering.

'Got a minute?

'I've got the rest of my life for you, my love.'

'Are you sure?' She went to stand by his side and put a hand on his shoulder. 'I felt you might have been bullied into talking about proposing. I didn't want you to feel I—.'

'Nicolette!' he interrupted. 'No one bullied me. I've been dreaming of asking you to marry me for months, if not years.'

'Have you?'

He pulled her into his lap and held her tightly. 'How could you think I wouldn't want to marry you?' He kissed her cheek. 'I love you!'

'I love you too. I mean, I really, really love you, James Brown.'

'I hope you do, Nicolette, if you're going to marry me!'

The end of the war came within days of Nicolette arriving back in England. The eighth of May, nineteen-forty-five saw a massive celebration across England. She celebrated with her friends at the SEO Headquarters. Cups of tea all round and some jam sandwiches were offered by the canteen. A few bottles of beer miraculously appeared, but that was as much as they were allowed.

The SEO needed to examine the evidence they'd gathered. The papers were being scrutinised by the bigwigs. The members of her unit were all called to give their opinions on the atrocities they'd uncovered, and Nicolette was asked whether she'd be willing to give evidence in court.

'Of course, I would, sir,' she told the examining officer.

'It might take years to bring some of these crimes to the courts. Would you still be willing to help bring these criminals to justice?'

'Sir,' she began, 'If it takes the rest of my life to trace these butchers, I will happily stand as an old woman and swear to what I've witnessed.'

'Good girl, Armaud. I'm glad we can count on you.'

She left the office with her mind filled with horrific memories. She recalled seeing James' poor face after he'd been tortured. Hearing of Henri's death. Witnessing the cold-blooded shooting down of her friend, Anna. Those were the crimes against people she knew and loved. There were hundreds more instances that she'd found evidence of. The people she read about were unknown individuals to her, but they'd all been loved by someone. They deserved justice.

'Was it rough, Knickers?' Taff caught up with her in the corridor.

'No, Taff. Not really.' She told him. 'Just makes me think, that's all. I get so angry sometimes.'

'We all do, Knickers. It goes with the territory, doesn't it?' He put his arm around her shoulders. 'When are you heading home?'

'Tomorrow, I think.'

'Will Falcon be going with you to meet the in-laws?'

She laughed at the use of James' code name. 'James will be travelling to London with me, yes.'

'When will you set a date?'

'You'll be the first to know, Taff.'

'I'd better be!'

Chapter 30: Revelations

The house was full of relatives, and the conversation switched between English and French as laughter punctuated the conversation. Nicolette was surrounded by love and merriment on the evening before her wedding. She and James had decided to wait, until the people they loved most could be present at their ceremony. James' brothers had both been demobbed by the end of September, and Felicity had made it home in October. Joseph was based at Biggin Hill and secured leave for the whole event. Her French family had made the trip from Verdun, but her American Aunt had sent a telegram of congratulations with apologies that they couldn't make it.

The wedding had been arranged for the Saturday before Christmas Eve and would be held at the register office in Weybridge, a few miles from her home. James' family all came from nearby Shepperton, so the arrangements had been easy to organise.

Fitting the visiting family into the Thames Ditton house was a squeeze, but Collette wouldn't hear of them going to a hotel. Elizabeth shared Nicolette's bed with Collette and Felicity and Nicolette were accommodated on borrowed mattresses on the floor. Uncle Edwin shared the largest bedroom with the oldest cousins, Antoine and Pascal, and Gaston shared with Joseph. Her Aunt Sabine and Uncle Francoise took the smaller bedroom at the back of the house.

Collette had suggested that she and Edwin should not sleep as man and wife while the visitors were there. She didn't want to confuse the extended family. Felicity seemed quite accepting of the new relationship, which confused Nicolette even more. She couldn't understand how two sisters could so easily switch their emotions. Felicity had loved Edwin but left him when she went to nurse in Africa. Collette professed to having always loved Edwin, even before she married Maurice. Now Edwin and Felicity were divorced, and Collette would marry him in the New Year. Nicolette was glad they planned to keep the news a secret from the French side of the family. Even though, Elizabeth knew of the love tangle; it would be very difficult to explain to the rest of them.

'I knew there was something between you and Mr Brown when you came to Verdun, that time.' Elizabeth interrupted Nicolette's thoughts and smiled over the rim of her sherry glass. She turned to Collette, 'They tried to deny it, but I could see the attraction.'

Collette almost dropped the sherry bottle. 'What!' She stared at Nicolette in bewilderment. 'When did you go to Verdun with James? I thought you hadn't known him long.'

'It's a long story, Mum.' She still referred to Collette as her mother because she couldn't get used to calling her, Aunt Collette. 'I was helping him get back to Britain. Was that in forty-two, Grand-Mère?'

'No, I think it was forty-one, Nicolette.'

'I thought you were in Northern France.' Edwin pointed out.

'I was.' Nicolette was beginning to feel uncomfortable. 'We were in Normandy for a short while.' Nicolette shook her head as it filled with images of the night she rescued James from the torture cage in the town hall. 'Can we talk about something else, please?'

Antoine came to her side and put his hand on hers. 'James told me what you did, Nicolette. We spent many hours on the road together when I took him south. I think he loved you from the very moment you saved him.'

'You saved him?' Felicity's eyes glowed with interest. 'How romantic.'

'There was no romance involved, Aunt Felicity!' Nicolette shook the remembered images from her mind. 'Believe me! It's not a subject I want to talk about.'

Edwin coughed to clear his throat. 'I think we should leave it there. Nicolette has made her feelings clear. Now who wants a top-up? Collette, you have the bottle, pass it around dear, will you?'

Nicolette gave her uncle a nod and a small smile. He didn't know the details of that awful night, but she knew he would know enough of war to realise what she might be hiding from her family.

'I can't wait to see your dress, Nicolette. I hope you'll be wearing a white gown.'

'No, Aunt Sabine. The dress is blue and quite simple in style.' She had James' imagined proposal in her mind when she chose the outfit. 'I spent so long in men's clothing that I would feel very strange in anything too elaborate.

A flashbulb went off in her head and her mind filled with the image of the elegant suit with the specially designed hat she had worn to kill the German officer. She shuddered and gripped her glass tighter. When would these flashbacks stop? Why couldn't she leave the past behind her?

'Is it true that you'll not be having bridesmaids?'

'That's right, Uncle Francoise, but we will be having an eight-man guard of honour.' She smiled as she thought of her commando friends. All seven of them would be attending.

They'd begged beds for the weekend from their connections in London. They had taken Rene under their wing and made him an honorary member of their unit. They'd even managed to get a uniform for him so he could look the part. She had been surprised to hear he had made it to London. The young French boy had never been outside Normandy until now.

Marcus had been invited but wrote to say he couldn't make it. She would have loved to see the older man again. He'd been like a father to her before she joined forces with the commandos. She'd won the grumpy soul over, and in time, she and Anna came to love him as if they'd really been his daughters. The smiling face of Anna came to her mind but was quickly replaced by the photographic memory of her being shot in the back and falling, face down to the ground. The glass of sherry fell from Nicolette's hands as if in slow motion. She watched it falling. The glass bounced away, but the golden sherry spread over the rug like a spreading bloodstain.

'Oh, Nicolette!' Collette hurried to get a cloth. 'I suspect your nerves are getting the better of you, aren't they?'

Nicolette watched Collette fussing as she mopped up the stain and picked up the fallen glass. She shook her head. She was getting married the next day. She had everything to live for. Her future was full of hope and promise, but it seemed her past wouldn't let her move on.

'Perhaps we should retire.' Elizabeth suggested. 'We have a long day ahead of us, and I suspect we won't be going to bed early tomorrow.'

'Good idea, Elizabeth.' Uncle Edwin agreed. 'Come along boys, I'll take you up.'

Antoine, Pascal and Gaston kissed their mother and grandmother before following the older man.

'Sleep well.' Joseph bent to peck Nicolette's cheek. 'This will be your last night of freedom, Sis!'

She smiled with trembling lips. Freedom meant so much more to her now than it ever did before. How could she explain to the people around her? How could she put into words what was happening in her mind? The world was free of war, but she couldn't shake the war from her head. It clung to her like a heavy coat weighing her down.

She watched the family leave, one by one until only she and Felicity remained in the living room.

'I'm glad we have some time alone, Nicolette.' Felicity sat beside her on the couch. 'I think I owe you an explanation, and I haven't had much of a chance to talk with you since I came home. It's all been a bit hectic, hasn't it?'

Nicolette sighed and shook her head. She knew what Felicity was going to say. At one time, it would have been the most significant conversation she would have with the woman who gave birth to her, but now the facts of her birth didn't seem the least bit important.

'You don't have to explain anything. Grandma Elizabeth told me everything.'

'No, she didn't.' Felicity insisted. 'She couldn't have because she doesn't know the truth of it. Nor does Collette.'

'Elizabeth told me that my father was an Australian doctor. You don't have to be ashamed, Aunt Flissy. I do understand, you know.'

'No, you don't, my dearest girl.' Felicity put a hand to Nicolette's face. 'I've kept a deep secret all these years, and it weighs me down.'

Nicolette recognised the feeling. 'I know how that feels, Aunt Flissy.'

'Is something wrong, child?' Felicity sat beside her. 'You've been a bag of nerves all night. It's more than wedding nerves, isn't it?'

Nicolette nodded.

'Are you having second thoughts? Wartime romances don't always work out, you know. No one would think badly of you if you wanted to call it off.'

'No, it's not that, Aunt Flissy. I love James very much.'

'Then what is wrong?'

'I can't get the war out of my head. It's as if there's a film of awful memories playing in the background of my mind, and I keep seeing the screen.'

'Oh, my love.' Felicity took Nicolette's hand. 'That's quite normal. You've been through such a lot, haven't you?' She patted the hand she held. 'I know you don't like to talk about it, but it would help if you did.'

'How?' Nicolette couldn't see that talking about her experiences would do anything other than burden other people with the horrors.

'Listen, Nicolette. I've seen my fair share of disagreeable sights. I'm not immune to the suffering I witnessed. My dreams are full of memories, and some of them date back to the first war.'

'I didn't know.' Nicolette gazed at her aunt with a puzzled frown. 'Do you still have nightmares about Verdun?'

'Not as much now as I did in the first days after we came to England. The bad memories fade, and I learned to replace them with good ones.'

'How do you do that?'

'Focus on something good that happened. I'm sure you can think of something.'

Nicolette searched her mind and remembered the time she was in the orchard at her grandmother's chateau. James told her he loved her. She smiled.

'That's more like it.' Felicity patted her hand again. 'Now, every time you get a flash of a bad memory, you must concentrate on a good one to chase it away.'

'Will that work?'

'What have you got to lose?'

'I'll try that. Thanks, Aunt Flissy.'

'And you must talk about your experiences. James will be going through the same thing, you know. Perhaps if you discussed this with him, it would help both of you.'

'He hasn't said anything.'

'Have you?' Felicity asked with a knowing smile.

Nicolette shook her head.

'Don't have secrets between each other, Nicolette. Be open and honest. You'll feel much better, and your relationship will be so much stronger.'

'Talking of secrets,' Nicolette said, 'What were you going to tell me?'

'Come.' Felicity tugged on Nicolette's hand. 'I need to make a confession. You will be tying yourself to James tomorrow. You'll be starting a new life with the man you love, but it will all be based on lies if I don't get this awful secret off my chest.'

'What are you talking about?'

'Come with me, Nicolette. Collette and Elizabeth need to hear this too.' She pulled Nicolette's hand and drew her to her feet.

Nicolette followed her aunt up the stairs.

'I can't go through this more than once. I need to tell you all together.' Felicity took a deep breath and opened the door to the

254

shared bedroom. Collette and Elizabeth were both already under their covers.

'I have something to tell you.' Felicity announced. 'You can all hate me at the same time. I hope you can find it in your hearts to forgive me but if I have to move out and start again somewhere else, then so be it. Whatever you think of me, I can't carry this burden any longer.'

'You're scaring me, Aunt Felicity.'

'What's got into you, Flissy?' Collette sat up on her mattress. 'I hope you're not going to make things difficult by mentioning the recent changes in our household.'

'You don't have to hide your divorce from me, Felicity.' Elizabeth said, arrogantly, as she pushed herself to a sitting position. 'I know all about your love triangle with Edwin.'

Felicity shook her head. 'This secret goes much further back, Tante Elizabeth. I can't let Nicolette marry without her knowing her true parentage. It wouldn't be fair to her.'

'You're too late, Felicity.' Elizabeth gave her a haughty glare. 'I already explained your dirty little secret.'

'I know what you think of me, Elizabeth.' Felicity squared her shoulders. 'You are right. I've always worn my heart on my sleeve. I fall in love too easily, and I often chose the wrong man to love. If that makes me a flirt, or a woman of loose morals, then I'll hold my hands up. I am all of those things.'

'You don't have to do this, Flissy.' Collette reached out to her sister. 'We can't help who we love.'

'No, but perhaps I should not have loved the same man that you loved.'

Collette huffed impatiently. 'I thought we weren't going to mention Edwin!'

'I'm not talking about Edwin.'

'Then who are you talking about, Aunt Flissy?' Nicolette asked.

'Antoine.' She let the name sink in before she spoke again. 'I was in love with Antoine.'

'My Antoine?' Collette whispered.

Felicity nodded.

'When?' Elizabeth asked. 'Before they were married?'

'And after.' She hastened to add, 'I'm so sorry, Collette. He said he loved me and that we would be together after the war. He—! No, *we* didn't want to hurt you. I told him he had to choose between us, but he couldn't make that choice. He loved us both, you see.'

'What about the Australian?' Elizabeth asked. 'You openly admitted that you were sleeping with him. Are you saying that you slept with each of them during that time?'

'Oh, my God!' Collette looked at Nicolette. 'She could be the child of either one of them!'

'No, you're wrong. I know who her father is. I didn't sleep with Alain in the months before Antoine was killed. I couldn't. I loved Antoine!'

'Are you saying that Antoine is my father, after all?' Nicolette asked.

Felicity nodded. 'Yes.'

'Why didn't you tell me?' Collette asked.

'Would you have taken her if you'd known what I'd done to you?'

Collette stared at Nicolette. 'How do I know what I would have done more than twenty-five years ago?'

'You could never have forgiven me for sleeping with your husband.'

Elizabeth drew a sharp intake of breath. 'What makes you think she can forgive you now?'

'I hope she can.'

Nicolette looked to the woman she had known as her mother until a little while ago. 'Mum?'

'I don't know what I think.' Collette hung her head. 'It all happened so long ago. We were different people then. We lived in a different world.'

'Antoine was still my son and still your husband, Collette. Are you going to let this, this *tramp,* get away with this?'

'Antoine is not without blame in this, Belle-Mère.' Collette pointed out. 'She says he loved us both.'

'In the same way that Edwin loved us both, Collette. It seems we attract the same men don't we?'

'But Edwin is not Antoine!' Elizabeth said.

'Perhaps not, Belle-Mère.' Collette sighed and went on, 'But you know that I love him. You may as well know that I plan to marry him in January.'

'Oh, my goodness! What a performance!' Elizabeth put a hand to her throat. 'I don't know what to say!'

'You don't have to say anything, Grand-Mère. Accept the situation. I have done.' Nicolette found it difficult to feel anything about the family squabbles. It all seemed so unimportant now.

'Collette loved Edwin, Edwin loved Felicity, now he loves Collette again. Felicity has stepped back to allow them some happiness. Just as she did when she gave me to her sister.' She turned to Felicity. 'It can't have been easy to give me away.'

Felicity gave Nicolette a tremulous smile. 'It wasn't so difficult because I knew Collette would love you and I would still be in your life.'

'So you really are my grand-daughter?' Elizabeth's eyes glittered. 'You are Antoine's child!'

'I can't understand why none of you could see it.' Felicity said. 'She is the image of her father. She has Verdun blood flowing in her veins.'

'She has my hair.' Elizabeth smiled. 'I always wondered how that could be.'

They heard a soft banging on the bedroom wall. 'Will you girls be quiet, please? We boys are trying to sleep!'

'Sorry Edwin.' Collette called back through the wall, and then turned to Felicity. 'Perhaps we should end this right there.'

'Do you forgive Flissy, Mum?'

'Do you?' Collette asked.

'I love you all. It doesn't matter whether I call you Aunt or Mum.' She turned to Elizabeth. 'And you were always my grandmother, even when I thought you weren't.'

'Then I suppose we'll keep this as our little secret.' Elizabeth huffed. 'This family has so many that one more won't hurt.'

'Really!' Felicity grinned. 'Are you sure? I mean, I was expecting fireworks and tornados. I can't believe you're all being so understanding about this.'

'Perhaps the cold light of day will make us think differently tomorrow, Flissy,' said Collette. 'But for now, let's get some sleep. Our daughter is getting married tomorrow.'

Chapter 31: Love and marriage

Nicolette had little time to reflect on her newly discovered heritage. She fell asleep, thinking of her French father and the convoluted affairs of the people in her life. She hoped her life with James would be less complicated. She loved him, and he loved her. It was as plain as that. Except that her feelings for him were sometimes overwhelming in their intensity. How could his love for her be as strong as the love she felt for him? She could only take his word for it that he would love her for eternity. His eyes told her that he loved her. She felt safe with him. She couldn't wait to marry him.

She listened to the family laughing downstairs as she got ready for her big day. She combed her hair and pinned the simple, pale-blue hat in place then tugged the white netting down over her eyes. She stood to smooth the blue, tweed skirt of the dress over her hips. Her grandmother had given her a white fur cape to wear, and she had white shoes and bag to complete her outfit. James might recognise her because he'd seen her in civilian clothes many times in the last months, but her commando friends were in for a surprise. She grinned at her reflection in the mirror as she imagined their reactions.

She turned to answer a knock on her bedroom door. 'Ready, sweetheart?' Collette came in and gasped. 'My, you look stunning.'

'Thanks, Mum.'

'Do you still think of me as your mum?'

'You *are* my mum!' Nicolette went to hug the woman she'd always known as her mother. 'No quirk of biology can change that. You brought me up.'

'I'm glad you feel like that. I thought things might change after you learned what happened.'

'Do you feel differently about me after last night?'

'You mean since I learned that Antoine is your father?'

Nicolette nodded. 'It was a lot to take in.'

'In a way, it makes me feel closer to you. Strange as that might sound.' Collette smiled. 'I know he cheated on me but I think, if I am honest, I always suspected he didn't love me as much as I hoped he would.'

'Did you love him, Mum?'

'I thought I did, but I think I was more in love with the *idea* of being in love, if you can understand that.'

'How do you know the difference?'

258

Collette looked pensive for a few seconds. 'Did you love Robert? Or did you only *think* you loved him?'

'I see what you mean.' Nicolette smiled. 'I did think I loved him, but now I know what love really feels like, I know that I didn't love him at all.'

'You love James?'

'With all my heart and soul.'

'Then let's go tell him, shall we?' Collette held out her arm. 'Edwin will be so proud to give you away.'

The ceremony didn't last long enough. Nicolette said her vows and listened to James saying his to her. He slipped the ring on her finger, and the deed was done. The family gathered around to congratulate the couple, and they were herded outside to make way for the next wedding party.

James held her back until the guests had gone through the door, and then took her arm. 'Come with me, Mrs Brown. We have a guard of honour waiting outside to congratulate us.'

'Did they all make it?'

'They more than made it, Nicolette. They tracked down Bones, Bing and Baldy, too. Though, Bing will be in a wheelchair.'

'Really! They're all here?'

She stepped outside into the pale December sunshine and heard a thunderous cheer from the airmen lined up on either side of the door. They raised their rifles and made an arch for the newly married couple to walk through. She smiled at each of their faces as she walked slowly down the archway they'd made. Tears were rolling down her cheeks when she reached the end. She bent to kiss Bing on his cheek to avoid being poked in the eye from the end of his rifle.

'Ah, you great softie!' Bing shouldered his weapon. 'Congratulations, Knickers.'

She turned to her new husband but caught sight of the young Frenchman. 'Rene!' She flung her arms around him. She switched, to speak French, 'I'm so glad you made it. How are you?'

'Happy to be free, and happy to be here.' Rene hugged her tightly. 'I almost didn't recognise you, Lucille.' Rene winked. 'Or should I call you Nicolette, now?'

'I think she looked better when she was my nephew!'

Nicolette spun around. 'Marcus!' She ran into the arms of the older Frenchman, and fresh tears rolled down her face. 'I thought you couldn't come.'

'How could I miss your wedding, ma petite fille?'

'When did you get here? How long will you stay?'

'Rene and I will stay for a few days. These kind gentlemen have offered to look after us and show us the sights of your lovely city.'

'But we'll take them to your wedding party first, Knickers.' Ginger called.

'Thank you, boys. You don't know how happy I am to see your ugly faces.'

'Well, ain't that charming?' Deadly grinned widely. 'It's not so long ago that we couldn't tell the difference between you and us lot.'

'She scrubs up well, Deadly,' Ginger nudged his friend. 'Doesn't she?'

'Falcon is a lucky man,' said Taff.

'Don't I know it?' James put his arms around Nicolette and kissed her full on the lips.

The airmen began to wolf whistle.

'Now, then, boys!' Edwin held up his hand. 'Let's have a little order, shall we. Do you all know how to get to the venue for the party?'

Nicolette waved to her family and friends as the wedding car pulled away from the register office.

'How are you feeling, Mrs Brown?' James asked.

'Overwhelmed, Mr Brown.'

'Happy?'

'Very.'

'No regrets?'

'Not yet!' She grinned and leant against his shoulder.

'We can look to the future, Nicolette. This day can be the start of the rest of our lives.'

'If only it were as simple as that, James.' She felt the heavy cloak of bad memories settle on her shoulders. 'We lived through some awful times to get to where we are today. Can we ever forget those horrors? They still haunt me, James. Do you feel the same?'

'I do, Nicolette. I don't think we'd be human if we didn't think of those memories from time to time.'

'I can't seem to *stop* thinking of them, James. They scare me. I can't seem to let them go.'

'Listen, my love.' He kissed her temple. 'Whatever has happened to get us to this point can now fade away. We have to let the horrors become distant memories. We'll help each other to forget the bad memories. We'll put them behind us. What matters is what happens from here.'

'I know you are right, James. I'll try to concentrate on the present. I want to be the best wife you could wish for.'

'You already are.'

'I love you, James Brown.'

Nicolette had danced with her husband, and then took turns with all the commandos. She had her toes crushed more than once. She'd sat on Bing's lap while he rolled his wheelchair around the dance floor. She'd danced with her brother, her uncles and her cousins. She'd even danced with her mother but so far, Marcus had not joined the dancing. Nicolette glanced at the older Frenchman. He was sitting alone, holding a small glass of brandy. She felt drawn to him. He looked so lost and sad.

'Marcus?' She sat beside him. 'Are you feeling all right?'

'Oui, Lucille. Sorry, I mean, yes, Nicolette.'

'I forget who I am too, sometimes.' She laughed and patted his arm.

'We were different people then. It was a different life. The world has moved on, but it is difficult to move with it.'

'Marcus!' She took hold of his rough hand. 'That's exactly how I feel too!' She gazed into his eyes and saw the sadness there. 'I keep having flashes of memories about my time in France. Don't get me wrong, I don't want to forget those times. Horrible as they were. I can't forget the friends I made or the things I had to do. Those people, and the work we did together, they changed me. They made me who I am today. They must have changed you too.'

'I was a simple farmer, Nicolette. War was a distant memory. I fought at Verdun, you know.'

'You did!' She was amazed to hear him tell her this.

'I was a young man, then. I thought I would never have to fight again.'

'But you did fight again, and you helped us win again.'

'At what cost, though?' Marcus looked into his glass. 'Please God it will never happen again.'

'Dance with me, Marcus.' She tugged on his hand. 'Please.'

He put his glass down and allowed her to walk him to the dance floor. 'I warn you, I'm no great dancer.'

She laughed and looked at the group of commandos. 'You can't be any worse than them.'

He took her in his arms, and they began a slow waltz. She rested her head on his shoulder, and he guided her around the wooden floor.

'Remember when I first met you, Nicolette?'

'When I jumped into your life?' She giggled.

'I thought you were a young British upstart with more manners than sense.'

'Did you?' She knew he didn't have a high opinion of her, at first.

'But you grew on me like a rash!' He shook her hand gently. 'You got under my skin and itched like a flea bite!'

'You make me sound horrible!'

'You made me care for you, Nicolette. Just as Anna made me love her. I felt you were the children I never had.'

'Oh, Marcus! We both loved you too. You do know that, don't you?'

'I hoped.' He shrugged. 'An old man can dream.'

'It is no dream, Marcus.' She hugged him tightly and kissed his cheek. 'I never knew my father but if I had, I would want him to have been like you.'

'It gladdens my heart to hear you say so.'

James came to whisper in her ear, 'I think we should be leaving soon.'

'But the party!' She didn't want to leave all her friends. 'I've barely had time to catch up with everyone.'

'We have the rest of our lives, Nicolette. Your family and our friends will always be close enough for us to visit.'

'France is not so far away, Nicolette.' Marcus gave her hand to James. 'My house will always be open to you and both.'

Nicolette leant to kiss the older man on his cheek. 'We will come to visit you in spring, Marcus.'

'I'll be happy to see you.' He kissed her forehead.

'One last dance before we go?' Nicolette asked, putting her free hand on her husband's shoulder.

James pulled her close and stepped out with her. They circled the room and felt all the eyes of their guests watching them.

'I am the happiest man alive, today.' His eyes held hers hypnotically.

'And I am the happiest woman.'

'I love you, Mrs Brown. Did I tell you that enough today?'

'No Mr Brown, I don't think you did.' She grinned. 'Why don't you tell me again?'

'I love you, Mrs Brown. I love you, Mrs Brown. I love you, Mrs Brown.'

THE END

Women of Verdun, the back story.

If you've enjoyed this book, you might like to read the first two books in the series.

Book one, Belle, tells the story of Nicolette's French grandmother.

Belle is nineteen in the late nineteenth century. The world is changing rapidly, but in France, in the district of Verdun, life flows at a slower pace. Belle is in love with her childhood friend and hopes he feels the same way. While visiting the Exposition Universelle in Paris, in the most romantic place in the world, Julien proposes but to her disappointment he does not speak of love.

Belle settles for a marriage of convenience, but realises her mistake when she discovers the husband she adores has a terrible secret that could ruin both their families. Can she find the courage to confront him? How can she love him after such a betrayal? How will she protect her family?

Book Two, Belle's Girls, focuses on the complicated relationship between Nicolette's aunt and mother.

In the middle of the First World War, Collette is afraid for her fiancé, Antoine, who is fighting to save the town of Verdun. They should have been married by now, but the war put a halt to their plans.

Her sister Felicity is secretly in love with Antoine but hides her feelings. Only their mother knows of her pain, but Belle is too involved with helping to feed the stricken soldiers to offer support to her youngest.

Felicity helps in the casualty station in the grounds of the chateau, assisting the Australian nurses to care for the injured and dying. Collette helps her mother and finds herself drawn to the dangerous work of taking food to the front line.

The turmoil of war changes the lives of the two French girls who are both in love with the same man.

Who will Antoine choose and what will the consequences of that choice mean to the family?

About the Author

Pearl A. Gardner has enjoyed some success with short story fiction, winning some national competitions. Her articles and stories have been published in popular magazines, both fiction and non-fiction, but she is concentrating on full length works now.

Pearl has a wide ranging and eclectic author list that includes many genres, from chick lit romances to science fiction, which she writes under the author name of P.A. Gardner

The following is not a comprehensive list, so if you really would like to see more work by Pearl A Gardner, simply search for her name in Amazon.

Published works

Published fiction and non-fiction novels by Pearl A. Gardner

The Scent of Bluebells – A World War Two romantic saga- In spring of 1939, eighteen year old Amy falls in love with Jimmy and life seems full of promise for the young girl from a northern mill town. War was brewing in Europe, and it would change her life forever.

Through the following five years of turmoil, Amy endures heartache and loss. Her husband returns briefly and leaves her pregnant with his child. She writes to him of the news but shortly before the baby is born, Jimmy is reported missing in action and presumed dead.

After more than a year with no further news of her missing husband, she slowly begins to enjoy freedom and independence like she'd never known before.

The war continues with no news of Jimmy and she dares to love again.

Will this love survive the war?

Will Jimmy be found?

A Snowdrop's Promise – A World War Two romance- At twenty-four-years old, Agnes felt she was headed for a spinster's life. Being taller than most lads was a disadvantage, but she didn't mind being the wallflower while her petite and pretty cousin drew men like a moth to a flame.

When Agnes fell for a tall Irishman's charm, she thought she had found the love of her life. When Andrew asks Agnes to marry him, she has no idea where his proposal will lead them. Her Catholic father would not permit a Protestant son-in-law and he refused to listen to their pleading.

The young couple continued to meet in secret, and when Andrew decided to talk to Agnes's father and try and win him around, none of them could have anticipated the outcome, or the repercussions of that fateful meeting.

War breaks out, giving a frightening and eventful backdrop to Agnes's life of secrets and lies. She lives in fear of the truth emerging, to ruin the lives of her children, but eventually begins to feel that the truth may perhaps lead to her salvation.

Can she face up to her fears and disclose the secrets of her past?

Pearl A. Gardner

Ella's Destiny – A romantic saga with a hint of sci-fi and a touch of time travel- War is imminent when Ella Stevens applies to join the Eden Venture in the hope of saving her teenage children and salvaging her failing marriage. Amid riots and unrest the family travels to their designated camp where they prepare for a future beyond anything they could have imagined.

During a perilous journey through space and time, Ella realises her marriage can not be saved, but is determined to fulfill her dream of finding a better future for her children. Arriving at the fresh new world, filled with hope and endless opportunity, Ella begins to build a life without her husband. However, the settlers soon discover that Eden is not the paradise they hoped it would be.

With no escape from the hostile and dangerous environment, survival becomes a priority. Ella embraces the challenges of her life with a new-found courage and moves into a future that no one could have predicted.

It's Penguin Shooting Day – A true diary account of the first weeks following brain injury. From my son-in-law, Simon's, point of view, he awakes in a bizarre place full of strangers and doesn't know why he is there. His yesterday is ten years ago and the only memories he has between then and now seem to be no more than hazy fragments. However, his first words to his wife, Natalie, when he wakes from the coma are, 'I love you, honey.' Even though he doesn't remember who she is, he knows that he loves her.

Amazingly, his emotions are still intact even though his memories don't support them. He has no recollection of his wedding day, or of his daughter's birth but the love he feels for his wife and child are overwhelming in their intensity.

So we use Simon's emotional strength and Natalie's inspirational positivity to form the foundations of a future we can only begin to imagine.

Pushed on the Shelf – a romantic comedy. Forty-something Trisha is reeling from the shock of being dumped by her husband, Robert, aka DISCWIFF (Dick in Sports Car With Foot Fetish.) Trisha now has to support her two children financially, as DISCWIFF has set up home with TITSNOBB (Tits no Brain Bimbo) and left her in a house that is about to be repossessed.

With no qualifications or experience, the job market looks bleak but she is determined not to go under.

As Trisha struggles to hold together all the threads of her unravelling life, her emotions get in a tangle when the owner of the local flower shop takes a keen interest in her and she agrees to go out on a date with him.

Trisha feels like her life is being lived inside a pressure cooker that's ready to blow a gasket. Something has to give, but what?

They Take our Children, Book One, The Truth Revealed

Soft science fiction / family saga about alien abduction. - Courtney is a brighter than average young woman but is otherwise as ordinary, happy and well adjusted as any other girl her age.

On her sixteenth birthday, Courtney's neurotic mother, Helen, calls her a monster in a fit of rage. The teenager runs off, causing panic in the family. Courtney's father, Gavin, has long suspected something sinister hiding in his wife's history but nothing could have prepared him for the truth. Helen's father, George, tries to reveal what he knows about the mystery but the family find it hard to accept his far fetched version of events as realistic.

Weaving between past and present the facts about Courtney's shocking alien origin are exposed and the search for whole truth begins.

They Take our Children, Book Two, Taking Control

Second book in the two book series about alien abduction. - Courtney's family are drawn into the murky world of ufology experts. Subterfuge and concealment become a part of their lives as they search for the secret to open the gateway to the second dimension where they hope to meet face to face with the aliens who abducted Courtney's cousins.

Talk of government agencies and 'above top secret' organisations makes them fearful but when they discover how much information has been covered up about the alien abductions, they become even more determined to take control and find the missing children.

Discover more about Pearl A. Gardner
www.pearlagardner.co.uk

Connect with Pearl A. Gardner

On Goodreads
https://www.goodreads.com/author/show/7350328.Pearl_A_Gardn
er

On Facebook
https://www.facebook.com/pearlagardner

On Twitter
https://twitter.com/PearlAGardner

Dear Reader,

I really appreciate that you took the time to read this work of fiction. I hope you enjoyed it.

I would be grateful if you could leave a review of the book on Amazon, Goodreads or your favourite review site.

If you have not enjoyed this book, or found faults with the work, please feel free to contact me to let me know how I may be able improve your reading experience of this novel.

Very best wishes from the author,

Pearl A. Gardner

Proof

Made in the USA
Charleston, SC
19 October 2015